Praise for *The L*
of Orkney series

For *The Red Sun:*

2016 International Book Awards: Fiction: Young Adult Finalist

2015 USA Best Book Awards: Best Cover Design: Fiction, Winner

2015 USA Best Book Awards: Children's Fiction, Winner

Beverly Hills Book Award: Best Juvenile Fiction, Winner

IBPA Benjamin Franklin Awards: Best New Voice Children's/ Young Adult, Silver Medal

Readers Favorite Awards Children Preteen: Silver Medal Winner

"This fast-moving adventure—the beginning of a trilogy—is sure to appease mythology fans who are outgrowing Percy Jackson's antics and looking for darker, weightier storytelling. **VERDICT:** A great choice for middle school collections."

—*School Library Journal*

"*Percy Jackson* meets Norse mythology in this captivating and unique adventure."

—*Foreword Reviews* (4 stars out of 5)

"*The Red Sun: Legends of Orkney* by Alane Adams is a book that will take children on a roller coaster ride of adventure and fantasy where whimsical and menacing creatures and witches will enthrall readers."

—Readers' Favorite (5 stars out of 5)

"This novel may appeal to young readers who have enjoyed other 'chosen one' fantasy stories: It moves along at a speedy clip, and preteens will likely identify with Sam's anger and frustration with the world . . . it's a high fantasy tale that maintains a quick pace..."

—*Kirkus Reviews*

"*The Red Sun* is a roller coaster ride of adventure, Norse mythology, magic and mayhem. Between Sam facing awesome villains in the magical realm of Orkney to teachers turning into lizards, I had the best time doing the voiceover for the audiobook. Don't miss out on this terrific story!"

—Karan Brar, actor on Disney's *Jessie* and *Bunk'd*

"Alane Adams is the brilliant mind behind the *Legends of Orkney* series . . . Adams' knowledge of the Norse myths lends itself to an intricate story full of legend and mysticism . . . For *Percy Jackson* fans."

—Hypable

"8 Middle Grade Books to Fall For During School Season"

—BuzzFeed

"Alane Adams weaves a rollicking tale of adventure, filled with magic and mayhem, in *The Red Sun,* first in the *Legends of Orkney* series. Adams combines elements of Norse mythology and Umatilla tradition to send her young protagonist, Sam, on a unique quest to find himself and to save the entire realm of Orkney in the process."

—*Clarion*

KALIFUS RISING

LEGENDS
OF ORKNEY

KALIFUS RISING

ALANE ADAMS

spark
press

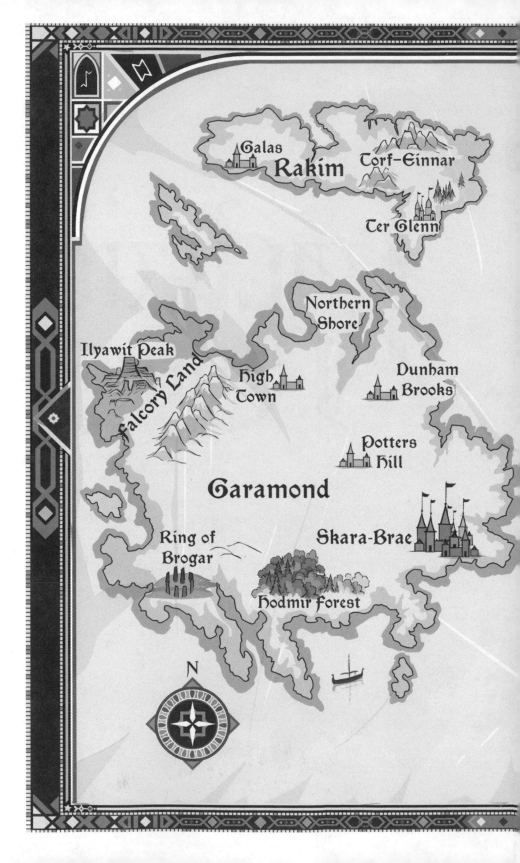

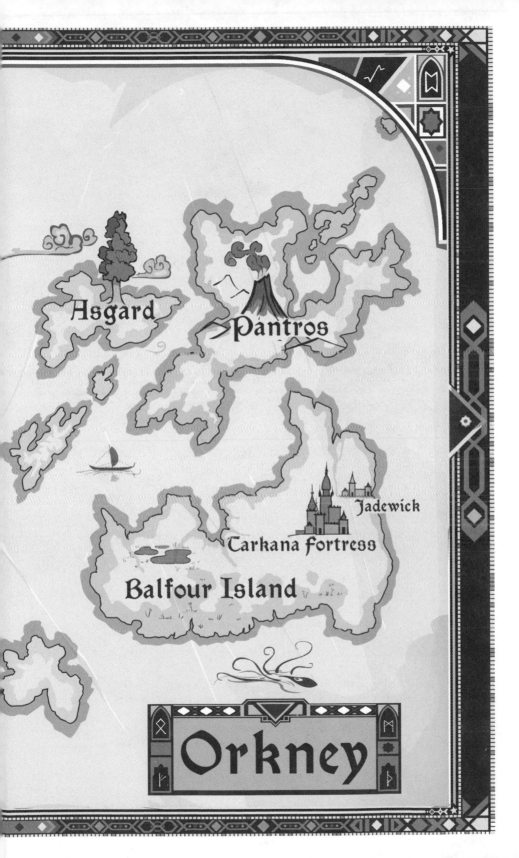

Published by SparkPress, a BookSparks imprint,
A division of SparkPoint Studio, LLC
Tempe, Arizona, USA, 85281
www.gosparkpress.com

Published 2016
Printed in the United States of America
ISBN: 978-1-940716-84-8 (pbk)
ISBN: 978-1-940716-85-5 (e-bk)

Library of Congress Control Number: 2016938631

Cover design by Jonathan Stroh
Cover and Map Illustrations by Jonathan Stroh
Author photo © Melissa Coulier/Bring Media
Interior design by Tabitha Lahr

For Ben

KALIFUS RISING

Volgrim Fortress

Ancient Days . . .

Prologue

The red sun hung like a blister on the horizon. Lingering crimson streaks of sunlight spread toxic fingers over the land, snuffing out every form of life they touched. By the next day, all living things in Orkney would perish if the poisonous curse afflicting the sun was not stopped.

Desperation gripped Catriona as she kneeled before her father, Rubicus, the powerful Volgrim he-witch she adored and feared. He was a massive man, broad-shouldered, with a thick beard trimmed to a sharp point. Deep grooves were etched in his face, like someone had chiseled them. His heavy brocaded coat, embroidered with silver thread and emerald stones, exuded nobility. He sat on his throne, an intricately carved work of black marble embellished with twisting shapes of Omeras in flight. The spike-tailed winged creatures that graced the Volgrim crest were as fierce and dark as the witches they served. Scattered around him were dozens of discarded tomes he had been poring over.

"Father, what is your plan?" Catriona grasped his rough hand and brought it to her cheek in search of comfort.

Rubicus jerked his hand free. "Plan? You think I planned for this?" He stood, pacing the chamber they occupied in their stone fortress overlooking Skara Brae. Rich murals lined the walls depicting ancient battle scenes. A fire burned in the fireplace, even though the day had been searing hot. Rubicus thrust a boot in the fire, dislodging a log and sending sparks shooting upward. "I was supposed to become a god! I cursed the *sun*. It rains death down on this realm. Odin should bow to me!"

Rubicus and Odin had been rivals for centuries. Each vying to best the other. The curse on the sun was Rubicus's latest attempt to outdo the god. To earn a spot next to him in Valhalla. But the curse had quickly spiraled out of control, like a raging fire fanned by winds. And now, all of Orkney was in danger of extinction.

The sounds of a battle raging outside the walls drew Catriona to the window. She stared down at the hordes of Valkyrie warriors amassed outside their fortress gates. The Valkyrie were guardians of the gods, Odin's private army. Immortal female fighters that were relentless in combat. They wore gilded armor and rode atop white horses whose thundering hooves made the very ground shake. Leading the Valkyrie was Odin himself, resplendent in an ornate breastplate and bearing a golden sword.

Nearly every Volgrim he-witch was engaged in defending their home, even those too young for the fight. Like Catriona's brothers. Green witchfire lit up the battlefield, but their enemies' numbers were far greater. Odin appeared unbeatable. He waded effortlessly through the line of he-witches, his sword flashing and glinting in the last rays of sunlight, making his way toward the gates. Even Rubicus's guardians, the famed Safyre Omeras, a specially bred line of the black-hearted creatures who breathed fire and were loyal only to Rubicus, were being brought down by the flaming arrows launched by the Valkyrie.

"Odin advances," Catriona said, gripping the ledge of the window tightly. "He bears a strange sword."

The odious god swung the weapon in a mighty arc. In a flash of blinding light, the golden blade cleaved through an entire line of he-witches guarding the entrance.

Catriona turned away in horror. Rubicus joined her, taking in the sight with an angry hiss. "Odin wields the Sword of Tyrfing. Forged by the black dwarves in Gomara, deep in the Skoll Mountains. Its blade never fails to cut down its opponent."

Catriona's heart clenched. She clasped her hands, searching the battling masses. Where were her brothers? Her uncles? Surely their great magic would protect them, even from Odin's powers. Another Safyre tumbled from the sky, crashing into the ground with a spray of dirt and screeching agony.

"We must help them, Father. Go down there and fight," she pleaded.

Rubicus laughed harshly. "And share in their fate? Look at them. They fall like stalks at harvest."

Catriona turned to stare up at her father. "Surely you won't abandon your sons?" Maksim. Leonis. Young Jinmar. Their faces floated into her mind. Even a selfish brute like Rubicus would not forsake his own flesh and blood. "You are responsible for this curse," she reminded him, then instantly wished she could take back her words at his sudden flash of rage.

He flung his hand out and flicked his wrist.

Immediately, an invisible iron band cut her airway off. She gasped, reaching for her throat.

His eyes were burning emeralds as he stepped closer to her. "I did this for them!" he shouted. "Odin wishes to throttle our power. Force us to bow down to him. I will never kneel before him, and neither will they, do you hear me?"

Catriona futilely tried to draw a breath in, but Rubicus's magic was too strong. She nodded, hoping to appease him. Black spots appeared behind her eyes before he relaxed his hand. Catriona sagged in relief, dragging in air. But she was undeterred, desperate to save her brothers. "Then let your sons inside our fortress. You've locked them outside the gates, fighting a war that can't be won."

The lines in Rubicus's face grew deeper as he clenched his fist in frustration. He kicked at the discarded tomes. "I was trying to buy time. To see if I could find a way to end this curse, but I failed. It has grown too powerful for me to control."

Catriona was at a loss. Her father had always been invincible. "What will happen?"

"We will perish. Everyone and everything in Orkney. Unless . . ."

"Unless what, Father?"

A muscle worked in his jaw as he clenched out the words. "Unless I die, and every he-witch along with me. It is our blood that formed this curse. Our blood alone can end it."

Catriona recoiled in horror. "No. There has to be another way. What if we went to Sinmara?" Sinmara, maven of the underworld, had given Rubicus a ruby ring that had helped create the curse on the sun.

But Rubicus appeared resigned, his eyes distant as he watched the last glimpse of the shimmering sun drop below the horizon. "There's no time. Odin will be inside the gates in minutes. We have shown him we are a threat to his precious mankind, and now . . . now he will erase us from existence." Rubicus turned to face Catriona. "You are my last hope. I must die for you to live, to carry on our line."

"No," she said, clutching his arm. "I can't bear to lose you."

Rubicus cupped her face with his hands. "Fear not, Daughter, we will rise again. It may take generations, but the world has not seen the last of the Volgrim witches. Mark my words: one day we will rule mankind in place of Odin."

Catriona grasped his cold hands and spoke with a certainty she had never felt before. "I swear, Father, on all I hold true, that your line will live on. I will make it so."

Pride brightened her father's grim face. "I may not be able to save your brothers, but you can save your sisters and cousins." He clapped his hands loudly.

They turned to look as a line of young girls entered from Rubicus's private chambers. In front was Catriona's knock-kneed sister, Agathea, sporting that ugly streak of white hair she'd had since age twelve. She held baby Vena, who squalled inconsolably for the mother who had died giving birth to her. And their cousins: Bronte, the oldest of the group, a sworn spinster and master of potions. Then spindly Beatrixe, mute since the day Rubicus had stricken her silent for talking back to him. The other three cousins, Paulina, Nestra, and Ariane, huddled together in a tight knot.

Catriona's resolve hardened as she studied them. She would take them into hiding. Run from Odin until she grew strong enough to destroy him.

There was a pounding on the door to their fortified tower below them. The young witches screamed in fear.

"Rubicus!" It was Odin. His booming voice shook the walls with rage. "You will answer for this curse upon my world!"

Rubicus swept Catriona close, pressing a kiss to her forehead. "Take them, my darling daughter, and run. Keep them safe."

She looked up at him. "Where can we go? We are hated by all in Orkney."

He put two fingers to his mouth and whistled shrilly. Outside, the thunder of beating wings could be heard. A shadow darkened the window as a Safyre Omera landed with a thud on the sill. Rubicus gripped Catriona's arms. "Go to the farthest ends of the earth if you must until you are ready to strike." He strode to a cabinet in the wall and opened the door. He took out a small jeweled chest and raised the lid. Inside, on a velvet bed, was a dagger made from black obsidian decorated with ornate carvings and a polished silver hilt. He lifted it reverently and then quickly sliced deeply into his palm. As blood welled up, Catriona paled.

Her father murmured words, waving the blade over his palm. The small pool of blood began to swirl, then a thin trail lifted up, twisting and wrapping like a snake around the blade. Crimson smoke billowed out and enveloped the knife in a cloud. Rubicus murmured faster, his eyes fierce as he circled the knife over his palm until the cloud dissipated in a sizzling clap of thunder. When the air cleared, he put the weapon back in the case and handed it to Catriona. "The last of my dark magic is contained in this blade. With this you can defeat Odin."

Excitement seized her. She wrapped her hands around his, clasping the blade. "Then let's do it, Father! Kill him now!"

But the Volgrim he-witch dashed her hopes. "The dagger is powerful, but it is no match for the Sword of Tyrfing. And it won't end this curse on the sun. The time for revenge will come, Catriona, and you will execute it in my name."

He grabbed his sword down from the wall and strapped it to his waist, then drew the giant blade.

The door crashed open as Catriona herded her charges to the window, loading them onto the back of the Safyre. She took one last glance over her shoulder as her father flung himself at Odin. Up close, the god was as broad-shouldered and fierce as Rubicus. Blue eyes blazed out from under bushy white eyebrows. Odin swung his golden blade, aiming straight for Rubicus's head.

Unable to tear her eyes away, Catriona would relive what happened next for centuries.

Her father fumbled to get his weapon up, and the Sword of Tyrfing unerringly found its target. When it was over, Catriona turned away and urged the Safyre skyward, arcing up and away from the fortress, steeling herself against the pain.

A fire had been lit in her heart, a raging hatred toward Odin and his precious mankind. She now lived for the day when that fire would consume all of Orkney.

Chapter One

North Shores of Garamond

Present-Day Orkney

A burst of green fire exploded the branch over the boy's hiding spot. Samuel Barconian, youngest member of the Orkadian guard at age thirteen, flinched, brushing smoldering splinters from his hair. He had to move, and fast, or end up incinerated into a pile of ash. Breaking from his hiding place, he sprinted across the clearing, weaving side to side to avoid the blasts of crackling energy that tore up the ground around him.

Sam dropped behind a fallen log for cover and tried to catch his breath.

War had come to Orkney, the last sanctuary for magic in all the nine realms of Odin. Black plumes of destruction could be seen for miles, staining the azure skies. The flocks of sheep that normally grazed on the verdant hillsides had fled the scorching witchfire. Dozens of sleepy villages had been burned to the ground, driving the helpless Orkadians from their homes.

Catriona, that queen of evil, was extracting her revenge. A witch so nasty Odin had trapped her and seven of her cronies inside stones for all eternity. Until Sam had messed that up and released them when he tried to save his father. Known as the Volgrim witches, they wielded an ancient magic darker and more potent than anything Sam's old adversary, Endera Tarkana, had ever attempted.

There was Bronte, a wizened hag, stooped with age, able to whip up deadly potions that raised putrid boils. Crafty Agathea, with her wide stripe of white hair, who bespelled the beasts they used in their attacks. And smelly Beatrixe, who could wipe you out with just her stench. One whiff of her made Sam want to puke. She reeked of sulfur and rotten eggs, but more importantly, she could shoot acid from her fingertips, melting whatever she touched. A handy gift Sam admired from afar.

The others—Paulina, Vena, Ariane, and Nestra—were like deadly tentacles, extending the reach of Catriona through all of Orkney.

After their escape, things had been quiet for a few months. While the shattered inhabitants of Orkney were still recovering from the deadly effects of the ancient red sun curse Sam had triggered on his twelfth birthday, the Volgrim witches holed up in the Tarkana fortress on Balfour Island, training Endera's young acolytes to be a lethal force. And then the attacks had begun. Catriona sent her Volgrim cronies out with the young witchlings to wage war on Orkney, along with a legion of vicious creatures: swarms of bat-like shreeks that pecked and clawed their way under your skin, packs of Shun Kara wolves that hunted and snarled at your heels as you tried to fight, and droves of sneevils.

The sneevils were the worst of them. Bristly fur covered their ugly hides. Curved tusks jutted up from their lower jaws just waiting to rip a person apart with one hook of their snouts. But right now, sneevils were the least of Sam's problems.

Another stump exploded next to him, scorched by a blast of witchfire. He had to get his butt moving. He rubbed the leather pouch that hung around his neck. A gift from his father, Robert Barconian. *There was a hero*, he thought. Inside, it held a shard of Odin's Stone, a powerful talisman imbued with Odin's magic, now destroyed except for this last piece.

Sam gripped the pouch tightly. Today, they would capture Agathea and strike a blow into Catriona's vengeance plan. Then the witches would know that Samuel Elias Barconian, Lord of the Ninth Realm, Son of Odin, son of Robert Barconian, was a force to be reckoned with. He would avenge his father and send Catriona and her ancient cronies back into the netherworld they had emerged from. Then he, too, could call himself a hero.

Sam peered around the edge of the log.

Agathea had been leading her acolytes on a series of raids along the northern shores of Garamond, Orkney's largest island and home to its capital city of Skara Brae. The witches were getting more and more brazen. Burning crops in daylight. Unleashing their beasts to terrorize. Then retreating to some hole where they waited to launch their next strike.

Captain Teren, the stalwart leader of the Orkadian Guard had a dozen of his best men creeping up the slope. If all went right, their ally, Gael of the Eifalians, would arrive along the flank side with his band of skilled archers. Their orders were to capture Agathea and bring her back to Skara Brae.

They were counting on Sam to stop her. With his growing magical powers, he was their only hope at trapping the witch and using her as leverage to get Catriona to stop this war. Being a witch wasn't something Sam liked to brag about. Not when just about everyone in Orkney hated witches. But he couldn't very well shut it out. The words of spells lit up like fireflies in his brain. The more he used his magic, the stronger it grew, like a virus multiplying in his veins. And the truth was, he secretly liked having magic. What kid wouldn't like the ability to shoot fire from his palms?

Captain Teren signaled to Sam across the clearing, pointing up at the tree.

There.

A nasty little witch hid in the branches. She was preparing to launch another blast of witchfire.

Got you. Sam closed his eyes, centered himself, and then

stepped out. He threw his hands forward, channeling the surge of power that coursed through him. A stream of virescent fire exploded from his palms, blasting the branch to pieces and sending the witch spinning through the air to land with a hard thud. Sam raised his hands to finish her off but hesitated as he saw how young she was. In a blink, she rolled behind the tree and sprinted to safety up the hill.

"Coward," she taunted as she ran off.

Fuming, he watched her go, fighting the temptation to follow after her and finish the job. He could have incinerated that witchling to a pile of ash. But he couldn't bring himself to win that way. Wouldn't. He would not become like Catriona. Killing without mercy. But it was frustrating to know the witches believed him weak because he showed his humanity.

With a sigh, he hurried after Teren. The captain led his band of soldiers stealthily up the hill toward Agathea's roost. Suddenly, a thundering sound made the ground shake. Teren's men let out cries as the witches used magic to send a wall of earth down the mountain, tumbling boulders and pinning the men underneath. Sam did his best to deflect the debris, stepping forward and thrusting with his palms, sending a wave of energy across the field, but he quickly tired.

He had learned that magic was like a muscle. The more he used it, the stronger he got, but it had its limits. It was exhausting. Witches like Catriona seemed to have never-ending deposits, thanks to the centuries of training they had before being locked up in stone. Sam was still a novice; if he used too much magic, he grew lightheaded and jelly-kneed. He needed to get better fast, because every time he failed, people got hurt.

As the dust settled, Teren rallied his remaining men forward. Sam raced up the far side, darting through trees. His breath came in ragged gasps. He had one thought on his mind: get to Agathea and cast the containment spell he had been practicing before she fled. He heard the whisper of the wings before he saw them. Black rain poured out of the sky, armed with fangs and claws.

Shreeks.

The men cried out as the flying vermin latched on and bit. Sam turned back toward Teren to help. Shreeks descended on him, biting at his neck and arms. He winced at their sharp nips. He swung the pouch holding Odin's Stone over his head, combining its magic with his own to create a powerful windstorm. "*Fein kinter*," he cried. *I call on my magic.* "*Fein kinter, ventimus, ventimus.*"

The wind blew off the flying rats, sending them spinning into the air like black boomerangs, giving the men a fighting chance to slash at them with their swords.

Too late, Sam realized the witches had lured him out into the open. *Dumbhead.* A rain of fireballs arced up over the trees and came down, aimed directly at him. Two of the soldiers closest to him fell to the ground, aflame, writhing in pain. Sam threw his hands out, shouting, "*Escudo!*" and sent every ounce of his magic into forming a shield over them.

It was one of the newest spells he had mastered; a bubble of gleaming energy formed, deflecting the deadly rain. Sam murmured to himself, focusing his strength on keeping the shield over the men around him. His arms trembled, even as adrenaline flooded his veins, adding extra gas to his magic. Teren shouted encouragement, but his voice was muffled as if it came down a long tunnel. Finally, the blasts of flaming globules slowed, then stopped.

Sam's shoulders drooped with fatigue as he lowered his hands. But the witches weren't finished with them. While they were huddled, a pack of sneevils had surrounded them. His magic spent, Sam drew his sword, followed by Teren and the handful of men left: the redhead, Heppner; brawny Tiber; dark and wiry Speria; the jokester, Rifkin, sporting his bald pate and gold earring; and the steadfast Galatin. They closed together back-to-back in the center of the clearing, while eight, then ten, then a dozen sneevils crawled into the open, their lips drawn into a snarl. Ivory tusks curved wickedly at the ends, tipped with sharp points ready to gut them.

"Steady," Teren said. "Wait until they draw close."

In a burst of black smoke, Agathea appeared behind the creatures. A thick white streak marked her swath of ebony hair. Her band of acolytes stepped out from behind the trees around her.

"Go, my pretties, feast on some fresh blood," she cooed to the sneevils, urging them to advance. "The traitorous witch-boy will make a delicious meal."

The beasts circled closer to the heroes, heeding her call. The sneevil closest to Sam bared its teeth and charged. Without hesitating, Sam drew his sword up between two hands and plunged straight down, pinning the sneevil to the ground.

"Kill them!" Agathea screeched. The pack of sneevils attacked with vicious snorts, tossing their heads to gore the men. The young witches blasted the small band of fighters with bursts of witchfire. Sam deflected the blasts, but he was fatigued. His arms shook with the effort. Then a volley of arrows appeared, arching high in the sky, aiming directly down at the witches.

Their Eifalian ally, Gael, had arrived with his archers. Their skill with bows made them fearsome foes. Sam almost shouted with joy as the arrows found their marks, making the acolytes shriek in pain.

Agathea took her attention off Sam's group to deal with the Eifalians. Their pale figures moved stealthily through the trees, keeping up a stream of deadly arrows. Agathea puffed out her cheeks and blew hard, sending a tornado of wind across the clearing. The Eifalians tumbled backward, their shots careening away. Teren and his men battled the sneevils, but they were in danger of being overrun. Agathea turned back to Sam and his companions, gathering her hands in a whirling motion as she created a large ball of witchfire.

Agathea was about to kill them all, and she would feel nothing. No remorse. No regret. She was a cold and heartless witch. Anger built inside Sam. He had to stop her. No matter what it took. But his witch-magic was spent.

Then he had it.

"Gungnir!" he shouted, and held up his hand. His palm tingled. There was a familiar crackle of energy, and then—in a flash of light and heat—his fingers were wrapped around the solid shaft of Odin's spear. At that moment, all thoughts of mercy were shoved aside. All Sam felt was the raw power of the spear and the thought of making sure Agathea never bothered them again.

Sam threw the ancient weapon with all his might. It whizzed through the air across the clearing, heading straight for Agathea's heart.

Chapter Two

Agathea's eyes grew wide at the sight of the danger. There was no time to conjure herself away. She was as good as dead. But in a blur of motion, she grabbed the nearest witch and pulled her close, using the girl as a shield. As promised by the gods, Gungnir found its target, only Agathea cheated death. The young witch was understandably shocked to see the spear in her chest. Sam recognized her.

Perrin Tarkana.

Endera Tarkana's daughter. Horror rooted him to the spot. The spear began to glow, sending sparks shooting in every direction as it vibrated in the girl's chest, and then in an explosion of bright light, it disintegrated into flying pieces of wood. Sam flinched, throwing his hands up to shield himself as stinging shards peppered his skin. When he lowered his arms, Perrin had vanished.

Agathea used the moment to spirit herself away in a cloud of billowing smoke. Agathea's acolytes scattered like roaches exposed to the light. Only the most powerful of witches had the ability to conjure themselves away. The sneevils halted in their tracks, sniffing the air as if confused.

Teren and his men charged the beasts, waving their swords. Without Agathea to control them, the animals turned and ran.

"What did you do, my lord?" Teren asked, a grin lighting his face. The men surrounded Sam, patting him on the back.

"I called on an old friend," Sam said through numb lips, staring at the spot where the young witch had been slain by his hand. Guilt and remorse were like twin slivers driven into his skull, making his head pound. "The Gungnir spear. It was a gift from Odin. It comes when you call it, and never misses its target." But this time it had. And now, all that remained was a pile of splinters.

Gael came up in a flurry of robes, along with some of his men. The Fifalians had pale skin and long white hair they kept tied back in leather laces. Their aquamarine eyes were over-sized, gifting them with the ability to read auras and see deception. Gael always acted like Sam's aura smelled like old gym socks.

"We failed to capture Agathea," Gael said tightly. "You were supposed to stop her from leaving." He looked disapprovingly over Sam.

Sam sighed. Nothing he did would ever please Gael. Not after that whole mess with the red sun curse.

"Don't be so hard on the boy." Teren put his hand on Sam's shoulder. "He fought bravely. And we sent the message that we are not to be trifled with."

Gael remained terse. "We shall see. An artifact of Odin was destroyed. That is a bad omen. There will be consequences, mark my words." He took his leave of them, citing an urgent need to head north to his home island of Torf-Einnar.

Sam gritted his teeth at the unfairness of it. They needed his help to stop the witches, but he still knew so little about how to wield his magic. And now he had destroyed a gift from Odin. *Way to blow it big time, Baron,* a voice mocked him inside his head. He still thought of himself as Sam Baron, the boy from Pilot Rock. Being the son of Robert Barconian was too much to live up to at times.

Teren led their small surviving crew south to the capital fortress, Skara Brae. As they rode, Gael's words rang in Sam's ears. The temporary victory felt fragile, as if at any moment a great and terrible power would be unleashed on the world. Ever since Odin had swept these few precious islands into his Ninth Realm, Orkney had struggled to find a peaceful balance between the magical creatures that lived here and the witches' raging thirst for power. Worry gnawed at Sam like a nest of rats that had taken root in his intestines. He had liked the power of wielding the spear, willing to take Agathea's life without hesitation. Was he already becoming cold and heartless like them?

The blond figure of Teren rode up next to him. Teren was not only the captain of the Orkadian Guard, but also a patient teacher and friend. He had taken Sam under his wing these past few months, showing him how to swing a sword and carry himself in battle.

"You all right, Samuel?" His keen eyes searched Sam's face. "You seemed upset earlier. It's not your fault Odin's spear was destroyed."

Sam shook his head. "It's not the spear—I mean, that's bad, too. But I knew that girl. Her name was Perrin. She was Endera Tarkana's daughter."

Teren's eyebrows rose. "That witch is a mother?"

Sam grimaced. "I know. I couldn't believe it either."

He told Teren how he had come face-to-face with Perrin one day in the forest. After skirmishing for days, both sides were worn out from lobbing firebombs and arrows at each other with no clear winner. Sam was resting against a tree trunk when someone plopped down against the same tree.

He held his breath, drawing his dagger as the unseen witch took a long drink.

"I know it's you," she said into the silence.

He gripped his weapon, palms sweaty.

"So you can put your skinny little blade away. I'm not going to kill you today."

Sam waited, not daring to move.

"But I am going to kill you one day," she whispered, and then she turned so her face was an inch from his.

He was surprised by how pretty she was. Dark green eyes framed a slender face with overripe red lips.

Her fingernail extended into a sharp blade. She drove the tip of it into the soft flesh under Sam's chin. "I could end your life right now, Son of Odin." Her voice was mesmerizing, trapping him in a fog of inaction.

"So why don't you?" Sam asked, feeling the sting. He'd seen that fingernail trick before, but his brain felt like it had been fried to a crisp.

"A favor to your friend, Howie. He's more than he seems. He tamed one of my mother's rathos."

Sam found himself entranced. "Your mother? Who is she?"

"Endera Tarkana. She would kill you outright." Perrin withdrew her finger and leaped to her feet before Sam could recover from his shock. "See you soon, brother witch. Next time, one of us will die."

Sam was left speechless. That's where he'd seen that trick. Endera had used it on him once. *How could someone as ruthless as Endera be a mother?* he wondered. Howie had mentioned Perrin. The witchling had been kind to his friend when he had been locked away in Endera's dungeon, sending him hot scones and little notes.

And now she was gone by Sam's own hand.

"A second later with the spear, and it would have been all of us dead," Teren said gently. "Agathea was not going to stop."

Sam faked a smile, giving Teren a weak thumbs-up. The soldier rode off to the front of the line, leaving Sam to his glum thoughts. The thrill of holding Odin's spear had been replaced by this wrenching guilt. It was a lot easier to wipe out a legion of zombies by holding a game controller than to fight in a real war.

Homesickness swamped him with a vengeance. He tried to remember Pilot Rock and his carefree days riding his bike, wind in his face as he and Howie raced each other to school, but the memories were faded, like they had happened to someone else. He was changing. Inside. The side effect of using potent magic.

A sense of wrongness settled over Sam like damp fog, and he spent the day gloomily wondering who was going to punish him first: Odin for destroying his ancient spear, or Endera for offing her daughter with it.

At long last, after a full day's ride, the horses crested the ridge overlooking Skara Brae. Red flags snapped in the breeze. The stone fortress looked serene and impregnable, built on the cliffs overlooking the blue seas below. Sam had a sudden vision of smoke billowing up from the turrets. He reined his horse in. The vision felt real, more premonition than daydream.

Teren turned in his saddle to look at him. "Everything okay, my lord?"

"Yes," Sam lied. He forced a smile. "Go on, I just need a moment."

They were within a stone's throw of Skara Brae. Teren nodded and urged the rest of the horses on.

Sam's breath caught in his chest. Something felt wrong. He searched the skyline. The glittering blue coast. The outline of the city. Nothing seemed untoward. His mare stomped her foot as the other horses headed toward buckets of well-deserved oats.

"Hold on, girl." He turned around in his saddle and spied a clump of trees.

Kicking his horse in the ribs, he urged her away from the gates. He circled the first trunk then entered the thicket. The sound of the ocean faded. Sunlight filtered through the trees, lighting up tiny dust motes. The crumbling remnants of a wall indicated a building had once stood there.

Sam reined the horse in as he saw a figure seated on the low wall. Her pale hair gave her away.

It was Vor. Goddess of Wisdom.

"Vor!" He dismounted and strode three paces to her, dropping down on his haunches to look into her sightless milky eyes. "It's good to see you."

"Samuel." She smiled and laid her hand on his arm. "Look how you've grown."

"What is this place?" he asked, looking around at the tumbled moss-covered stones.

"This used to be the Volgrim fortress, before it was torn down. Rubicus created the red sun curse here."

Sam shuddered. Rubicus had been about the worst kind of he-witch imaginable, and he was Sam's great-great-grandfather. "I killed Perrin Tarkana today," he blurted out.

Vor's smile faded, replaced by a worrisome frown. "Taking a life is a heavy burden. It will leave a black mark on your conscience, like a stain you can't wash out."

Sam wanted to shout at her that he had had no choice, but it wouldn't change the guilt he felt. Vor was right; it left a stain on him. "Why did the Gungnir explode?"

"When the Gungnir struck the wrong target, the magic in it was destroyed." She hesitated, then went on. "Samuel, I'm afraid you have set in motion a chain of events that cannot be stopped."

The blood ran out of Sam's legs. He sank down onto the mossy ground. "What do you mean?"

"You have shown yourself to be a threat. You nearly killed Agathea. Catriona will be forced to take action."

"I'm ready. I know who I fight for."

"No, Sam. You are still a child, one born of two powerful bloodlines. With every spell you cast, you become more and more attracted to the power being a witch gives you. Without your mother to guide you, I worry where it will take you."

It was like she knew his deepest fears. "So what can I do?"

But Vor turned her head sharply, as if she heard a distant noise. "I must leave." Her image fluttered. "Odin would be angry at me for interfering."

"Wait!" he cried. "Vor, what's going to happen?"

For a moment, he thought she wasn't going to answer. Her body was transparent. She was dissolving into shards of light. And then she whispered, "You must face the darkness inside you."

"What do you mean?"

Her voice came from a great distance. "If you fight it, you will lose. Surrender and you might win." The next instant, she vaporized into iridescent points of light.

Sam sat in the clearing long after she was gone, waiting for her to come back and tell him everything would be okay.

He spent the next few days mulling over Vor's words, ducking out of training to lie on his bunk, staring at the ceiling. What did she mean by facing the darkness inside him? He was one of the good guys. Sure, there were moments he felt a raw power tugging at him, like when he watched a friend die in battle, or witnessed the destruction the witches unleashed on the land. In those moments, outrage flooded his veins, making his hands tremble with a need to lash out. But he kept it under control. Because he didn't want to be like them. And he would never stop fighting for Orkney.

Finally, on the third day, Heppner dragged Sam out of his bunk, insisting the boy join them at supper. As Sam walked alongside, he stepped in a puddle, which was strange, because it hadn't rained in days. His feet rooted in place as if turned to stone. Black liquid crawled up his legs, spreading around his calves like thick tar. Coldness seeped into his bones as the black goo climbed past his knees to his waist to his chest. He felt frozen, like he had swallowed ten gallons of ice cream all at once. His voice clogged in his throat. He tried to shout at Hep to help him, but he couldn't move or even speak.

Hep turned and saw the danger Sam was in. He ran to the boy's side, but before he could reach him, the blackness swallowed Sam up.

Chapter Three

Pilot Rock, Oregon

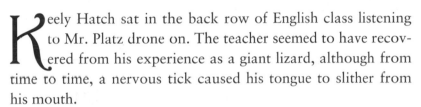

Keely Hatch sat in the back row of English class listening to Mr. Platz drone on. The teacher seemed to have recovered from his experience as a giant lizard, although from time to time, a nervous tick caused his tongue to slither from his mouth.

Howie leaned over to whisper in her ear. "You wanna come to Chuggies later? I'm working the counter. I can get you some free chili fries."

Chuggies was a burger joint owned by Howie's uncle. He let Howie work there after school. "You know I think that place is disgusting," she whispered back.

Howie just grinned, his curly hair falling over his forehead. He pushed up his glasses on his nose. "Leo said he would stop by. He said he had something important to talk about."

That got her interest up. But then, everything about Leo was interesting to her. After they returned from their adventures in Orkney, Leo's father, Chief Pate-wa, had transferred Leo back to the Umatilla school. Now they only saw Leo when he came to town. Keely had expected her dad to be beside himself with worry after her weeks' long disappearance, but Sam's mom, Abigail, had bespelled him and Howie's parents into believing they were away at a special camp for gifted students. The school had received a glowing report from the "program" Abigail had invented, and besides having to catch up on schoolwork, the matter was closed. Forgotten. As if it had never happened. As the bell rang, Keely trailed behind Howie into the hallway, thinking about Leo and Sam and witches, when a figure bumped into her.

It was Ronnie Polk, the bully who lived to torment Howie. His nose was slightly crooked from the time Sam had pounded him into the ground. His eyes were mean, small for his face, and he reminded Keely of a sneevil. Ronnie wore his pants three sizes too big. They hung so low on his hips, half his underwear showed. Two of his ugly friends slammed Howie against the lockers while Ronnie rummaged through his backpack, taking his lunch out and opening the sandwich.

"Lookee here. Grape jelly. This is gonna look nice smeared all over your face."

Keely stepped forward, ready to give Ronnie a piece of her mind, but Howie stayed her with his hand. "I got this," he said, before turning to face Ronnie, his eyes large behind his glasses. "I think you should stop picking on me."

Ronnie sneered. "Or what? You gonna tell your mommy on me?" His pals laughed along with him.

"Naw. I'm going to tell everyone you sleep with the lights on because you're scared of the dark."

Ronnie's sneer faded. "Shut up. I am not." His buddies hooted at the idea, and he joined in, though his laugh sounded a bit strained.

"No?" Howie jerked his arms free and stepped closer to the bully. "Then how come when I ride my bike past your house at night, the light is always on?"

"That's a lie." Ronnie dropped Howie's jelly sandwich and balled his hands into fists. "How about we take it outside?"

Howie raised his hands. "I'm not going to fight you. I'm

going to prove it. We'll go in the gymnasium and turn out all the lights. See who lasts longest. If I lose, you can take a free swing at me."

Keely waited for Ronnie to take Howie up on his offer, but the bully backed away, shaking his head.

"It's just a trick to get me into trouble. I'm outta here." Ronnie swaggered off, trailed by his two loser friends.

Keely raised her eyebrows at her friend's sudden bravado. "Way to go, Howie. But he ruined your lunch."

Howie whipped a candy bar out of his pocket and waggled it at her. "No problem. I always carry a supply of Nut Buddy's." He tore the blue wrapper open and took a bite. "You know I've faced off against bigger than Ronnie," he said around a mouthful of nougat. "I mean, Sam and I did defeat a whole band of witches single-handedly."

Keely smiled at his boast. "What do you think Sam is doing right now?"

"If I know my man Sam, he's probably mowing down some witches."

Keely replayed her memories of Orkney. Most of them were harsh, like being locked in Endera's dungeon with filthy rathos. But there were good ones. Being pulled on a raft by dolphins. The witch-girl Mavery. The day they had played in the ocean. "Do you ever wish you'd stayed? Back in Orkney?"

Howie didn't hesitate. "Every day. I even dream about it at night."

"Me, too." The dreams had started a week ago. The same one every night. "What do you see?" she asked.

"A big bird flying across the sky, like an eagle, only it's not."

Keely's breath quickened. "You're dreaming about a iolar. Rego had one as a pet. But you never saw a iolar when you were in Orkney, so how could you be dreaming about one?"

Howie shrugged. "What do you dream about?"

"I keep seeing this beautiful lake surrounded by trees, but I'm sure I've never been there." She sighed. "Sometimes I want to scream out loud that witches and magic really exist, but who would believe me?"

"Just me. And our wolf-brother Leo. So maybe I'll see you after school?"

She hesitated. "I need to get in some practice at the archery field, then I should get home. Get dinner for my dad. But I'll try."

They parted ways, and Keely went on to her next class. Her life after school consisted of two things: continuing her practice with a bow and taking care of her dad. Leo had taught her the basics back in Orkney, but she had been unskilled, and largely helpless. Next time, if there was a next time, she planned to be able to hold her own. Besides, it took her mind off the empty house she went home to.

Ever since her mom had died, it had just been her and her dad. She kept things normal as possible around the house. Doing the shopping. Fixing his favorite meals. Ironing his shirts. But they both missed her mom like crazy. And a gnawing guilt made it hard to talk about. A secret Keely kept and never shared out loud. She just tucked in her chin and carried on like everything was great. She could win an Oscar for her long-running performance of *Life Is Just Fine, Thank You Very Much*.

After school, Keely decided to pay a visit to Sam's mom. Keely kept a notebook on everything she knew about Orkney, peppering Abigail weekly with questions about the realm. Abigail had tried and tried to get back to Orkney, but even with her magical powers, she had not found a portal after the stonefire had been destroyed. Keely trudged up the steps to Sam's house. The lawn looked overgrown. Maybe Abigail was waiting for Sam to come home and mow it. She pressed the doorbell.

No answer.

Keely peered through the window. A pile of mail spilled over on the floor. By the looks of it, several days' worth. Had Abigail left town? Or had she found a way back to Orkney? Disappointed and more than a little frustrated, Keely decided to skip archery practice and head to Chuggies. At least Leo would be there.

As she pushed open the door to the restaurant, the smell of fried foods made her wrinkle her nose. Howie was at the register helping a couple of kids order. His curly hair poked out from under a white cap, and the red bowtie of his uniform made his Adam's apple stick out.

Keely waited till it was her turn, then stepped up to the counter. Howie's eyes lit up behind his wire-frame glasses.

"Ready for those chili fries?"

She snorted. "As if. Just a salad and drink. Where's Leo?"

"Not here yet. But he'll show. He promised."

Howie rang up her order, then handed her a cup. Another group of kids jostled her aside. She filled her cup at the soda fountain. No sooner had she sat down in a booth than a shadow fell over her. She looked up and then jumped to her feet.

"Leo!"

The tall lanky boy gave her a hug. Leo's jet-black hair was tied in a ponytail. His cheekbones were high, his chin square. His eyes were like dark chocolate. He wore his usual flannel shirt over a tee and jeans. He sat down next to her as Howie slid in on the other side of the booth, sliding a basket of chili fries in front of Leo and pushing a plate of salad toward Keely. The boys began scarfing the gooey pile down. Suddenly hungry, Keely ditched the salad and grabbed a cheese-covered fry.

"What's up, my wolf-brother?" Howie asked between bites. "We haven't seen you in a millennia."

Leo gave a tense shrug. "My father thinks I should spend all my time learning how to be a great chief. That fun is for people who don't have responsibilities. Sometimes I want to run away as far as possible."

Howie waved a fry at him. "What you need is another adventure, my man. A one-way ticket to Orkney to wrestle some sneevils, or take down a witch or two."

Leo leaned in, lowering his voice. "That's why I'm here. I've been having dreams. About Orkney."

Keely and Howie traded looks. Things were getting weird. Orkney weird.

"We've been having dreams, too," Keely said. "I keep seeing this lake surrounded by trees."

"I see one of those iolar birds," Howie added.

"What do you see?" Keely asked.

Leo hesitated. "I don't know why, but . . . I see us drowning under water." The color went out of his friends' faces. "Look, these might not be just dreams."

"What else could they be?" Keely asked, almost scared to know.

Before Leo could answer, the table began to shake, vibrating under her hands, making the fries skip across the surface. The overhead lights swayed wildly. Under her feet, Keely felt a rumble, then a loud crack echoed like a rifle shot. A jagged opening appeared in the tile floor, zigzagging across the length of the restaurant. Water shot out of the crack as if a water main had broken. Screaming patrons fled the restaurant as gushing water sprayed everywhere, dousing Keely and the others.

"What's happening?" Keely cried.

"I think it's an earthquake," Leo shouted over the ruckus, taking her hand and pulling her out of the booth.

The soda machine went crazy, spraying fizzy liquid from every nozzle. Behind the counter, the shake machine turned on and began to spin, spewing thick gooey liquid in the air.

"Where's Howie?" Keely asked. They looked around the deserted restaurant. There. Howie was lugging a bucket. He scooped up water and slogged it over to the sink.

"Howie, we have to go!" Keely shouted. They splashed to Howie's side, but he refused to budge.

"My uncle went to the bank and left me in charge. I can't let Chuggies go down the drain." He looked like a drowned rat, his drenched curls plastered to his face, but his chin was determined.

Keely took a good look around. Something was odd. The

restaurant was filling up too fast. Already the water was to their knees. Another minute and it would be at their waists. She tugged on Howie's arm. "Come on, we have to get out before we're trapped in here."

Howie resisted, but as the water surged higher, he dropped the bucket, looking dejected. He followed her and Leo toward the door, but the waist-high water dragged on them, pulling them back. The harder they pressed forward, the more the water tugged them in reverse, like an invisible current was sucking them in. Keely lost her grip on Leo's arm.

"Leo!" she cried in a panic, clutching at his hand. He grabbed for her but missed. The water swirled faster and faster around the restaurant, churning her like she was stuck in the spin cycle of a washing machine. The water rose higher, impossibly fast, until, moments later, she was floating, pressed up against the ceiling.

Leo bobbed next to her. Behind her, Howie flailed his arms, shouting for help. Keely had to think fast, or they were all going to drown.

"Take a deep breath and swim for the door," Keely shouted. Leo nodded, puffing his cheeks out. Howie looked panicked, but he plugged his nose as the water reached the ceiling and sealed them off.

The strange current tumbled and spun her, but Keely was determined to find a way out. The door was just over there. She could see daylight coming through the murky water. She just had to reach it and hope Leo and Howie found their way. She kicked herself forward, fighting the current, and headed for the light. A flickering image came toward her. It had a speckled body and swam close enough for her to see its gills. It looked like a trout of some kind.

What was a fish doing in Chuggies?

Keely kept fighting her way forward. Either the door was farther than she thought, or the water was pushing her backward. Finally, as her lungs were about to explode, the current died down. A strange light shone above her. She could see blue sky on the other side. Keely didn't have time to question where it came from. She kicked hard and broke through the surface, dragging in a lungful of air. She shook wet hair out of her face and looked around.

Chuggies was gone. And all of Pilot Rock. Replaced by a pristine lake rimmed by thick willowy trees. The lake from her dreams. The sun was just cresting above the horizon. A low mist clung to the surface of the water. In the distance, a snow-capped mountain rose. Ravens cawed a greeting from the trees lining the small lake. And then a large noble bird flew over, dipping down to snatch a speckled fish in its beak.

Keely nearly shouted with joy as she recognized the distinctive orange- and cinnamon-tipped feathers and the snowy white chest. That was a iolar. The same species as Rego's departed companion, Lagos.

Which meant they were back. In Orkney.

Next to her, Leo broke the surface with a loud gasp. "Where's Howie?" He spun around in the water.

Keely searched the area. Leave it to Howie to get lost. She was about to dive under to search for him when he popped up behind them, gasping for air.

Howie let out a whoop. "What's up, Orkney!" he shouted, pumping his fist in the air.

Keely sighed with relief, exchanging grins with Leo, and then the trio swam to shore. They wrung out their clothes, shivering in the brisk air.

"What just happened?" Keely asked, looking from Leo to Howie as she squeezed water out of her thick hair.

"It's what I was trying to tell you," Leo said. "Those weren't dreams we were having, they were premonitions. Someone was sending a message."

"I bet my buddy Sam did the old toilet-flush trick to get us back to Orkney. Obviously he needs our help," Howie answered, polishing his glasses and replacing them. Miraculously they had stayed on in that washtub. He looked a bit ridiculous in his dripping Chuggies uniform. The white shirt clung to his chest. The matching pants were mud-streaked and ripped on the knee. His red bow tie had come untied and hung limply.

Leo absently rubbed the twisting scar on his arm, the one he'd gotten from the Shun Kara bite the day he and Sam first met. "What if it's Endera up to her old tricks?"

Keely thought about it, then shook her head. "No. Endera didn't do this. Do you remember what Brunin said to us? Back on Asgard?" They had encountered a giant warrior bear named Brunin while exploring Asgard, one Mavery claimed was actually Odin.

Leo nodded. "He said the day would come when Sam would need us to stand by him."

"What if that day is now?"

Leo remained silent, skeptical.

Howie clasped his hands on their shoulders. "Listen, my buddy Sam has always had my back. Friends stand together—that's what he would say when someone bullied me. I say it's time we stood by Sam." He thrust one scrawny fist out. "To Orkney."

There was silence. Like it or not, they were here. Keely wasn't sure she was ready for an adventure of this size, but something prodded her on. The idea that Sam needed her to do this. To be brave when what she really wanted was to dive back in the lake and swim home as fast as she could. "To finding Sam," Keely said, placing her fist in the circle.

They waited, watching Leo's face, needing him to join in.

"To staying alive," Leo added ruefully, covering Keely's hand with his.

Chapter Four

"Hello? Is anybody there?"

Sam's words were met with silence. He had awoken to find himself lying on a slab of cold stone. He sat up, trying to adjust to the darkness. Where was he? His head was fuzzy, like his brains had been scrambled.

Think, Baron, he said to himself. *How did you get here?* Last thing he remembered, he had been walking along with Speria . . . or was it Heppner? And then he had stepped into some black goo.

Sam got to his feet and found his legs were wobbly, but held him. He reached for the familiar pouch he wore around his neck, but it was gone. Feeling bereft, he blinked in the darkness, wishing he had light. He rubbed his cold hands together and then snapped his fingers. A flicker of light appeared over his palm. It was weak, but at least he could make out his chamber.

There wasn't much to see: Roughhewn walls carved out of solid black granite. A stone floor spattered with the water that dripped down from unseen cracks in the ceiling. The air was oppressive, like there were fifty stories of cold unfeeling rock above him. A metal door had been notched in the wall. Sam shivered, feeling the cold press in on him.

"You got lousy service here," he joked out loud. "Where's

the double cheeseburger I ordered? And my extra pillows haven't been delivered. You're not going to like the review I leave online. Zero stars for this joint." His voice echoed off the walls, pinging back at him, piercing his skin like acid-tipped darts to remind him how alone in the universe he was.

Sam's eyes fell on the door. He ran his hands over it. The seams fit snug into the rock. There was no latch on the inside. Maybe magic could open it.

He stepped back, shaking out the tension in his hands. His light went out, but he focused on opening the door. Channeling his magic, he put all his energy into creating a spell that would get him out of this prison. He said the words aloud, to add strength to his spell, and because he needed to hear a voice, even if it was his own.

"*Fein kinter, terminus*," he said, then thrust forward with his palms. Emerald-tinged light shot from his palms and hit the door, which glowed brightly. Sam's hope flared, but then the magic crackled and pooled in the center of the door and then zinged back at him, zapping him so hard that his teeth hurt and his hands went numb.

So it was enchanted. Good to know.

He needed to think this through. Sam sat down, then laid back, staring into the darkness. If magic couldn't get him out, he would have to wait and see what the witches wanted. They had to be behind his kidnapping. Who else had the power to plant some kind of magical black tar and kidnap him? Only Catriona.

If Howie were here, he would find some way to make a joke about it. When Endera had locked him in her dungeon, Howie had befriended a rathos he named Bert. A tsunami of loneliness washed over Sam. He missed his friends. How long since he had last seen them? Six months? He remembered Keely's laughter around the campfire the night before they set out for Asgard. Mavery's little dance, her antics entertaining them all. And Leo, stoic and brave, but a true friend.

He wondered what they were doing. They had probably

gone on with their lives, and their algebra homework, and forgotten all about him. Howie had probably beaten all ninety-nine levels of Zombie Wars III. Heck, he was probably playing Zombie Wars V by now. Sam wallowed around in his self-pity until a strange sound made him turn his head. A skittering sound. Like something was crawling across the stone.

He tensed, his nerves firing on all pistons as he sat up, listening hard to decipher the noise.

There it was again. A soft scratching.

"Who's there?"

The noise stopped. Sam held his breath, waiting. When it didn't reoccur, he relaxed, about to lie down, but then he heard it again, louder this time. Bolder.

There was something in the cell with him. Sam's heart started beating faster. His hands were still numb, but he rubbed them together as the sounds got closer, trying to get his light back. He snapped his fingers. There was a spark, but nothing happened. He did it again, feeling the hairs on the back of his neck stand up as something brushed against his leg.

Fear made his fingers slick with sweat. He tried again, focusing everything on this one tiny spell. Light flared long enough for him to see his cell clearly.

It was crawling with scorpions. Dozens of them. As big as lobsters.

Deathstalkers, his mind supplied. He could tell by their oversized red bodies and the yellow bands across their pincers. Their tails curved up around their backs, tipped with lethal-looking stingers guaranteed to deliver a fatal dose of poison.

"Get back!" He scrambled away, but there were more behind him. They surrounded him.

Was this some kind of nightmare he was reliving? Endera had tried to kill him once by dropping a Deathstalker in his crib. Sam tried blasting them with witchfire, but his numb hands wouldn't work. The first creature bit him on the ankle.

He let out a yell as a fire burned in his blood. The venom

acted like nitroglycerin, sending his heart rate skyrocketing. His light flickered out, and he was left in the darkness. Another bit him on the thigh. He kicked them away, but they kept coming.

Catriona stared into the glowing malachite orb. She had uncovered it from the bowels of this moldering pile of stones Endera and the others called home. It had been covered in dust and cobwebs. A useless piece of glass to anyone else. In her hands, it came alive. Showed her what she desired most.

And right now, she desired watching the young witch-boy suffer. In the fog of the rounded glass, his body twisted and contorted under the ministrations of her deadly pets.

"Is he dead yet?" Agathea hissed over her shoulder.

They were in Catriona's private quarters, high up in the north tower of the Tarkana fortress. She had commandeered the entire wing. Rectangular openings carved into the walls allowed her to view the dank, steamy swamps below. Fat candles dripped wax on the stone floor. The light flickered as a cold wind blew in. It was raining out. Lightning slashed the sky. A stormy day, perfectly suited to her mood.

Annoyed at the interruption, Catriona waved her hand over the glass, sending the Deathstalkers away. "I didn't bring him here to kill him."

"You wish to torture him. Fine, let me unleash my rathos on him," Agathea coaxed, a white stripe of hair falling over her face. She drew an oversized rodent from her pocket. "They will eat him alive. Slow as you want," Agathea promised, lovingly stroking her pet.

Behind her, the voiceless Beatrixe waved her hands in the air, signaling her silent agreement. Wizened old Bronte ignored them, her bent figure huddled over a cauldron. She stirred it slowly, muttering one of her incantations.

Catriona seated herself on a broad velveteen chair in front

of the fire. "Calm yourself, sister. He is far more valuable to us alive."

"He tried to kill me," Agathea sulked, seating herself across from Catriona. "Perhaps you grow soft. The brat fights for those Orkadian filth."

Catriona gave her a look of such intense anger that the other witch shrank back in her seat. She raised her hand and made a fist. The rathos in Agathea's hands squeaked in agony, its eyes bulging.

"Sister, I am sorry," Agathea pleaded. "I didn't mean to offend."

The rat began to shake and then exploded into a puff of black smoke, drizzling ash onto Agathea's lap.

Catriona seethed. "You know what I desire, what I have plotted for centuries. Vengeance for our father."

"And you will have it, sister." Agathea trembled.

"Killing Odin is no small feat. He would never let us close enough. But at last, the key to Odin's destruction is in our hands."

Old Bronte cackled as her brew bubbled over. It gave off a cloud of steam that smelled deliciously of rotted beets and dried toad legs. "Odin's blood can take Odin's blood," she sang out, dragging her cauldron to her potion table.

Catriona smiled. "Exactly. Samuel Barconian spans both bloodlines." She stood and moved to the mantle, opening the jeweled case that rested there and lifting the heavy black dagger her father had imbued with his magic. "He is a Son of Odin and a Son of Rubicus. He alone can get close enough to place this blade into Odin's treacherous heart."

"Impossible," Agathea sniped. "He is just a child."

"The same child who released us from our prison," Catriona sniped back. She replaced the blade and paced in front of the hearth. "He has a darkness inside of him. I feel it. He fights it, but if he is pushed, he will turn to our side. The Deathstalkers are there to fill his veins with poison, turning him to our purpose and draining his soul of all hope. And because I enjoy watching him suffer."

Bronte's voice rose above the clatter of her potion making.

"The venom will do its part. We shall supply the rest." She opened a small glass vial, using a pair of tweezers to remove a long brown hair. "I have saved this for centuries, waiting for the right moment to use it."

Catriona hurried to her potion table. It was filled with jars and bottles with names even she didn't recognize. She studied the hair. "What is it? The hair of a sneevil?"

"A single hair from the head of Rubicus." Bronte dropped it into an empty goblet, then ladled some of the liquid from her cauldron and swirled it around. The liquid bubbled and frothed. A purplish fog trickled out, rising up in a snaking trail. "Behold the essence of his dark magic. One taste of this and the boy will forget every good thought he ever had." She held up a bottle, capturing the fog inside and sealing it with a cork.

Catriona's eyes glowed with excitement. "Nothing can get in our way once we put our plan into motion," she crowed. "Absolutely nothing."

Chapter Five

After hours of hiking through Orkney woods so dense only glimpses of sky peeked through, Keely declared themselves hopelessly lost. Trees towered overhead, their gnarled branches twisting and twining to form a canopy that kept the air dank and cool. Strings of feathery moss trailed down from the boughs. The ground was soft under feet with a thick layer of dead leaves. As they passed a fallen log, Keely spied a soggy blue candy wrapper and knelt down.

"Whoa, what's a Nut Buddy wrapper doing here?" Howie asked in awe.

Keely rolled her eyes at him. "I'm guessing you dropped it, dope. Obviously we're going in circles. And thanks for sharing." She shoved the wrapper at him, then plopped herself down on the log, feeling her frustration rise.

"I was hungry," Howie said with an unapologetic grin. "I found it in my pocket."

"Great," Keely huffed. "We're going to starve before we ever figure out why we're here." When they had struck off away from the lake, she had expected things to magically fall into place. But the exhilaration of finding themselves back in Orkney was fading, and reality was setting in. "We have no idea where we are, or how far the nearest town is. And what are our parents going to think? My dad is probably freaking out right now."

Leo knelt by her side. "Something powerful brought us here. I'm sure it will guide us forward. And there's nothing we can do about our families. We have to be patient and figure this out."

"Yeah, Sam's probably right around the next bend," Howie said confidently, yapping on about how excited Sam would be when he saw them.

Keely's ears picked up another sound. "Shh," she said, listening. The rumbling sound of a voice filtered through the trees.

"Someone's close by," Leo said, rising to his feet.

But Keely was already wading through bushes, following the sounds until she reached a clearing covered in soft grass sprinkled with blue wildflowers. A bright shaft of sunlight lit up an ancient stone well. A crow balanced on the battered shingled roof, bobbing its head at an old man. The man had a long beard that flowed to his knobby knees. He wasn't very tall, about Keely's height, and not much more than skin and bones. One eye appeared larger than the other. His white tunic was stained with age and time. A thick rope hung down from the well roof. The man hauled it up, until it dangled a wooden bucket dripping with water.

Shakily, he poured water from the bucket into a weathered wooden bowl and then hunkered down over the bowl, stirring it with one long, dirt-stained finger.

"Excuse me," Keely said.

He startled, knocking the bowl over, then cursed as the liquid seeped into the ground.

"*Feregen*, child. You don't sneak up on an old man like that. Now look what you did." Using a gnarled stick to lever himself up, he lifted the bucket back over the well and lowered it down again.

Leo nudged her, and she took the opportunity to draw closer.

"I'm Keely." She gave a hesitant smile. "This is Leo, and Howie. We're here. We made it," she added, in case her meaning was unclear.

"I know who you are," he muttered with a dark scowl. "Like I have nothing better to do than run around doing Odin's bidding. Don't just stand there, boy," he snapped at Leo. "Help an old man."

Leo stepped in and took the rope from him, lowering the bucket hand over hand.

"You were sent by Odin?" Keely's heart quickened. She exchanged excited glances with Leo and Howie.

"Odin and I have an arrangement." The old man snickered. "I plucked his right eye from his head, just like that." He snapped his fingers in her face.

Keely tried to remember the stories she had read in the library. Odin had sacrificed an eye to gain wisdom.

"You're Mimir!" she blurted out.

The old man danced a little jig. "Mimir the Wise, at your service."

"Who's Mimir?" Leo asked, drawing the full bucket to the ledge.

Pieces of the story came back to her. "According to legend, Mimir was an ancient sage who possessed great wisdom. Odin traded Mimir to the Vanir, frost giants who lived in an icy northern realm, in exchange for peace. Odin promised them a fountain of knowledge, but Mimir spouted nonsense. The frost giants were so angry, they sent Mimir's head back to Odin in a bag."

"Ouch!" Howie murmured, rubbing his neck. "So if this guy's Mimir, why's he still got his head?"

"Lost my head but not my brains," Mimir giggled, then raised his skinny arms, grabbed his ears, and tugged upward. A wet, popping sound rang out, and then he was holding his own head.

Keely's stomach rolled at the grotesque image. Howie made retching noises. Even Leo coughed to cover his discomfort.

The eyebrows on the decapitated head waggled as Mimir kept talking. "The Vanir did not like my advice. But then listening and hearing are two different skills. The Vanir listened, but they did not heed my words." With a forceful grunt, Mimir pulled his head back on his neck.

Keely trailed a hand along the stone wall. "If you're really Mimir, this must be your Well of Wisdom," she said, peering over the ledge. The inside walls were bearded with dappled moss. Two stories below, the water glimmered faintly. And then she saw something mysterious; a swirl of light on the surface that beckoned her closer.

Howie elbowed in next to her. "What is that?" The odd glow reflected on Howie's glasses.

"Magic," Leo answered, sounding awestruck.

A sharp clapping made them turn around. "Sit, children." Mimir waved them down as he sat himself on a rock. "Join an old man."

They left the well and sat in a half-circle before him.

"His head's on crooked," Howie whispered in Keely's ear. "Should we say something?"

Keely elbowed him to be quiet. "So are you the one that sent for us?"

Mimir puffed his cheeks out. "Maybe yes, maybe just a guess."

Keely gritted her teeth over his evasive answer. "We're looking for a friend, Sam Baron. Do you know where he is?"

Up on the well, the crow cawed harshly as if it understood the name. "You mean the worthless rat who stole this?" Mimir drew a battered horn from the folds of his tunic and waved it at her.

The Horn of Gjall. Keely recognized the runic symbols carved on it. Sam had stolen it from Odin to try to barter for Howie's life, but in the end he had chosen to return it rather than betray the god.

"I thought the horn belonged to Odin," she challenged, folding her arms. "You know it can summon an army of the dead."

"Ooh, are you planning on calling up some skeletons?" Howie asked, clapping his hands excitedly. "I'd like to see that."

Mimir poked Howie in the chest with one gnarled finger.

"Careful what you wish for, boy, or you'll see firsthand what an army of the dead can do. This horn has many powerful purposes. Odin lets me borrow it to conjure the wisdom he seeks. Your Sam almost handed it over to the witches."

"Sam helped save this realm," Leo reminded him.

Mimir snorted. "The witch-boy is reckless."

Leo's eyes flashed in defense. "He is a Son of Odin and—"

"—And because his father's father's father descended from Odin you think he deserves my respect?" Mimir was so upset, spittle flew from his lips. His face reddened as he ranted on. "He is also a Son of Rubicus, the evilest he-witch to ever walk the land. The boy's future is clouded. Every day I drink from the well, but I cannot see which path he will choose."

Keely leaned forward eagerly. "Then let us try. We can help."

Mimir folded his arms. "There is a price to pay to drink from my well. Odin sacrificed his eye." He shoved his face an inch from hers. "You have beautiful eyes."

She reared back. "I'm not letting you take one of my eyes. There has to be something else we can offer."

"It is not the price, but the sacrifice you make," he said craftily. "What do you value more than anything?"

"Besides my father, my friends," she said simply. Howie and Leo nodded. "But we're not sacrificing one of us," she added hastily.

"Then we have nothing to discuss." Mimir levered himself to his feet with his crooked stick. He packed his bowl and shoved the horn into a worn satchel he slung over his shoulder. "I told Odin it was a waste of time bringing you here, that you were nothing but earth children." He made the last part sound like the worst sort of insult. "And as usual, I was right." He spun on one knobby knee and began to trundle into the woods. The crow hopped down from the well, flying over to his shoulder, shaking its head at them accusingly, as if even it were disgusted with them.

"We don't need him," Leo said. "We'll figure it out on our own."

But Keely needed answers. "Wait!"

Mimir paused, cocking his head to the side.

"There has to be something we can give that doesn't include an eye or one of us," Keely pleaded.

Mimir slowly turned, folding his scrawny arms across his chest. "I'm listening."

She nervously twisted her hair around her fingers. It was long and thick and blonde. Her mother used to braid it every night before bed. Keeping it long made Keely feel close to her. "My hair. I'll cut off my hair. I haven't cut it since my mom died. It's the best I can do."

Mimir hesitated, scratching one hand over his chin as he thought it over.

"It's not much of a sacrifice," he finally wheezed, "but I can see that it pains you to lose it. It will do." He turned back to the clearing and dumped the contents of his satchel on the ground.

"What about us?" Leo asked, but Mimir waved him away.

"One is enough." The old sage fished inside his tunic and pulled out a knife. The handle was made of polished bone. The blade looked sharp, curved with a wicked point. He set the knife before Keely.

"What do I do?" Keely asked.

"You must make the sacrifice, and then you may drink from my well," he answered.

Keely's fingers trembled slightly. What if it didn't work? Or if Mimir was lying? She lifted a swath of her hair, hesitating.

Was she crazy for trying this?

No, she told herself, *Sam faced sneevils and biters and a pack of witches to rescue me.* She closed her eyes and began to saw back and forth.

Swack. A thick lock of hair dropped to the grass. She stared at it in shock, hardly believing she had just done this to herself.

"It's okay, Keely," Leo said, his hand warm on her arm.

"Yeah," Howie added. "We're right here."

Grimly, she lifted another hunk, gripping it tightly, and cut it off. She cut again and again, letting the clumps of hair fall in a heap around her.

When she was done, she ran her fingers through her shorn hair, torn by regret. It felt like she had lost a piece of her mother. She silently passed the knife back to Mimir.

The sage appeared satisfied. He tipped some water from the bucket into the bowl, then threw a handful of tresses in. The blonde wisps sizzled and turned into smoke as they hit the surface. He stirred the water with one dirty finger, then took the horn and scooped up some of the liquid. He held it out to Keely.

"Drink."

Keely took the ancient object. She looked down at the filmy surface and saw a reflection of her eye. Then something else, a spark of light that grew. Her reflection disappeared and the water glistened with promise.

Before she could change her mind, she lifted the horn to her lips. The water was cool and tasted sweet. She tilted it back, drinking deeply, and then closed her eyes, focusing on the answers she sought.

How do I help Sam?

But before the thought was fully formed, a vision slammed into her head.

Chapter Six

Keely was jolted by an image of ice and blizzarding snow. It was like she was there in the freezing hail. North. Sam's salvation lay in the northern part of Orkney. She saw a shield bearing a symbol with two bears. One bit the end of the other so they formed a circle.

Her body shuddered as images hit her in waves. There was a cave guarded by a strange eight-legged creature. The cave was filled with blue light from a full moon. It shone down on a shimmering pool in the center. In the bottom of the pool, a small white object glimmered like a fat pearl.

She needed to go to this place. The feeling was an overwhelming urge. Another, more violent shudder gripped her.

You are Chosen. The words echoed in her head, and she saw the journey she was to take. *The Seeker.* She was alone. Howie and Leo were not going with her. Fear turned her arms to rubber, and the horn slipped from her hands.

I'm not going without Leo and Howie. No way.

But the visions kept coming, one after another, flooding her brain like a movie stuck on fast-forward. Howie dressed in a soldier's uniform. *Orkney's Protector.* And Leo. *The Sacrifice.* She saw a golden cuff on the leg of a monster. It had the head of a giant lizard and the body of an armadillo. Darkness swirled around Leo, and in the darkness, she sensed a malignant evil like nothing she had ever felt before. A man's eyes glittered with mirth.

Arrows of pain pierced her heart as she saw Sam, writhing in agony in a dark cell, his only company a swarm of scorpions the size of lobsters. Then she glimpsed Mavery, her favorite little witch, with her head on a chopping block. A giant man stood over her cloaked in a black hood as he hefted an axe high over his head.

Keely saw armies advancing across snowy fields, giant men battling against Eifalian archers, bodies falling everywhere. And then a phalanx of witches arriving to wipe out the survivors. Tears ran down her cheeks as she saw army after army fall to the unstoppable forces of the witches, and at the front of them, standing by Catriona's side, was a dark-haired he-witch with a burning yellow gaze.

Sam.

It was like watching a horror movie, only she couldn't close her eyes and escape the bloodshed. Then something even more frightening made her gasp. Catriona and Sam thrust their hands in the sky. There was an explosion of bright light, blinding, like an atomic bomb had gone off. A jagged tear zigzagged across the sky, like the universe itself was splitting in half. As the light reached the ground at their feet, Catriona stepped through it, followed by Sam and her army of witches. Keely choked at the sight waiting on the other side.

Pilot Rock Junior High. Catriona stood outside the cafeteria, whirling in delight.

With a gasp, Keely opened her eyes. Mimir stared at her intently, his bony arms wrapped around his knees.

"Tell me what you saw. Tell me all."

Keely's throat clogged with emotion. "Sam's in trouble. The witches . . . they're tormenting him." She wiped the tears from her eyes as she relived the images of the scorpions swarming over him.

"Can he be brought back to the light?" Mimir asked, pinching her arm in a tight grasp. "Or is he is already lost to the witches?"

"Back off, old man," Leo warned.

Keely bit her tongue. No way she was going to tell Mimir she saw Sam tearing Orkney to pieces alongside Catriona. Because it wasn't going to happen, not if she and Leo and Howie did their part. She glared at the wise man. "Sam will never be one of them. My friends and I are Chosen Ones. I am the Seeker. I have to go north and find a pearl that can help Sam. Howie is Orkney's Protector. He has to guard Skara Brae until I return. And Leo . . ." Her voice dropped. "Leo is the Sacrifice."

She tried to stand, but Mimir's grip tightened, and his lips curved into an odd smile.

"Chosen, you say? Then our deal is not done . . ." He released her arm and plucked a feather from the raven, eliciting a sharp squawk from it. He moistened the tip with his tongue. Then he grabbed her hand, turning it over in his own. With the sharp tip of the feather's shaft, he poked her palm once, making it sting. She snatched her hand back as a drop of blood welled up. The crazy coot just laughed and handed Howie the Horn of Gjall.

"Here, boy. You said you wanted to see an army of the dead. As Orkney's Protector, you might need to before this is over."

"Suhweet!" Howie's eyes were wide with excitement.

"What about me?" Leo asked.

Mimir spat on the blade Keely had used to cut her hair, wiping it clean on his tunic before passing it to Leo. "Doubt you'll survive the beast that guards that cuff, but a blade comes in handy." He sniffed the air, looking suddenly wary. "Be gone now. These woods are full of dangers."

Leo tucked the blade in his belt and tugged Keely to her feet. "Come on. Let's go."

They headed back into the woods. Howie played with the horn, bringing it to his lips like he wanted to blow on it, but Keely slapped his hand. "Don't you dare. Put it away."

He tucked it in his waistband under his shirt, muttering that she was no fun.

"You said we were chosen," Leo asked. "That I'm the Sacrifice. What does that mean?"

Keely filled him in as best she could. "I saw a golden cuff on the leg of a monster. It had the head of a giant lizard and the body of an armadillo."

"Oooh, an iguanadillo," Howie supplied from her other side.

Keely elbowed him. "No jokes, Howie, this is serious. Leo has to defeat that . . . iguanadillo to claim the cuff, and if he survives . . . then the cuff will take him someplace dark, that's all I saw."

There was silence. The wind rustled the leaves in the trees.

Leo's eyes were wide, but he nodded, as if he were trying to reassure himself it was going to be okay.

"What about me?" Howie asked nonchalantly. "You said something about Orkney's Protector? That was a joke, right?"

But Keely wasn't listening. "Why's it so cold?" she asked, teeth chattering.

While they had been walking, a bank of fog had rolled in, spreading through the forest, casting a chill to the air and blocking the sun's warmth. A rustling of leaves made Keely's hair stand up. Then something cold and icy passed over her face.

"Wraiths!" Leo shouted.

His warning sent a chill through Keely. She had pages of notes on wraiths in her Orkney notebook after grilling Sam's mom about them. Undead beauties cursed to walk the land in eternity by the goddess Freya as punishment for their vanity. If you looked directly at them, they would pierce you with icy bolts shot from their eye sockets that sapped your life force. Sam bore a ragged scar on his shoulder from one he had encountered in the woods with Mavery.

"Don't look at them!" Keely called out. "They can't hurt you if you don't answer their call." They sat down in a circle, their backs pressed against each other. She pressed her fists into her eyes as Howie and Leo did the same.

The air grew thick and cold, sapping her of warmth. The whispering sounds of ghostly creatures flying through the mist made her suddenly wish she was back home in Pilot Rock safe in bed. Only Leo's presence next to her, and Howie's chattering teeth on the other side, kept her from running screaming into the woods.

Then it got worse; she began to hear them, murmuring to her, talking in her ear, telling her to lower her hands and open her eyes.

An irresistible craving came over her. A curiosity so deep, so intense, she had no will power to fight it. She *wanted* to look at them. The urge was overwhelming, a siren song playing in her head.

"See the wonders of the night. See the dead come back to life."

The dead come back to life? Keely had a sudden longing to see her mother. Cutting her hair off had brought her grief right to the top. Abigail's dire warnings not to look flew out of her head, replaced with a sudden need. What harm could it do to take a quick peek? What if she saw her mom? Just a glimpse would be amazing. Slowly, Keely lowered her hands. Her right eye fluttered open, and then her left.

Ghostlike creatures trailed around their group, wrapping themselves like gauze over each of them. They looked female, long wispy tresses curling behind them. Their faces were surprisingly beautiful, an ethereal image of what was once alive. She searched eagerly, seeking the familiar face, and then one of the wraiths locked in on her open gaze.

An arrow of awareness shot through Keely as if she and the creature were mentally joined. In that moment, Keely saw through its ghostly exterior into the heart of the creature, sensing a tiny spark that contained the wraith's humanity and compassion. And then the spark was crushed out. Keely gasped, realizing the danger too late as the wraith made straight for her. As it drew near, its face hollowed out, revealing a ghastly vision. Bony cheekbones and skeletal lips pulled back into a snarl. Keely threw her arm over her face, but the wraith shot a bolt of ice from its glittering eye sockets.

Keely shrank back, expecting to be impaled, but a blur of movement knocked her over. Leo jumped in front of her, taking the blow to his side. The wraiths circled over them, furiously thrashing and screeching as they prepared to unleash more of their deadly ice bolts. Desperate to save Leo, Keely flung her body over his.

"Stop it!" she cried. "He is a Chosen One." Her words echoed in the chill air.

Unexpectedly, the wraiths drew back and became still, floating in place as if her words held some kind of magical power. Then they screeched in unison, a piercing sound so loud it made Keely's ears hurt. They whirled furiously, lashing the kids with a chill wind, before joining into a single chain and disappearing into the murky fog.

Guilty horror filled Keely as a crimson stain spread across Leo's shirt. "This is all my fault." Her teeth chattered with shock. She wished she could go back in time and make everything better.

"It's okay, Keely." Leo's face was gray. "I'll be fine."

"No, it's not." Keely scanned her memory for every detail Abigail had told her about the undead maidens. "I need to pull it out. Their ice is filled with poison." She grasped the icy bolt and slid it free. It turned into vapor in her hands. Howie gathered some moist leaves and packed them in around Leo's waist.

"Hey, my wolf-brother, don't die on me," Howie joked, but he looked worried, his eyes big behind his glasses.

Keely pressed her hand on Leo's arm. "We're not going to let anything happen to you, are we, Howie?" She looked at Howie, needing reassurance.

Howie scoffed. "No way my wolf-brother is going down. Not without a gnarly fight. Soooo . . . about my path?" Howie asked nervously. "You didn't mean that part about being Protector and all, right? I mean, Odin probably picked me as Chief Nerd."

Keely shook her head. "Odin chose you as Protector of the Realm, Howie. You wore the uniform of the Orkadian guard. Without you, Skara Brae will fall."

"Are you serious?" Howie's face burned red with embarrassment. "If this is Odin's idea of a joke, the joke's on him because I'm not that guy."

Keely grasped him by his scrawny shoulders. "Odin put his trust in us, Howie. Us—not me, not Leo, all of us. I saw how you stood up to Ronnie Polk. You're not the same guy who used to get grape-jelly facials. Mimir gave you Odin's Horn of Gjall! He must believe you're trustworthy."

Howie smiled weakly, still unconvinced.

"What else did you see, Keely?" Leo asked, wincing as he tried to sit up.

"My job is to bring back that pearl. It's somewhere at the bottom of a pond. I think it's the key to saving Sam. I saw blizzards and snow. Oh, yeah, and a giant beast with octo legs guarded it." There was more to her visions, a lot more. But something urged her to hold back on the details. No need to burden them when they already had so much to deal with.

"Well, what are we waiting for?" Howie said, leaping to his feet. "We are the Chosen Ones, so let's get out there and do some Chosen work."

Chapter Seven

Howie might have been eager to get moving, but there was no way Leo was up to it. The sun was already sinking behind the trees, and Leo looked too weak to stand. "I'm actually pretty tired," Keely said, jerking her head at Howie so the lunkhead would notice Leo wasn't going anywhere. "I think we should stay here for the night. Maybe try to get a fire going. In the morning, we can figure a way out of these woods."

"I will be fine by morning," Leo said, though his voice was tinged with pain. "I just need to rest."

"No problem. I can get a fire going," Howie said, cracking his knuckles like popcorn.

Keely raised an eyebrow. "Serious? I didn't know you were a Boy Scout."

He shrugged. "I wasn't. But I did go to science camp. And they thought us nerds should know how to survive in the wilderness in case, you know, we got lost walking from the mess hall to rocket lab. You had to start a fire with nothing but a stick and some moss." He looked around the clearing. "And I think we have plenty of that here."

He scurried off, rummaging for the perfect piece of wood.

Keely turned back to Leo, putting her hand on his forehead. He was burning up. She took off her denim jacket and made a pillow under his head. "Get some rest. Things will be better in the morning."

He nodded, his eyes already drooping.

Keely sat back. Her stomach rumbled in protest. It would have been nice of Odin to give them a little advance warning so they could have at least packed snacks. And not saying goodbye to her dad was awful. He would be lost without her. Howie returned with an armful of wood and wads of dried moss. He busied himself with a rock, boring a hole into a log. Then he crumbled some dry moss in it and added a small piece of wood.

"Okay, let's see if the ol' How-master still has the magic touch."

Placing the tip of the stick in the small hole, Howie swirled the stick between his palms, spinning it back and forth. His tongue was clasped firmly between his teeth. Keely hovered, hoping for a miracle, but prepared to console Howie if his experiment failed. The sun was fading, and a fire sounded really good. Leo was sleeping, but his brow glistened with sweat.

"I think Leo may have an infection," she said. What would they do if he got really sick?

Howie shouted with glee. "Got it. Nailed it. Knew I could do it."

A tiny tendril of smoke rose from the log. He blew on it, pursing his lips and getting his face close. A little flame jumped up.

Keely smiled, feeling a surge of hope. Things would look better once they had a fire going. "Way to go, Howie."

He added some small twigs and fed it shreds of moss. "Come on, little fire, bring us some warmth. Hey, you don't think those wraiths are going to come back, do ya?"

Keely wrapped her arms around her knees. "No. But let's not think about it, okay? We have a fire now thanks to you."

Howie lay back, tossing some more sticks into the small blaze. "Bet you wish we could order some Chuggies chili fries now."

She laughed. "Are you kidding? I'd eat an entire Chuggies burger with all the fixings."

They chatted about food and what they would eat if they

could until the moon rose high and Howie fell asleep, head on his arm, huddled close to the fire.

As Howie snored, Keely mopped the fever on Leo's brow. He was restless, tossing side to side. Her careless mistake had nearly cost Leo his life. *Never again,* she swore to herself. Never again would she drop her guard like that. She turned her face to the moon, thinking about the pearl she had seen in her vision, wondering if it would be enough to save them all.

"We're coming, Sam," she whispered, staring at the moon until her eyes closed.

Fragments of dreams filled Leo's head, making him toss and turn. Visions of scaly beasts chasing him. A shiny gold cuff just out of reach. As he stretched to take it, he fell, arms pinwheeling as he dropped into a pit that never ended.

Leo gasped, opening his eyes.

Was he awake or asleep?

He sat up, gasping as the sharp pain of his wound lanced straight to his brain. Definitely awake.

Night had fallen, sprinkling the sky with bright stars. Keely and Howie slept soundly around the nearby campfire. Howie's snores sounded like a chainsaw. But that didn't stop Leo from hearing a branch snap in the surrounding darkness. His heart jumped, but his friends continued sleeping. What if the wraiths had returned?

I am a warrior of the Umatilla, Leo told himself. *I can stand.*

And so he did. "Who's there?" he called. Squinting to see in the darkness, a flicker of light caught his eye. A single spark.

"I'm not afraid," he declared, but it came out more like a whisper. Staggering forward, clutching his side, he headed for the strange glow.

The light twinkled and danced, enticing him closer. He stumbled three more steps and almost touched the sparkle before it floated up and out of reach. He staggered forward, reaching for the light just as it danced away. Again and again, he reached and missed. Finally spent, Leo sank to his knees.

"I am a warrior of the Umatilla," he said out loud. "I am not afraid."

A soft voice came out of the darkness, surprising him. "No, brave one, you need not fear me. I am a friend."

Leo felt the soothing comfort of a hand on his shoulder, a woman's presence next to him. He tried to rise from his knees, but the woman held him down. "Stay. The fever grips you. Let me help."

She placed her hands on his wound and pressed.

Her hair shimmered like white rain in the moonlight. Leo blinked, clearing the fog from his vision. Recognition hit like a breath of hope.

"Vor," he said hoarsely, gasping when her hand slipped inside the wound. The pain was intense, and at the same time, her touch was a relief. "It's you."

"Shh. Yes, brave one, I am here."

Leo had met Vor once on his first trip to Orkney. She had guided him on his journey to rescue Sam and stop the red sun curse. Her hands gently ministered to his wound, and when she withdrew, the skin began to knit, restoring itself. The fever faded from Leo's brow.

"Why are you here?" he asked.

Her brow furrowed. "Odin is acting strangely. I am troubled by his choices. Bringing children into battle. You nearly perished at the hands of wraiths on your first day."

Leo sat up, feeling stronger already. "Whatever lies ahead, I am ready. I won't fail Keely or Sam."

A sad smile passed over her face. "Brave one, it will be harder than you know. If you fail to stop Sam in time, I fear the worst . . . one of our own may be taken."

"One of your own? You mean a god?" Shock rippled through Leo. "How can that be?"

Vor shrugged imperceptibly, her blank eyes focused on a distant point. "Even the gods take foolish risks."

Leo absorbed her words. "What can I do?"

She hesitated, as if the words pained her. "You are the Sacrifice. You must do that which you were chosen for. But never give up hope." She opened her hand. In her palm, a white butterfly fluttered softly, hovering there. "When all seems lost, in the darkness, you will find my light."

A cold wind gusted. Vor turned her face toward it. Leo could swear he saw a cloud of fear in her sightless eyes. Then the goddess began to disintegrate. Her head, then her shoulders, then her gown. In mere moments, all that was left was a small pile of sand on the rock. The butterfly flitted around it and then flew off. Leo reached out to touch the sand, to see if it was real, but the wind blew the grains into the night.

Chapter Eight

Sam was dreaming. In his mind, he was standing outside in bright sunlight as the Orkadian Guard played a mournful song on their trumpets. It was the day of his father's funeral. All of Orkney was out to pay homage to a man they had admired and respected. Flags fluttered in the breeze, snapping in the salted wind that blew in from the sea.

He remembered the warmth of the sun on his face as he placed his father's regimental sword on the coffin. He wished his mother could have been there, longed for the comfort of her arms. Had Sam done the right thing by freeing him? It tormented him as the box was lowered into the earth. Maybe Sam should have left him in the stone. Maybe someone stronger than Sam could have saved him. He began to sweat as his dream turned darker, and images of his father beseeching Sam for help cascaded through his mind.

"Why, Sam? Why did you let me die?" Over and over his dad asked him that question, his face floating before Sam's eyes.

The wispy image faded away, and Sam awoke. His arms and legs bore the marks of vicious bites from the creatures that scuttled about in the endless dark. He shivered with cold even as his skin burned. How many days had he been left alone in this dungeon? *What if no one ever came back for him?*

"C-c-can I . . . ge-get . . . that ro-room service now?" he called out in the emptiness of his cell, teeth chattering, his body racked with tremors. "How 'bout a g-glass of ice wa-water?" Thirst made his tongue feel like rough sandpaper. How long could a person live without water? Three days? Four?

And then, after days of silence and isolation, the door to his prison slowly creaked open. He turned his head, straining to see who was there.

A woman stood in the doorway, carrying a brightly lit torch. "So you live."

Catriona. Her voice rasped like steel wool.

Sam squinted his eyes into narrow slits, waiting for the light to be tolerable. The old crone slowly came into focus. She wore a charcoal wool dress with pointed shoulders that covered her from her neck to her ankles. Long gray hair fell in waves down her back, wiry and untamed. Deep wrinkles lined the gray skin hanging in loose flaps on her face. Her lips were thin and slightly purpled, pursed into a tight line. Her eyes were the only vibrant thing about her, a blazing green that actually hurt to stare at.

She sauntered forward into the cell, placing the torch in a hole bored in the wall. With a crook of her finger, the door slammed shut behind her. "Tell me, how do you like this place? I spent a thousand years inside a rock. This is quite spacious by comparison."

"No complaints," Sam lied, struggling to his feet. He clenched his fists, forcing himself to stop shaking.

"You surprise me. My Deathstalkers can kill a man with one sting." She stopped a few feet away from him.

Sam shrugged like he didn't have a care in the world. "Endera tried to kill me with one of those overgrown roaches when I was a baby. Didn't faze me then, doesn't faze me now." That was a fat lie. Between the fever and the blistering pain, Sam's blood raged with a burning sensation that made every joint throb.

Catriona laughed, a jagged sound that scraped against Sam's ears.

"Then perhaps you would enjoy more."

She waved her hand, and a scuttling noise made Sam step back. From behind Catriona, the horrible creatures spilled out of the crevices, their crimson bodies crawling over the floor toward him, snapping yellow-striped pincers as they advanced. Beady black eyes glittered in the light. Their stingers were poised and ready to do their worst.

"Why are you doing this?" Sam asked, kicking at a Deathstalker that got too close.

Her eyes glittered with a deep malevolence. "It's time you took your rightful place at my side. Every day you linger here, your precious Orkney loses another battle to me. Join me, and the war can end today."

"You can't win," Sam said, kicking another Deathstalker away. "And you can't turn me to your side. Endera tried and failed. I'm a Son of Odin through and through."

"And a Son of Rubicus," she reminded, stepping closer to him. She chucked her fingers under his chin, lifting it so his eyes met hers. "My father's blood flows through your veins."

Sam jerked his chin away from her vile touch and took a step back. Up close, her evil was like a powerful force, emanating off her in waves. "What do you want? Why bring me here?"

Catriona spread her hands wide. "To open your mind to the possibilities of what you can do with all that glorious anger you carry. Why do you fight who you are? We are alike, you and I. We both lost our fathers at a young age. I watched him die, you know. Odin took his head off with one swing of his sword." Her face tightened as she replayed the memory, hatred oozing from every pore.

"Odin had no choice," Sam reminded her. "If he didn't stop Rubicus, the sun would have destroyed every living thing, including your ugly hide."

"Odin could have showed mercy," Catriona hissed, her gnarled fist clenched in his face. "After Rubicus died, I was forced to live in exile, running from one end of the earth to the other in search of a refuge. My sisters and I were outcasts. Alone. Hated by all. Perhaps you have felt that way?"

"No." Another lie. When the red sun had returned a second time, Sam had felt the withering hatred of those who blamed him.

A smile touched the corner of her lips. "I can tell when you're lying, boy. Don't worry, I understand you. You can't help who you are."

Her eyes were mesmerizing as she laid a hand on Sam's shoulder. He wanted to pull away from her hateful touch, but his legs didn't obey his orders.

"You remind me of him, you know," she whispered.

"Who?"

"Rubicus. You have his chin. And his temper."

Revulsion and denial flooded Sam's veins. "No. I'm nothing like him."

She withdrew her hand. "I suppose we shall see, won't we?" She snapped her fingers, and the door flew open. Sam hoped Catriona would leave the torch behind, but she took it, pausing in the doorway. "How many innocent lives will be lost today because you refuse to join me? Ten? A hundred? Pick a number, and my beautiful witchlings will make it so. You have the power to end this war, but you refuse. Which makes you just like Rubicus, so willing to let innocents die to save his own skin."

Her words stung like a flurry of Deathstalker bites, forcing Sam to bite down on his cheek to stop from howling at her.

"This is your last chance. Join me, and I'll send them away." She nodded at the army of scorpions.

Sam gritted his jaw, refusing to speak.

"Oh, very well, have it your way."

The door slammed shut, and the Deathstalkers began their march toward Sam.

After leaving the boy, Catriona climbed to the highest parapet of her fortress. She sucked in a bellyful of air. Entombed for centuries in her stone prison, she had dreamed of this freedom every single day. And now that it was here, she was determined to devour every moment life had to offer. Catriona threw her arms out, letting the elements whip her hair. Rain lashed at her face as she cackled in delight. She pressed cold fingers to her skin.

Wrinkled. Lined. Old.

But not weak.

She wound her hands around her head three times and then flung them up at the sky. A bolt of green lightning shot from her fingers, mixing with the lightning in the sky, creating an ancient dance. She laughed long and hard. It felt good to work out the kinks. Get the juices rolling.

War had invaded every corner of the land. Exactly as she had plotted. Raining down pain and suffering on those responsible for destroying her family and locking her away. They would pay, and pay, and pay some more until no morsel of flesh was left that had not tasted her revenge and choked on it. She would cut out the heart of Orkney and force it down the mewling Orkadians' throats until they retched with regret.

For you, Father, she whispered to herself.

A raven landed on the rail, bobbing its black head. In its beak it clutched a scrap of red fabric with strange writing. She fed it a tidbit of mincemeat from her pocket and stroked its black feathers. The ravens spoke to her. Spilled their secrets for the right price.

It let out a loud caw and squawked for minutes, chattering on.

Catriona fed it another morsel, feeling her anger rise as she absorbed the import of the news.

Odin was interfering again.

What kind of fool game was he up to, bringing those earth children back to the Ninth Realm? No matter. They were as helpless as newborns. A nuisance easily sacrificed. But still, there had to be a reason for this desperate maneuver. The old windbag was many things, but impetuous was not one of them.

Behind her the door creaked. She whipped her head around, wrapping her wet cloak to her body. "I do not wish to be disturbed," she snarled.

Her eyes clashed with those of her rival, Endera Tarkana. A scar ran across Endera's face, and more crisscrossed her arms, marks of her failed battle with the witch-boy when she had tried to destroy him at the Ring of Brogar. At Endera's side stood one of those flea-ridden Shun Kara wolves she favored. It growled low in its throat, as if warning Catriona to be polite.

"Endera. What do you seek?" Catriona kept her voice neutral. Endera was important, even if her grief was getting tiresome.

"The boy lives," Endera reproached.

"He is a useful pawn. When we are finished with him, he will die, like all pawns."

"You will not turn him," she said, stepping forward. "I tried."

"You tried and failed. I will not," Catriona decreed.

Lightning slashed the sky, lighting up the hatred on Endera's face. "You underestimate his strength."

Catriona's nostrils flared. An uncontrollable urge to crush Endera's windpipe under her hands swept over her. Her knuckles tightened.

Fear dilated Endera's pupils, turning her eyes black. "Kill me, hag, and every witch here will turn on you," she hissed. The Shun Kara snarled, stepping forward, snapping at the air.

Thunder roared in the background. The turret lit up with the flare of a lightning strike out on the bog.

Catriona glared into the angry depths of Endera's eyes. She had no fear of the animal; she could erase it with one snap. But now was not the time to assert her power, not until she was sure the coven would stand behind her. She relaxed her face. "I have no intention of killing you, Endera. If I did, you would already be dead. No, you are far too valuable to me. And as such, I promise you, the boy's life will be yours to take when I am finished with him."

"And your sister? Agathea is as much to blame for my misery."

"She can be yours as well. When we seal our victory, I will not stand in your way." The lie passed smoothly over her lips. Once Catriona sealed her reign over the coven, Endera would be disposed of. With a flurry of her skirts, Catriona swept down the stairs.

Chapter Nine

After Vor disappeared, Leo made his way back to camp and burrowed under some dead leaves, sleeping deeply until the sun had risen high in the sky.

Leo sat up and put a hand to his side. It was tender, but healing. So he hadn't imagined it—Vor had actually visited him during the night. Keely and Howie were nowhere to be found. He took a deep breath, closed his eyes, and murmured the prayer of his people.

"*P'ca tiicam, P'sit tuxin, k'alanawa.*" *Mother earth, Father sky, I thank you for this day.*

Laughter drifted through the trees. Leo staggered to his feet as Howie and Keely scampered back into the clearing. Keely held the tails of her shirt carrying some greens, while Howie carefully held a piece of dripping bark folded in a cone. But the bigger surprise was Keely's newly shorn hair. It had turned completely white overnight. Not exactly white. The tips looked like they had been dipped in silver.

"You're awake!" Keely said with a smile of relief. She dropped her supplies on the ground. There were some green tubers, a black cabbage, and a handful of jookberries. "But you shouldn't be up."

"What happened to your hair?" Leo asked.

Howie handed him the dripping bark cup. "Drink, my wolf-pack brother, before I spill it all."

Leo tipped it back, swallowing it down in three gulps.

"I have no idea why my hair turned white," Keely said, patting her pixie cut gingerly. "Howie think's it's a side-effect of drinking from Mimir's well. But really, you shouldn't be up."

"I'm better. Vor came to me last night and healed me." Leo lifted his shirt. The ugly wound was already closed over.

"Get out of here," Keely said, touching it in awe.

"She told me something strange," Leo said, lowering his shirt. "Can the gods die?"

Keely looked at Howie. He shrugged.

"I suppose they can," Keely said. "In the ancient days, when the gods still walked the earth, Odin was killed by Fenrir the wolf."

"But he's still around. Sam spoke to him," Leo said. "And we saw him on Asgard as Brunin."

"The gods are more than their human form." Keely sat on the ground and patted the spot next to her. Leo joined her as Howie poked a stick in the fire to stir the ashes back to life. "I'm guessing their powers keep their spirits alive here in the Ninth Realm, long after they're dead. They have a permanent home in Valhalla, which is somewhere over a rainbow bridge, if you believe what was written thousands of years ago."

"And if their spirit is . . . taken? What then?" Leo asked, pressing for more information.

Howie picked up a hunk of black cabbage and bit into it. "Taken?"

Leo put a warning hand on Howie's arm. "Don't eat that raw. It will make your belly ache."

Howie just kept chewing. "Dude, I got an iron stomach." He let out a burp.

Keely handed Leo some jookberries. "What do you mean, taken?"

Leo ate the berries, savoring their tart flavor. "I don't know.

It was something Vor said. That unless we stop Sam in time, one of their own will be taken."

"I know there are some gods that have moved on to the underworld and have not returned. Odin's son Baldur was lost to him. What do you think Vor meant by it?"

Leo shrugged, feeling uneasy.

After their simple meal, they stomped out the fire.

"So which quest first?" Howie asked. His stomach let out an ominous gurgle. He winced, looking a touch green, but carried on. "We going after Keely's shining pearl? Or fighting the iguanadillo for the cuff? I'm down for either."

"Sorry, Howie, I think we need to go to Skara Brae first," Keely said. "We'll need Rego's help to go north. If this island is Garamond, then we can't be far."

Howie sighed. "Great. Let my humiliation begin."

Keely was as shocked as Leo at the change in her hair color. Howie had noticed it first. She hadn't believed it until she had seen her reflection in the small stream they found. She looked Eifalian with the alabaster white color, but oddly, the ends were tipped in silver. Mimir. Was it as Howie said, a side-effect of drinking from his well? Or had the old sage done something when he jabbed her with the feather? And it wasn't just her hair. Her fingers tingled, like they were extra sensitive.

Howie led the way through the forest. Leo advised they keep the sun to their left to not get lost. Leo walked slower than normal, but he seemed to be mending fast.

"What about Sam?" Leo asked. "I mean, are you sure we shouldn't try to rescue him before we go on our quests? He could help us."

Keely thought about it, then shook her head. "No. Catriona is too powerful. I don't know why Odin needs us to go after these things, but he does."

"If it helps Sam, I'm in," Leo said. "He's saved my life more than once. And I believe he can beat Catriona if we help him."

Keely hooked her arm in his. "I agree."

Howie stopped abruptly, forcing Keely to bump into him.

"Howie," Keely complained, ready to shove him along. But he shushed her and grabbed her and Leo both by the collars and yanked them down into some brush.

"What is it?" Keely whispered.

"Look," he hissed, parting the branches.

Keely choked back a gasp. They had nearly walked into a nest of witches. There were six or seven young witchlings milling about in a clearing. They wore similar outfits, black leggings and tall boots with belted tunics. An older woman stirred a large cauldron that hung over a fire.

She clapped her hands, and a burst of purplish gray smoke rose up.

The smoke swirled and danced around, changing colors as shimmering silver streaks ran through it, zigzagging until there was the outline of a horrid face. Keely instantly recognized it. She had seen it on the battlefield the day Sam had released its owner from her stone prison.

Catriona.

Her voice boomed from her hovering image. "Dear Ariane. Odin has sent three earth children over. Find them and end them. They are close by. Odin must not be allowed to interfere."

The witch called Ariane shook her fist. "I will ferret them out and cook their flesh over my fire. They will not leave this forest alive."

The smoke dissipated, erasing Catriona's image. Ariane whirled around, pointing her finger at her young acolytes. "Why do you stand there? Find them. Bring them to me."

They sank lower in the brush. The witches scattered through the woods. One walked so close, she nearly clomped on Keely's hand with her pointed boot. Ariane was alone by the fire, stirring the steaming cauldron, and muttering to herself.

Keely looked at Leo. He jerked his head, motioning them to back away, but before they could move, there was a loud gurgling sound followed by a rumbling croak like someone had stepped on a toad.

Howie had burped.

They froze. Ariane kept stirring the pot, but her shoulders hunched tighter, and she snapped her fingers twice.

"So much for your iron stomach," Keely whispered to Howie, who shrugged sheepishly. "We need to go." They started to back away, but they ran into something solid.

Behind them, a trio of witches waited, green fireballs over their hands.

"Bring them to me," Ariane commanded from the clearing. "I have plans for them."

The closest witch beckoned with one hand. They clambered to their feet. Leo put his arm protectively around Keely's shoulder.

But Howie puffed out his chest, swaggering forward. "Look, ladies, there's enough of me to go around, no need to fight over me."

The witchling flicked her finger, and a blast of witchfire shot at Howie's feet. He yelped, dancing on one foot as he held the other one. The smell of burning rubber rose from his smoking tennis shoe.

They were hustled into the clearing. Ariane whirled around and eyed them up and down.

She had a large hooked nose and a wrinkled mole the size of a fat raisin on her chin. Her eyebrows were dark and bushy over a pair of smoldering green eyes that gave her a splash of color in an otherwise drab appearance.

"I'm making earth children stew, and I was missing the main ingredient." The witch tilted her head back and laughed. The acolytes joined in, cawing like a flock of crows.

"We're not your next meal, you ugly witch. We're here to stop Catriona," Keely said, even though at the moment, she had no idea how she was going to do that.

"Stop Catriona? Mere earth children? So, dearie, can you do

this?" She flung her wrist out and strewed red powder onto Howie's face. Immediately ugly boils popped up, bursting with fluid.

"Yow!" Howie howled, fanning his hands at his face. "Keely, do something!"

Keely was trying to think. "Stop that right now, or else you'll find out why Odin chose us."

Ariane's eyes danced with mirth. "I'm trembling. What will you do to me?"

"Not me. Odin. He'll . . . he'll . . ." Keely realized she hadn't a clue what Odin would do.

Ariane's bushy brows drew together until it looked like a giant caterpillar crawled across her forehead. "Foolish child, I will enjoy this far too much. Come, my witchlings, draw closer, watch and learn." The witchlings pressed in around the three heroes, pushing them closer to the fire.

"*Ala can tabra, sin mor fera,*" she hissed, waving her hands over the pot. Immediately, wisps of putrid-smelling smoke rose up, twisting and turning into thick tendrils, tinged with a violet shade. The coils rose up and then turned and wound around Keely like rope. The smoke plumes were strangely cold and had a weird strength. Like living branches, they twisted and twined around each of the three kids until they could hardly move, let alone breathe.

The acolytes joined in, repeating her words, raising their hands in the air. The smoke started to undulate, lifting the kids off the ground.

"Keely, what's the plan?" Howie squeaked out, his face an ugly blistered mess of weeping boils.

"I'm thinking," she said, wriggling, hoping to loosen the tightening coils around her.

"Think fast," Leo said. "I can barely breathe."

Just when Keely thought things couldn't get worse, Ariane threw her hands to the side, drawing her struggling prisoners toward the fire, a maniacal grin on her ugly face. It looked like she was trying to dunk them into her cauldron, which was crazy because the pot was too small. But no sooner had Keely thought that than the pot grew, swelling wide until it was the size of a hot tub. Fizzing liquid steamed and boiled, pocking the surface with bubbles.

The tendrils of smoke lowered them closer to the surface until Keely's feet skimmed the boiling liquid.

"Keely!" Howie squealed.

Think, Keely, don't die here. Not yet. Not until you've done something amazing with your life.

And then she had a thought. The wraiths had beat a hasty departure when she had shouted they were Chosen Ones, as if in some way their lives mattered. In the brief moment she had made eye contact with that undead beauty, she had glimpsed a spark of humanity, right before it tried to kill her. Maybe they would help. What did she have to lose? They were about to be boiled into witch stew. She closed her eyes, sending a silent message.

Please, help us! We are Odin's Chosen Ones. It cannot end here. I know you saw me back in the clearing. I know you tried to kill me. But you stopped. If you can hear me, please help. I'll do anything.

She waited, hoping, as her feet dipped in the water. She drew them up, fighting to stay above the surface. Rising steam made her sweaty and hot. But nothing happened. No shrieking ghouls came. It was over. She had failed.

And then an icy prickle ran up her spine.

And what will we receive in return?

The ghastly voice was like a whisper across her skin.

I will plead your case with Odin, she replied. *Please. Help us.*

Ariane flung her arms wide. "And now, earth children, you will die." She moved to clap her hands together, to drop her prey into the pot, but the clearing was suddenly filled with the sounds of screeching. Ghostly figures flew through the air, dozens of them, with their hideous faces and streaming ephemeral hair. The acolytes screamed, fleeing the icy bolts the wraiths shot out of their empty eye sockets. Ariane looked stunned, her mouth a large O.

"Back off, get away," she squealed, trying futilely to blast the wraiths with witchfire, but there were too many of them.

Three wraiths headed straight for Keely, Leo, and Howie. Keely screamed as the hideous face got close, but the wraiths didn't impale them with poisonous ice bolts. Instead, they shot at the enchanted coils around them, splintering them and making them dissipate.

Released, they began to drop into the boiling water, but another set of wraiths scooped them up and set them on the ground before zooming back to attack the witches.

Ariane let out an undulating cry, sending a cloud of smoke up around the encampment. The air was thick, making it hard to breathe. Keely clutched Leo's and Howie's hands as they fell to their knees, choking and coughing.

The wraiths continued their attack, filling the murky air with eerie wailing. And then there was a burst of green light and everything went quiet. As the smoke slowly dissipated, Keely got to her feet. Leo stood next to her. Howie had his face buried in his hands, his shoulders hunched over.

"Is it over?" he moaned.

Keely grabbed him by the arm, dragging him to his feet. "Yes. I think they're gone. Let me see those boils." His face was blistered and swollen, but he brushed her hand away.

"I almost got us killed," he said, tears running down his cheek. "I shoulda listened to Leo."

"Hey, stop it," Keely said. "I got Leo impaled with an ice bolt because I opened my eyes. The point is, we got through it. Thanks to some nasty wraiths."

"Where did the wraiths come from?" Leo asked.

"I called them."

His eyebrows shot up. But he didn't say anything.

Adrenaline pumped through Keely's veins. She still couldn't quite believe her desperate plan had worked out. "So, I think we've had quite enough adventure for one day. It's time we found our way out of this forest and got Howie to Skara Brae."

"You're leaving me there?" He looked woebegone with his patchwork of throbbing red boils and tear streaks cutting a trail through the dirt on his face.

"Don't worry, Howie. We survived an attack by wraiths and avoided being boiled alive by witches. How much worse can things get? Come on, I have a good feeling about this direction." She set off through the trees with a spring in her step. Defeating Ariane had given her confidence. Calling the wraiths had been an act of desperation, but it had worked.

Maybe she could figure this out before it was too late to rescue Sam.

Chapter Ten

Sam was losing his mind. Day after day of being locked in a stone dungeon with not even an old *Gamer* magazine to flip through did that to a guy. He had paced from one end of his cell to the other, searching for an escape, hurling his magic at every crack and crevice to find a way out.

And he had gotten absolutely nowhere.

Water dripped from the ceiling, driving him bonkers with the tiny plonking noise, but he had finally figured out a way to capture the drops in his boot. At least now he had a few sips of smelly feet water every few hours. Hunger was making him hallucinate. He would stare at a rock and imagine it was a giant cheeseburger. It was getting so bad he found himself drooling over a hunk of granite, about to bite into it before he had snapped himself out of it.

If Catriona's plan was to turn him into a stark raving lunatic, it was working.

The Deathstalkers had a daily ritual of attacking him, but Sam had gotten smarter, lining up an array of rocks for ammunition to nail them the moment they poked their scaly heads out of a crack. He had tried using witchfire, but in his weakened state, the rocks were more effective. Still, a few of them always managed to slip past and get a nip in before he stomped them or kicked them away. And with every sting, venom loaded up in his system until it felt like his blood was made of gasoline. One more bite and he might just explode . . .

The last attack had cost him. He had been dozing, dreaming about a thick-crust extra-cheese no-anchovies pizza, when they had scuttled their way in, and by the time he had gotten to his rock supply, several of the venom-tailed arachnids had bitten him. Now, he lay on his back on the cold stone drenched in sweat and raked with fever, but he couldn't stop shivering. His teeth chattered uncontrollably. The scorpions had left after doing their worst, returned to their hidden nests.

He couldn't take another second of being alone.

"Is anyone there?" he yelled.

His voice echoed back at him. He shouted until his throat was raw, but no one answered. He remembered back when he was younger, maybe in fifth grade, when he had stayed home alone with a fever. His mom had been called in to work. He had felt this same helplessness as the fever rose and there was no one there to stop it, until he had phoned her, sobbing. That day, she had rushed home to give him medicine and a cool towel for his forehead.

Not this time.

Sam almost missed Catriona in that moment. The silence was killing him. The inescapable horror that no one was listening. That no one cared.

"Please," Sam moaned, "just somebody answer me."

Isolation pressed in on him like a suffocating blanket until a yawning chasm opened up in him. More painful than the stings was the growing certainty that no one was coming for him. His friends had forgotten him. His father was dead. And his mother might well have been on another planet. He was completely alone.

As Sam closed his eyes in despair, he sensed a Deathstalker slither from the cracks. He had just fought off the last round. He had nothing left to fight with. It skittered forward, crawling across the stone slab. It reached his boot and crossed the toe, inching up his leg. Sam shuddered, waiting for the bite. Why fight the inevitable? Maybe he should just give up. But some part of him held out, fighting back. Was he not a powerful witch? Was he just going to lie there and take it from a bunch of overgrown roaches?

"Stop," he whispered. "I command you."

Oh, really, Baron? he instantly mocked himself. *Talking to overgrown insects.*

But the little beastie stopped, its pincers waving as it perched on his knee.

Sam sat up. His hands were shaking, but he conjured up a small light. He studied the nasty creature. "Really? That's all it takes, is to say *stop?*" He laughed, a harsh sound that sounded more like a moan.

The Deathstalker just stared at him with its tiny black eyes. Its tail was still coiled toward its head, waiting to strike him with its venom-laden tip.

But Sam couldn't quash the bubble of laughter that rose up, a mixture of joy and despair, and maybe a touch of insanity. "If you really want to do me a solid, get me something to eat."

The creature waved its claws at him as if it were receiving a signal and decoding it.

"Yeah, I'm thinking a big cheeseburger with a side of fries," Sam mocked, realizing he had finally lost his mind. He was talking to a Deathstalker.

I've gone totally insane.

But the creature retreated and scuttled down Sam's boot, then scampered across the floor, disappearing into one of the cracks.

Alone again. At least the nasty thing hadn't bitten him this time.

Sam extinguished his light, unable to sustain it.

For a moment, he felt deserted. Then the noises came again. The scrabble of countless claws. An army of Deathstalkers skittering toward him in a clattering storm.

A new wave of dread came over Sam, swamping him with damp fear and resignation.

Good job, Baron. This time they're actually going to kill you.

He braced himself for the attack, hoping to find the strength to fend off the bites. But he had nothing. Nothing at all.

"Okay," he announced, feeling tears sting at his eyes, wishing he had a chance to say good-bye to his mom. To Keely. Howie. Leo. "Just make it fast. I'm ready for a change of scenery," he joked morbidly.

The creatures crawled in a line up his leg, up his chest, hovering below his chin. He closed his eyes, holding his breath, afraid they were going to crawl inside his mouth and burrow into his brain. But the thing that happened next was inexplicable: a crust of bread brushed against his lips. He could smell the yeast and the wheat.

Sam opened his eyes and saw the dim outline of something on his chin.

A Deathstalker.

He opened his mouth to scream, and the small sliver of bread promptly went in his open jaws. It tasted heavenly, melting on his tongue. Better than a Chuggies Deluxe with extra bacon. Sam gaped as swarms of the creatures carried miniature snacks in bucket-brigade fashion.

These Deathstalkers that had stung him for days, tried to kill him with their lethal venom, were now saving him. Another one brought him a bit of jerky in its pincer. Tiny bits of meat, fruit, and bread landed on his lap.

Why were they helping him? What reason could they have for their change of heart? Sam was wary of trusting them, trying to puzzle it out. Had they stung him so many times he was now one of them? Or had their venom changed him somehow? An uneasy feeling settled over him as he watched the growing tribute pile. Vor's words echoed in his mind: *If you fight the darkness, you will lose.*

Perhaps the Goddess of Wisdom was right. Maybe it was time to stop fighting his inner demons. The ones he kept tethered when he showed mercy, when what he really wanted was to unleash his full powers. Maybe it was time to do as Vor had said and let all that darkness out.

Sam closed his eyes, drawing in a deep breath, and stopped fighting the venom that flowed through him, instead embracing it, accepting it into every fiber of his being. It was like uncorking a bottle of soda that had been shaken violently. Powerful pulsating magic fizzed in his veins. He could control these creatures, he realized with growing certainty.

"*Nistrasa, nistrasa venimus, fealty,*" he hissed. *Bow to me, bow to me, my venoms*, he called, feeling his muscles swell with newfound power.

The Deathstalkers lined up in a row on the dungeon floor, tails poised over their heads. Waiting to obey.

Sam called on the creatures to feed him. To infect him with more of their poison. He would submit to the darkness in him to stay alive.

But he could control it, the same way he could control the Deathstalkers. And turn away from it when he was safe again. Because the darkness would never rule over him.

Never.

Catriona studied her glowing orb, cackling to herself in delight as the boy drew on his dark magic. He had been near giving up, and she had felt her plan unraveling. She couldn't allow that. This boy was the key to victory, and time was running short.

So she had urged the Deathstalkers on. Bent them to his will. Let him think it was he who commanded the creatures.

So quick to believe, she mused. *He craves the power.*

The old witch smiled as the boy's eyes glowed with the yellow venom that flowed in his veins. Not long now, and he would belong to her completely.

The door to her chambers was flung open, interrupting her reverie. A lanky witch strode in, waves of ebony hair flung over her shoulders. She wore riding breeches and tall black boots under a flowing cape. Vena. Ever the dramatic one. Agathea scurried in after her, followed closely by Beatrixe and Bronte. All had the same frozen look on their faces, a look of fear Catriona had not seen since her father had been alive.

Catriona rose from her seat. "What is it? What has happened?"

Vena crossed to her side, clasping her by the forearms. "Sister, I bring terrible news. Nestra and I got tied up fighting off Falcory warriors." She hesitated, and then added, "Nestra didn't make it."

There was a moment of silence. Agathea let out a wail. Beatrixe just twisted her hands over and over. Bronte's hunched shoulders slunk deeper before she wordlessly retreated to her precious workshop, clanging vials and bottles around.

Rage filled every pore in Catriona's body, sending seismic shudders through her as she exploded. "I will string up every one of those Falcory savages by their intestines and let them twist in the wind! I will burn the entire countryside with witch-fire until not a living thing grows! I will starve them, and then when they are on their knees begging for mercy, I will feed them to the sneevils." Catriona's chest was heaving as she finished her tirade.

Vena didn't cower. Oddly, she smiled. "Calm yourself, sister. Lovely as that sounds, let me take revenge. I can change every one of their lowly cattle into horrible beasts with gnashing teeth longer than their forearms. I can turn their house pets into deadly menaces that spit poison in their soup."

Catriona's rage simmered to a low boil. She sat herself down on the sofa next to Agathea and stared at her youngest sister, turning her words over in her fertile mind. Ever since she was a young witchling, Vena had excelled at making transfiguration potions that could change harmless creatures into deadly ones. Rats became flying shreeks. Ordinary boars became vicious, gut-tearing sneevils. Vena had single-handedly created some of the most awful creatures Orkney had ever been plagued with.

Catriona snapped her fingers at Beatrixe, who seemed locked in a trance.

"Fetch our sister a drink. I believe I have just the task for her special talents."

Beatrixe crossed to the serving tray by the fireplace and poured Vena a glass of brandy. Vena tossed the drink back in one long swallow, then slammed the glass down on the low table, wiping her mouth with the back of her hand, and waited for Catriona to speak.

"We are winning this war today, but the tides could shift at any time. There are only eight of us—seven now with Nestra gone. What we need is an army loyal only to us," Catriona crooned. "An army of fearsome men that will seal our victory and turn our enemies' will to dust."

"Where will we find an army like that?" Agathea sniped. "The Balfin ranks are full of spineless men with no will to fight."

Catriona leaned forward. "Then Vena will change them."

Vena looked from her to Agathea in confusion. "Change who?"

"The Balfins."

"Into what?"

Catriona threw her hands in the air. "Use your imagination. Make them stronger than ten men, with teeth sharp as a sneevil's tusk. Make them an army to be feared," she crowed. "It will be your greatest masterpiece."

Agathea was speechless. From her potion lab, Bronte let out a loud cackle of pleasure. Even Beatrixe looked pleased, her eyes bright with the idea of destroying their enemy.

Vena clapped her hands like a little girl. "Ooh, I like it. I like it very much. I've never changed a man before, but I believe I know just the potion. It will take some time to find the right ingredients."

She leaped up and spun in a circle, arms flung out, tilting her head back as her laughter filled the air. She spun faster and faster and then disappeared in a cloud of smoke. Long after she left, her laughter echoed in the room.

Chapter Eleven

Keely's spirits continued to rise when, after less than an hour of walking, the trees thinned out and they came upon a heavily rutted road that was bound to have a lot of traffic. Or so said Leo after studying the tracks. To the south, a distant plume of black smoke rose into the sky, as if something large were burning.

After a quick vote, they turned away from the smoke and trudged along the lane. Minutes later, a wagon came careening down the road. As the driver cracked his whip over the team of horses, Leo waved his arms to slow it down. The wagon thundered past them, leaving only a trail of dust. They were about to continue on, but a loud rumbling sound caused them to turn. This time there wasn't just one wagon, there were dozens, all loaded to the brim with household items and packed with people clinging on for their lives.

The wagons passed by in a blur of whips cracking over horses' heads and frightened faces of passengers. Finally, the horde thinned out until the last wagon came into sight.

"This one, Leo," Keely urged.

Leo jumped out into the road, waving his arms. But the driver either didn't see him or seemed bent on running him down.

Then an ear-splitting whistle sounded, and the horses snorted wildly, rearing up as the driver wrestled to get control.

It was Howie. He had two fingers in his mouth, his cheeks puffed out like a blowfish.

"Whoa, whoa, hold up, girls." The driver calmed the horses, reining them in, and the wagon came to a stop an inch away from Leo.

"Are you crazy?" Keely stormed, glaring up at the driver. "You could have run him over."

The man had leathery skin like he spent his days in the sun, and he wore a straw hat pulled down low over his face. His wagon was piled up with a rickety tower of furniture and a few dusty sacks of grain. "When a man's running for his life, it's wise to stay out of his way," he griped. "In case you haven't noticed, there are witches everywhere."

Keely almost laughed. Boy, had she ever noticed. "Look, we need a ride to Skara Brae. Can you take us there?"

His eyes narrowed. He looked over his shoulder, as if worried the witches were right on his tail. "I might be able to. For a price. Can you pay?" He held out a hand. It was grubby and stained with dirt.

"No."

He immediately picked up the reins and whipped them over the horse's backs. The wagon lurched forward, but Keely wasn't giving up.

"Hey!" She grabbed the harness of the nearest horse, jerking him back. "I didn't say you wouldn't get paid."

He eased up on the reins.

"I'm listening."

"We're going to see Captain Teren of the Orkadian Guard. He will pay for our safe transport."

The man skewered his lips to the side, expressing his skepticism loudly. "You lot know the captain of the Orkadian Guard?"

"Yo, man," Howie chimed in. "The captain is my bud's bud. He will be, like, mucho apreciado for your help."

The man ran a hand over his rough chin, then nodded his head toward the back. "Get in. If you're lying, I'll take it out of your hide."

Keely didn't hesitate. She clambered over the side and landed on some hard sacks of grain. Leo and Howie quickly followed. With a jerk, the wagon was off. They made themselves a little nest among the sacks and one by one fell asleep.

Keely awoke with a jolt. She had been dreaming she was a wraith, flying through the sky with soulless eyes and bony arms. She rubbed her eyes, looking around. The stone walls of a city rose before them. Red flags snapped in the breeze.

She elbowed the boys, rousing them awake.

Howie's face was split by a gaping yawn that exposed his tonsils. The boils were beginning to fade but still left round welts across his cheeks. "Are we there yet?" he asked.

The wagon driver shouted to the horses to stop as they crossed a bridge to the gate.

A sentry called down from the ramparts. "Who seeks entrance?"

"Name's Milligan. I've got a delivery of grain. The last you'll be receiving from me. The witches burned my crops to the ground, same as the last ten wagons that came this way."

"Who're they?" the sentry asked, still suspicious, pointing at the children. "And why are they dressed funny?"

"Them's here to see the esteemed Captain Teren."

Keely waved up at the guard. Howie saluted him. Leo just nodded.

"How do I know they're not witches in disguise?" the sentry asked.

Milligan leaned over in his seat and spat on the ground. "Because I would have executed them on the spot and put their heads on a pike if they were. Now open the gate before I climb up there and make you."

The man conferred with another guard, and then they disappeared. The gate rolled upward, and the wagon rumbled through, past the city walls.

There was no welcoming party awaiting them. Instead, they entered into a city that appeared under siege. Citizens scurried about, clutching children by their hands, looking scared as if they expected the witches to attack at any moment. The shopkeepers they passed cast wary glances at them. Many were busy boarding up their windows. A smell of fear and desperation tainted the air. They clattered along paving stones until they entered a large open square. A lofty building rose up with the words GREAT HALL etched in stone over the columned entrance. A tower rose from either side, one with a bell, the other with a clock.

The square was lined with shops and other less-imposing buildings than the Great Hall. The smell of cinnamon teased Keely's nostrils as they passed a spice shop. A butcher had a single hunk of meat on display, dangling from a metal hook. The stables held a handful of horses, attended to by a young man in dungarees. He nodded at her as they rolled on by. A burly soldier eyed them suspiciously from the doorway of the armory. He was built like a lion with a mane of blond hair.

"How are we supposed to find Captain Teren?" Keely asked.

"No worries, lass, I know where to find the captain," Milligan called out over his shoulder. "Only one place he'd be this time of day."

Milligan drove the cart down narrow cobblestone streets. Glum faces peered out behind curtains on the second floors. The farmer drew up the wagon outside a large muddy field. In the center, a tall blond figure fired orders at the dozen or so men lined up in ragged uniforms attempting archery practice. Keely snorted as they fired arrows off in every direction but the targets—she could do better blindfolded. The man turned, frowning as they approached. It was Teren himself.

"You're Sam's friends," he said when they drew near enough. "But what are you doing back in Orkney?"

"I brought them," Milligan bragged. "And now, I'd be expecting my payment." He held out his grubby hand.

Teren's frown deepened. "You brought earth children to Orkney? What are you, some kind of wizard?"

"No. Just a farmer with no farm. Got the last of my crop on that wagon. Thanks to those witches, I've got no home to return to."

Teren's face softened. He put a hand on the man's shoulder. "Then you are welcome here inside these walls. Here," he unclipped a satchel from his side and shook out two coins. "Take this, find yourself a room. We could use more men in the fight."

Milligan took them, scowling before he grudgingly nodded. "I'll just see to my business, and then you can count on me. And a lot more like me coming this way."

As Milligan trudged off, Teren turned to the kids, pointing at each of them in turn. "Let me see, you're Keely. Howie. And Leo. But why are you back in Orkney?"

"Odin brought us," Keely said. "We've been chosen to help save this land."

His eyebrow rose. "Chosen? How so?"

"Well, we met Mimir and—"

Suddenly a dark-haired moppet tackled Keely and nearly knocked her backward. "Keeeeely! I knew it was you."

"Mavery?"

The witchling broke into a grin. Keely grabbed her and swung her around. "It is you! What in the world are you doing here?"

Mavery had the same impish look, but her ragged clothes had been replaced with a neat gray frock over black leggings and soft boots. Her dark locks had been trimmed evenly and tucked behind her ears. And she was at least an inch taller.

"I live here, silly. Me and Sam have to stick together. We're the only good witches around, you know."

Behind Mavery, a stumpy figure hurried into the arena. Rego. Sam's stalwart friend and companion. Keely had never been so happy to see a dwarf in her life. A small iolar perched on Rego's shoulder, eyeing them curiously with a sharp tawny gaze.

"Why am I not surprised to find you three in Skara Brae?" Rego announced, a grin splitting his whiskered face.

Keely ran forward to give Rego a hug. The bird squawked, startled by her approach, and flapped its wings wildly.

"Hush, Lingas." He reached up to scratch the bird's snowy belly. She had leather jesses around her ankles, keeping her tied to him.

Howie high-fived Rego. "Dwarfmaster, what's up with my buddy Sam?"

A shadow chased over Rego's face. "Sam is out of our reach. You shouldn't have come back here. Last time, the witches used you against him."

"We were brought here," Leo answered. "Odin called us back. But perhaps we should discuss it privately?"

The recruits had all stopped their archery practice and were milling about, listening in on their conversation with open curiosity.

Teren nodded. "Aye, let's move this into the armory. Better to keep it amongst ourselves until we know what this is all about. There are many in Skara Brae I do not trust."

Rego grunted. "Beo will want to be there."

Teren scowled but agreed.

Chapter Twelve

Keely would have rather been taken to a place with a hot shower and room service, but at least the armory was warm and dry. There was a crowded bunk room attached to a small dining hall that held a long rough table. The place smelled like a locker room. Grungy piles of dirty uniforms competed with mounds of unwashed chainmail for floor space. A trio of sputtering candles dripped wax all over the table. Four soldiers were seated eating a meal. The remains of a cooked chicken sat on a platter. Keely's stomach rumbled, but the carcass looked picked clean.

Teren made quick introductions. "Keely, Leo, Howie, meet my most trusted men. This is Galatin." Galatin stood and shook their hands. He was young, maybe nineteen, with close-cropped hair. He had the battle-worn look of an experienced soldier in spite of his youth.

Next was Heppner, a carrottop with a swath of freckles. Then Speria, dark, silent, and slender as a whip. Both men nodded curtly. The largest of them was Tiber, the beefy blond man she had seen in the doorway of the armory. He folded his arms and just grunted at them. Lastly, Teren introduced them to Rifkin. The soldier had a shiny bald head and a large gold hoop hanging from his right ear. A beard covered most of his lower face, ending in a tiny braid at his chin.

"Pleased to meet you," Rifkin said, jumping up and pumping Keely's hand, and then moving on to shake Leo's and Howie's. "Welcome back to our esteemed land."

Rego entered with Lingas on his shoulder, leading a hawk-faced man and a boy their age. The man's black eyes darted from person to person in the room. Small silver hooks dangled iolar feathers from his earlobes. A javelin was strapped across his back, tipped with a long and pointed flint arrowhead. His chest was bare save for a beaded leather vest. His face was fascinating, marked by a hawk-like beak famed for giving the Falcory exceptional sense of smell. The boy was a carbon-copy of his father, down to the beaded vest and silver earrings, though his feathers were smaller. As they stepped forward, Keely saw the man favored his left leg.

While Rego settled Lingas on her perch, Teren turned to the newcomers. "Meet Beo, and his son, Jey. Beo is the Falcory representative to the High Council. He was wounded fighting off a nest of witches. Took down one of the Volgrim hags with a javelin through her cold heart, and then removed her head just to be sure she was really dead."

Beo nodded curtly, arms folded. He stood apart from the group. Jey mimicked his father, folding his arms, but his eyes darted around the room, passing over Howie like he was of no consequence to linger appreciatively on Keely, then moving on to Leo. Keely could feel tension rise in the room, as if the two boys were somehow locked in a silent competition.

"Tiber, keep an eye on the door. I don't want any listening ears," Teren ordered as he waved them into chairs. Tiber went to the door, cracking it a hair, leaning his bulky body against the doorjamb. When they were seated, the captain cleared his throat. "These earth children claim they have been chosen by Odin to help us defeat the witches."

There were some snickers under hands that quickly covered

mouths. Even Rego let out a little chuckle. Irritated by their lack of respect, and more than a little put out that no one had offered her a meal or a hot shower, Keely stood, planting her hands on the table.

"Look, I know it sounds crazy, but someone flushed us back to Orkney. We didn't even get a chance to say goodbye to our families. Then we met Mimir in the forest, and he let me drink from his well. We've been attacked by wraiths, and we outsmarted a witch named Ariane, who wanted to boil us alive. So I'd appreciate it if you'd give us some respect. And something to eat. We're starving." She sat back down with a huff.

There was stunned silence. Rego broke it with his chuckles. "Mimir, you say? You'd have to make a sacrifice . . . of course . . . the hair." Rego eyed her pixie cut. He let out another chuckle. "A sprite of a girl taking on a crafty old coot like that. You're lucky it didn't cost you an eye."

"My apologies for our lack of manners," Teren said. "Speria, go fetch them another chicken. There's nothing but bones left on the plate."

Speria left and returned with a glistening, steaming chicken that smelled like it had just been pulled off a spit. Keely's mouth watered as he set it down. The three kids scrambled to tear off hunks. For once, Keely didn't give a thought to manners, biting chunks of meat off the bone and savoring the feeling of filling her belly. When she was done, she wiped her hands on her soiled jeans and used her shirt to wipe her chin.

Teren leaned forward. "Tell us what you saw when you drank from Mimir's well. You can speak freely. I'd trust these men with my life."

"I saw two bears in a circle," she began, "one swallowing the other's tail."

Rifkin slapped his thigh, his gold earring glinting in the candlelight. "That's the mark of the Vanir."

"The Vanir? You mean the frost giants of old?" Rego looked doubtful. "I didn't think they still existed."

Keely felt a chill of apprehension. The Vanir were the tribe that Odin had once traded Mimir to. The ones who had cut off his head.

"Oh, they exist," Rifkin said, eyes wide as he spoke. "Giants with the strength of ten oxen. They live in Rakim, an icy realm north of the Eifalian kingdom. Rifkin knows 'em too well." He tapped his temple. "It's so cold, your eyeballs freeze solid if you open them in a storm, that is, if the troll-hags that live in the woods don't cut your heart out with their stone daggers first."

Every person in the room gawked at Rifkin, mesmerized by his vivid tale.

"What?" he said, blinking under their collective gazes. "I grew up in the northern territories. I've heard these stories since I was a babe."

"Go on," Mavery nudged Keely. "Tell us the rest."

"I saw a cave. A giant beast with lots of legs guarded it."

"That's Audhumla," Rifkin whispered. "He guards Ymir's cave."

"Who's Ymir?" Leo asked.

"Ymir was the creator of the cosmos," Rifkin answered. His eyes glittered with excitement as he told the story. "He was killed by his three sons: Odin and his brothers, Vili and Vi. When he died, he spit out the sky. His hair became the trees." Speria and Heppner joined in, chanting in unison, "And his bones the mountains, his sweat and blood, the seas."

"A child's nursery rhyme," Teren scoffed.

But Rifkin was undeterred. "Legend has it Ymir's bones were thrown into the Cave of Shadows. It's said to hold the greatest treasures of this world. What I wouldn't give for five minutes inside and a sack to carry all that gold," he added dreamily.

Keely went on. "In the cave, I saw a pearl at the bottom of a pool. It glowed with a bright light."

"A pearl?" Speria raised a skeptical eyebrow. "What good is a trinket?"

"Yeah, how's a pearl going to stop witchfire from turning

you to ash?" Heppner chortled, elbowing Speria. "You going to get a string of them and make yourself a pretty necklace?"

Mavery leaped up, throwing her hand out, and sent a tiny blast of witchfire at Heppner, singeing the end of his nose. "Be nice, or next time I'll turn you to ash myself."

Heppner's face turned as red as his hair. A black streak marked his nose. "Why you little witch, I oughtta . . ." He shoved his chair back, probably intending to throttle the girl, but Teren held his hand up.

"Enough. Look, this is a nice tale, but the Cave of Shadows is nothing but a myth."

"Begging your pardon, Captain, but the Cave of Shadows is real as this cup," Rifkin said grimly, knocking his tin mug sharply against the table. "I stood outside it once myself. And mark my words, that pearl she speaks of? That's the Moon Pearl. Every child of the North knows it holds the essence of Ymir's heart. I'd stake my life on it."

Teren hesitated, a spark of hope lighting his eyes. "And you really think this pearl can help us defeat the witches?"

"Not just defeat the witches, bring Sam back to us," Keely said firmly. "He's out there. We can't forget that." They were all silent a moment as they thought of their friend. "We were each given a task. I am the Seeker. I have to go north and retrieve this Moon Pearl. I am going," she added, in case that wasn't clear. "But I could use some help."

"And the others, lass?" Rego asked.

Keely cleared her throat before announcing the rest. "Er, Howie's been chosen as Protector of the Realm. Skara Brae will fall unless he makes a stand here."

Speria and Heppner erupted in laughter, although Heppner eyed Mavery warily. Galatin remained silent, but his lips twitched with amusement.

Teren's eyebrows arched so high in disbelief they almost disappeared under his sheaf of blond hair. "Is this some kind of joke? Look at him—he can barely lift a sword."

All eyes turned to stare at Howie. His cheeks reddened, but he just grinned, spreading his hands wide. "Teren, my man, Odin chose me to be Protector of the Realm. Not my fault, just my fate. You're either with me or against me. And trust me, you don't want to go against The Howmeister."

Teren looked like he wanted to explode. Howie's fingers twitched at his waistband. Keely knew he was itching to pull out the Horn of Gjall and show them what he could do, but now was not the time to call an army of the dead. She put a hand on his arm and caught his eye, shaking her head.

Fortunately, Rego intervened.

"Captain Teren, surely you could use some extra hands around here," the dwarf said quietly. "The boy could be of service. What about you?" Rego asked, turning to Leo.

"I am the Sacrifice," Leo said grimly. "Keely saw a golden cuff guarded by a monster I must defeat. When I do, the cuff will take me someplace dark."

Beo spoke for the first time. "This monster. What does it look like?"

"A cross between an iguana and an armadillo," Keely said. "Why? Do you know it?"

Beo nodded curtly. "That is the she-she-kana. It lives on the edge of the Falcory lands deep inside a mountain known as Ilyawit Peak."

"I'm not afraid," Leo said.

Next to Beo, his son Jcy snorted, as if that was the dumbest thing he had ever heard.

"*Ilyawit* means *death* in our language," Beo said dryly. "All who have ventured inside have only scattered bones to show for their bravery. The she-she-kana guards the Draupnir, a golden cuff that has the power to free someone from the underworld. The beast is invincible. The boy will never defeat it alone."

Teren drummed his fingers on the table. "What say you, dwarf? You believe these earth children speak the truth?"

Rego rubbed his whiskers. "How else can you explain their arrival here? If they're back, its Odin's doing, mark my words."

"Maybe this is our chance to end this," Teren said with fire in his voice. "Beo proved the Volgrim witches are not invincible when he took off that hag's head. If the gods have favored us with hope, then we cannot turn our backs on it." The captain abruptly rose to his feet. "I'll need volunteers to escort these children on their quests."

Rego stood. "Tiber and I will take Leo west to the Falcory lands to find this cuff he speaks of."

"I'll guide you," Beo said.

"Father, your leg," Jey argued. "You can't ride. Let me go." Jey's voice was brash, confident like his father's. "I know the way to Ilyawit Peak."

Beo shook his head. "No, Jey, it's too dangerous."

Jey drew himself up tall. "I am thirteen. A man. You have trained me for this. Where others have failed, I will not."

Teren stepped in. "Beo, we could use your help here. Lord Orrin is up to his usual trickery on the High Council. With Gael absent, you are my only ally. Send the boy as a guide. Tiber and Rego will enter the beast's lair alone."

Beo put his hand on Jey's shoulder, affection softening his hawk-like features. "You are sure?"

Jey nodded, his dark eyes sparkling with excitement.

That settled, Rego pointed at Rifkin. "Rifkin knows the northern territory, so he should travel with the girl."

Galatin spoke up. "I will accompany Rifkin."

Teren turned to his remaining men. "Speria, Heppner, you stay in Skara Brae with me; I can't be left alone with all these recruits. I would accompany you myself, but there are politics afoot here, and we must tread carefully. No one is to speak of this outside this room, understood?"

The men nodded.

"Then you must leave now," Teren said. "Every moment

you linger inside the walls risks discovery and answering questions before the High Council until we reach old age."

Keely's head spun. She had really been looking forward to a shower, maybe a good night's sleep.

Mavery piped up. "I'm going with Keely. She'll need my help."

"No!" Keely's voice was harsh. "You can't come. It's too dangerous, and . . . you're too young. You'll just be in the way." Her words were deliberately hurtful, but the vision she had had of Mavery's head on a chopping block gave her no choice. The imp had to stay back where she was safe.

Mavery looked like she wanted to spit nails at Keely, but the men were already scraping back from the table as Teren issued his orders.

"Rego, Tiber, rustle up some horses from the stables for your journey. Galatin, you and Ritkin commandeer one of our ships. It's the fastest way to the Eifalian kingdom. I'll send word to the fleet captain."

Keely tried to think of something to say to Mavery to make her feel better, but the witchling ran out of the room, her face red and tear-streaked. Keely sighed and turned to give Howie a goodbye hug, but Rego interrupted, holding the young iolar on his arm. "I have a favor to ask, lad," he said to Howie. His voice was gruffer than normal. "I want you to watch over Lingas while I'm gone. She's too young for a journey like this, and untrained."

Rego thrust his arm out. The bird screaked loudly at Howie, opening its mouth wide and snapping at him when he reached out his fingers.

Howie snatched his hand back. "Uhm, are you sure? Maybe she could just go with Keely?"

"Nonsense, she won't like the cold. Here," he lifted the bird onto his fist and held her out. "Just take her." He sniffled loudly, as if parting from his pet pained him.

Howie slowly raised his fist, mimicking Rego. The bird hesitated, her tawny eyes sizing Howie up, and then she delicately stepped over onto his hand. He tentatively lifted her to his shoulder.

"Who's a pretty bird?" Howie cooed. Lingas promptly bit down on his ear, drawing a sharp yelp from him. She let out a soft cackle, like she thought it was funny.

"She's a bit feisty, but you'll get used to her antics," Rego said. "She likes to hunt squirrels, but keep her tied up with her jesses," he pointed to her leather leggings, "until she's bonded with you."

Howie rubbed his ear wryly and nodded.

Teren approached and clasped Howie on the shoulder. "Apologies for my words earlier, lad. What with defending an entire realm and fighting spells I can't even name, I've been a bit knackered."

"Yo, I get it. No need to apologize," Howie said. "Just point me and Lingas here in the direction of a hot shower and a comfy perch, and I'll let you get back to biz."

"Oh no. No, no. That won't do." Teren shook his blond head and tapped Howie on the chest. "Not for the Protector of the Realm and his noble bird."

"Yeah," Heppner said, mirth lighting up his freckles, "the Protector would want to be near the men."

"Training with them," Speria added, waggling his dark eyebrows.

"Bunking with them," said Heppner.

"Side by side," Speria finished.

"Starting with cleaning their gear." Teren stripped off his breastplate and chain mail and dumped his armor in Howie's arms. "Have this lot polished and cleaned by morning. Make sure my sword is sharpened. And run over to the blacksmith and ask him to adjust the chest piece. It's feeling tight. And keep that bird on a leash," he added warily, "or I'll roast it for Sunday supper."

The men laughed as they left Howie in the armory clutching all the gear they stacked on him.

"No problem," Howie said to their backs, as Lingas pecked his ear again. "I'll just take care of this and meet up with you later. You know, so we can talk strategy and stuff."

Leo slapped him hard on the back. "You can do this, Howie. Just do your duty and be brave."

"Sure thing, my wolf-brother. You just worry about that iguanadillo."

Howie looked like he was about to cry. Keely gave him a quick peck on the cheek. "Don't worry so much. You're going to do great. Remember, Odin chose you." She dropped her voice. "And whatever you do, don't show anyone the Horn of Gjall. It's not a toy, Howie. In the wrong hands, it could be disastrous."

He gave Keely a weak thumbs-up, juggling the armor. "Got it. Lips are sealed. I'll see ya when I see ya."

Leo tugged on Keely, but her eyes fell on the far wall of the armory. "Not yet, Leo." She strode over to the wall and lifted a large bow down. It was beautiful, carved from polished yew. "This time, I'm going to be prepared."

Leo grinned as he took another bow carved from redwood. They each took a quiver of arrows before they hurried after Rifkin and the others to the stable.

Outside the armory, Keely pulled Leo to a sudden stop.

"What is it?" His brown eyes were full of concern.

Keely gripped his arm. "When I had my visions, there was more. A lot more I don't dare tell Teren. When you get the cuff, it will lead you to a place with no life. There's someone there, waiting. I don't know who. But he's in there, and he's bad news. Do you hear me, Leo? Very bad news. Stay away from him."

Leo nodded, and they moved on to the stable. Rego had his own pony, a reddish horse smaller than the others. Tiber rode on a tall black steed. Jey leaped on the back of a painted brown and white horse. He and his father briefly clasped arms. Beo removed his javelin and the case it hung in and handed them over to Jey. A flash of pride lit up the boy's face as he slung it around his shoulders.

Beo led a sturdy pinto over to Leo. "You can ride bareback?"

Leo nodded.

"Then take my horse. He will ride straight and true."

Leo grabbed a fistful of mane and lithely pulled himself up on the back of the horse.

Keely reached out and took Leo's hand, pressing it to her face. "Be safe. I think you might have met someone as tough as you," she joked, looking over at Jey. His dark eyes studied them coolly from the back of his horse.

Leo didn't smile, ever serious. "I won't let you down. I'll find this golden cuff, Keely. I swear on my honor."

She smiled, about to say goodbye, when he leaned down and brushed his lips against hers, light as a feather. She was left stunned as he rode away, scattering a flock of ravens that pecked in the dirt.

Jey's eyes flared at Leo's show of affection. He kicked his horse with a sharp thump and jumped in front of Leo to lead the way.

"Come along, lover girl," Rifkin ribbed, holding the stable door open. "We've a boat to catch."

Galatin threw a hooded cloak over her, cinching it under her chin. "Speak to no one. If anyone asks who you are, you are an Eifalian student visiting."

Keely nodded and followed him down side-alleys to the harbor. She had barely set foot in Skara Brae and was already being secretly whisked away. But she wasn't completely alone. She had two of Orkney's finest with her. And Sam was out there. Waiting for them to be the heroes this time.

Chapter Thirteen

I *am alive.*

Sam repeated that mantra as he paced in the dark hole Catriona had thrown him in. He snapped his fingers, and a ball of light appeared over his palm, giving him a glimpse of dark shadows and solid rock before it went out. He did this over and over. He hated the darkness, but he couldn't sustain his magic. His brain was too jittery, like he had drunk an entire swimming pool of Mountain Dew.

Catriona had not returned, but he could feel her malignant presence in his cell. Like she was watching him every second. He picked up one of his pets, letting the scaly creature crawl over the back of his hand as he imagined sending the Gungnir spear through *her* evil heart. A smile crossed his face.

She wanted him to join with her.

Never, he swore to himself, setting the scorpion down. He was one of the good guys. No way she was going to change that about him.

But you are changing, a voice whispered in his head. *Every time you use magic. Every time you smile as you think of a way to extract vengeance. You're becoming more and more like me every day.*

He tensed. Was that Catriona in his head? He snapped his fingers. Not even a spark. Snapped them again. His fingers were slick with sweat. Darkness pressed in on him, suffocating him. Then a familiar laugh made him stop in his tracks.

"Keely?" He whirled around, but there was no one there. It came again, from another corner of his cell. He spun, trying to catch a glimpse of her.

"Where are you?" Had Keely come to rescue him? Joy made his heart race.

He held his breath, desperate to hear her laugh again, and then as the silence stretched out, he realized he was hallucinating. After days of captivity, his mind was beginning to crack. That was what Catriona wanted. To break his spirit. He needed to rest. Get his wits about him.

He was about to lie down when a flickering image appeared before him. Sam blinked, pinching his arm to see if he was dreaming. A ghostly Keely stood in his cell. She was talking to someone. Leo's face came into focus next to her. Leo was on horseback. It was like watching a grainy black-and-white movie. Keely smiled up at Leo.

Leo's voice was tinny but clear. "I'll see you soon," he said. And then Leo leaned down and kissed her.

Sam's eyes bulged out, unable to look away. The image shifted, and he saw his friends swimming under an azure sky. Even Howie had joined in the party, letting out a loud whoop. Sam's heart beat wildly out of control as the movie repeated again and again. Leo kissing Keely. Howie laughing. Acting like they didn't have a stinking care in the world.

While he was locked in this hole.

See how they've forgotten you, the voice whispered in his ear. He could almost smell Catriona's fetid breath.

"I know you're doing this!" Sam shouted. "Get out of my head!"

You are nothing to them.

Sam knew Catriona was trying to mess with his head, but he couldn't quell the outrage that rose up in him.

Because it wasn't fair. Sam had saved Keely! Saved Leo! Saved everyone! And they just forgot about him like he was yesterday's newspaper, trash to line a birdcage with.

He shook himself to clear his mind. "You can't make me hate them. I won't let you win."

His cell grew quiet, and for a moment, he thought it was over. And then another image flickered to life, this time showing his mother working in the mill back home. She was laughing, going about her work as if her life was perfectly fine.

Why hasn't she returned for you? Why has she abandoned you? The voice was a crooning whisper in his head. Even when Sam plugged his ears, the words still got in.

"She would have come back if she could," he shouted, his voice echoing off the walls.

But she's a powerful witch . . . the voice answered.

Sam broke into a sweat. His hands began to shake. Catriona was wrong. Just because Abigail was powerful didn't mean she could return to Orkney. *But was she even trying?* Doubt seeped into his bones like tiny needles prickling his soul. He tried to calm his breathing, hoping the torment was over, but the sound of another familiar voice began to play.

Sam slowly raised his head, dreading what he would see. The voice was his father's, Robert Barconian. He lay on the battlefield, his uniform dusty and bloodied.

"Why did you free me and let me die?' he asked, beseeching Sam with one hand. "Why?"

Sam bit his lip so hard that blood flowed across his tongue like a bitter paste. The image of his father reaching for him played in a cruel loop, and he couldn't look away. He sank to his knees, wishing it weren't true. Wishing he could call Catriona out for another lie.

But he couldn't.

Sam was forced to relive the awful guilt that came from knowing he had killed his dad just as surely as if he himself had stuck the blade in. A moan left his lips as rage pounded in his head. Painful, blinding rage. He clutched his temples, writhing in the darkness, until he finally unleashed his scorching pain in a howl so loud it would have split the walls if they hadn't been hewn from uncaring stone.

High up in her room, Catriona smiled, watching Sam through her magic glass as he thrashed about, trying to reject the disturbing images in his mind. She let the spiteful thoughts pass softly through her lips . . .

"Why did you free me then just let me die like that?" she whispered . . . and then watched through the glass as the words reached Sam's ears, filling his head with poison. Fanning the flames of his rage. Endera had been a fool. The boy was as easy to break as a matchstick.

He let out a powerful scream, and her glee turned to shock when her precious glass orb cracked down the center, then exploded into a mass of shattered pieces.

She stood before the pile of broken glass in disbelief. He had destroyed it with only his rage. Then her lips curled into a smile.

Soon this powerful weapon will belong to me, Catriona gloated.

A fluttering sound came at her window. A pair of ravens settled onto the ledge, pecking about for food.

"What news do you bring me, my beauties?" She scooped them up, letting them perch on her shoulder. The glistening black birds jabbered raucously into her ear. She fed them bits of bread from her breakfast as she encouraged them. "Yes, tell me," she whispered. "Tell me everything."

After Ariane's failure to eliminate the earth children, Catriona had called on one of the many eyes and ears she had planted inside the Orkadian ranks. Her fists closed and constricted as she took in their news. So Odin thought sending the girl to Ymir would help him? That feeble brat was no match for the savage Vanirians. The frost giants would crush her like an insect. Still, Odin did not ordain heroes casually. She would take no chances.

"Tell the traitor the girl is to be killed," she instructed her black minions. "She must not be allowed to reach the Cave of Shadows." She released the birds back into the night.

She chewed over the ravens' other bit of news. Odin was sending one of the earth children after a rare prize. The Draupnir cuff. Odin had fashioned it to retrieve his son from the underworld. A tempting artifact to someone who had lost a loved one . . .

The perfect plot came to a boil in Catriona's mind. To retrieve the cuff, the boy would have to cross the dire wastelands to the Falcory lands. Ariane was nearby and could take her revenge out on him for their dear sister Nestra's death at the hands of the Falcory.

But she will need help.

Catriona smiled as she looked out the narrow opening cut into the stone walls. This side of her room overlooked the courtyard. Endera stood talking to a small group, no doubt complaining about how Catriona was running things, seeding her words of discontent.

The truth was, Endera was more than a little disappointed in how her ambitious plans to free her ancestors had turned out. In her power-addled mind, Endera had thought Catriona would bow to her in gratitude.

Fool, Catriona scoffed.

This Volgrim witch was at her peak. Her power was unmatched. Endera could pit the entire coven against Catriona and it would not matter. But a divided coven would prevent them from achieving their ultimate goal. So perhaps a trip away would do Endera good. Some place far from her allies within the coven, chasing after an impossible prize until Catriona had sealed her rule of the Tarkana Fortress. Kill two birds with one stone.

And it will be all her idea, Catriona plotted.

She immediately called a meeting of the coven.

Within an hour, nearly two hundred witches had assembled in the Tarkana Hall in the shadow of the oversized spider. Catriona seated herself on the throne, a replica of her father's. Once she sealed her rule over the coven, she would rename the place Volgrim Hall. The other witches obediently took their seats around her in their chairs. News of Nestra's death had spread, casting a pall over the gathering. Beatrixe and Agathea sat close by. Bronte refused to leave her potion-making. The fussy hag was too old to coerce, and Catriona had let it be.

Endera was joined by her fellow Tarkana witches: the aging Hestera; the young, simpering Lemeria; and a handful of lesser witches who appeared uneasy with the power struggle that gripped the coven.

Catriona clapped her hands twice to bring the meeting to order. "Sisters, you've all heard the tragic news of Nestra's passing. The inhabitants of this world shall pay dearly for their actions, I assure you. But today I bring ill news of Odin's interference. The earth children are back from Midgard."

There was silence, and then Endera spoke in a bored voice. "The friends of the witch-boy? They are hardly a threat."

"Alone, no. But in Odin's shadow they are to be feared. Ariane was unable to defeat them. Somehow these friends of his summoned wraiths. Even now, the girl makes her way to Rakim to find Ymir."

Murmurs of disbelief greeted her words.

Endera's eyes narrowed. "She'll never survive the frost giants. No human can."

Catriona suppressed her joy at how easily Endera was led. "Too right, Endera. But just in case you're wrong, I've planted a traitor in her midst."

Endera's eyes grew cold at the inference she might be wrong. But before she could speak, Catriona stood, facing the assembly, her voice booming. "But that is not our only problem. Odin sent one of his heroes to seek a golden cuff. He must be stopped. Ariane is close by, but she could use help."

Catriona let her words hang in the silence of the Tarkana Hall. Not one witch uttered a sound.

But the knuckles on Endera's hands turned white as she gripped the arms of her chair. "Golden cuff? You don't mean the Draupnir?"

Catriona turned her head slowly toward her adversary. "I believe that's the name, yes. The very same cuff fashioned by Odin to free his son from the underworld." It was so gratifying to watch Endera's tortured emotions. She would not be able to pass up the power the cuff offered. Not with her daughter trapped in the underworld, soon to be lost forever. "The Draupnir has been lost for centuries. But if the boy retrieves it, who knows what power these children will gain."

"I will go after him," Endera said, rising. "Ariane can use my help."

Catriona concealed her satisfaction. Ariane would redeem her failure to eliminate the earth children by killing Endera long before the upstart made it near the cuff. "Are you sure, Endera? I could use you here."

Endera laughed bitterly. "You'll count every second hoping the Falcory kill me like they did Nestra."

Catriona seethed at her cruel jibe. Nestra had been not just her cousin, but also an old and dear friend. "As you wish, Endera. The coven will be ever grateful for your help."

Endera rose and began to walk away and then stopped and turned slowly. "What of the other boy, the one they call 'Howie'?"

The queen of witches cackled long and hard before answering. "Odin made him Protector of the Realm. The boy is a laughingstock. He will be the first casualty when we ride into Skara Brae and take their capital city."

Chapter Fourteen

Howie stared glumly around the weapons room. The armory consisted of the men's dining hall, the musty barracks, and this dump, currently piled up with muddy swords and grimy shields. Keely and Leo had barely been gone five minutes, and Howie was so lonely he wanted to howl. He had to pull it together or he was going to sob all over the armor Teren had dumped in his arms. His only companion was Rego's bird, and so far all Lingas had done was bite him.

The iolar sat on her perch, watching Howie closely while he hefted a grimy chest plate onto the table and picked up a wire brush, scraping off the mud and grime. He had been given an oversized shirt that hung down to his knees and breeches that were a size too big, but it was a step up from the rather rank and smelly Chuggies uniform.

"You've got it easy, Lingas," he said. "I mean, you were born a fighting-machine with that beak of yours and those talons. Look what I've got," he indicated his scrawny form. "Not a scrap of muscle."

Before Lingas could squawk at him, a man burst into the room, followed closely by two men dressed in black uniforms. These weren't Orkadian soldiers. They looked like Balfins, the ones that had guarded Howie during his time at the Tarkana Fortress. The man wore a long red robe with heavy gold brocade. His eyes were sharp under thick eyebrows, and a scar ran along one cheek, giving him an air of danger. All told, he reminded Howie of a weasel.

"What can I do ya for you?" Howie said nonchalantly.

"Boy, where is Captain Teren?" the man snapped. "I heard a rumor there were outsiders inside the city walls."

"The captain is out training the troops, my man. It's just me here."

"My man?" He sauntered closer, eyeing Howie with an appraising look. "It is proper to address me as Lord Orrin. I am the High Regent here. Which you would know if you were from here. What did you say your name was?"

"Who, me? I'm just the armor-cleaner guy," Howie said, growing uncomfortable under Orrin's pinpoint stare. "Just blew into town."

Orrin's furry brows rose in surprise. "You're an earth child. What brings you back? Wait, let me guess, you're here to save your friend." He tilted forward, lowering his voice like they were sharing a secret. "It won't work, you know. Catriona will never let him go."

"She won't have a choice once we complete our missions," Howie bragged without thinking. Orrin's eyes flared. Howie could have slapped himself in the head. Teren had told him to keep his fat lips zipped, but he'd blown it already.

"Missions. So the rumors are true. Odin has chosen his heroes. Which are you? The Seeker? No, no, the Sacrifice. You look a bit like a lost lamb."

The two guards snickered.

Howie flushed. "Actually, I'm the . . ." He cleared his throat, working up the courage to say it.

"The . . . ?" Orrin raised one eyebrow, waiting.

Howie forced out the words. "The, uh, you know, Great Protector of the Realm."

One corner of Orrin's lips rose in a sneer of contempt. "Great Protector, is it? I see. So you must have superior fighting skills?"

Howie fiddled with the armor, avoiding Orrin's eyes. "Well, sure. Obviously." He tried to think of something, *anything*, he could brag about. "I play a mean game of Zombie Wars. Wiped out a legion of undead armies on my way to getting the top score." Howie had the sense of mind not to mention the horn Mimir had given him that actually could command an army of the dead. It was currently buried under Howie's dirty clothes.

Orrin's voice dripped with disdain. "And will a 'top score' in Zombie Wars help defend us against an army of witches?"

This Orrin dude was obviously pushing his buttons, but Howie was tired of people picking on him. "Yeah, I get it, I don't exactly look the part. That's cool. Who knows what Odin was thinking? I mean, he is a gaaaawd, and all, so you know, I expect he has it under control."

The High Regent waved a hand. "Or perhaps Odin has his own agenda. What about your friend? The he-witch. I hear he is a prisoner in the Tarkana dungeons. You don't worry about him?"

Howie shrugged. "Sam can take care of himself."

Orrin stepped closer. Howie smelled cloves on his breath. "There is a rumor that colonies of Deathstalkers live within the Tarkana walls."

"Hey, man, I was there myself. No scorpions. Just giant rats." Howie shuddered as he remembered them, although his buddy, Bert the Rat, had grown fat eating his crusts.

Orrin tapped his chin as if he were thinking. "Ah. You were in the upper cells. There are lower ones. Deeper underground. But, if you're not worried, why should I be? And with you on guard here at Skara Brae, I guess he is very much on his own."

Orrin stood directly underneath Lingas's perch. Howie was about to warn him that was probably a bad idea when Lingas let out a burp. A dribble of bird vomit erupted from her mouth and landed on Orrin's red robe, splotching it with what looked to be squirrel entrails.

Howie couldn't help it. He snorted with laughter. Orrin looked angry enough to rip Lingas's head off, but the bird bared its beak at him as he reached for it, and the weasel-faced official retreated.

"Be careful the Great Protector doesn't need protecting," he spat out, wiping his robe in disgust as he left the room, followed by his men.

Lingas cackled and then tucked her beak in her chest and promptly started snoring.

Howie picked up one of the swords and gripped the handle in his hands. Orrin was right. He should learn more about being a warrior. The sword was so heavy, his arms trembled under the weight, and the tip sagged to the armory floor.

A peal of laughter rang out behind him. The back entrance, the one that led to the barracks, stood open. A girl leaned against the doorjamb. Maybe twelve. Thin as a reed with long brown hair tied back tightly. She wore breeches instead of a skirt, with short black boots. She carried a stack of clean uniforms she hung in a cupboard.

Hello, cutie pie.

"You're holding it wrong," she taunted.

Howie leaned on the sword, trying to act casual. "Yeah, I'm just, you know, getting the feel for it. The captain is counting on me to help win this war."

She walked slowly along the rack of swords, running her finger across the blades. "I could beat you blindfolded with a wooden spoon," she challenged over her shoulder.

Howie's common sense, the part that recognized he knew absolutely nothing about swordplay, was promptly overridden by his desire to impress this girl. So without thinking, he yanked a set of wooden practice blades from the bin and tossed one to her. "I'm warning you, I beat all seventeen levels of Sword Master III. Plus the bonus content."

The girl caught the blade with one hand. "Do you always speak such nonsense?" she asked, slashing the air smoothly with it.

Howie's mouth went dry. That had looked pretty polished. "I—"

"Let's have a go." She bowed and extended the tip of her sword to him, crouching slightly. He mimicked her stance, but it was her eyes that drew his attention. They were a toffee color with a fringe of thick lashes. And just as steady as her blade.

Howie met her thrust, but she parried fast as lightning, leaving him stumbling over his feet. Every attack he tried, she countered, moving like a nimble-toed dancer. It was obvious within seconds she outclassed him by a hundred miles, and that what he had learned playing video games was of absolutely no use in a real fight.

After she had knocked the sword from his hand three times and allowed him to retrieve it, Howie finally surrendered.

"Where'd you learn to fight like that?" he panted, slumping against the table.

She gracefully sliced the air with her sword before she sat next to him.

"My father. He was a great swordsman. A member of the Orkadian guard. I used to come here with him to practice."

"Was?"

Her gaze, which had been so direct, now drifted away and darkened. "He died a few months ago. Ambushed on patrol by some nasty witches." Her voice was laced with a mixture of spite and grief.

"I'm sorry."

"Me, too." She swung her legs and waited for him to speak.

"I'm Howie." He stuck out his hand. "That's Lingas." He indicated the snoring bird.

"Selina," she said, slipping her slender hand in his. "You're not from here, are you?"

"Nope. I'm from good ol' Pilot Rock, Oregon. A place with hot showers, flush toilets, and cable TV."

She pulled her hand free as her voice turned cool. "You're friends with the he-witch." It sounded like an accusation.

"That's me. Sam's best bud."

Her face turned cold. "Where's your 'bud' now? No one's seen him in weeks. They say he's gone and joined the witches."

"No way!" Howie's voice rang with conviction. He might not think much of his abilities as Great Protector, but he had a ton of confidence in his friend. "Sam's one of us. Catriona's got him locked up in her dungeon. I'm here to help find him and save Orkney. Odin sent for me himself. Made me Protector of the Realm." He waited to see if she would laugh at him, but she didn't even blink.

"Then why are you hiding out here in the armory with only a iolar for company?"

"You mean besides my total lack of skills?" Embarrassment stung his cheeks. "You saw me; I can't fight worth beans."

"So that's it? You're just giving up?" She jumped down and paced in a circle, taking practice swings with her sword. "Some Protector you are."

He slid off the table. "Who said I'm giving up?"

"I say it." She circled him. "What will you do about it?" She slapped him on the thigh from behind with the flat blade of her sword.

"Ow!" He jumped and turned to face her.

"Show me something, Protector."

His leg stung from her smack. "Stop it."

"Make me." She hit him again, this time on the arm.

He stepped back, feeling his face turn red. "I don't want to hit a girl."

She slashed the air three times with the sword, all the while advancing on him. He stumbled back and, in full-blown humiliation, fell on his bottom.

Selina stood over him. "Why are you so scared?"

"I'm not scared." A sweat broke out on his upper lip. He was scared. But he didn't want to admit it.

"Then hit me."

"No."

"Hit me!"

"No!" Suddenly he wanted to cry. And the Howmeister made it a rule not cry in front of girls.

"You're a coward is what you are." She put the point of her sword under his chin and lifted it.

She was looking at him the same way Ronnie Polk and his buddies did when they picked on him. A simmering fury rose within Howie as she shook her head in disgust and turned her back to walk away.

"Take that back," Howie demanded, scrambling to his feet. He clenched his fists, feeling frustrated and angry and afraid.

She paused, cocking her head to the side to look at him. "I fight for my father's honor. Who do you fight for?"

Howie knew the answer without having to think. "Sam. He's my best friend. He's stood up for me so many times I lost count. I'd do anything to be the one standing up for him."

She threw him a sword. "Then fight. Odin picked you. Have a little faith."

Howie gripped the sword. Confidence trickled into him. Tapping the sword to his forehead, he bowed. "Come on, chiquita, show me what you got."

Selina grinned, tipping her sword and mirroring his bow. "It will be an honor, Lord Protector."

Chapter Fifteen

Keely stared wistfully at the receding island of Garamond. Things had happened so quickly, she had hardly had time to catch her breath, let alone realize she had parted ways with her two most trusted allies. She worried about leaving Howie alone. He was sorely lacking in confidence. Leo. Well, he would probably defeat the iguanadillo in two shakes and be back in Skara Brae before Keely even got close to the Cave of Shadows.

"Where are we headed?" Keely asked as the two men quickly set the sails and caught a stiff ocean breeze. They had taken possession of a small skiff Galatin said was used for scouting missions. It was bare bones, with only a tiny cabin below deck. It was designed for speed, not comfort.

Galatin answered from his position at the helm. "North to Torf-Einnar."

Torf-Einnar. She tried to remember her Orkney geography. "Isn't that where the Eifalians live? I met Gael before." Gael was the Eifalian representative to the High Council. From what she could recall, he didn't always approve of Sam, but he was a good person.

Galatin nodded. "We'll be needing their help to go north to Rakim where the Cave of Shadows is. Gael's father is King Einolach. Their territory borders the frost giants. They've been enemies for centuries, but the Eifalians know the ways of snow and ice."

"So we're talking cold," Keely said.

"Colder than a witch's heart," Rifkin muttered next to her as he unfurled a sail.

"And you really think they'll help us?"

Galatin gave the wheel a spin as the wind caught the sails and the skiff picked up speed. "Once they understand the importance of our mission."

Rifkin winked at her. "Personally, I think they'll toss us into the street like dishwater. The Eifalians have no love for the Vanir."

A giant yawn split Keely's face.

Galatin jerked his head at the hatch. "Go down and get some rest. We'll sail through the night. Should make Torf-Einnar by late morning if the winds are kind."

Keely didn't argue. She took a bunk below and promptly fell asleep. Her sleep was dreamless except for one recurring vision.

The Moon Pearl. It glowed like a celestial night-light. She wanted to touch it, feel its soothing power, but it was just out of reach.

When she awoke, sunlight streamed through the small porthole over her bed. She rubbed away the smudges and looked out with wonder. They were approaching the coastline of a beautiful emerald island. Torf-Einnar. Stone cliffs streaked with creamy layers of pink and beige rose up from the water. Along their rim, fresh snow dusted the tops of towering pine trees. In the distance, white-capped mountains beckoned. Beyond those mountains was the Moon Pearl. Keely could feel it calling to her.

Brimming with excitement, she climbed up onto the deck. Galatin stood at the helm. Rifkin swung in a hammock.

"Good morning, little mouse," Rifkin said cheerfully.

Galatin tossed her a hard biscuit. "Eat this, Chosen One. You'll need to keep your strength up. The journey ahead will be difficult."

"I can do it, you know," she said, meeting his eyes. "I'm not afraid."

His eyes narrowed. "Then you're a fool. Fear's what keeps you alive on the battlefield." He spun the wheel sharply. "Rifkin, get your lazy bones moving. We're nearly there."

Keely turned away, gripping the railing with one hand. Galatin's words chafed at her confidence. Of course she was scared, but that wasn't going to stop her from going ahead. She nibbled on the biscuit, watching as a dolphin crested the wave next to the ship. Keely smiled, remembering their adventure to Asgard and how Mavery had gotten the dolphins to haul their raft across the sea. Poor Mavery. Keely hated hurting her feelings like that, but what choice did she have?

As Keely leaned on the rail, something moved out of the corner of her eye. She tensed, imagining one of the rathos she had encountered in the dungeons at the Tarkana Fortress. Did the ship carry the same vermin? There was a rolled-up sail stowed in the helm of the ship. It was moving slightly. Too big for a rathos. Suddenly suspicious, Keely marched over to it and pulled it away.

"Hello."

Mavery's beaming face looked up at her. She looked pleased with herself and not the least bit put out at being discovered. Her hair stuck up in clumps, and her gray dress was rumpled from hiding all night under the sails.

"Mavery! What . . . you're supposed to be . . ." Keely sputtered for words.

Galatin and Rifkin heard the ruckus and made their way forward. Galatin had a thunderous look as Mavery got to her feet. "You were told to stay in Skara Brae, witch."

"No, I was told I couldn't go with you," Mavery said saucily. "No one said I couldn't catch a ride to Torf-Einnar. I felt like paying a visit to King Einolach."

Rifkin snorted. "Good friends with the king, are you? A little witchling like yourself?"

Mavery just gave that sweet smile and turned her back on them, holding on to the rail as the skiff cut through the water.

Galatin shouted at Rifkin to get back to sailing the ship, and the two girls were alone.

Keely put a tentative hand on Mavery's shoulder. "I'm sorry. About yesterday."

"It's okay. I know why you did it." Mavery kept her eyes on the approaching shores.

"What do you mean?"

She snorted. "I'm not stupid. You drank from Mimir's well. You saw things that are going to happen. You musta seen something bad. Real bad to not want me to go, because we're friends . . . right?" She finally turned to look up at Keely.

Keely saw the shining look of need in the girl's eyes, and she wrapped an arm around Mavery's shoulders. "Yeah. We're friends. And you're right. The things I saw . . . they're pretty ugly."

Mavery turned back to the horizon, looking pleased. "That's okay. I've survived lots of things I wasn't supposed to."

They were silent a moment. "What happened?" Keely ventured. "You know, the day the witches tossed you overboard. Why did they do it?" Mavery had been abandoned by the Tarkanas and left to drown. An old sea captain named Jasper had plucked the girl from the frigid waters.

The girl's face paled. Her lip trembled slightly. "Because they knew."

"Knew what?"

"That I wasn't like them."

"But you're . . . a witch."

"Yeah, so?"

"So what made you different?"

Mavery took the barely nibbled biscuit from Keely and held it in her palm. "Sometimes what you see on the outside is not what's in the inside." She cracked opened the biscuit. A tiny delicate flower nestled in the center. Its pink petals unfurled in the light. Mavery lifted it and began plucking the petals, dropping them one by one in the water. "I'm not a Tarkana witch. I was a foundling. Left on the steps of the Tarkana Fortress. They musta seen something in me they didn't like."

"So who are you?"

Mavery's eyes were bleak as she stared out at the sea. "Someone nobody wanted. Look, we're here."

The ship came around an island point, and the city of Ter Glenn burst into sight. A picture-perfect fairy castle sat atop a large outcrop of rock. Dozens of turrets rose up, impossibly tall and beautiful. Green banners flapped in the breeze. A small town was nestled along the seawall. The whitewashed buildings were capped by red-tiled roofs. An armada of boats lined the wharf. Men crawled over the decks, loading supplies and polishing brass. More than a dozen soldiers patrolled the ramparts.

The Eifalians were nothing if not well-armed. Surprising for such peaceful people. Then Keely realized . . .

War was coming.

A depressing thought settled over her. What good were warships against the power of the Volgrim witches? Catriona could probably incinerate them all with one sweep of her hand.

They nosed in among the large ships. Keely had barely set foot on the dock when a boy with a sheaf of hair even whiter than hers dropped down next to them from the sidewalk above. He landed on his feet light as a cat. He had an elfin face—thin, pointed chin, and eyes bright as the blue sea.

"What are you doing back here?" he said, planting his hands on his hips as he glared at Mavery.

"None of your beeswax, Theo."

"Who's your friend?" He switched his glare to Keely.

"Hi, I'm Keely." She stuck her hand out, but at the mention of her name, he took a step back.

"You're an outsider. You don't belong here. This is not your world."

"I came to help my friend, Sam," she explained.

"Well, I hope he dies," the boy snapped. "He ruined every-thing."

"Back off, Theo," Mavery said, raising her hands. "Before I give you a good blast of witchfire."

"Theo." A sharp voice came from above. Keely looked up and recognized Gael leaning on the railing. The Eifalian frowned with disapproval.

Theo pushed Keely backward before disappearing under the riggings of a boat. Keely flailed, spiraling over the edge of the water, but Mavery grabbed her arm with two hands and pulled her back to her feet.

"What was that about?" Keely asked as they walked up the dock.

"Theo's just a spoiled royal brat. Ignore him. That's what I always do."

Keely wondered why Theo hated Sam so much. Something about his eyes was haunting. A grief that she recognized.

Gael awaited them at the top of the gangplank. At his side was a beautiful woman. She was tall and elegant with a regal air, and her skin was pale, almost translucent. Her oversized eyes were a sparkling blue, kind but searching as they passed over Keely. Gael bowed low, his aqua-colored robes glimmering in the light. "Welcome to Torf-Einnar, Keely. This is my wife, Rayan."

Rayan squeezed Keely's hand gently. "Gael has told me much about your adventures. I apologize for my nephew's behavior. He has not been himself lately."

"That's all right. It's nice to meet you." Keely curtsied awk-wardly, feeling underdressed in her jeans and the soiled denim jacket she had been wearing since they arrived in Orkney.

Rayan turned to Mavery with a warm smile and put a fond hand on the girl's shoulder. "Nice to see you again, Mavery. We so enjoyed your last visit. I told Captain Teren that there is always a home for you here."

Mavery flushed and curtsied.

"Come, let us proceed to the palace," Gael said. "My father,

King Einolach, awaits your audience." His eyes lingered on Keely's silvery white hair, but he made no comment on the unnatural color.

The two girls were ushered into an ornate carriage drawn by four prancing horses. Galatin and Rifkin mounted their steeds and rode alongside. Mavery sat close to Keely as Rayan filled them in on the scenery.

"Ter Glen is our main city. The Eifalian kingdom is a tiny one, but powerful. Many of our people live in small hamlets nearby where they can mine the goods we trade and grow our food."

Pressing her face to the glass, Keely took in the fanciful sights. People milled about dressed in colorful robes. Some wore bright turbans wrapped around their heads. All stopped and bowed as the royal carriage passed by. The cobbled streets were spotless and lined with shops with funny names she didn't recognize. One had a picture of shiny green beetles with a sign announcing TRILLYWIGS SOLD HERE under it, while another pronounced a NEW SHIPMENT OF PHORALITE.

They rattled over the cobblestone road up the hill to Ter Glen, a breathtaking palace. The pristine walls were whitewashed, sparkling in the sunlight reflected from the ocean. They entered through tall gates and came to a stop outside a gabled building with red roof tiles. Shutters were thrown open, and flower boxes made colorful splashes. Everything appeared built with exquisite care, down to the intricately carved doorframes.

Gael helped Rayan out, then extended his hand to Keely. She could feel callouses on his finger pads similar to her own. Gael must have been an avid archer.

"Mavery, you know the way to the guest quarters. Please show the young miss to her room," Gael suggested with an elegant wave of his arm.

"And don't be late for dinner," Rayan added with a fond smile.

The witch-girl curtsied and grabbed Keely's elbow, pulling her through an archway. They headed down an endless corridor from where Keely caught glimpses of the sea as they skipped across an open-air bridge. She wanted to stop and soak it all in, but Mavery dragged her along, turning left and right until Keely was completely lost. Finally, the path ended at a round thatched cottage.

Mavery pushed open the door and waved Keely in. "Here you go."

It was a single room. Simple, but elegant. The walls were smooth, bare of any design. A large bed frame carved from white birch took up most of the room. Next to it, a tall dresser held an oval-shaped polished stone mounted on a stand. Keely ran her finger over the surface. It glowed a soft warm pink.

"It's a soul crystal," Mavery boasted, proud of her knowledge. "The Eifalians use them to read people's auras and do healing."

Keely caught a glimpse of herself in a small mirror on the dresser. She touched her hair, feeling the spiky tufts. The color was like liquid metal. She could easily pass as an Eifalian.

Fresh clothes were laid out on the bed: thin suede leggings, a silken undershirt, and a sweater made of the softest wool. A velvet cloak hung on the wall the color of hunter green, beautifully embroidered with gold filigree and capped with a fur-trimmed hood. Fingering a pair of tall boots, Keely was amazed at how light they were. Even the gloves fit perfectly, the soft leather stretching around her fingers.

"How come you know so much about this place?" she asked.

Mavery gave a shrug. "I'm an orphan. I got no real home of my own. Gael and Rayan, they thought, maybe . . ."

"They wanted to adopt you?"

Mavery scowled. "Stuff and nonsense. I'm a witch. They're Eifalian. And Theo's a brat. I tried it for a couple weeks, and you know what happened? Sam got taken by the witches. So I hightailed it back to Skara Brae where I belong. In case Sam needs me."

A bell rang twice.

"You should wash up and get dressed," Mavery said, wiping away the tear that had escaped. "The king don't like it when you're late." She ducked out the door before Keely could get a word out.

Chapter Sixteen

Keely washed up and changed as quickly as she could, glad to be rid of her filthy jeans and dress in something clean and warm. The new pants fit snugly. She slipped easily into the boots and pulled the sweater over the silken undershirt.

Running a stiff brush through her hair, Keely felt a flutter of nerves. How did one act around a king? Curtsy? Bow? Wrapping the cloak around her, she opened the door, then hesitated, unsure of her direction. There was a nip in the air that had her pulling the cloak tighter. The sun was already sinking low in the sky. Days were short here in the North. She took a step onto the grass, and immediately, tiny lights came on, glowing dots heading off to the right.

Keely knelt down and studied the source. A little green beetle perched on a blade of grass.

These must be trillywigs, Keely marveled, recognizing it from the advertisement in town.

She touched its back, and it shuttered closed, folding a pair of mottled green-and-blue wings over its head. She let it go, and it unfolded, glowing again.

"Wow," she whispered. They were like fairy lights showing her the way.

She followed along the trillywig trail, retracing her steps to the main palace. A curving stairway lit up as she approached. Holding the rail, she climbed slowly, gasping when she entered a wide atrium.

The spectacular room was surrounded by majestic white stone pillars. There were no walls, no ceiling. The stars had come out. A thin crescent moon shone down. White cloth stretched between the pillars was buffeted by the breeze blowing in from the crashing ocean below. Torches flickered in the salty air, adding a magical glow to the space.

In the center of the atrium, a man sat on a high throne made of alabaster stone. Curving whale bones rose up behind him. This must have been King Einolach, Gael's father.

As she drew closer, Keely noticed a number of Eifalians seated cross-legged on scattered rugs at the feet of the king. Their eyes were closed, and each held a soul crystal in the palm of his or her hand. Around each of them an aura swirled, a dim glow that charged the air with a tingling energy that made the hair on Keely's arms stand up.

Gael and his wife waited alongside Mavery and her two Orkadian escorts. Beside Rayan, Theo stood in a formal outfit of purple velveteen and a gold sash tied at his waist. His face was neutral, but his eyes glittered with an intense dislike. Keely took her place in line next to Mavery.

A gong rang out, reverberating in the stillness. The assembled group of Eifalians lifted their heads as one, and the air quieted down.

King Einolach held an ornate staff made of whalebone. At the top was an opaque crystal the size of a goose egg that glittered in the reflected white of the room. He raised the staff and stabbed it into the stone floor one time. The crystal glowed and then burst into a rainbow of soft colors that spread out over all of them. As the light hit her face, Keely was bathed in a feeling of soothing serenity.

Gael stepped in front of his father's throne and bowed.

Mavery dropped into a curtsy, elbowing Keely to follow. Keely awkwardly bent her legs and imitated her.

"Greetings, Father," Gael began. "I bring you guests from across the sea. Ensign Galatin and his associate represent the Orkadian Guard."

Galatin and Rifkin made appropriate bowing motions. King Einolach waved his hand at them. He was old—really old—but still majestic. His fair skin was deeply lined. White hair fell down his back in waves. He wore a luminous crown made from mother-of-pearl, swirled with shades of pink and blue and gray. His robe was woven with tiny crystals that shimmered like a living tapestry. On his left hand, a large opal stone caught the light, winking at Keely like a wise eye.

Gael continued. "And I present to you, Miss Keely of the Fifth Realm."

The king breathed deep. "Ah yes, the world of men. Yet she looks as if she could be Eifalian. You have the hair of a healer. Only the greatest healers bear silver tips in their hair."

Galatin stood, waving his hand at Keely. "The child drank from Mimir's well. She says that Odin selected her and her two earth companions to help us in our fight to defeat the Volgrim witches."

The king leaned forward to inspect her. His eyes were a cerulean blue, taking in every inch of the girl. He held out his staff. The crystal at the top shot out rays of light that washed over Keely. The tingling she had been feeling ever since her hair turned white intensified, spreading from her fingers up her arms through her whole body. Her scalp prickled, as if her thoughts were being probed. Not just her thoughts. Her motives. Her heart. Her temper.

Her secrets . . .

After a long moment, King Einolach raised his head and fixed her with his gaze.

"You have lost someone close to you."

Keely hesitated, feeling a familiar stabbing pain. "My mother."

"I sense a dark spot inside you, something you hide."

Keely pasted a smile on her face. "Things happen. That's all."

Einolach's fingers tightened on the knob of his staff as if he were irritated by her evasion. "These things that happened, you feel responsible. Why?"

Keely's toes curled in her boots. She wasn't going to bare her soul in front of all these people. Not here. Not now.

As her silence stretched out, the king gently added, "There is freedom in sharing your burden."

The thought passed through her before she could stop it.

I killed my mother.

Einolach's eyes widened, as if she had spoken aloud.

Thankfully, Gael stepped forward, interrupting the moment. "Father, we must discuss—"

But King Einolach raised his hand, cutting Gael off, and he drove his staff into the ground once again. "We will share a meal before we discuss official matters."

Keely sagged with relief as attention turned away from her. A table was brought in, carried by silent workers with shaved heads, dressed in white robes. They appeared to be trainees, acolytes to the Eifalian council members.

"Theo, please show Keely to her seat," Rayan said, putting her arms around the boy's stiff shoulders and pushing him gently forward.

Theo stuck his arm out stiffly, and Keely hesitantly put her hand on his arm. He led her to the table, then pulled her chair back, scraping it across the marble floor. He bowed, then waved her into the seat.

She sat down, then leaped to her feet as pain shot through her. Theo's eyes were triumphant as she bit back the squeal of pain.

Gael swooped over to her side. "Is there a problem?"

Theo paled, looking suddenly young and vulnerable.

"No." Keely palmed the pointed shell Theo had left on her seat, hiding it in her hand. "I was just waiting for you to sit down."

Gael nodded and moved on, ushering Theo into a seat across from her and taking his place next to the boy. Keely carefully checked her chair and sat down, squeezing in between Mavery and Rifkin. Theo glared at her from across the table, but she gave him a sweet smile and turned her attention to the delicious-smelling food that arrived. Servants bore trays of roasted lamb surrounded by boiled potatoes and the ever-present pungent black cabbage. Keely dug in, finding eating a welcome distraction from the king's interrogation.

At the end of the meal, Mavery let out a small burp. It echoed around the table, drawing a glare from Gael and a gasp from Rayan.

"My compliments to the chef," she said cheekily.

The king surprised everyone by letting out his own small burp and raising his glass. "To the chef," he said. He winked at Mavery, clearly having a fondness for the orphan.

Unburdened by ceremony, the assembled group let out a collection of burps, large and small. Rifkin swallowed air and cut loose a foghorn. Galatin didn't join in, or even smile. He just swirled his glass of wine like it was poison. *Crankypants.*

As the dishes were cleared, King Einolach sat back in his chair. "Tell me . . . what help do my guests seek from the Eifalian kingdom?"

Galatin stood, clearing his throat. "The Volgrim witches are waging a war we cannot win, not without powerful magic at our side. Samuel Barconian gave us an edge. Without him, our losses mount. Even if the Eifalians and the Falcory join us, Catriona appears unstoppable. This earth child says Odin sent for her and her friends to help end this war and bring Sam back."

A hushed silence fell over the group. The seated Eifalians whispered among themselves.

Gael spoke next. "Father, Keely was gifted by Mimir with visions. She saw a path to defeating Catriona, but it is a path of great danger. One that . . ." he hesitated, as if he were choosing his words carefully, "one that requires seeking out the frost giants' help."

At the mention of the Vanir, King Einolach's face went taut.

Ramming his staff into the ground, he pointed a finger at Gael. "Never," he said forcefully. "Never will I ask those barbarians for help. We have an agreement that has not been breached in centuries. We do not travel beyond the Skoll Mountains, and the Vanir do not stray into our lands. That is the way it is."

Keely leaned forward. "Your Highness, we have no choice. Sam has been taken by the witches. If they turn him . . ."

"Yes, I have seen what he is capable of," the king said angrily. "He nearly destroyed our world once."

Theo abruptly shoved his chair back with a loud scrape. "I say let him die. He deserves it."

Rayan stood smoothly and went to Theo's side, putting her arms around his shoulders. "Hush, Theo. Come along. Its time you went to bed."

She led the boy away, but not before he cast one last withering glance at Keely.

Keely waited until Theo was gone before she renewed her plea. "I can save Sam, maybe even stop this war, but I have to go to the Cave of Shadows and ask Ymir for the Moon Pearl." Keely waited for a reaction. The Cave of Shadows was a thing of myths according to Rifkin. They might just laugh themselves silly.

The air vibrated with the outpouring of thoughts from the seated crowd. Keely's pores tingled with it, feeling doubt and disbelief scrub against her skin like a scratchy blanket.

The king rested pale hands on his staff. His voice was kind, but skeptical. "So you intend to find the creator of the universe? All by yourself? And just ask him to hand over the very essence of his heart?"

Keely swallowed back her nervousness and nodded. "I know it sounds crazy, but Odin named me the Seeker. I can do this. Because if I don't, and the witches turn Sam, they'll use him to draw on the most ancient magic in this realm. They'll destroy everything and kill everyone until they reach their ultimate goal."

"And what is that?" the king asked.

Keely hesitated. She hadn't yet said out loud this part of the vision she had glimpsed at Mimir's well. The vision of Catriona and Sam ripping the sky apart and stepping through to stand in front of Pilot Rock Junior High.

Mavery elbowed her. "Just say it," she whispered.

Encouraged, Keely turned to face the king and spoke words that sent a shockwave through the palace. "To release Orkney from the Ninth Realm."

Chapter Seventeen

An uproar broke out over Keely's outrageous statement. Heads turned as conversation hummed. Fear and shock filled the room. The king called for silence, rapping his staff twice before the room quieted.

"What do you mean, child?" he demanded. White fury emanated from him in waves that rolled over her like a hot wind, like it was her fault as the messenger. Even Galatin and Rifkin looked stunned.

Keely thought of Leo, riding off to face an uncertain future. And Howie, left behind in Skara Brae to be a leader, when he had no confidence in himself. She had to do as well as them, or better. She remembered something her mom had said once: *Fake it till you make it*. She cleared her throat, rose to her feet, and raised her voice to add strength to her words.

"I mean, whatever force keeps Orkney here in the Ninth Realm, the witches are going to try and break it. Orkney would be returned back to my world." She looked into the king's blue eyes. "Into Midgard. Making the two realms one again, the way it was before Catriona was put into those stones at the Ring of Brogar."

The king slumped back in his chair. "No. It is not possible. No one in Orkney has the power to undo Odin's magic. The force that separates us from earth will never be broken. Odin made sure of that."

"You're wrong. Sam has the power. I don't know how, but he does," she said, slumping down in her seat, her legs weak. "If he aligns himself with Catriona, he will help her undo Odin's magic and return Orkney to earth. I saw it when I drank from Mimir's well."

The king was thoughtful. "A millennia ago, your world and ours were one, you know. We magic folk had existed on earth since the dawn of time. But Catriona was filled with hatred toward mankind, a way to punish Odin, I suppose, for killing her father. She and her cronies used their magic in evil ways, burning cities to the ground, creating poxes, terrorizing entire countries in her mindless need to punish humans. Odin had no choice but to take action. Magic had almost destroyed the world once with the red sun curse. Catriona seemed bent on destroying it again. She had to be stopped. And so Odin arranged for her to be trapped in stone for eternity. But Odin no longer believed magic and mankind could safely coexist, so he brought these islands from earth into the Ninth Realm and created this place, this refuge for magic. You see, child, Odin would never allow Orkney to be returned to earth. Mankind is safely under his care."

"What if Odin's not here? What if something happens to him?"

There were audible gasps at that. Einolach's eyes narrowed to flint. "Like what?"

Keely bit down on her tongue. Vor's words to Leo that one of their own would be taken only painted Sam in a worse light. She changed tactics. "Look, if Odin has it under control, then why did he bring us here? What is he afraid of?"

The king didn't answer. Instead, he closed his eyes and passed his staff side to side. As the crystal at the end began to glow, a light spread out, filtering like a hazy cloud over the heads of every member assembled. Keely felt the prickle on her scalp. Then she heard strange whispers, like the other's thoughts were being drawn into the cloud. The air grew thick with it.

Dangerous.

Preposterous.

Impossible.

Every cell in her body tingled with that strange new feeling she had, like her nerves were hypersensitive. There was plenty of scoffing, but there was also fear underlying the thoughts. As the king drew on the collective thinking of the Eifalian court, he raised both hands, moving them like a conductor before an orchestra. A hum vibrated the air as the whispers swelled into a loud buzz like a swarm of bees. Keely felt herself swept up in it, as if her mind was adrift in the same current.

Then King Einolach stood abruptly, and the buzzing was cut off. He waved his staff over the group. "I have collected the auras. I will sleep on it. In the morning, you will have my decision." He left with a swish of his robes, followed by an entourage of Eifalian council members and attendants.

When the atrium had cleared, Gael bowed slightly at them. "I believe my father will take your counsel to the elders and seek their wisdom. We have not crossed the border between Torf-Einnar and the Vanirian kingdom of Rakim in many generations. Both sides took a blood oath to remain apart. If it is broken, there will be war. My father must be sure it is the right path."

Galatin bowed stiffly in return. "Soon he won't have a choice. The witches will be on his doorstep, and he will be at war, regardless. We appreciate your hospitality and assistance, Gael, but we must head north, with or without your approval."

The Eifalian gripped Galatin's arm. "You think you can face those savages alone and survive? If this girl is truly chosen, then it is our duty to see she is protected. You think two soldiers alone can do that against the Vanir?"

Galatin's jaw clenched. "I do not intend to fail, nor will I disobey my orders." The soldier nodded curtly and left the room. Rifkin slid Keely a nervous glance before scuttling after Galatin.

Keely was left with Mavery and Gael.

"You must be tired from your journey," Gael said calmly,

sweeping his arm forward. A thousand tiny trillywigs lit up. "If you follow this path, you will find your way back to your chambers."

On impulse, Keely leaned forward and gave him a quick hug. "Thank you, Gael. Please speak to your father. I know he listens to you."

He held her away from him. "Your hair," he said hesitantly. "When did it turn that color?"

Keely raised a hand self-consciously to her tufts. "After I sacrificed it at Mimir's well."

He looked like he wanted to say something more, but all he said was, "Curious." Then he bade them goodnight.

Mavery slipped her hand in Keely's, and together they walked down the path of delicate lights. Everything on this island appeared fairy-light and whimsical. The sconces on the wall were shaped like conical snails the size of oranges. Whorls of pink, yellow, and green rose to a familiar sharp point. So that's what Theo had put on her seat. When she reached for one, it glowed amber and vibrated under her touch.

"Those are phoralites," Mavery explained. "They're much prettier than trillywigs." She chattered on about life at the palace as they walked down the path to Keely's quarters.

A voice hissed from a tree branch overhead. "You could have ratted me out."

Keely knew it was Theo without looking up. "I don't rat out my friends," she said.

"I'm no friend." He dropped down from the tree and landed like a cat blocking their path, his white hair shining in the dim light. "And I wish the witches would just blast your friend to pieces."

Exasperated, Keely folded her arms, studying him curiously. "What did Sam ever do to you?"

Theo's lip trembled. He suddenly looked like he wanted to cry. Keely took a step forward. "Are you all right?"

But Theo backed away, his eyes glistening with unshed tears, and without another word, he ran off.

Mavery grabbed Keely's arm and hurried her forward. "Told you, he's just a spoiled royal brat."

Keely hesitated, wanting to go after him. The boy seemed upset, but right now she had bigger problems on her mind. She let Mavery drag her to their small dormer. A phoralite glowed next to the bed, casting a golden light. Two nightgowns had been laid out. The air was chilly, so they quickly changed and slid under the covers. Keely waved her hand over the glowing snail, and its shell dimmed and went dark.

"Mavery, why does Theo hate us so much?" She stared up at the ceiling, seeing his sharp face. "And don't tell me he's just a spoiled brat."

Mavery plucked at the sheets. "It's no big deal. It's just the red sun, you know, it hurt a lot of people."

Keely rolled on her side. "Did it hurt Theo?"

"No, not Theo exactly."

"Then who?"

Mavery sighed. "His mom, okay? When the sun was at its worst and food ran out, she left Ter Glen to help the people in the outer villages. But she didn't make it back alive."

Keely didn't say anything. She couldn't. She knew exactly how Theo felt. That horrible hollow feeling. Waking up every morning those first few months and, for just a second, forgetting your mother was gone. Then remembering and feeling the loss all over again. "No wonder he hates us," she whispered. She was Sam's friend, which made her Theo's enemy.

"Yup," the witchling murmured, but her eyes were already closing.

Keely stayed awake for a long while, staring at the ceiling and thinking about Theo and his blue eyes. She thought of her dad and how worried he must be. She hadn't even been able to leave him a note. What would he think? That she had been kidnapped? That she had run off and left him?

She must have fallen asleep, because she awoke to a scraping sound. Her eyes flew open. Moonlight glinted off Rifkin's bald head. The jovial soldier had a crazy look to his eyes. Something glinted in his hands. *Was that a knife?* Keely was about to scream when Mavery popped up next to her.

"What's going on?"

Rifkin whipped his hands back, and whatever he held disappeared. "Time to go."

"I'm coming," Mavery said, eagerly throwing back the covers and hopping to her feet. "So don't even think of stopping me because I'll just follow you."

Keely didn't know what was worse, bringing the witchling and putting her in danger, or leaving her behind, knowing full well she would follow them and maybe put herself in worse danger. She shook her head in defeat. "Don't say I didn't warn you."

"Galatin's not going to like it," Rifkin grumbled.

"I'll deal with Galatin," Keely said. "Wait outside." For the moment, she wanted Rifkin as far away as possible.

Rifkin harrumphed and stepped outside while the girls quickly threw on their clothes.

As she dressed, Keely's mind spun. Had she just imagined that look in Rifkin's eyes? He was normally so jovial and easy-going, but in that moment . . . it was like he had wanted her dead. She wrapped the heavy green cloak around her shoulders and pulled on the fur-lined gloves. A small bag for laundry hung on a hook. She took it down and pried the phoralite off the wall. The bottom of it was soft. Keely ran her finger over the tiny cilia that allowed it to stick to the wall. It glowed under her touch. She tucked it in the sack, and then on a whim, she added the soul crystal that sat on the dresser.

They snicked the door quietly behind them and tiptoed down the corridor. The light was dim. The sun had not yet risen. Trillywigs lit up along the path.

They followed Rifkin through a side entrance that led into a narrow alley. A servants' area, less elegant by far than the rest of the palace. Galatin awaited them at the stables with horses ready, saddlebags bulging with supplies, and a pile of thick furs lashed to the back.

"Why are we leaving so early?" Keely asked, shivering in the frigid air as Mavery let out a wide yawn.

Galatin didn't meet her eyes as he answered. "I overheard Gael speaking with his father. Einolach is going to forbid us to head north. What's she doing here?" he nodded curtly at Mavery.

"Mavery's coming. No point leaving her behind, she'll just follow us." Something was off. Her newly heightened senses told her Galatin was lying. He was nervous, and a pulse was beating in his neck. "Are you sure he's going to forbid us? Gael seemed like he wanted to help."

Galatin snapped at her, clearly annoyed. "Look, we go now. Are you up to it or not?"

She was. But unless she was mistaken, one of her escorts had tried to kill her, and the other was lying. How was she supposed to know who to trust? "I am, but—"

Galatin cut her off. "No buts. We ride. Now."

Rifkin jumped up on his horse and held out his hand. Keely hesitated, but he gripped her wrist roughly and pulled her up. Galatin lifted Mavery behind him. Without another word, they clattered down the cobblestone alley.

When they came to the city gate, Galatin dismounted and spoke quietly to the guard on duty. They seemed to know each other. Galatin passed the guard a small satchel. A moment later, the gate was opened, and they left the city walls behind as the sun was just cresting over the spires.

"Was that a friend of his?" Keely asked Rifkin.

"Galatin met him at a pub last night. They came to an arrangement." He winked at Keely over his shoulder. "A small bag of gold, and he looks the other way."

Something about this whole situation troubled Keely. Maybe it was the thought that Rifkin had wanted to kill her, or Galatin's sudden urge to leave without a word to anyone. She exchanged a glance with Mavery, but the witchling just shrugged.

The sun began to rise, melting the frost on the ground and bringing a slight warmth to the chilly air. They left the main track and took a rutted overgrown trail that led into a thick forest of ancient pine trees. Rifkin's head was bare, as if the cold didn't bother him, though particles of ice clung to his beard. Ahead of them, the Skoll Mountains rose menacingly, capped in snow and an ominous layer of gray clouds. The Cave of Shadows might as well be on another planet it was so far away. The enormity of Keely's journey hit her like a ton of wet beach sand.

Think positive, Keely told herself, eyeing the steep grade ahead of them. Maybe this would work out. Maybe she would get to Ymir and she could plead her case. Make him see reason. Then an image of the eight-legged beast that guarded Ymir's cave flashed before her.

Or maybe this beast, Audhumla, would eat her head for breakfast.

Chapter Eighteen

Leo's blood boiled. Not because the sun beat down on his head. No, it was three days of being ignored by that arrogant Falcory kid that had about pushed him over the edge. Jey led the way, hardly speaking to Rego or Tiber, back straight as a ruler, his eyes firmly pinned on the horizon.

Leo made the mistake the first day of trying to be friendly, riding up alongside Jey and asking him what it was like being Falcory, wondering how it compared to his own experience as Umatilla. Jey's answer had been curt. "Being Falcory is a supreme honor. I will make a great chief someday." In fact, whenever Jey did speak, he began just about every sentence with, "When I am chief . . ." as if he had never had a moment's doubt in his life. Apparently, Jey's father hadn't drilled into Jey's head, like Leo's father had, that the most important trait a chief had was humbleness.

The final insult had come this morning. Jey had gone hunting with his javelin before sunrise, without inviting Leo, and returned to dump a limp pheasant on Leo's lap, ordering him to clean it. Leo had been about to throw the bird in Jey's face when Tiber had stepped in, quietly taking it and plucking it clean.

Tiber was like that. Large as a barn, but humble as a church mouse. He never complained and was always eager to pitch in.

Jey could learn a thing or two from the Orkadian, if he ever noticed anyone but himself.

If Jey wanted to be ignored, Leo would ignore him. Once he led them to Ilyawit Peak, Jey could take a long hike off a short cliff as far as Leo was concerned. According to Rego, the Falcory lived on the far western shores of Garamond. The towering pine trees around Skara Brae thinned out to scattered brush and the sharp smell of juniper. Sand and rock replaced the loamy soil of the forest, and the temperature rose steeply. For the first time, Leo felt at home in Orkney. It reminded him of the Umatilla lands back home. Open. Free. He could breathe out here.

Water was scarce, so they preserved every drop, keeping the horses fresh and limiting their own intake. The sand beneath them was soft, making it slow going. The air cooled as the sun settled low on the horizon, casting a pale orange glow. In the distance, a jagged red peak impaled the sky.

"Is that where we're headed?" Leo asked.

Rego grunted, bouncing along on his pony next to him. "Aye. The boy says that there's Ilyawit Peak." His eyes slid over to study Leo. "This Sacrifice business leaves a bad taste. You sure you're up for this?"

Leo shrugged. "Back home, everyone expects great things from me because I'm the son of a chief. It always makes me want to do the opposite. But here, no one expects me to succeed. And now I want to prove them wrong. Is that weird?" His words had a bitter ring to them, and Rego's eyebrows arched up.

"Sounds like you've got a load on your mind. I've got a set of ears and nothing to fill them with if you care to share."

Words exploded out of Leo. "My father has my whole life mapped out for me. He's never once asked me if it's what I want to do. He's given his whole life to serving our people, and he expects me to do the same. Some days I want to run away as far as possible."

Rego was silent. His lips puckered and relaxed as if he were chewing the words over. Finally, he said, "If honor is such a burden, why are you riding toward certain death just to help your friends? Sounds to me you're a lot more like your father than you let on."

Before Leo could absorb the truth of his words, Tiber pulled his horse up.

"What in Odin's creation is that?" The brawny soldier pointed into the distance.

A dark mushrooming cloud clung to the horizon. The cloud was a turbulent mass of dust that sent stinging sand across the desert.

"Haboob!" Leo shouted over the growing rumble of wind and churning sand. Haboobs were sudden sandstorms that ripped across the plains around the Umatilla wastelands. He had been caught in the open once and had been nearly flayed alive. The distant red hills blurred and then disappeared entirely in a furious brown cloud. Leo slid off the horse. Rego grunted at the cloud and then angled his round girth off his pony, sliding to the ground, joined by Tiber.

Jey turned his horse around, leaping down to confront Leo. "It's just a sandstorm," he snapped. "It will pass."

"No. It's much worse. Look," Leo said curtly, holding his hands over his brow to block the swirling sand. The sky had grown ominously dark. The roiling cloud of sand was bigger than any storm he had ever experienced. "We have to let the horses go."

"We need them," Jey argued, but Leo slapped the horses on the rear.

"They'll find their own shelter. We need to take cover."

"You're not in charge!" Jey said, his face reddening as he jumped in front of the horses.

Leo was about to flatten him, but Rego stepped in.

"No time for squabbles, boys. The storm is almost on us. I say let the horses go and make our way to shelter."

No sooner had he spoke when the burgeoning cloud lengthened out into the shape of a giant worm, growing longer and thicker by the second. Sudden dread made Leo's heart skip in his chest as a swirling black hole opened at the head, a giant, sightless mouth. Sand spiraled up off the desert floor into the maw like it was a Hoover vacuum. Small rocks flew up, then shrubs and mesquite trees swallowed up into the void.

And it was headed their way.

"Take cover!" Rego shouted. Tiber whooped at the horses, sending them scattering.

Leo spied a small mound of boulders. With any luck they were large enough to protect them. He ran, Tiber and Rego on his heels. Jey hesitated a moment longer, as if transfixed by the storm, and then the Falcory boy was after them, quickly overtaking them and leading the way to cover. The edge of the sand storm reached them before they had made it ten steps, swirling sand in their eyes and blasting them with hot air. Leo could barely make out the mound of boulders. Behind them one of the horses squealed in panic. He looked up and saw it flying through the air, helplessly sucked into the giant black hole.

Then Tiber grabbed Leo by the collar and dragged him forward, tossing him into the pile of stones.

"Hold on tight," Rego shouted over the wind. They wedged themselves between rocks and waited.

With a roaring sound like a race car engine, the mouth of the strange storm passed over them. A rock next to Leo lifted and then took off like a slingshot.

Rego shouted for help. The dwarf's feet had left the ground. He clung to a rock, but he was being sucked into the vortex. Tiber let go with one hand and grabbed the dwarf by his chest mail. The beefy soldier clung to the dwarf as the ferocity of the storm reached its high point, deafening them with the thunder of sand and wind. Tiber seemed to be winning the battle, and then the storm increased another notch. Rego was torn from his grasp, cartwheeling through the air. Tiber lunged for him and lost his own grip, instantly sharing the same fate as the dwarf.

Leo shouted in horror, but his two allies were gone. Moments later, the wind lessened, and the roaring subsided until only a passing gust stirred the air. Leo stood up, brushing the coating of dust from his hair and face. His ears were full of sand—everything sounded muffled. He shook out the grit, then looked around for signs of Tiber or Rego.

"Rego?" he shouted.

"They're gone," Jey said without a trace of emotion. "We need to find the horses." He brushed past Leo and retraced their steps.

Leo stared after him. They had just watched two friends get sucked into a black hole, and Jey acted like they had gone for a walk. He shook his head, suddenly grateful he was nothing like the heartless Falcory, then followed after the boy. They spotted a mound across the dune. Jey dropped to his knees and brushed away the sand.

The vacant eyes of Jey's painted horse stared up at them. Jey said nothing, just gritted his jaw and pretended that losing his favorite horse didn't bother him. The waterskins tied to her had broken in her fall and spilled into the sand. The tip of a stick stuck out of the ground. Jey dug down, letting out an excited yell when he pulled his prized javelin out. He slipped it back into the leather case he wore.

"I've never seen a storm like that," Leo said, breaking the silence.

"That's because it was witch magic. They must be looking for us." Jey put his fingers to his lips and let out a whistle. He sniffed the air with his beak, wrinkling his lips as he filtered the smells. "The horses are all dead," he said in that clipped detached voice. Then he turned and started to jog.

"Hey, where are you headed?" Leo called.

Jey answered without slowing. "To the mountain to get that cuff. I made a promise to my father."

Leo hurried after him, grabbed Jey by the shoulder, and spun him around "Stop. We have to look for our friends."

Jey's dark eyes glittered angrily. "No. We have to get to Ilyawit Peak and recover the Draupnir. Or are you running away from that like your responsibility to be a chief?"

Shame flooded Leo. "You heard that?"

"Yes." He looked at Leo with disgust in his flinty eyes. "A Falcory would never turn his back on his tribe. We have honor. We are not cowards."

Leo's jaw tightened. "I'm not afraid."

Jey pushed him. "Prove it."

Leo pushed him back. "Knock it off. I said I'm not afraid."

Jey's fingers curled into fists, as if he were about to take a swing at Leo, and then he took a step back. "I won't dishonor myself by hitting you. Keep up if you're coming." Jey turned and sprinted across the sand.

Leo glared at his back. He had no choice but to race after him or be left alone in the middle of this desert. But before he followed, he stopped and said a silent word for Rego and Tiber, praying that they had landed safely somewhere.

The two boys pushed on, neither one admitting to fatigue or thirst. The sun was like an oven, baking them to a crisp. All moisture had been sucked from the air. Leo's mouth felt like it was made of dried cardboard.

Finally, after two punishing hours, Leo called a halt. "I give. You're better and faster than me," he gasped, dropping to his knees. "I can't go on. I need water."

Jey slowed and then stopped. His shoulders went up and down as he panted for air. "You lasted longer than I expected." A small sound of admiration tinged his voice.

Leo would have smiled if his lips weren't cracked and dry. "Look, I can't do this without you. We would have more success if we worked together. As a team." He let the olive branch dangle.

"Agreed." Jey stuck his hand out, and they clasped arms.

"We need water," Leo said, tasting the grit between his teeth.

"See that mound of rocks?" Jey pointed to a distant clump of boulders. "There will be water there."

"How? An underground spring?"

Jey grinned, flashing white teeth. "No. My father's secret stash. The Falcory cross the desert all the time. We prepare for the worst. Last one there has to carry the water."

Jey took off in a sprint. Leo chased after, but even with his longer legs, Jey easily beat him to the boulder pile. The boy pushed a rock aside, revealing a small hole in the ground. He reached in and pulled out a bulging waterskin. Uncapping it, he tilted it back, pouring water down his throat before passing it to Leo.

Leo drank greedily. "I think I like your father," he said with a satisfied burp.

Jey took the waterskin and capped it tightly before settling himself down in the shade of a boulder. He looked up at Leo. "The girl is pretty. You like her, don't you?"

Leo's mind flashed to Keely, and he shrugged. "Keely's my friend."

Jey grinned jauntily. "I will steal her from you some day." He folded his arms, tucked his chin on his chest, and promptly fell asleep.

Leo sat awake, staring at the distant red peak as the sun set behind it, thinking about iguanadillos and the very real possibility that being the Sacrifice would end with his death.

Chapter Nineteen

Leo and Jey walked through the night, stopping to rest and take tiny sips of water. By dawn's light, they were at the base of Ilyawit Peak. Rocks pressed in on either side as they wended their way along a narrow animal trail that led up the mountain. Strange insects called out with sharp chirps. Hidden birds screeched at them from small rock caves.

They refilled their waterskin from a brackish stream that trickled out of a boulder. The water smelled like rotten eggs, but it was better than nothing. They climbed to a flat mesa where the smell of decay permeated the air. Burned and blackened trees dotted the rocky plain. The bones of long-dead animals, picked over by carrion, lay scattered in heaps. Red-gulled vultures hovered over a misshapen lump, squawking their displeasure at the interruption.

A rock wall rose three stories above them. Cold air flowed from the dark opening at the top, down the cliff face. Through the pungent smell of the offal Leo could detect the sulfurous odor of the she-she-kana lair.

It was time to face his destiny.

There were handholds cut into the side of the cliff. Neither boy spoke. Jey began to climb, pulling himself easily from hold to hold. Leo followed, feeling his stomach in knots. With each advance up the wall, Leo was less and less certain about his ability to tackle this beast that had now grown to the size of a tanker truck in his mind.

Too soon, he levered himself over the lip of the cliff. His knees were shaking as he stood next to Jey. The black hole of the entrance yawned like a menacing trap.

Leo hesitated. "You promised your father you wouldn't go inside. I can do this alone."

Jey just laughed. "I'm not letting you have all the glory. Besides, I didn't promise him. I just didn't argue with Captain Teren when he suggested it." Jey rolled his shoulders. He held up the javelin in one hand, thrusting it high as he let out a loud whoop. "Beware, she-she-kana, your doom awaits you!" he shouted.

Leo pulled out the curved knife Mimir had given him. It felt ridiculously small in his hands. Together they stepped inside the hole. It reminded Leo of Sinmara's underworld prison. He let his eyes adjust to the darkness. He could make out uneven ground. Rocky outcrops pressing down from the ceiling would crack open his head if he wasn't careful. They moved forward, on alert for the slightest noise. The tunnel came to a bend and split into two trails. The left trail led downward; the right tilted upward at a slight incline. They stood, uncertain, neither wanting to be parted from the other.

Leo spoke first. "I'll go right," he said softly. "You go left."

For once, Jey didn't argue. It took another ten minutes of maneuvering and stumbling before Leo emerged on a narrow shelf of rock overlooking a large chamber. The walls of the cavern were phosphorescent, giving off a natural glow. Steam rose from an oily pool of water in the center and disappeared through a circular opening that offered a glimpse of sky. Crystal stalactites hung from the ceiling, emanating the same internal light. Scattered bones littered the floor around a smooth, rounded indent where the monster no doubt slept.

There was no sign of the she-she-kana.

Jey appeared below, walking across the chamber floor to the

edge of the pond. The boy spied Leo above him, shrugging as if to say he didn't know what to do. Behind him, the water rippled. Out of the center, a creature emerged. The she-she-kana was as big and ugly as a tank. Broad and squat with mottled green skin, it had taloned feet and a short neck. Tiny eyes were placed well back next to a pair of small slits for ears. Its snout was blunt, consisting mostly of a wide pair of jaws lined with two rows of sharp teeth. A thick plating of scales like armor crossed its chest and torso.

It really does look like an iguanadillo, Leo thought, with his first real frisson of fear. Then a glint of light caught his eye, and his heart rate ratcheted up. There. On its hind leg. A golden cuff gleamed.

"Jey!" Leo hissed a warning, jabbing his finger to point over Jey's head.

The Falcory boy turned around and stumbled backward as the she-she-kana bore down on him, moving fast on its stubby legs. Jey threw his javelin, but it bounced harmlessly off the beast's scaly plates. Leo took a running leap off the top of the ledge, soaring through the air to land straight down onto the creature's head as its jaws widened to devour his friend.

Gripping the scaly creature with his knees, Leo raised his knife high, then plunged it into the beast's right eye.

The creature bellowed, rearing up on its hind legs, and tossed Leo off as it pawed furiously at its wounded eye. Leo held onto the knife but lost his hold on the beast. He landed hard on his backside, feeling the wind knocked out of him.

The iguanadillo's deafening yowl echoed off the walls, knocking down loose rocks that tumbled around them.

"It's got a soft spot under its chin. If I kill it, the Draupnir is mine!" Jey shouted, then he charged forward, clutching his javelin. "Come and get a taste of me, you ugly beast!"

The she-she-kana turned at Jey's voice. It was quick and agile for such a squatty creature. It scampered forward like a lizard. Jey drew his arm back and launched his javelin, aiming squarely at the beast's soft underthroat, but the creature dropped its head, and the javelin sailed past. Fast as lightning it whipped its head up, and a long silvery tongue streaked from its mouth, snatching Jey and rolling him up like a sausage in a bun. Jey let out a shocked scream as the she-she-kana tossed its head back and opened its jaws wide to swallow the boy. All Leo saw of Jey were his legs kicking to get free.

"Leo, help!"

The beast swung back and forth, attempting to guzzle Jey whole. In another few seconds, Jey would be dead. With its head up, its vulnerable spot was exposed. This was his chance. Leo ran forward, clutching his knife. He jumped onto one bent foreleg of the beast and thrust upward with all his might, aiming for the tender spot. The curved blade went in all the way to the hilt. He thrust harder, pushing deeper, feeling the blade slice through tendons and flesh.

Green, gooey blood sprayed on him, making him gag. The beast kept on its feet, determined to choke Jey down its throat. It staggered forward, raising one taloned foot to crush Leo. Leo rolled sideways and dodged the attack but then had to roll again as the creature came crashing down on its side, hitting the ground next to him with a tremendous thud that shook loose another cascade of rocks.

A long, foul gust of air was squeezed from the dead beast's lungs as its enormous body deflated like a popped balloon. It was silent in the cavern save for dripping water. Leo jumped to his feet, wiping the beast's blood from his eyes and searching for his friend.

"Jey, where are you?" He pried open the creature's massive mouth. The jaws were foamy, covered in sticky saliva. With both hands, Leo shoved up on the upper jawbone. The slack, silvery tongue rolled out, spilling the Falcory boy onto the floor.

"Jey, say something!" Leo cried, rushing to his side.

After a long moment, Jey sputtered, spitting out beast saliva and wiping goo from his eyes. "Took you long enough. Thought I was going to have to come out the other end."

Leo grinned. Nothing dented this Falcory. He stuck his hand out and pulled Jey to his feet.

"I was going to claim it for myself, you know," Jey said quietly. "I didn't think you deserved a prize like that, but you saved my life." He nodded at the dead beast. "Take what you came for—you earned it."

Leo walked to the back of the she-she-kana. The cuff glinted at him. He hesitated, his hand hovering over the golden object. If he claimed it, his quest would go on. To the darkness that awaited him. Jey's father had said the Draupnir had the power to bring someone back from the underworld. Was that Leo's next stop? A visit with Sinmara, mistress of the underworld? She had lost her hand last time when Rego lopped it off to get at her rings. She would not welcome him back, that was certain.

Leo gingerly touched the Draupnir with his fingertips. The cuff warmed slightly at his touch, and his resolve hardened. If it meant bringing his friends back together, he would do it. Rego's words came back to him. Maybe the dwarf was right, maybe he was a lot more like his dad than he realized. The thought gave him the courage to put both hands on it and pry it apart. The cuff came loose easily. He held it, staring at it in awe. Smooth and heavy, without markings or scratches. Perfection.

Leo slipped it over his wrist and up his arm. It went as far as his bicep, and then it softened and tightened around it, as if it was fitting itself to him.

The Draupnir was his now.

With a loud crack, the she-she-kana shrank, shriveling up before them, as if whatever magic had kept it alive all these centuries was gone. When it was finished, it was nothing more than a pile of dust and bones.

Jey peered at the gleaming artifact on Leo's arm. "Now what?"

Leo looked down at the cuff. A new challenge awaited him: figuring out where the cuff was going to take him next. He had a feeling that would prove more dangerous than retrieving the Draupnir from the she-she-kana.

Chapter Twenty

Sigmund Degroot was not a terribly brave man. He rather despised swords and all manner of brutish battle. Left to his own devices, he preferred to wander among the swamps of Balfour Island, studying plants and cataloging them in one of his beloved journals. But his father commanded the Balfin army, and Sigmund was expected to follow in those lofty footsteps. And now, with the full-scale war the witches had started with all of Orkney, every able-bodied Balfin had been conscripted into the Black Guard to join the witches for a final secret invasion.

The seaport town of Jadewick had become crowded with young men from every village and township on the island, assembling and training in preparation for the pending invasion. Sigmund sat at the bar inside Flanner's Tavern, glumly nursing a glass of soured milk as he sketched his latest finding into his journal. He shipped out at dawn, joining the front line on Garamond. He'd never left Balfour Island before. On one hand, exploring new lands was exciting—who knew what exotic flora he would find? On the other hand, exploring those new lands as a soldier, with enemies out to kill him, was enough to send shivers down his not-so-sturdy spine.

Across the tavern, his fellow recruits were busy whooping it up, chasing everything in a skirt, but all Sigmund could think about was the pain of curtailing his field studies. He took a sip of his warm milk, savoring the sour taste. Why, just today he had made an extraordinary find in the swamps that adjoined the Tarkana Fortress. A rare plant not seen in decades. The *Ophrys insectfera* flower resembled a common housefly with its black-ish-red petals that drooped like wings from a small rounded bulb. If he wasn't shipping out tomorrow, Sigmund would have spent the next few days searching for more *Ophrys* specimens and adding color to his meticulous sketches.

A figure slid onto the stool next to Sigmund. The smell of lilacs lifted his head from his sketches. He expected to see one of the barmaids chatting him up, but this woman was no serving girl. She was beautiful and exotic like one of the rare orchids in his books. Her hair tumbled in waves of black ebony down her back. She wore a velvet green dress cinched tight, emphasizing her tiny waist. Her eyes were a matching green, holding a spark that made his shyness evaporate.

"Who are you?" he asked, his blood fizzing with a curious excitement. Part of his brain registered that she was a witch, but the fact didn't scare him for some reason.

"I am Vena," she answered. "I hear that you are the expert on local flora, and I see my sources were correct." She laid one slender finger on his newest sketch. "Tell me, Sigmund, where might I find this lovely plant?"

Her voice was irresistible, like warm honey.

"How do you know my name?"

Vena smiled and put a hand on his shoulder. "Don't be coy. Speak up."

Sigmund swallowed hard. His mouth felt dry as dirt. "Out behind the . . . in the swamps behind the fortress."

"Take me there," Vena said, grasping him firmly by the arm.

To Sigmund, this woman was more intoxicating than a deadly nightshade. He would have swooned if her hand weren't clamped so tightly on him. She had impressive strength, and a sliver of worry needled his addled brain. Witches came into the tavern on occasion, but none as powerful as this. "I would, milady, but . . . but I leave on the morrow. Joining the battle, you see."

"Then we must go immediately." With that, Vena stood and walked out of the tavern, ignoring the catcalls and whistles from the rowdy group that pelted Sigmund with rude comments as he stumbled after her.

Clear your head, Sigmund, he thought as he drew in a breath of cold night air.

As much as he hated to disappoint this beautiful creature, the trip through the swamps was impossible at night. One wayward step and they could sink into a bog of quicksand. Notwithstanding the terrible creatures that hunted at night.

"Mistress Vena, regrettably we cannot make the journey tonight—" he began, but the words stuck in his throat as she grabbed him by his shirt and hauled him close. For a second, he expected a dazzling kiss. But instead, the witch opened her mouth and blew a small puff of green gas that enveloped his face and made Sigmund dizzy, then weightless.

He tried in vain to call out for help before losing consciousness.

When Sigmund opened his eyes he was flat on his back, the ground soft and squishy beneath him. Unfamiliar night sounds filled the air. As he sat up and looked around, he saw a ghostly green glow across a small clearing. Trees and branches grew in knotted twisted tangles.

I'm in the swamps, Sigmund realized. *But how did I get here?*

Two horses stood by. Had he ridden here? His mouth tasted as sour as the milk he had been drinking, but he was otherwise okay. The beautiful Vena was kneeling beside some plants, her hand casting a green glow over them.

Sigmund recognized the clearing. He had been here earlier today. He stumbled across toward her. "What are you doing? How did you find this place?" he asked, hoping she wasn't destroying the precious flowers by picking them.

"I followed your rather pungent scent. Now, hush." Her hands kept moving as she muttered strange words under her breath, intensifying the glow around the flowers. She reached inside her bodice and pulled out a small glass vial and opened it, sprinkling some of the purplish liquid on top of the flower.

Sigmund drew closer to see what she was doing. *Ophrys insectfera*, the fly orchid, was moving under the green glow of her hand, undulating and swelling rapidly in size. The potent liquid sizzled everywhere it touched the plant, emitting a putrid white gas that veiled Vena's dark magic ritual. From the swollen bulb of the plant, a buzzing sound could be heard growing in intensity until, with a loud pop, an explosion of furious black flies erupted through the haze. They were unnaturally large, with glowing green eyes. They bobbed in the air above Sigmund. He swatted at the insects, terrified. The horses snorted in fear, tearing lose from their tethers and fleeing in the night. But the witch didn't flinch.

"I owe you a debt of gratitude," Vena said, rising to stand by him. "I've been traipsing about these swamps for days searching for a plant such as this. Now my transmutation potion will spread like wildfire across the Balfin army."

"P-p-potion?" Sigmund stammered, swatting at the cloud of flies around his face.

Her lips curved into a smile, but her eyes had that predatory look to them, like he was a mouse and she the hungry hawk. He should run, his brain said, but Sigmund felt curiously weak, as if his limbs were frozen in place.

"Yes. You're the perfect candidate. Come, let's see if it works . . ."

She snapped her fingers, and the cloud of flies came to a halt, hovering over Sigmund's head, and then settled on him. He swatted at them more vigorously now, but they swarmed him, invading every part of his body—crawling under his clothes, into his ears, his nose, biting him with tiny nips.

What is happening to me? Sigmund silently screamed.

A cracking jolt of pain shot through him as the potion reached critical mass in his bloodstream. His body began to tremble and shake with overwhelming energy. His fingers extended and swelled, growing coarse hairs on the backs of his knuckles. Muscles bulged under his shirt, tearing at the fabric seams. He screamed in agony as his body underwent a radical transformation from human to something monstrous.

Sigmund dropped to his knees, hands in the mud, clutching at the ground to hold onto reality. All around him the thick mass of flies grew larger and louder as more insects erupted from the blooming orchids, each one a carrier of Vena's potion.

"Please make it staaaaawwww . . . !" Sigmund cried, but his plea was cut short.

His jaw ratcheted forward from his skull, distorting his normally placid features into something primal and grotesque. His brow jutted, eye sockets expanded, and new, tusk-like fangs sprouted from his lower gums, evicting the old human teeth. His nose flattened out as his nostrils expanded, allowing him to breathe in greater quantities of air. The hair on his head thickened and lengthened, falling in coarse waves to his shoulders. Heaving sobs filled Sigmund's chest as his precious journal fell from his now-tattered shirt into the mud and sank from sight.

And then, as soon as it began, the buzzing stopped. The biting flies settled on the branches of the trees, painting them black, and Sigmund's transformation halted. The unimaginable pain receded, and an inhuman strength surged through him.

"Rise," Vena commanded the abomination at her feet. "Rise and swear allegiance to me."

Sigmund raised his oversized head to see the witch's eyes feverish with excitement. He found he shared her emotion, enthralled with his newfound power. He slowly raised one of his brawny arms, staring at the thick black hair that now covered it, clenching and unclenching a gnarled fist that had grown two sizes. He clambered to his feet, feeling his joints creak with the added muscle. His enlarged heart pumped blood through his veins like a giant steam piston. He pounded one fist against his chest, testing his newfound strength, and opened his mouth to shout, "Yes!" But the noise he produced was an animal-like grunt.

Sigmund was surprised, but he liked his new language. It was raw. Ferocious. He craned his head back and ratcheted his mouth wide, unleashing a roar that rattled the leaves in the trees.

Vena smiled, looking pleased with her handiwork.

"Now, Sigmund, let's go share my potion with your daddy and his spineless Balfin soldiers. Together we'll build a Volgrim army to be proud of."

General Degroot sat atop his horse, irritably looking down on his battalion. He was dressed in his impeccable uniform made of black leather, adorned with silver epaulettes. On top of his head he wore the high-tip silver helmet as befitted a general. His men were neatly outfitted and in perfect formation. But where was that worthless son of his? If Sigmund was out wandering the swamps in search of his precious plants, Degroot would have him publicly flogged. He had warned the lad not to embarrass him, not in front of the men he commanded. Especially today, of all days.

A surprise inspection had been called by the queen of witches, Catriona. The general didn't care for her. Hestera had always been more accommodating and had a spot of affection for him. From what he had seen, Catriona hadn't a shred of humanity in her cold heart. Still, Degroot wanted to impress, hoping to gain favor with this new lot. His men looked sharp enough, five thousand strong, standing steady in neat rows that filled the vast plaza outside the Tarkana fortress. They were dressed in full battle armor; even the horses had metal chest shields and ornamental helmets to protect them in battle.

Degroot's horse reared nervously as a black cloud swirled out of thin air right before him, and a witch emerged from the roiling darkness.

She was stunning to behold, with long locks of hair and a pretty face. Degroot recognized her as Vena, one of Catriona's fellow Volgrim witches. The general straightened in his saddle.

"Mistress Vena." He bowed his head. "I understand you wish to inspect the men." Behind her, on top of the fortress rampart, a row of witches came into view. In the center, Degroot saw the imposing figure of Catriona. He felt a thrum of excitement, saluting her with two fingers to his brow.

Vena ambled forward and ran one hand over the nose of his horse.

"General, I've already looked over your men, and I must say, I find them utterly . . . pathetic."

The general bristled at her insult. "Madam, many of them are newly joined. Give them some time to season."

"We have no time to give," Vena said sharply. "Every day the Orkadian army destroys one of our sister witches. We are few next to their numbers."

"The Balfin army will easily destroy their defenses with the added charms provided us," General Degroot said smoothly, fingering the shiny disc that hung around his neck. A large fly landed on his cheek. He swatted it away.

The beautiful witch laughed. "Those charms will not guarantee defeat of the Orkadian army, not when they drag in the Eifalians and the Falcory. But fear not. I have a plan—rather, a potion—to ensure that your men are worthy of defending our coven."

"Potion?" Degroot seethed with irritation. "War is not won with potions. It's won with strategy and superior strength." Another strange fly landed on the back of his hand. Before he could swat it, the dratted thing bit him. He yelped at the sharp sting, slapping at it. Just then, a loud buzzing noise caught his attention. The sky grew dark, the sun eclipsed by a swelling black cloud that flew over the heads of his men. The men moved uneasily, eyeing the pulsating cloud. Even the horses stomped their feet, some rearing up and snorting.

"Let me show you how this war will be won," Vena said, turning and clapping her hands.

The gates of the Tarkana fortress opened. A hulking figure appeared, lumbering steadily toward them. Black plated armor was strapped across the beast's chest, leaving thick, hairy arms bare.

Degroot had faced vicious sneevils and had even survived a giant akkar attack, but he had never seen anything as grotesque as this. "By the gods, what is that?" he whispered.

The figure grunted loudly, slamming one fist to its chest. The bushy hair on its head extended along its cheeks, nearly covering the skin on the face. A pair of sneevil-like tusks jutted up outside the lips from the bottom jaw. But there was something curiously familiar about the monster. So much so that General Degroot ignored the stinging bites of the pernicious flies on his face and arms, leaning forward on his horse as he peered into the eyes of the creature. He had seen them before. But not like this. Fierce, like a wild animal was trapped inside.

It can't be, Degroot told himself. But his instincts told him it was.

"Sigmund?" The General's voice cracked. "Is that you?"

The monster let out another roar, raising one fist in the air.

With a twirl of her hands, Vena took charge of the roiling swarm of flies and shouted, "Feast on them, my little parasites. Feast away!" She spun in a circle, dancing wildly until she disappeared into a cloud of smoke.

By now the General's men were under heavy attack from the flies and running helter-skelter in every direction. Still stunned by the ghastly sight of his mutated son, Degroot barely acknowledged the bugs covering him from head to toe, crawling into every orifice and delivering their toxic serum to his blood, which had begun to hum with a strange and powerful cadence. As the first ripple of change tore through him, he was bucked off his horse, which shook and screamed in a shrill whinny.

General Degroot lay in the dirt, writhing and shrieking, trying in vain to throw off the blanket of flies on him. "Help me, Sigmund," he screamed, but Sigmund's hulking figure stood silently over him, watching as his father twisted, trying to crawl toward his horse. The beast lay on its side, quivering as flies settled on it in a black canopy. Before Degroot could reach it, the horse stood up. Its armor had somehow melted into its body, molding with the horse and becoming part of its hide. Reddened eyes were mad with power as the horse reared up, pawing at the air.

Instead of being terrified, anticipation rippled through the general. Here was real power, not those petty trinkets the witches gave them. The tall silver helmet was melded to his head. His veins pulsated with pure energy. A twisted smile creased his face even as the agony of his swelling bones and stretching flesh tore an anguished cry from the depths of his guts.

When the transformation was complete, a new vision of the world awaited Degroot. Pushing himself to his feet, the General stood and surveyed his new army. The once-thin hair on top of his head was now thick and fell down his back. As the last of his men and their horses went through the change, they began to rise up like him, looking around at the formidable new breed of Black Guard soldiers.

General Degroot put one hand on his son's shoulder. Finally, he had a son to be proud of. Sigmund nodded at his father and then let out a triumphant howl. His voice was joined by the throngs of soldiers awaiting his command.

Chapter Twenty-One

From the parapets of the Tarkana fortress, Catriona beamed with triumph as Vena appeared at her side. "Well done," she murmured, clapping her hands slowly in appreciation. "You've done more than even I imagined. Now we finish turning the boy to our side and win this war." With a whisk of her skirts, she headed down to the dungeon.

The subterranean hallway was lit by torches placed every ten feet along the wall. A shadowy figure huddled outside Sam's cell door. Dear cousin Bronte. The crone clutched the vial filled with purplish fog in her fingers.

"You're sure it will work?" Catriona asked.

Bronte nodded. "It will do its part. The boy must supply the rage."

"Then we have nothing to fear—this Samuel Barconian has rage enough for ten men," Catriona said drily. She waved one hand in front of the door, and the lock fell open. "Wait here until I give the signal." Snatching a torch from the wall, Catriona pushed the door open. The torch cast a beam of light across the rumpled figure curled up in a ball on the ground. Several Deathstalkers hovered, fleeing the light and leaving their scattered tidbits.

If Catriona's heart had retained any feeling, she might have felt pity for the boy. He looked bereft and feeble. But there was no room for pity, not when the final descent onto his dark path awaited him. She entered his cell, slamming the door shut behind her.

At the sound of the door, Sam lifted his head blearily from the stone. He squinted in the sudden bright light, then made out Catriona's wrinkled prune face. Crazily enough, he was actually happy to see her. One more day of solitary confinement and his mind would turn to pea soup.

But what does she want this time? More torture?

"At last, the maid is here with my breakfast," Sam said insolently, pushing himself up to his feet. He swayed slightly. "I ordered a double stack of blueberry pancakes, like, two weeks ago."

Catriona said nothing. Something told Sam this wasn't a social call.

He kept his banter up. "So did you come to escort me to my new room? One with a flat-screen TV and a king-sized bed? Oh, and I'd like a view of the swamps, please."

Catriona didn't seem fazed. "For a boy who has endured such betrayal, it is hard to imagine you can stand."

Wariness made Sam's guts tighten up. "What betrayal?"

She gave a tiny shrug of her shoulders as she sauntered closer. "Tsk, don't pretend you didn't see them together. Laughing, having a lark without you."

The muscle in Sam's jaw was the only thing that moved. He didn't look at Catriona. Flashes kept splitting his head open. Images of Keely. Leo. Sharing a kiss while Sam lived in this dank hole with only vermin for companions. He hated Leo at that moment.

"Yes, Leo, isn't it? And you thought he was your friend?" Catriona chortled as Sam's eyes flared with rage. "Leo's interest lies in the girl, not you. Who can blame him, really? You're nothing but a lost cause, are you not?" She leaned in. "Just say the words, Samuel, and I will curse him with putrid boils the size of melons that will leach the treacherous life from him."

Sam bit down on his tongue, refusing to be baited.

But Catriona didn't stop her torment, circling him and poking at him. "Or perhaps we should snip out that worm, Howie? The one who professes to be your best friend. But is he?"

She let the question linger. The only other sound in the prison hole was the sound of water dripping from the ceiling.

Drip. Drip.

It was like acid, eating away at his confidence. But then Sam remembered his trump card.

"You're brainwashing won't work on me. My friends would do anything for me, same as I would for them. But it doesn't matter, witch, because they're not in this realm, so you can't touch them." Sam gloated as he finished.

"Oh, but they are."

Sam stared at her warily. What was her game? Keely, Leo, and Howie were all safely back in Pilot Rock. He had sent them there himself.

A sly grin came over Catriona's face. "Didn't you hear? Your friends have returned. Odin brought them back. They call themselves the Chosen Ones." She held out a scrap of red fabric.

Sam took it, hardly believing his eyes. It was Howie's red bow tie. The one he wore on his uniform at Chuggies. It even had the logo printed in the fabric. Keely, Howie, and Leo were here? They hadn't forgotten him at all!

He couldn't stop the grin of joy as he faced his adversary. "Then give it up, Catriona. Beat me, feed me to your scorpions, do whatever you will, but I will never serve you. My friends are gonna bust me out of here, and then I'm gonna put you back inside a stone prison worse than the last one."

Sam waited for Catriona to erupt, but she looked at him with pity in her eyes, clucking softly.

"Poor Samuel, so misled. You think your friends are here to save you."

Sam tensed. "What are you saying?"

"The Tarkana fortress is not hidden. And yet, who comes for you?" She spread her hands wide. "Do you see your heroic friends breaking down my gates?"

Sam struggled for an answer. "No, but—"

"But . . . but . . . but . . . face it, witch-boy, Odin didn't bring your friends back to save you."

"Then why?"

"Why indeed. Why would a god send children to certain death?" She snapped her fingers, and a set of chairs appeared. She sat herself down and waved him into the other. He sat because, truthfully, his legs felt weak.

"What are you talking about? Odin wouldn't hurt my friends."

"Wouldn't he? Do you know what he's done? Odin named that scrawny one as Protector of Orkney."

Sam flinched. Why would Odin choose Howie to protect his realm? That was like asking a mouse to guard the lion's den.

"So. He must have had a good reason."

Catriona snorted softly. "Please, Samuel, even you can see how ludicrous that is. When I ride into Skara Brae with my army, he will be crushed under my boot heel. But if that doesn't convince you, then hear this: Odin sent your Keely to Rakim to face the Vanir. Did you know the Vanir can tear a man in half with their bare arms? If the freezing cold doesn't kill her, those ruthless frost giants surely will."

Sam wanted to tell her to stop, but his tongue felt nailed to the roof of his mouth. Every word she spoke carved into his skin. Why would Odin put his friends in such danger, instead of sending them to rescue him?

Catriona fanned herself, as if she was getting overheated. "And don't get me started about poor Leo. I hear he is destined to return to Sinmara's underworld, where he will surely perish." She shook her head, as if she couldn't comprehend the truth of her words. "Dear boy, Odin has sentenced your friends to certain death."

Sam bit his lip. It didn't make any sense. "No, he wouldn't do that. Odin will help them."

Catriona leaned forward in her chair, resting her chin on her hand. "Did he help you save your poor father when he could have?"

Ouch. The knife of guilt twisted in Sam's gut. He gaped like a fish on a hook, then stuttered out, "N-no. But that . . . that was my fault."

Catriona's eyes widened. "Was it? I mean, Odin is a *god*. An all-powerful god. Why did he care so little for you that he let your father die?"

Splinters of pain made him dizzy. "I don't know."

"Perhaps you should ask him. Because it seems to me he let you take the blame."

Had he? Had Odin done that? No. His brain was scrambled. But something, maybe all that scorpion venom, fueled a sudden rush of anger. *Why hadn't Odin done more to help? Robert was Odin's kin.*

"You see it, don't you," Catriona crooned. "Odin has abandoned you, and now he has sent your friends to their death."

Sam dug his nails into his palms, clenching his fists so tight he winced with the pain. "No. I don't believe you."

"Fine. I will prove it to you."

She withdrew a satchel from the folds of her skirt and poured a pile of green glass onto the ground. "You have magic. Use it. See for yourself I am not lying."

Sam stared at the pile of glass. He didn't know what it was, but he felt a connection to it. For the first time in days, magic flowed under his fingertips. He closed his eyes, holding both hands over it, willing it to reform. When he opened them, glass swirled up in a long trail, spinning faster and faster as the pieces knitted together to form a ball. Light illuminated the interior of the globe, casting a green shadow over Sam's hands.

Catriona looked excited. She held a hand out underneath the glowing ball, holding it in place. "Excellent. Now ask to see what you desire."

Sam didn't hesitate. "Show me Keely," he said.

The glass swirled and grew cloudy.

He stared hard as an image of Keely came into focus. She was surrounded by hulking giants. Those must be the Vanir. One held a knife to her neck. Next to her was the little witchling Mavery, looking terrified. Sam couldn't bear to watch. Sweat broke out on his brow.

"Show me Leo."

He leaned closer, holding his hands around the swirling glass as if he could reach inside and touch his friends. He jerked as Leo came into view. His friend swam in a dark pool surrounded by dead souls that had not yet crossed over. Leo looked terrified and alone.

Sam wiped his brow. "Show me Howie."

Howie stood in the middle of a battle wearing armor two sizes too big. An apelike creature bore down on him with a sword, about to take his head off.

Sam drew his hands back with a gasp, shaking with horror. The globe went dark in Catriona's hands, then turned into a pile of shattered glass that trickled through her fingers.

She grabbed Sam's hand, clasping it between her leathery palms. "These are Odin's plans for your friends. They came to save you, but who will save them?"

Sam hesitated, wanting to draw his hand back but unable to escape her grasp. "How do I know these aren't lies?"

Catriona shook her head slowly, then thankfully released him. "You know they are not. But these things have not yet happened. Their fate is not etched in stone. You have but to say the word, and they will all be saved."

His eyes locked on hers, searching for deceit. "How?"

"Join us, and we will show you how to end Odin's rule on this land."

Sam felt the knife twist harder in his gut. He couldn't betray Odin. But Odin had surely betrayed him by bringing his friends back and sending them to face dangers beyond what they could handle. Sam had heard stories about the Vanir. Stories soldiers like Rifkin shared around the table at night. The Vanir were bloodthirsty and ruthless. How would Keely ever survive that? And Leo. Sam ran his hand through his hair, seeing Leo's lifeless eyes. He had looked lost. Like he had given up all hope.

Anguished, Sam leapt to his feet and paced the cell as Howie's face swam before his eyes. Howie was Sam's best friend, but he was weak. He couldn't even lift a sword, let alone swing it to defend himself. If Sam didn't stand by him, who would?

He turned to face Catriona. She perched on the edge of her chair, like a cat waiting to lap up a bowl of rich cream.

"And if I don't?" he asked, knowing the answer but hoping, praying there was another way.

She smiled, a satisfied grin that revealed blackened teeth. "Then your wretched friends will get what they deserve. And you will spend eternity in this hole knowing you stood by and did nothing."

There was silence after she spoke.

Drip. Drip.

Sam's head hung as he wrestled with his thoughts. "And you swear on your life that if I . . . if I join with you," he struggled to say the words, hating every one of them, "that they will be safe. You promise."

"I cannot promise anything, Samuel. If you change paths, the future will be rewritten—that much I can promise. The choice is yours."

Sam digested her words, but he knew there was only one choice.

Vor had said that to win, he had to surrender to the darkness inside him. Well, he was about to throw himself headlong into the deep end. He lifted his chin to face her squarely. "What do I have to do?"

A look of triumph passed over Catriona's face. "Accept a push in the right direction. Let me open your eyes to what real power feels like." She stood. With a wave of her hand, the chairs disappeared. She clapped her hands, and the door to the dungeon swung open as a whole passel of witches filed in. They formed a circle around Sam, holding hands, singing a shrill refrain. Their voices rose higher and higher, echoing off the walls of the small cell until they became painful to hear.

Sam put his hands over his ears, needing to escape the wretched noise. His eardrums felt on the verge of exploding.

Catriona began chanting, moving in a circle around him, her hands waving, eyes closed as she concentrated. "*Mordera, mordera invidiam. Mordera, mordera invidiam,*" she repeated, her hands moving over her head.

Sam could only watch in dread to see what fate awaited him. The old one, Bronte, uncorked her vial, and a malevolent purpled fog billowed forth. The witches kept up their caterwauling. The fog passed over their heads, forming a thin trail that snaked toward Sam. Instinctively, he turned his head away to avoid it as it teased his nostrils, but Catriona grabbed his head and held it.

"*Mordera invidiam*, Samuel Barconian, Son of Odin, Son of Rubicus, and now, Son of Catriona."

The purplish fog slipped into Sam's nostrils. He shuddered, but she held a hand over his mouth so he had no choice but to keep breathing it in. His throat burned. His eyes watered with the harsh acidic smell.

Sam struggled to get away, but Catriona's grip was like an iron manacle. He kept inhaling until his head grew light and dizzy. His muscles turned to rubber as his strength slipped away. After endless moments, he gave up the fight, letting the noxious fog flood in through his nostrils.

Catriona ceased her chanting, and the hags stopped their singing. For a moment, the cell was blessedly quiet.

Drip. Drip. Drip.

Sam could hear his heart beating like a bass drum. He wondered if anyone else could hear it. He opened his eyes, but there were three of everything. Three Catrionas. Three sets of Volgrim witches. He rubbed his eyes with his knuckles and then found it better if he only opened one eye.

"What did you do to me?" he said, but his voice sounded muffled, like he had a mouthful of peanut butter. He felt detached, as if his spirit had left his body.

Was he dead? Was this what it felt like?

My heart's beating, he reasoned. *I can't be dead.*

But he couldn't feel anything, couldn't move. The witches raised their arms into Vs, like they were victorious.

What had they won?

And then it began. Visions clawed at Sam's mind. Phantoms probing with long black fingers driving needles into his brain. Voices came in his head. *Who are you? Who are you?* they asked.

His eyes were open, but a thick mist clouded his vision. Sam took a step forward. Cold gray fog pressed in on him. He waved a hand to clear it away.

"I'm Sam. Sam Baron," he said out loud.

The chilly mist didn't clear. He took another step. Hands grabbed at him, cold fingers trailing along his skin. He jerked away. He couldn't make them out. But they were there. Faceless bodies reaching for him.

Liar, came the voices, whispers and accusations echoing in the dark. *Liar. Liar. Liar.*

"I am Samuel Barconian," he shouted, spinning around to find the speaker. "Is that better? I am the last Son of Odin."

Liar, liar, liar.

He spun back, taking three steps forward, and stumbled over his own feet. He covered his ears, muffling the hateful voices. "Who am I then?" he shouted. "Huh? Who am I?" The rage flowed easily. Like old times.

A witch, came the whispers. *One of us.*

"No," he argued, gripped with a desperate need to be heard. "I am not one of you."

Of them, came the mocking whisper. *Of them, among them, one of them.*

"I am a Son of Odin," Sam shouted, but the words tripped on his lips. *Who was he again?*

Odin is dead, came the whispers. *You killed him.*

"Me?" A flood of guilt nearly drowned Sam where he stood. What had he done? "No, I would never. He is a god. He cannot be killed." Sam dropped to his knees. He put his hands on the floor. It was real. Cold and hard. Substantial. He pressed his face to it, letting the tears run down onto the surface.

Dead. Odin is dead. Dead is dead. Of us, among us.

"I did not kill Odin," Sam persisted, feeling the tears burn a trail on the stone like acid.

But you will, came the voices. *You will kill him. You will, you will.*

"My name is Samuel Barconian, son of Robert Barconian," he whispered.

Your name is Kalifus. Son of Rubicus, Son of Catriona, came the voices.

Kalifus, Kalifus, Kalifus, echoed the voices. *One of us.*

Sam hesitated. Was he? Was he who they said he was? He put the letters together in his head. Let it pass his lips.

"Kalifus," he whispered. And in that moment, like a lock tumbling into place, he knew it to be true.

Mercifully, a deep and powerful sleep took him away.

Chapter Twenty-Two

My name is Kalifus. I have no family, no loyalty other than to my coven. I have one purpose, one mission: Serve the witches.

The words played over and over in Sam's head, as if they had been planted there like evil seeds. He couldn't shake them off, nor could he tell if they were his thoughts or someone else's. He was too tired to fight it. Countless hours had passed, maybe days since Catriona had delivered her potion and left Sam alone in his cell.

His brain was glitching, flashing between the old Sam and the new one. *Kalifus.*

Keely. Leo. Howie. That's why he was doing this, he remembered, but he couldn't hold onto the thought. Instead he just kept getting bombarded with images of his friends carrying on without him.

Laughing. Playing. Living life while he was locked away in this dungeon. He hated the old familiar anger that rose up in him, but if he didn't let it out, it festered inside like a poison.

The Deathstalkers brought him food, but he had no patience for their ministrations.

"Get out!" he shouted, kicking at two that offered him crusts of bread. Hunger gnawed at him. Thirst drove him mad. But Catriona did not return. *Why?* he wondered. Was she going to starve him to death? She could have killed him long ago if that was her desire.

It's like she was testing him. A slow smile came over his face. That was it. Catriona was testing to see if her little experiment had worked. If he had chosen his path. Sam's brain hummed as he stitched together a plan. He would play the part of Kalifus. Act the role. Just enough to convince her he was on her side. Then he would be Sam again.

Gathering his strength, he channeled everything he had into a lungful of air. "I am Kalifus," he roared to the empty space of his cell. "I demand that you release me so that I may serve you!"

His words echoed off the walls.

At first, nothing happened. And then, a tingle reached his fingers. A burst of energy like static electricity ran through him, sending fine tremors over his skin. Something inside of him rose up, as if his magic was being supercharged.

This is cool.

As his veins zinged with the potency of the magic, Kalifus closed his eyes and concentrated, willing the cell door that held him prisoner to swing open. Energy crackled the air, snapping like flags flapping in the wind. Then with a bright green flash, the door flew off its hinges, clanging against the far wall.

Surprise made him gape for just an instant, then a rush of exhilaration moved him forward.

Freedom. After weeks of banishment, Sam was leaving his cell. Unused muscles strained in protest as he stepped into the deserted dungeon corridor. He thrust his hand out, lighting the wall torches one after another to guide him toward his destiny. He followed the lights to the surface, climbing carved stone steps until he pushed open a heavy door.

Faint recognition flickered in his mind. The dimly lit court-yard with its slender trees and iron-rod benches.

Tarkana fortress. Following his instincts, Sam shuffled along the corridor leading to the grand hall, where Endera had once tied his friends up as bait for her ravenous spider.

The corridor was deserted. The moon shone half-full over the courtyard. There were no guards posted outside the towering set of doors that barred entrance. Sam waved his hand and pushed with his newly amped-up magic. The doors swung open on well-oiled hinges. Inside, the hall was alive with swaying shadows as the incoming surge of air flickered the torches lining the walls.

He staggered forward past alabaster columns, feeling stronger with every step. The floor was made of white marble, swirled with clouds of red, as if it had absorbed the blood spilled on its surface. Giant tapestries lined the walls, depicting long-ago scenes of battles won. His eyes passed over one of Rubicus, kneeling before a glowing red sun. At the far end of the hall, the witches were assembled on the raised dais, silently waiting while Sam made his way toward them. The giant spider perched in her web behind them, spinning thread with her long hairy legs, waiting for a victim that he was confident would not be him on this day.

A large throne occupied the dais, made of black marble and intricately carved with the twisting shapes of Omeras in flight. From this place of honor, Catriona held court. She dominated the room with her electrifying power.

To her right sat one of the Volgrim witches, Bronte, eagerly looking their new pet up and down. To her left, the old Tarkana hag, Hestera, glared at him, unimpressed. He recognized other witches flanking them: young Lemeria, the one who had made his feet dance long ago. Agathea. Vena. Beatrixe. But no Endera.

Maybe she's been banished, Sam fervently hoped. *Or better yet, executed.*

He came to a stop in front of the dais and waited.

"Who are you?" Catriona asked. Her voice echoed in the recesses of the hall.

"I am Kalifus," he answered loudly.

"Kalifus." The witches repeated his name, murmuring to each other.

"Kal-i-fus," Catriona said, crooning his name. Her eyes were green slits, studying him warily. In her fingers she grasped a small leather object. Recognition hit him. It was his father's pouch. The one that held Odin's Stone. A sudden longing to hold it gripped him, but he fought it. Catriona studied him, watching his face closely.

"You desire this?" She swung it from the string that held it. His eyes followed it. He did, but he shook his head.

"I have no use for it," he said.

"He lies," Hestera accused. "I can see it in his eyes. You've not turned him; he's simply playacting."

Catriona's fist clenched tighter around the pouch. "Are you pretending, Kalifus?"

"No."

"Good. Then you won't mind destroying what's inside." She dumped out the small shard of stone and placed it in his hand. She sat back on her throne and waited. Every witch seemed to hold her breath.

The stone sat on his palm, warm and vibrant. It was a piece of his father. A talisman of Odin. He couldn't destroy it. The witches were all staring at him. If he wavered here, he would never gain their trust. Slowly, Sam's fingers curled around the stone. He clenched it tightly, then directed his magic toward it, trying not to cry as a fine sand trickled onto the dais. When he was finished, he opened his eyes and stared wordlessly at the tiny pile of sand.

"See, Hestera? He cares nothing for his father's precious gift to him. Now, whom do you serve?" Catriona asked.

He dropped down onto a knee, clenching his fist over his heart. "I am blood of your blood. Son of Rubicus. Son of Catriona. I can serve no other." Like a doctor with a probe, she poked at his thoughts with her magic, searching his intentions. He ruthlessly squashed Sam's existence, the part of him that longed to lash out at her. He raised his head and met her eyes. Victory gleamed in them.

"Do you hear that, sisters? The boy has chosen sides." Catriona's voice was thick with triumph.

Hestera gripped her emerald-tipped cane. "He is still an abomination. A danger to us all."

Catriona rose to her feet. "Silence, or I'll turn you into a pile of ash myself." She raised one threatening hand at her challenger.

Argument broke out among the witches from both sides.

Sam rose and sent a blast of crackling witchfire at the wall of tapestries, incinerating the image of Rubicus kneeling before the sun. As the woven fabric crumbled to ash, the witches stopped chattering. All eyes turned on the witch-boy.

"Tell me how to earn your trust," he demanded.

The witches offered no response.

"I am not one of your pets." Stalking forward, he sent a blast into the web, incinerating half of it and sending the hulking spider scurrying back into the corner. "One day I will rule over this coven."

He stopped before Catriona. Her glittering green eyes returned his stare. "Very well. You shall have your chance. There is one more test."

"I will not fail you," Sam said, thrumming with the power the witches had unlocked with their noxious gas. "What must I do?"

"Do that which you were born to do. Kill Odin."

Her words staggered Sam, taking him by surprise. He recalled the words spoken in his dungeon, but he'd thought they were part of an evil dream to torment him. "No one can kill a god."

She waved him off dismissively with her hand. "Then you are not Kalifus, Son of Rubicus. You are weak. And those earth children will die, each of them, painfully and alone, thanks to your failures."

Desperate determination filled him. "I never said I wouldn't try." He stepped forward. "Tell me what to do, and I will find a way." He'd let the witches think he was going to kill Odin. Once he was on Asgard, he would be able to reason with the god. Hatch a plan to defeat Catriona once and for all. Catriona must not suspect. He would be Kalifus with every thought, every action.

She smiled with satisfaction. "Take this knife." She held out a dagger made of polished black onyx. "It belonged to my father, Rubicus himself. It holds a dark power, enough to bring Odin down. I would kill Odin myself, but he would never let me close enough. You, he has a fondness for—the old Samuel Barconian, that is."

Sam took the ancient weapon. The blade was decorated with carved symbols of their magic totems. It was heavy. Powerful. "How will I find him?" he asked, tucking it into his waistband. "His island is hidden, constantly moving."

Catriona tossed him a familiar satchel. He opened it and found the heavy compass Endera had given him on his first journey to Asgard. The device was contrary, but with some luck and patience, it had deigned to shown him Odin's secret location. "Where did you find this?" The last he had seen it, Rego had taken it to be stored in the archives under the Great Hall in Skara Brae.

"Not everyone is united in their support of Orkney," Catriona sniffed. "I have a traitor among them, one who does my bidding. It is far too valuable to collect dust in that hole."

Excitement made his heart jump. "With this, I can find Odin anywhere he's hiding. All I need is a ship."

"The Balfins will take you." She clapped her hands, and two hulking figures stepped out of the shadows. "As you can see, we have enhanced them to better suit our needs."

Shock turned Sam's blood to ice. These were the creatures the glass orb had shown Howie facing off against. They were big as Neanderthals, with bulging foreheads, recessed eyes, and massive jaws. Their noses had flattened out like someone had punched them in. Thick black hair stuck up in every direction from their heads. A pair of sneevil-like tusks jutted up from their bottom jaws. Muscles bulged under their armor, straining it to its limits. They let out loud grunts, ramming their lances into the stone in greeting. So that part of the vision was true. Which meant the other parts probably were as well.

"They're all like this?" Sam asked in fearful awe.

Catriona just smiled and nodded with pride.

The witches are going to win this war, Sam realized with a sinking horror, *unless I find a way to stop them.*

Lemeria clapped her hands giddily. "Tell him, my queen, tell him of our plans."

A ripple of pleasure made Catriona appear younger as she addressed Kalifus. "Once Odin is dead, then we will have the power to destroy the magic that separates our world from that of mankind. We will once again rule over Midgard. And you, boy, are going to seal our victory. Come, sisters, we must prepare for our coming battle. Kalifus, these Balfins will escort you to your ship."

Catriona stood with a swish of her skirts and swept off the dais and out of the room, followed by her cronies, leaving Sam with the Balfin monstrosities. Horror left Sam rooted in place. Destroy Odin's magic? Could she do that? *If Odin was dead, she could.* His feet were like lead as he turned to follow, but he paused when he spied the small pile of sand. Grief rippled through him.

Turning to his escorts, he tested his powers. "Wait for me outside." When they hesitated, he drew a ball of witchfire and threw it at their feet, forcing them to stumble back. "Disobey again, and I will incinerate you." They fled, leaving him alone.

Sam swiftly knelt down and scraped the traces of sand into the pouch Catriona had discarded. Slipping it around his neck, he hid it under his shirt.

Asgard awaited, and with it, a divine appointment with Odin.

Chapter Twenty-Three

The armory soon became Howie's second home. That is, when he wasn't out on the training field being beaten to death by Teren's trainees. They used him as a punching bag during matches, expecting him to dodge the thrust of every sword and hold on to a shield while they pounded him with maces. He had bruises up one side of his body and down the other. They didn't even let him hold a sword, but he had polished a hundred of them to a bright sheen.

And then there was the armor. Lingas sat on her perch entertaining him with her incessant bird chatter, while he spent hours cleaning off mud and grime. As soon as he finished one lot, they brought another in, filthier than before. The only fun he had was the few hours he snatched in the early morning to take Lingas out flying in the fields outside the gates. He loved to watch her soar high in the sky. She didn't listen to a thing he said, but she regularly delivered offerings of rabbits or small squirrels, which he passed onto the cook in the kitchen in exchange for extra servings of stew.

Not that I have time to eat, Howie grumbled to himself, as he rubbed a cloth over a sword. His arms ached. He slept on a mattress of straw that poked and made him sneeze. The truth was, he didn't feel anything like a Protector. *More like a slave.*

"Time to train," Selina announced as she pranced in, looking fresh as a daisy.

Howie groaned. "Again?"

"Yes, Howie, again. Unless you want to lose to the witches on the first swing."

"How are we supposed to defeat magic with a bunch of swords? What's the point?"

"You can't give up just because it's hard, Howie. Come on, move it, lazy bones."

Howie wearily set down the armor he was polishing and picked up a training blade, tipping it to his forehead and saluting Selina.

"Okay, give it your best shot."

He parried her first thrust but missed the second.

"Faster," Selina ordered, smacking Howie with the flat side of her wooden sword.

"Easy, chiquita, we're just practicing," Howie reminded her. He was sweating, his shirt damp and clinging to his bony frame. Bruises pocked his arms and legs.

They continued on, working well past sundown, as they did every night, training like the entire pack of witches was going to descend on them any minute.

"You're slow, Howie. You have to move like a cat," she said, dancing from foot to foot. Lingas squawked in approval, flaring her wings in support.

Howie rolled his eyes. He wished with every bone in his body that he had Selina's agility, but, no matter how hard he worked, he was clumsy as ever. *Why did Odin choose me to be Protector?* he thought, as she knocked the wooden sword from his hands for the umpteenth time.

"What's wrong?" she asked as she bent down and picked up his weapon.

He took the sword from her but didn't answer, just gripped it.

"You doubt yourself," she stated.

"Every day," he said glumly, letting his sword arm drop. "Even Lingas doesn't listen to a word I say."

She put one hand on her hip, flipping her long dark hair over her shoulder. "So you're saying Odin was wrong to choose you."

He nodded, swallowing the lump in his throat. He spread his arms wide, looking down at his scrawny form. "Hello, Selina, I'm not exactly hero material."

"That's because you're looking at the wrong place. In here," she lifted the tip of her practice sword and poked at his heart. "This is what matters. Are you a coward?"

"No."

"So I ask again: Was the all-knowing father-god wrong?"

Howie sighed. "Naw, I guess he was just being optimistic about my prospects." He slashed his blade through the air and took a fighting position. "Show me your cool parry move again."

The next day on the training field, Howie was receiving his usual pummeling from the recruits. They seemed to enjoy beating on him with their practice swords until he crumpled to the ground. At the moment, he had two bruisers thrashing at him with ferocious intent, as if they were in a hurry to get on with something more challenging. Even Captain Teren looked bored, standing on the sidelines, talking to Speria.

Howie thought about all the reasons he should just go down and end this quickly, but Selina's words echoed in his head. *Was Odin wrong to choose you?* No. Odin didn't make mistakes. Which meant these bozos weren't just disrespecting the Protector of the Realm, they were dissing the Creator of the Realm himself. He had seen these lunkheads practice often enough. He knew their moves to a tee. And all that armor polishing and practice sword fighting had given him some newly added muscles.

Feeling suddenly energized, Howie dug his feet in and rose up under their swords, throwing them back with a thrust of his shield. They were startled, trading bemused glances. With a shrug they attacked again. But this time, Howie ducked and swung his leg around, taking one of them down hard. He grabbed the soldier's blade and drove upward with the hilt, the way Selina had taught him, and knocked the wind out of the second one.

The only sound on the practice field was the two recruits lying on the ground gasping for air. Everyone else watched in stunned silence.

Finally, the sound of clapping came from the sidelines. "Howie, you've been practicing," Teren acknowledged with raised eyebrows.

Howie strode over to the captain of the guard, picking at his nails nonchalantly. "Yeah, maybe a little."

"I think it's time you took on more responsibility."

Howie drew himself up tall, ready for Teren to put him in charge of a battalion of men. "Anything you want, Teren, my man."

"Excellent. You can be my squire."

Howie blinked. "Your squire?"

"Yes, it's quite an honor." Teren's eyes twinkled.

The ever dour Speria joined in, leaning one arm on Howie's shoulder.

"A lot of great soldiers started as squires, lad," he said, waggling his dark brows. "Even me."

"So it's a promotion?" Howie said, looking from Teren to Speria. "Because I'm really tired of polishing armor all day."

Teren laughed. "Oh, you'll still be polishing armor. But being my squire is the highest honor I can pay you. It means I will train you myself. In return, you will attend to me every day."

"You mean polish your boots," Howie said despondently. Being the so-called Protector of the Realm had so far been one big disappointment.

"Yes. Clean my boots . . . but you get to stay in my quarters in the Great Hall."

Howie perked up. The men's barracks were drafty and cold and smelled like trolls' feet. "Is there hot water?"

"There will be when you draw my bath for me." Teren grinned, showing his white teeth.

"What about Lingas?"

"The bird stays in the armory," Teren said sternly.

Howie hesitated, then shook his head. "No can do. The bird and I are a package deal. It's both of us or neither."

Teren glared at him, but before he could argue, Heppner came up and pulled him away.

"See that the bird doesn't disturb me," he tossed over his shoulder.

Howie saluted him, grinning up at Lingas. "We just made it to the big house, my friend. We're in the lap of luxury now."

The bird squawked and nipped Howie's ear, but it didn't dent his excitement.

A few hours later, Howie missed the barracks.

His new bed had more lumps than the old one. More straw poking him. Howie pounded his sawdust pillow and turned on his side. Teren occupied a spacious room with a four-poster bed for the captain and this narrow bunk in the corner for his squire. A large changing area was screened to give privacy. A carved oaken wardrobe held various sets of uniforms and fancy clothes. But while the surroundings were an improvement over the barracks, there were annoying drawbacks.

Howie lay wide awake as wind whistled through the walls. Doors creaked. Shutters rattled in the windows. Teren snored like a hibernating bear. And with Lingas snoring away on her perch next to his bed, the racket was in stereo.

Howie sighed. *Sleeping Beauty couldn't nap in here.*

He pulled the old horn out from under his pillow, the one Mimir had given to him. The Horn of Gjall. Not so fancy up close. It was full of dents. Dirt pitted the carvings. He held it to his lips, puffed his cheeks out, and pretended to blow on it. He imagined himself controlling a massive army of zombies in an apocalyptic battle against the witches. He was almost asleep, a dreamy smile pinned to his face, when a scratching noise made his eyes open. It sounded like someone tapping lightly on the door. He raised his head and looked over at Teren, but the taskmaster was out cold.

Shoving the horn under his pillow, Howie threw back his woolen blanket and stood uncertainly, shivering in the chilly night air in the castoff long johns Teren had supplied him. He had to roll up the sleeves and ankles, but it was an upgrade over the grungy nightshirt he had in the barracks. His bare feet recoiled from the cold stone as he tiptoed to the door and cracked it open.

Dim torches glowed in the hallway. He stepped into the empty passage and heard the noise again. Now the sound was clearer. A scratching sound like someone filing their nails on the stone. It came from around the corner.

He knew he should go back to bed, but curiosity won out. Howie crept to the end of the corridor and peered both ways. More torches flickered, casting long shadows. The hallway appeared deserted. Then he saw something small and green, like a furry monkey, scrambling around the bend.

"Hey, wait up," Howie called. He hurried after the creature.

When he turned the corner, he didn't see the little pest lying in wait, one leg stuck out.

Howie tripped, falling face-first on the stone. He threw his hands out to break his fall, but instead of hitting solid ground, Howie tumbled through space. He let out a long yelp that squeaked all the air out of him. His legs went over his head, his elbows knocking against his knees as his arms flailed, trying to find some kind of grip.

"Heeeeeeelp!" he shouted. His voice echoed in whatever freaky bottomless pit he had fallen into. Wind rushed past his face, making his eyes stream tears. His glasses slipped to the end of his nose and then fell off, lost to the void. Probably better not to be able to see the ground when he splattered.

After a long agonizing minute where Howie anticipated his death every other second, he decided it was time to man up. Gathering his courage, Howie shouted into the nothingness, "I am Protector of the Realm, and I order you to stop!"

In an instant, his falling slowed to a crawl. The wind stopped making his eyes burn. He was still descending, but it seemed likelier he would survive the landing.

"That wasn't nice," Howie said loudly. "Not cool, monkey man. You set me down gently, you hear me?"

Snickering laughter reached his ears, but Howie's feet dropped lower, and he drifted slowly to a stop until he touched ground.

He breathed a deep sigh of relief. Then reality set in as he took in the fact that there was sand beneath his feet and unbound blackness all around him. Wind ruffled his hair. Salty ocean sprayed on his cheeks. A crab scrambled over his toes, making him step back. As his eyes adjusted to the darkness, Howie could just make out a sweeping coastal shoreline. In the distance, a gigantic tree was outlined against the purplish night sky.

Behind him, he heard that same tittering laughter.

"Who's there?" Howie called, whirling around.

"Who's there?" the voice answered, followed by a long snicker.

Howie squinted. Without his glasses, everything was blurry. The clouds parted overhead, and a sliver of moonlight revealed a creature standing on a rock near the edge of the dense foliage that formed a barricade along the beach.

Pale green fur covered its body. It wasn't anything like a monkey, Howie realized. Or any other kind of creature he had ever seen before. Long drooping donkey ears hung down past its chin. Its large almond-shaped eyes glittered with mirth. It was double-jointed, allowing it to chew on its own toenail, which it did with some gusto. Something glinted around its eyes.

"Hey, those are my glasses," Howie said.

"Those are *my* glasses," it answered, pushing them into place and continuing to chew on its toenail.

Howie took two steps forward, his feet sinking into the wet sand. "This isn't funny."

"This isn't funn-eeeee," the creature answered, stretching out Howie's words. It proceeded to laugh long and hard, rolling back and forth across the rock.

Howie felt the first prickle of anger. This pest was highly

annoying. But two could play at that game, and if there was one thing Howie was good at, it was being annoying.

"You're a jerk," he said.

"You're a jerk," it mimicked, sitting up.

"No, you are."

"No, you are."

"I said it first."

"I said it second, and two is bigger than one." It held up two spindly fingers.

Howie rubbed his chin, as if he were thinking. "So you're saying you're number two. Sounds like you're poop to me."

The creature's jaw gaped open, and then it started laughing so hard its face turned purplish. When it recovered, it wiped away fat tears of mirth.

"Well done, Master Howie. Well played," it said, sounding more intelligent than Howie had thought it was. "My name is Fetch. It is an honor to meet a Chosen One." It handed over Howie's glasses.

He took them, wiping them clean with the sleeve of his long johns before putting them back on. "Hey, how do you know my name?"

The creature leaped to its feet. "You think it's chance that you are here on Asgard?" It waved a hand at the island behind them.

"This is Asgard?" Howie gasped. "Then that giant tree over there is the Yggdrasil tree? Does Odin want to see me?" Awe tinged his voice.

Fetch rolled spindly shoulders. "Asgard, yes, but only a Son of Odin can approach his Superior High Being."

Howie slumped. "Too bad, it would be cool to meet the dude. So what can I do ya for? Why'm I here?"

Fetch raised a finger. "A gift have I to present to you from Odin."

Howie brightened. "A gift, you say? Lay it on me." Maybe Odin was giving him some mighty god spit like he gave Sam with his Fury. Invincibility was a cool superpower he could most definitely handle.

Fetch cleared its throat, drawing its slight figure up as tall as it could reach until it was eye level with Howie. Its voice boomed with gravity as it spoke.

"I hereby gift you with the Sword of Tyrfing." Fetch looked down at empty hands and snapped its fingers. "One moment."

Fetch dove into the bushes, rummaging around, then gave an excited sound of discovery before climbing back up on the rock, dragging an old rusty sword. "I present to you the Sword of Tyrfing." It bowed its head low over the proffered sword, waiting for Howie to take it.

Disappointment made Howie droop. Rust had eaten holes in the scabbard. The hilt was tarnished black with age. It looked like something you could pick up in a second-hand shop for a few coins. Fetch drew the sword out of the scabbard, and Howie's hopes sunk deeper. The blade was pitted and dull.

He put a hand out to stop Fetch. "Dude, that's a pile of rust. Tell Odin, no thanks. I want something cool, like a shield of invincibility or a flaming sword."

Fetch trembled, looking over its shoulder in fear. "Dear Sir, you must take Odin's gift. Do you not know how angry his Royal Godness would be if you refused?"

Howie sighed. This was worse than any hand-me-down he got from his brothers. Odin clearly thought so little of him that he was offering Howie a rusted old broken-down useless weapon.

"Yeah, sure, whatever." He took the sword from Fetch, tucking the blade back in its scabbard without looking at it. Selina would laugh her pants off when she saw him wielding this. It would probably crumble to pieces the first time he faced a witch.

Fetch cleared his throat again. "There are rules, caveats, stipulations on its proper use. Tyrfing once belonged to Odin's grandson. The blade was forged by a pair of black dwarves—Dvalinn and Durin—who cursed the blade with three evil quests."

Howie's interest was piqued. "Evil quests, you say? So the blade is, like, enchanted?"

"Not anymore. The third quest was completed by King Agantyr of the Goths when he destroyed an entire army of Huns."

The creature seemed eager for Howie to jump on the excitement train, but Howie slumped again. So it wasn't even enchanted. A used-up second-hand hunk of rust.

"There's more—" Fetch offered, but Howie waved him off.

"Never mind, little dude, I got four older brothers. They don't call me Hand-Me-Down-Howie for nothing. Tell Odin thanks and all, but can I go home now?" A wide yawn split his face. Sleep made his eyes heavy.

Fetch's fingers fidgeted nervously. "You do not wish to hear the rest?"

Howie shook his head, fighting another yawn. "Naw. Just tell him mucho apreciado. I'd like to get back to my bed before the sun rises." His eyes felt too heavy to keep open. If he stood here much longer, he might actually fall asleep standing up. He had done it once before waiting for his turn to use the bathroom. With nine brothers and sisters, a guy could fit in a good nap standing in line.

Fetch hesitated and then nodded. "As you wish, Master Howie. As you wish."

But Howie couldn't keep his eyes open any longer. His chin hit his chest, and he began to snore.

Chapter Twenty-Four

Howie was dreaming about battling witches with a fistful of French fries when a cup of cold water splashed on his face abruptly woke him up.

Teren stood over him looking impatient. "Your first day as my squire and you've overslept. And your bird made a mess. I expect you to clean up after it."

Howie sat up, groggily rubbing the sleep from his eyes. "Is it morning already?" Lingas squawked at him from her perch, letting him know it was high time for her to be out flying.

"Lord Drabic and the esteemed High Council demand our presence. Fetch me my dress uniform."

Howie groaned, shaking his head to clear away the fog. That was some dream. Visiting Asgard in his sleep. He sat up, swung his legs over the bed, and planted his feet on the ground. He wiggled his toes. There was sand across the top of his foot.

"Haven't got all day, Howie." Teren stood in his skivvies, tapping one foot, waiting for Howie to bring him his clothes.

Howie was still processing the fact that there was sand on his feet. "Dress uniform—is that the one with the shiny buttons?" He scrambled out of bed and opened the wardrobe where Teren stored his clothes. Hanging there was a sharp-looking uniform with a row of brass buttons, shiny red epaulettes, and gold trim on the red fabric.

"That's the one." Teren snatched it out of his hands and went behind the screen to get dressed. "You have a uniform as well," Teren said loudly. "It's hanging on the door of the wardrobe. Put it on. You have to look the part if you're to be my squire."

Howie opened the other wardrobe door, then froze. His eyes went toward Teren, but the captain was busy getting dressed.

Hanging from the wardrobe hook was the old rusted sword Fetch had given him. *So it wasn't a dream.*

"What do you think?" Teren called out cheerfully.

Howie's eyes went from the sword to the outfit that hung next to it and groaned. A pair of satin purple breeches was matched with a frilly shirt and green vest. "Um, you expect me to wear this?"

Teren popped his head around the screen. "I do if you expect to eat today." He gave Howie a wink and went back to his dressing.

Shedding his long johns, Howie quickly slipped the breeches on, crossing his fingers they wouldn't fit. But of course, everything was just his size. The shirt he buttoned on had a ruffled collar that went up to his chin. A black belt cinched at his waist. He caught a glimpse of himself in the mirror over the bureau. It was official. He looked ridiculous.

"Well, well, look at you." Teren grinned at Howie's obvious discomfort. "Not quite complete, though." He took a broad floppy hat from the dresser and placed it on top of Howie's curls. "Now that's a squire. Come along, mustn't keep Lord Drabic waiting. He'll get too far along in his cups to make sense." Teren paused, his eyes going to the rusted sword. "Where on earth did you find that old thing?" He lifted it off the hook.

"Uhm, in the armory. I thought . . . you know . . . I would try it out."

Teren laughed. "Oh, Howie, you are ever entertaining. Do

strap it on. Then come along, we're late." He held it out to Howie. Howie had no choice but to accept it.

He strapped the sword to his belt, suddenly grateful there were no camera phones in the Middle Ages. What little street cred he had left back in Pilot Rock would be quashed if a photo of him in his squire outfit and junky sword ever found its way onto the Internet.

He spied something odd in the mirror. Was that a scroll of paper tucked into the hilt? It was. Howie unrolled it and squinted to decipher the spidery handwriting:

A single act of bravery can change rust to gold.

Fetch had left a medieval riddle for him. Great. Like Howie had time for puzzles. He crumpled the note into a ball, tossing it into the bin, and hurried to the door.

Lingas screaked loudly, bringing him to a halt.

"Sorry, girl, important business. I'll take you flying when I get back. Pinkie swear." He held up his little finger and then quickly shut the door on her complaints. He hurried to catch up with Teren, one hand on his floppy hat. A servant walked past in the other direction, and Howie flipped the ridiculous item onto his head.

A guy had to have some decency.

The captain strode past the main hall to the chambers where the High Council met. Teren paused outside a set of double doors and put his finger on Howie's chest.

"Stay in the background and keep quiet. I don't want you to draw attention to yourself. There are many in this room I do not trust."

Howie nodded and zipped his lips, then mumbled something unintelligible to show his mouth was sealed shut.

Teren threw open the door and strode in with his squire in

tow. Howie glimpsed a roomful of important people and then ran smack into a serving girl. She carried a tray loaded with drinks that went flying. Howie's feet went out from under him. He fell backward, crashing into a guard who stood sentinel at the door, causing the guard to tumble onto a table that held serving dishes, sending the meeting's elaborate meal crashing to the floor.

Every eye in the room turned on Howie as a plate spun in place for an excruciating few seconds, making a wobbling noise before it mercifully stopped.

Teren hung his head in utter disgust.

"My bad," Howie said, scrambling back to his feet.

The captain jerked his head for Howie to go stand in the corner of the room. Embarrassed, Howie slouched off, wishing he could disappear. Teren continued on toward the large table that took up the center of the room. The Orkney VIPs assembled around the table and took their seats.

Howie slumped against a column. Frankly, he wasn't all that impressed by the meeting hall. For all its political importance, somebody had seriously skimped on the decorating budget. An Orkney banner featuring the white heron hung from the ceiling, but it was moth-eaten, and the heron was gray with dust. The meeting table was plain oak with scratches and stains like the one in his kitchen. A brown mouse ran across the floor, nabbed a stray crumb, and disappeared into a crack in the wall. Two chairs were empty, leaving three men seated around the table with Teren.

Beo impatiently spun a blade on his fingertips. The Falcory flicked a glance at Howie, his black eyes giving no indication they had met. A guy with a triple chin sat at the head of the table, fat hands shaking as he poured some red wine into his goblet.

That must be Lord Drabic, Howie reasoned. Head of the High Council. His skin was pasty like he had never spent a day in the sun.

The third guy had a shaved head and was dressed in the

black robes of the Balfin. Howie recognized his slippery face from his days at the Tarkana Fortress. Emenor. Endera's lackey. He had an urge to plant his fist between the guy's eyes. Then a man came out of the shadows and took a stand behind Drabic. Lord Orrin. Howie's heart kicked up a notch as Orrin's weasely eyes pinned on Howie. He felt like a bug under a microscope.

"Captain Teren, I don't believe everyone here has met your squire," he said, smiling broadly.

"Howie's just a boy I'm training, Lord Orrin," Teren said casually, pouring himself a ration of wine. "Shall we begin?"

But Orrin didn't let it go. Folding open his hands, he strolled toward Howie. "Now, now, I've spoken with the boy. Not only did he survive incarceration by the witches, but he also tells me he's been chosen as Protector of the Realm."

His statement was greeted by soft chuckles. Even the guards posted at the door had a laugh. Howie burned with embarrassment. It was one thing to be the butt of Heppner and Speria's jokes, but these windbags hadn't earned the right to make fun of him.

Teren laughed along with the group. "Stuff and nonsense. Just a story the boy likes to tell."

"I wonder . . ." Orrin stopped an inch away from Howie. His eyes bore directly into Howie's, making him squirm. "He does seem a bit puny to defend us all." His eyes drifted downward to the weapon at his hip. "And he is armed with nothing but a rusted blade."

Drabic spoke up. "Come, Orrin, leave the boy alone. We have important business to discuss."

Orrin smiled and leaned in to whisper in Howie's ear. "I've asked the kitchen to prepare a stuffed iolar for dinner. I hope you'll join me." He turned away and smiled at the High Council. "You are right as always, Lord Drabic. Emenor, please share your news with the Council."

Howie's heart rate returned to normal as attention shifted to the Balfin. Orrin was dangerous, like a viper waiting to strike. If Orrin touched that bird . . . well . . . Howie's hand went to the hilt at his side. Rusted or not, old Tyrfing would find a final resting place deep inside Orrin's gut.

Emenor was tugging at his collar as if it were too tight. "As you know, the Balfins have remained neutral in this senseless war with the witches."

"Neutral?" Beo slammed the tip of his knife deep into the wood of the table. "You shelter them."

"We have no choice if we wish to survive, Beo," Emenor hissed back. "But I bring good news. The witches have sent word they wish to discuss a ceasefire. A treaty. They will end their assault on Orkney in exchange for being left alone."

Conversation instantly broke out. Howie felt a buzz of excitement. A truce was a good thing. The war would end, and maybe Sam would come back.

"Why would they agree to it?" Teren rose from his chair. "Swords and arrows are useless against their trickery. My men are beaten back and pummeled at every turn. The witches are fewer in number, but their powers grow. It is only a matter of time before they set their wicked eyes on Skara Brac. If the Black Guard joined with us, we could root them out once and for all."

All eyes turned to Emenor. The Balfin's bald pate gleamed with a sheen of sweat. "The Balfins may be well-armed, but we do not believe in war," he said haughtily. "Not until all efforts at diplomacy have failed."

"A treaty is good news," Drabic said, raising his glass and taking a long drink. "It means they're afraid of us."

"What if he's lying?" Beo said, pointing at Emenor. "There have been rumors of beasts on Balfour Island. Passing ships have reported seeing monsters that walk as men."

Orrin stood calmly behind Emenor. "Mere ramblings by seamen with sun-addled brains. Emenor is a member of this council. He deserves the benefit of your trust. Lord Drabic has agreed to go to Balfour Island and meet with Catriona herself.

Captain Teren, you will take a squad of your best men and accompany Drabic."

"No. I cannot leave the city," Teren said adamantly. He planted his hands on the table to face Drabic. "Skara Brae is our last stronghold. Refugees flood our streets. If I take my men, it will be completely unprotected. The witches will have the perfect opportunity to attack. If Gael were here, he would never allow it."

"It wasn't a request, Captain Teren. And Gael is not the leader of this council, I am," Drabic said irritably. "You will follow your orders or be removed from your post as captain of the guard. Emenor and Lord Orrin have graciously agreed to oversee the protection of the city."

Howie snorted to himself. Skara Brae was safer in his clumsy hands than with that pair of snakes in charge.

"What say you, Beo?" Teren said stubbornly, looking to the Falcory to bolster his plea.

"This war cannot continue," the Falcory said, pulling his knife from the table. "I agree with you, Captain Teren, it could be a ruse, but a truce may be our only hope. I would accompany you, but I must return to my people and bring them this news." His eyes bore into Teren's. Howie read the message loud and clear: Beo was worried about the fate of his son, Jey.

Back in Teren's chambers, the soldier cursed and kicked a chair over. Howie walked an irritated Lingas to the window and let her loose, then plopped down glumly on his cot.

"So you're leaving?" Howie said.

Teren ran his hand through his hair. "It seems I have no choice. Orrin is up to no good, and Drabic is too foolish to see it."

"So don't go," Howie urged. "Tell Orrin to get stuffed!"

"If I do, they'll boot me out of the city and strip me of my title. No, I must see this through."

"Then you'll need your squire." Howie pasted his trademark grin in place to hide the fact his knees were knocking against each other with fear.

Teren cocked an eyebrow. "Are you sure you're up for it? There are all sorts of dangers out on the road. Witches. Sneevils . . ."

Howie shrugged. "Eh, sneevils are just overgrown pigs with bad teeth. Maybe we can barbecue one for supper."

A fierce look of respect came into Teren's eyes. He gripped Howie tightly by the shoulder. "I've watched how hard you have worked and trained. Never complaining. It would be an honor to have you ride alongside me. This will be your first test as Orkney's Protector."

For once, Teren's lips didn't twitch when he used Howie's title. Howie considered that progress. Half an hour later, he lugged their two satchels to the courtyard, where a company of men were assembled. More than a dozen of Orkney's finest were suited up in their Orkadian uniform, including the redheaded Heppner, who would accompany them. They carried their swords, and each man had a powerful crossbow strapped to his back with an ample supply of the iron bolts with razor-sharp tips. If it was a trap, Teren obviously planned to be able to fight back.

Lord Drabic arrived, complaining loudly about everything, insisting he could not survive without a wagon full of fancy rugs, several barrels of wine, and two mealy-faced servants to attend to him. Teren gave in and strapped the extra items onto the roof of his carriage.

When they were finally ready, Teren mounted his horse. "You're in charge now, Speria," he said, leaning down to clasp the wiry soldier's hand. "Protect my city while I'm gone."

"Yeah," Heppner smirked from his horse, "have fun babysitting that lot."

For once, Speria's dark eyebrows didn't waggle with humor. The soldier looked gloomy as he bade them farewell. "Worry about keeping yourselves in one piece. The city walls will hold off any army those witches bring for weeks."

"Let us hope you are right," Teren said grimly.

Just then, a familiar voice rang out. "Howie! Where are you going?"

Howie turned. "Selina. Hey, I'm just, you know, heading out on a top-secret mission with the captain. You'll take care of Lingas for me, won't you?"

She nodded and flung her arms around his neck. "Be careful."

Howie felt himself flush to the roots of his hair as she kissed him on the cheek, and then she turned and ran into the crowd.

"Someone's got a fan," Speria teased as he boosted Howie up to his horse.

Howie tried to look the part of confident hero as he picked up the reins, shaking them firmly. "Okay, giddy up. Hit it. Let's get this show on the road." The stubborn animal just stomped one foot, not moving.

Heppner rode by, swatting the horse on the rear, and it took off, nearly unseating Howie as it loped out the gates. Howie clutched the saddle horn, praying he didn't fall off and send the crowd into gales of laughter.

They clattered over the bridge and turned south. The horses' hooves clipped sharply over the stony road. Howie rode between Teren and Heppner. He turned in his saddle to give the city one last look.

"Think we'll ever make it back here?" he asked.

Teren kept his eyes straight ahead. "It's not too late for you to turn around."

Howie snorted. "And miss out on all the fun? You heard Beo. There might be monster men ahead. Yippee-ki-yay."

Teren didn't have to know Howie was completely and utterly terrified at the idea of meeting a monster man in person.

Chapter Twenty-Five

Keely stood in a field of snow. The air was still and quiet around her. Nothing moved. The world was gray and barren, devoid of all living things. She didn't know how she had gotten here. Where were the others? Galatin? Mavery? Even that lout Rifkin? She opened her mouth to call for them, but nothing came out. *You're dreaming*, she said to herself. Before she could pinch herself awake, Keely heard a familiar voice calling for help.

It was Sam. He was in trouble. She tried to move in the direction of his voice, but a strange paralysis gripped her.

Then he was there, running across the field of snow toward her. Chased by a swarm of wolves nipping at his heels, their haunting howls breaking the silence. Shun Kara wolves, Keely realized with a sinking dread. Witches' pets.

"Help me, Keely!" Sam cried, glancing frantically over his shoulder at the approaching pack. "Make them stop!"

Keely tried to run, but it was as if the snow were cement. She could only watch helplessly as the wolves brought Sam down right in front of her. Sam was screaming, begging her to help him. Her helplessness was agonizing. Then the pack of wolves transformed into a black cloud, swirling around Sam and swallowing him up.

The screaming stopped, and Sam went silent. Keely waited, feeling her heart thunder in her chest.

Then the cloud evaporated, and Sam stood before her alone, head bowed. His clothes were torn, and his arms scratched and bloody. When he raised his head, fear curdled her blood. His eyes glowed yellow, glaring at her with a venomous hatred. "You let them do this to me. This is your fault," he said, and then he shot a hand out to grab her neck, choking her with a ferocious grip.

With a scream Keely awoke, grabbing at her throat, breathing rapidly. Sam was changing. She could feel it in her bones. The dream had been a warning. They were running out of time to find the Moon Pearl.

The campfire was dead, buried under several inches of fresh snow. It covered the ground, making the world a single color, as if an artist had dipped a paintbrush and plastered every tree and rock with splashes of crystal white.

Oh, and it was cold.

Bone-splintering cold.

Keely pushed back the furs and rubbed her eyes. Every muscle in her body ached after days on the back of a horse and sleeping on the hard ground night after night. She couldn't decide which she missed more at that moment, hot showers or a mattress. Mavery snored in a ball next to her. Rifkin was nowhere in sight. He had been nothing but friendly toward her since they'd left Ter Glenn, but she couldn't erase the sight of him hovering over her with that crazy look in his eyes. Galatin was already loading their horses. He gave her a sharp look but said nothing. She couldn't read him. He seemed loyal to their mission, but she was pretty sure he had lied about his reasons for rushing them out of Ter Glenn in the dead of night. They were nearing the top of the pass that would lead them to Rakim. Keely shivered, realizing they were about to enter into an even more treacherous stage then they were in now.

The sun was a leaden disc, hidden behind a thick layer of

clouds. Gripped with a sense of urgency, Keely nudged Mavery awake. The girl was buried in the bottom of the furs.

"Come on, Mav, time to go."

Mavery groaned and then popped her head up. "It's too cold," she said, before sliding back under the fur.

Keely ripped the furs off, glaring down at her. "Maybe you should have stayed back in Skara Brae."

Mavery grinned up at her. "Then you'd be here all alone with no friends."

Keely shook her head, but she couldn't help smiling. The imp had an endearing way of getting under her skin.

Mavery stomped her feet into her boots and ran her hands over the cold remains of the fire.

"Can you get it started?" Keely asked, shivering as a sharp wind blew across the camp.

The girl looked slyly up at her. "Only if you say, 'Mavery, I can't do it without you.'"

A sudden rush of tears made Keely drop her head. "I don't think I can do it at all."

"Aw, I was only kidding. What's wrong?"

"I had a dream. About Sam. He's in trouble, Mavery. He needs us, and we're running out of time."

The girl put her hand on Keely's. "Then we'd better get moving," she said calmly. "But first I need some breakfast." She clapped her hands and shoved them into the cold ashes. A spurt of flame erupted, singeing Mavery's hair and sending her falling back on her behind.

"Nice job," Keely praised, warming her hands over the crackling flames. She threw in another log. The fire cut through the icy air, making it easier to breathe.

Mavery stretched like a cat next to her. "What's to eat? I'm starving."

"Same thing as yesterday. Mashed oats with a side of stale bread. I'll try to hunt us a rabbit later." Keely's skill with the bow had advanced greatly since she'd been practicing. She had managed to keep them fed with a fresh supply of meat. Keely scooped some snow into their pot and waited for it to melt before adding the last handful of oats. She threw in a pinch of salt and some sugar from the precious little supplies they had left. It was runny, but Keely ladled a bowl for each of them. Rifkin returned with an armful of firewood and a ready smile.

"Well, good morning, little ones. I see you've served up a fine breakfast." He took his dish and spooned it in greedily.

Galatin ate silently, picking at the thin gruel. "We're near the summit," he announced. "Then we'll be in Vanir territory. They'll be no more fires after this."

They had climbed high above Ter Glenn. As cold and difficult as it was, the woods held their own beauty. Bushy-tailed squirrels with thick silver coats ran up and down the trees, chattering at them like they were intruders. Gray-feathered birds flew sharply through the trees, sending out trilling calls to each other. The birds had a black stripe across their face, like a mask. They were small and sang a lilting chorus. As one dive-bombed her head, Keely ducked.

"What kind of bird is that?" she asked.

"That's a Northern shrike, child," Rifkin answered.

"It's beautiful."

Rifkin laughed. "Not so beautiful when they pluck your eye from your head and eat it for breakfast."

She watched the shrike dive-bomb the forest floor and come up with a squealing rodent in its beak. Jeez, was everything in Orkney dangerous? Even the most beautiful things seemed to have a dark side to them.

Keely ventured a question that had been on her mind. "How are we going to find the Cave of Shadows? Is Rakim very big?"

"I'm going to lead us there," Rifkin boasted. "I know the secret to finding it."

"Tell us," Galatin said sharply.

"Now why would I do that?" Rifkin's eyes glinted greedily.

"You might decide to cut me out of the deal. Just take my word, I've stood outside it, but I lacked the particulars to get inside."

Keely frowned. "Particulars? Do you need a key?"

Rifkin bellowed with laughter. "No, child you need to have the blood of an Eifalian. They're the sacred guardians of Ymir's cave."

Keely blanched. "But none of us are Eifalian. How are we going to get in?" She could just imagine fighting through blizzards and snow to stand outside the Cave of Shadows, only to be denied entrance.

But Rifkin seemed nonplussed. "Oh, you'll get us in, little mouse. You've got a bit of Eifalian in you."

She bristled at Rifkin's diminutive nickname for her but focused on his words. "I don't have Eifalian blood. I'm not even from this place."

Galatin interjected, pointing at her head. "Your hair tells me different. King Einolach even noticed. Rifkin's right. You've got a drop of it somehow."

Keely's hand rubbed across her palm where Mimir had poked her. Had the old coot given her what she needed to succeed?

An animal howled through the trees. Galatin stood up to listen. Mavery turned to look worriedly at Keely. Her nose was red with cold. A sharp wind blew a flurry of snow across the trail. Clouds had rolled in, blotting out the weak sun. Fat snowflakes began to fall.

"Maybe we should go?" Keely said. She slipped her head through her bow and tucked the quiver of arrows over her shoulder.

"For once I agree with the child," Galatin said. "Chosen One, you ride with me today."

They quickly mounted up and began their climb. There were no trails, only towering silver ash trees that whispered as their branches shimmered in the stiff breeze. Shrikes whistled and trilled as they darted in and out of the trees. A layer of crusty snow covered the ground. The only noise was the crunch of hooves as the horses broke through the rime.

Galatin spoke softly over his shoulder. "I know you didn't approve of my decision to leave without Gael's help. You should know, I lied about hearing the king forbid our passage."

Keely stilled, listening.

Galatin's voice dropped to a whisper. "But I had my reasons. If the king had read our auras again, he would have learned I—"

But Galatin stopped mid-sentence, cocking his head sharply to the side. The chattering birds had gone silent, as if a switch had been thrown. Their horse snorted, its nostrils flaring as if it smelled something foul.

Out of nowhere, a rock pelted Keely on the back. She yelped in pain as another glanced off her temple. Mavery and Rifkin were also under attack from a volley of stones.

Their horse reared up as a rag-covered, misshapen creature launched itself at them, rolling in a ball and landing on two feet. It was squat and short. Its face was mottled with warts and scars. The creature's hair was grizzled and gray, standing up in wiry tufts. One snaggletooth hung over its bottom lip. From the shape of it, Keely guessed female.

"Troll hags!" Galatin shouted, drawing his sword. "Don't let them get the horses."

Chapter Twenty-Six

Galatin slashed at the creature, but it dove to the side. It had yellowed nails longer than Keely's pinkie, disgustingly green mottled skin, and hands that dragged on the snow. It hurled another rock at Keely's head. Galatin kicked the horse and charged the troll, trying to run her down. Keely pulled her bow to her hand, nocked an arrow, and let it fly, but her arrow went wide as the troll nimbly rolled between the horse's legs. The horse let out a scream and then dropped to its knees. Keely desperately held on to Galatin but lost her grip as he went flying over the horse's head.

As Keely tumbled, she glimpsed the troll underneath the horse. It had used a rudimentary stone dagger and stabbed it deep in the animal's belly. It grinned at her, revealing crooked black teeth. The horse tried to stand, but it staggered and then rolled over on its side, pinning Keely underneath.

She desperately pushed on it, feeling the weight crushing her. The troll leaped on top of the horse, scrambling over it to get to her. Keely could smell a fetid odor like rotting cheese. The troll made horrible grunting noises like a wild beast. Galatin lay nearby, unmoving. She called out for help, but Mavery and Rifkin were surrounded by a pack of trolls. Rifkin slashed his sword, impaling one, while Mavery shot bursts of green witch-fire at the others.

Keely's attacker's black eyes narrowed in glee upon seeing the girl pinned and helpless. The troll raised the knife over its head to kill her, but a loud thunk made Keely blink. An arrow buried itself dead center in the troll's chest. With a look of surprise, the wretched little hag toppled backward onto the ground.

Skinny arms grabbed Keely from behind and pulled her out from under the dead horse. She caught sight of white hair and then a blur of motion as another arrow was fired. It caught one of the troll hags in the shoulder. The awful creature screeched, and her remaining allies stopped attacking to see who the shooter was.

Keely finally got a proper look. Her eyes grew wide in shock.

It was Theo. Looking dashing in leather leggings, wrapped in furs, the irritating boy who had disliked her on sight now loomed above her like a pint-sized warrior. Matching leather straps bound the fur tightly to Theo's arms. His gloves went up to his fingertips. He carried a longbow and nocked another arrow. With steely precision, he let the feathered arrow fly. The second troll was hit square in the chest, knocked down with a squealing grunt.

The remaining troll hags scrabbled away into the woods on all fours as Theo kept up an onslaught of arrows. Rifkin chased after them with his sword, shouting curses at them.

"You saved me," Keely said, stepping forward to embrace him. "But what are you doing so far from home?"

He looked at her with earnest eyes. "I came to take you back with me. Eifalians cannot enter Rakim. You mustn't break the treaty!"

"But I'm not Eifalian," she said, "I'm from Midgard."

A frown crossed his forehead. "I don't understand how, but you are. I can feel it. So can my uncle. And the Vanir won't care what the truth is; you look Eifalian."

"I can't go back. Sam needs me to do this."

Color slashed his cheeks as anger rippled through him. "I command you as heir to the Eifalian kingdom to return with me."

"Theo, I'm sorry—"

But he backed away from her, ashen faced. "Then war will begin. And it will be all your fault." He turned and ran through the trees down the hillside.

"Theo, wait!" Keely cried, but behind her Mavery let out a cry.

"Keely, Galatin's hurt!" The girl was bent over their leader, who lay still as a corpse.

Rifkin emerged from a copse of trees, limping and cursing. "I'll go find our other horse. You tend to Galatin," he called to Keely.

Keely joined Mavery and rolled the soldier over. She gasped at the deep gash on his temple and quickly pressed a clump of frozen snow to it while Mavery got a fire going. The girl boiled some snow, adding precious meat to make a broth. Rifkin returned with the other horse, tying it off to a tree before joining them at the fire.

They were silent, all three staring at the unconscious figure.

Keely ladled broth into a cup and spooned some into Galatin's lips.

"Galatin, can you hear me?" she asked.

There was no answer from him.

They kept the fire going and waited for Galatin to wake up. The troll hags must have left the area because the birds resumed their calling. Mavery sat with her arms wrapped around her knees, staring into the flames. She was scared. Keely could see it in her eyes. Rifkin sat with his arms folded, whistling to himself like he wasn't worried, but the lines around his eyes were deep.

How did I get myself into this? Keely wondered with mounting dread. *And what was Galatin about to tell her? Was Galatin a traitor? Who could she trust?*

A pair of ravens flew through camp, their blue-black bodies nearly taking Keely's head off.

Rifkin got to his feet. "I think I'll stretch my legs. We're running low on wood." He took off whistling through the woods.

"I should try to get us a rabbit," Keely said, determined to keep busy. Where was her bow? She must have lost it when the horse had reared up. She searched in the snow and then sagged with disappointment. The precious bow was broken in half. Two jagged pieces hung from the bowstring. It was useless, but she uncovered her satchel in the snow.

Keely grabbed the bag, struck by an idea, and went back to the fire. She knelt by Galatin and rummaged in the sac. She pulled out the pink soul crystal.

"Ooh, I didn't know you brought that!" Mavery crowed.

The crystal glowed faintly in Keely's hands. She had an urge, a sense that the crystal could help Galatin. King Einolach had said she had the hair of a healer. She removed her gloves and held the crystal over Galatin's head, passing it back and forth over his wound.

"What're you doing?" Mavery asked.

"Shh." Keely was concentrating. It was probably a stupid idea, and she didn't want Mavery to laugh at her, but if the king was right, then maybe, just maybe, she could use the crystal to help Galatin. The pink stone glowed under her hands. She concentrated on sending healing thoughts toward him. Her skin tingled as a faint shimmer of electric energy ran up her spine to her shoulder and down her arm into the stone. It glowed brighter, casting a rosy glow over Galatin's face. Shock mingled with awe as she realized it was working.

His eyes flickered, and then opened.

She pulled the crystal away, smiling down at him.

"Look who's awake."

Galatin sat up, woozily rubbing his head. The bruise was yellow and black, but his eyes were clear. "Is there any water?"

Keely poured him some in a cup and held it to his lips. His hand shook slightly, but he managed to swallow the whole cupful.

"Where's Rifkin?"

"Getting wood."

"You were about to tell me something important," Keely began, but another pair of ravens took flight through the trees, flapping their wings and sending out a harsh caw. Rifkin sauntered out of the woods, clutching a few sticks.

Galatin laid into him. "Rifkin, you shouldn't have left the camp unattended. If the troll hags had returned—"

The soldier dropped the wood by the fire, glaring at his comrade. "Glad to see that knock to your head didn't affect your personality. If they had come back, we'd all be dead. One sword wouldn't stop them."

"He's right," Keely said, gripped by a sudden terror that the troll hags were going to pounce any second. "I don't even have my bow anymore."

There was silence save for the crackling of the fire.

Galatin cleared his throat. "It's not all bad. We still have one horse. I just need some rest, and then I'll be ready take on the troll hags if they come back."

Rifkin harrumphed loudly. "It's not the troll hags I'm worried about." He licked his finger and held it up. A layer of frost formed on it instantly. "Feel that drop in temperature? A storm's coming. The ache in my bones tells me it's a bad one. If we don't find shelter, we'll freeze to death in our beds."

Galatin stood, staggering slightly, one hand to his head before he steadied himself. "Then we must ride. Immediately. Get across the pass and find shelter."

"I wasn't finished," Rifkin said. "The troll hags scavenge in the forest and sell their secrets. They will have told the Vanir we're coming. As soon as we cross the pass, we'll be in their territory. They'll be waiting to pluck us like fattened berries on a bush."

"Then we'll fight them."

Rifkin spat into the fire. "There are two of us, saddled with children. Against frost giants that could tear your head off with one swipe of their hand. There's no fighting them. There is only surrender."

Galatin stared him down and then closed his eyes. "We've made it this far. I say we keep moving. Find shelter and see if we can make our way past the Vanir."

With a disapproving snort, Rifkin shrugged and loaded the horse. Mavery and Keely rolled up their furs and handed them off. As Keely turned away, Rifkin gripped her arm and yanked her in close.

"You want to find Ymir and the Cave of Shadows, you best be ready to run."

"What do you mean?" Keely whispered.

"Galatin's going to hand you over to them on a silver platter. No one in their right mind goes up against the frost giants. They're too powerful. Sneak around them, outsmart them," he tapped his forehead. "That's where I come in. You and I can make it on our own."

"I can't leave Mavery behind," Keely said, watching the witch-girl dance around the camp.

Checking that Galatin was busy with his gear, Rifkin jerked Keely within an inch of his face. "You want to get that Moon Pearl or not?"

"Yes."

"Then be ready when I say *run*."

Chapter Twenty-Seven

By midday, they were nearly to the pass separating Torf-Einnar from Rakim. Galatin steadfastly led their lone horse with Mavery on top as temperatures fell and a stiff wind picked up. Rifkin and Keely followed behind, trudging steadily uphill through the snow-covered trees. Between gasps of air that burned her lungs, Keely mulled over Rifkin's words, liking him less and less as the hours passed. Whatever happened, she wasn't leaving Mavery behind to face the fate Keely had glimpsed in her vision.

After a short rest at the pass, they began the treacherous job of making it down the other side without falling into the steep abyss that rimmed the trail. How far down they would fall was impossible to know because a gray fog covered the valley below. Keely caught glimpses of a dark river winding through more forest.

She lost count of the number of times she slipped on the slick surface and fell to her knees. Worse, the storm Rifkin had warned about moved in, hurling sleet in their faces and slowing the horse to a crawl. Galatin lifted Keely into the saddle, ignoring her objections that she was fine, and told her to hang on. Mavery wrapped her arms tight around Keely's waist.

The wind cut through the thick furs they wore like they were nothing more than fine silk. Growing up in Pilot Rock, Keely had never imagined such cold. Her skin burned like it was on fire. She pulled her hood tighter, not daring to open her eyes in the keening storm. They made slow progress. With each minute, Keely ticked off another part of her body she could no longer feel. Toes, gone. Fingers, numb. Nose, frozen.

"There!" Galatin shouted.

Keely peeked out through stiff fingers.

A darkening in the white ice. An opening.

Shelter.

Galatin lifted her down, and Rifkin held Mavery. They trudged through the wind and snow to the opening in the ice. The cave was a mere slit in a granite wall, too small for their horse to enter. Keely looked at the animal over her shoulder, wondering how long it would last before it froze, then slid down a steep plane of rough rock into a broad cavern. Behind her, Mavery followed, then Rifkin and Galatin.

It was pitch black. Keely took the phoralite out of her bag and warmed it in her hands. It glowed faintly, enough to see the interior of their safe haven.

Cobwebs patterned the ceiling, glittering with ice. There were scattered piles of sticks and dead leaves that had blown in. Rifkin pushed them into a pile.

"Can you light a fire, child?" Galatin asked Mavery. The girl's teeth were chattering so hard that the sound echoed off the ice-covered walls.

Keely reached for Mavery's shoulder and gave it a squeeze. "Come on, kiddo, we need some warmth," she coaxed.

"Oh, n-n-now you're gl-glad I-I'm here," she stuttered out.

Mavery knelt down and stuck her hands in the pile and muttered, "*Fein kinter, calla fi.*"

Nothing happened.

"Come on, witch-girl," Galatin said sharply. "We need heat."

"I can do this," she insisted, "just be patient, would ya?"

The two men backed off.

The witchling turned to Keely. "I'm too cold to think up my magic," she whispered. "I need your help."

"What can I do?" Keely asked.

Mavery shrugged. "I don't know, but you're different than before. Not just your hair. Your aura, too. You don't just look Eifalian, you feel Eifalian to me. And they have their own kind of magic. You used the soul crystal to help Galatin."

Keely knelt down next to her. "Fine. I don't know if I can help, but I'll try." Keely stuck her own hands over the pile. "What do I say?"

"Say what you feel."

"How?"

"The words come from inside you." Mavery took Keely's hands in hers and planted them on the ground. "Magic is you needing something and believing it can happen."

"Well, right now we need fire," Keely said, "so let's make it happen."

Keely closed her eyes and imagined the biggest bonfire she had ever seen. It was the last time she had gone camping with her parents, before her mom had gotten sick. She remembered the crackle of the flames on her face and the smiles on her mom's face as they toasted a bag of marshmallows. She could smell the burnt sugar now.

"You're doing it," Mavery whispered, and she squeezed Keely's hands.

Keely smelled the smoke from their fire that night and the burning sage that had singed her nostrils. Logs had popped and snapped as a desert wind blew across the mesa.

Another log popped, loudly, spitting sparks that tingled Keely's skin.

She opened her eyes. Three faces stared at her across a blazing fire.

Keely jerked her hands back, suddenly realizing they were still in the flames. They should have been burned to a crisp, but they didn't hurt. And they weren't cold anymore. She could feel her fingers again. Galatin grinned at her. It was the first time Keely really saw him smile. It was nice. It made him look younger.

"Well, looky here, the little mouse has some magic in her," Rifkin said.

They huddled around the small blaze, sheltered from the wind screaming outside their chilly nest. Keely's stomach was so empty, it was hollow. The only sound was the chattering of Mavery's teeth.

When their eyes grew too heavy to keep open, Galatin and Rifkin made bookends around the two girls. Keely slept in fits, finding snatches of rest between shivers. It felt like the night would never end. She cradled the phoralite in her hands, enjoying the tiny yellow glow. Every so often, Galatin would toss another stick on the fire. Their little pile dwindled until there were only a few twigs and scraps left.

Outside, the wind howled like a legion of banshees, whipping in through the narrow opening and crawling under the fur to chill them where they lay. Keely looked at her hands—her magical hands—and wondered if Odin had made a huge mistake when he had chosen her for this job. At this rate, she wasn't going to make it out of this cave without freezing to death. How would she ever face the frost giants or find Ymir and his Cave of Shadows?

Sleep finally overtook her. When Keely opened her eyes, something had changed.

It was quieter outside. The wind had calmed to a murmur. A dim gray light, the first sign of day, filtered into the cave, illuminating dark granite walls layered with a shiny covering of ice.

Galatin stood up, swaying slightly. "I'll go look for wood."

But for once Rifkin took charge, jumping to his feet. "No, you sit down and rest. The girl and I will go." He nodded at Keely.

She slipped her cloak over her head and put the phoralite back in her satchel. Mavery huddled under the furs, her lips blue with cold.

"I'll be right back," she said to the girl.

Rifkin pushed her up and out of the cave then climbed after her.

The world was completely white, covered in frozen sheets of snow. Their poor horse was a frozen statue, head down as if it were grazing in the snow.

"This way, child." Rifkin took off, striding across the terrain, his boots crunching on the crusty surface. She followed as best she could, trying not to slip. They entered a small stand of trees. The snow was softer and deep.

Rifkin kept going, plodding steadily, as if he was in a hurry to get somewhere.

"Wait up," she called. "Where are you going?" There were branches here, poking up out of the snow, but Rifkin charged onward.

"Keep up, little mouse."

Keely struggled to wade through waist-deep snow, feeling it slide into her boots. Panting, she had finally caught up with him when behind them, back on the trail, shouts rang out.

The sound of hoofbeats carried across the crisp air. Had someone come to rescue them? Keely stopped and turned around.

There were men, all right, but not the rescuers she hoped.

The Vanir had arrived. Through the trees, Keely could make out giant men circling the mound of snow where their horse was buried, investigating.

These men were larger than a team of hulking linebackers. They wore fur skins as capes. Long, wild chestnut hair ran down their backs. Their barreled chests were bare, as if they didn't feel the cold. They had horses the size of Clydesdales they rode bareback. The animals wore shiny silver face guards and tail ornaments woven in the hair.

Keely was about to shout a warning to Rifkin and Mavery, but a hand closed over her mouth.

"Keep quiet, girlie. You don't want the Vanir on our heads, do you?"

That's when Keely realized Rifkin had planned this. He must have known the Vanir would come once the storm cleared. She bit down on his thumb, and he jerked it back, cursing. She started to run, but he tackled her in the snow, crushing her under his weight and burying her face in the powder.

When she came up, he held her in a tight grip, keeping his hand over her mouth and a knife to her throat.

"Not a word, or I'll cut you and leave you here to die," he whispered.

She watched in horror as Mavery was pulled kicking and screaming from the cave. Then Galatin was dragged out between two of the frost giants. He appeared unconscious. Or worse.

One of the giants backhanded Mavery to silence her. Keely screamed into Rifkin's hand as the witch-girl was knocked off her feet, flying into the snow. She was tossed up on a horse like a bag of grain while Galatin was loaded onto another. Then the giants took off in a thunder of hooves.

Rifkin finally released Keely.

"Sorry about the knife," he said, without sounding the least bit apologetic. "I couldn't have you getting us caught."

"You knew," she said, giving him a shove backward. He just laughed.

"I warned Galatin the Vanir would attack. He didn't listen."

Keely shoved him again, not caring that he was bigger and had a knife. "You knew they'd be taken. We should have saved them."

"And then what? We'd be on the back of them horses, too, and for what? Rifkin doesn't get caught." He tapped the side of his head. "I'm too smart for that."

"We have to go after them."

"We have to find the Cave of Shadows—or have you forgotten about your little quest?"

No, she hadn't forgotten. But she couldn't abandon Galatin and Mavery.

"I did this for you, girlie. If we're going to save this realm, you're the only one who matters now."

Keely crossed her arms defiantly. She hated his logic, but he was right.

"What will they do with them?" she asked.

His eyes shifted downward. "The Vanir won't kill them. Not right off, anyway. They'll want to know why they're here, and if the Eifalians sent them."

"And if they think that?"

"Then things will get ugly."

Bile rose up in her throat. She hadn't eaten anything, but Keely couldn't stop the retching that gripped her stomach. She sank to her knees and dropped her head. The thought of Mavery being hurt was awful. She should have insisted the girl stay in Ter Glenn. Had her locked up in a dungeon. Her hands fisted in the snow. The only chance she had of saving the little witch now was to go forward. Find Ymir and figure out a solution to this whole mess. She looked up at Rifkin. She had to know something before she took another step.

"Back in Ter Glenn. You were going to kill me, weren't you?"

Rifkin scowled, looking away. But he didn't deny it.

"Why?"

He laughed bitterly. "Let's just say the witches can be very persuasive. And they pay well."

"You're working for Catriona!" Shock ran through her. She got to her feet, backing away, ready to fling herself on the mercy of the frost giants. Anything but this despicable traitor.

He stubbed a finger at her. "You should be thanking me. When she sent her ravens to check up on me, I told those brainless birds to tell that witch you were dead. So no one's looking for you, little mouse, and now ol' Rifkin can get his payday when you help me break into that treasure trove."

Keely turned her face away from him, listening to her heart racing in her chest. The wind blew through the trees, sending a chill down her spine. Every fiber of her being wanted to walk away through those trees, but she didn't move. If she did, her chances of reaching the Cave of Shadows dropped to nothing.

She came to a decision. "I'll go with you on one condition. You have to swear that once we get the pearl, we rescue Mavery and Galatin. And don't lie; I can read your aura." Keely's Eifalian powers were still tiny, but she had enough for her to sense the lip service Rifkin was about to feed her. "You need me, as much as I need you."

He turned red, glowering at her. "That's foolish—"

She grabbed him by his thick coat, shaking him as hard as she could. "Swear it, or I'll go after them myself right now, and you'll never see the inside of that cave or get your hands on all that treasure."

He looked annoyed but reluctantly grunted his assent. "I suppose we could swing through Galas on our way back home. We'll need to steal a ship."

"Promise." She stared into his red-rimmed eyes, searching for deceit.

"Cross my heart." He drew his fingers in an X across his chest. "So, you coming with me or not?"

Rifkin was undoubtedly the worst kind of traitor, but right now, he was Keely's best option for completing her quest. "Yes. But if you call me *little mouse* again, I'll cut your tongue out in your sleep."

Chapter Twenty-Eight

With the Draupnir wrapped tightly around his arm, Leo felt invincible. He had killed the beast and recovered the golden cuff Odin had tasked him to find. He wished for a moment that he could tell his father about his heroic feat. Make him proud. But Chief Pate-wa was a world away.

Jey knew of a nearby Falcory village a day's walk, maybe two, where they could get horses. The two boys laughed and joked about their adventure as they followed a narrow animal trail through scraggly mesquite, past piles of red boulders, making their defeat of the she-she-kana bigger by the moment.

The attack, when it came, caught them both by surprise.

With his heightened senses, Jey smelled the change in the air first—the odor of brimstone that swept in with the witches a moment before the attack. He tackled Leo as a volley of flaming thorns the size of tent stakes pinged into the ground around them with lethal force.

As Leo recovered from the shock of being slammed to the ground, Jey twisted in pain, clutching at the burning thorn protruding from his shoulder. Leo thrust his arm under the boy and together they ran to the shelter of some rocks. The sound of cackles added haste to his feet. A pack of witches was encamped in a circle of mesquite brush barely visible through a thick ring of thorned trees.

"Sorry, Jey, we need to get this out," Leo said. Jey was pale, his eyes pools of pain, but he nodded at Leo.

"Go ahead. I'll be fine."

Leo put one hand on Jey's good shoulder to brace himself. The boy stifled his groan of pain as Leo pulled the still-burning thorn free. He tied off the wound as best he could with a strip of leather he cut from their waterskin. They leaned against the boulder. They could hear the witches rustling in the brush, drawing closer.

Jey sucked in a deep breath. "I still have my javelin. I'll make a distraction. Then you run like the she-she-kana is after you. Once you get to the trees, head north. The village is close by; I can smell the campfires."

"No," Leo answered swiftly, "I won't leave you behind. You'll die."

Jey rolled his shoulders. "I'm a Falcory. It takes more than a few witches to bring me down."

"Let me stay and fight with you."

Jey grasped Leo on the shoulder. "You have to get the Draupnir where it belongs. You can't run away from this responsibility."

Leo blinked once then nodded. Jey was right. Keely and Sam were counting on him to follow the cuff to where it led him.

Jey studied the terrain. "There's a ravine over there. It follows a dried-up river. If you get to it, you'll be out of the line of fire. On the count of three, I'll charge their camp. Don't look back. And don't stop running till you find that village, understood?"

Leo's throat locked up with thick grief. This was a suicide mission for Jey.

"I'm sorry," Leo began, but Jey gave him a shove.

"Go on, get ready." Jey had his javelin in one hand. Leo stared at it, knowing this was the end of his friend, but feeling helpless to do anything about it.

Jey counted down, then, with a warrior yell, charged toward

the witches' camp. Leo set off in the opposite direction in a blistering run heading for the safety of the ravine. He was almost to the rim when a zinging fireball passed by his ear. It exploded the ground in a bright orange flash, knocking him off his feet, tumbling him down the steep incline. He landed in a clump of prickly cacti. The stinging barbs barely penetrated his consciousness. He rolled over, ready to run, but an old hag stood over him. Leo's heart sank. It was Ariane. The Volgrim witch who had threatened to turn them into stew. Her caterpillar-like eyebrows arched in recognition.

"Well, well, the earth-child who escaped me."

Leo swept his leg out, hoping to catch her off guard, but she was too fast. Quick as lighting she did a backflip, landing in a crouch. Leo had half a second to leap to his feet, but she had vanished. He spun around too late. She pounced, spewing her feral breath on him. A cloud of gray vapor enveloped him in a choking mist. He coughed, feeling dizzy. Tingling numbness spread through his limbs. He tried to stay upright, but his bones were spaghetti, and he collapsed to the ground, staring helplessly up at the witch.

Ariane withdrew a wicked-looking dagger from the folds of her skirt. "And now, earth-child, it's time to pry that cuff off your arm."

"Not so fast, Ariane."

Endera appeared in a cloud of black smoke. Behind her, a half dozen bristling, snarling Shun Kara wolves streaked down the ravine to her side. Their lips were raised, baring their teeth in a vicious grimace.

Ariane hissed at her. "Endera. What are you doing here?"

"Catriona gave me orders to retrieve the Draupnir." Her eyes went greedily to the cuff on Leo's bicep.

Ariane snorted with laughter. "Funny. My orders were to kill you on sight."

But Endera didn't look shocked at her words. In fact, Leo could see she expected it. If Ariane hadn't been the worst sort of witch, he would have shouted a warning, but as it was, he couldn't move a muscle.

"A pity you didn't listen," Endera said, and then she snapped her fingers.

Too late, Ariane saw the trap Endera had set. While Ariane was focused on Endera, the Shun Kara had moved in, surrounding her. At Endera's signal, they leaped in unison, taking the witch down in a pile of fur and snarling growls.

Ariane let out a terrifying screech of pain—she was barely visible under the wolves' gnashing teeth—and then there was a small puff of smoke, and the animals stopped their fighting, confused as they snapped at air.

Ariane had vanished.

"Get up," Endera ordered Leo.

Leo stood woozily. The effects of Ariane's spell were beginning to wear off, but he had no strength to run.

"If you want to live, do as I say." He could hear the keening cries of other witches approaching. Endera waved her hand at the wolves, muttering *"Sinfara niemen."* The wolves backed away and disappeared up the rocky side of the ravine toward the sound of the witches. Their howls echoed in the afternoon, followed by sharp shrieks of pain.

Endera pulled a long silver chain from her neck and looped it around Leo's wrist and then her own.

"What are you doing?" he asked. "Why are you helping me?"

The look that crossed her face would have frozen a lava flow. "I'm not helping you. I'm helping myself. Hold your breath," she added as she snapped her fingers. A cloud of black smoke engulfed them. Leo caught the whiff of rotting eggs, and then they were gone.

It happened in a blink. It felt cold and devoid of light, as if they were hurtling through space. Then they hit the ground. Hard. Endera landed on her feet easily, but Leo tumbled. The chain binding them snapped. He gasped for air as if he hadn't breathed for an hour.

"What . . . what just . . . happened?" he stammered, slowly sitting up. His elbows were bleeding, scraped from the porous black rock they stood on. A large, familiar shape rose behind them, and a trickling sense of dread took seed. "We're on Pantros," he said. So that was it. He was headed into the underworld.

"What do you think the Draupnir does?" Endera said, grabbing his elbow and yanking him to his feet.

"Brings someone back from the underworld."

If she was surprised by his knowledge, she didn't say anything. She passed her hand over the chain wrapped around Leo's wrist. It glowed red, singeing his skin before it snapped to connect with hers, reforming the link. She started walking, jerking him along.

"Stop."

Leo dug his feet in and jerked back on the chain, forcing her to turn around. He ignored the flash of rage that turned her eyes to daggers.

"I'm not taking another step until you tell me what you're doing."

The nail on her index finger extended into a sharp point. She tilted his chin up. "I could kill you this second and leave your body for the vultures to pick over."

"Then do it," Leo breathed. "Get it over with already."

When Endera didn't immediately act, hope spurred his voice. "You need me alive for some reason. You could take the cuff off my arm, but you haven't, so just tell me what you want, and maybe we can help each other. You tried to kill one of the Volgrim witches you worked so hard to bring back. Why?"

She glared at him, eyes glimmering with a rage that threatened to snap at any second.

"I am the leader of our coven!" she snarled. "I didn't bring back those hags so Catriona could take it from me." She drove the nail of her finger deeper into his throat.

Leo held himself still. She was a hair's breadth away from cutting his throat. Something had changed her from the Endera Tarkana they had faced before. That witch had been unflappable.

"That doesn't explain why you want the cuff."

A flicker of pain made the heartless witch look suddenly vulnerable. "Your friend, Sam, tried to kill Agathea with the Gungnir spear, but Agathea sacrificed my daughter Perrin to save her own life. The Draupnir can get her out."

Leo hid his shock. Endera hardly struck him as the motherly type. "And what do I get in return for helping you?"

A slow smile spread over Endera's face, one of cunning and pure malice. "My promise that when I get back to Skara Brae, I will do to Catriona what I did to Ariane."

"Your Shun Kara let Ariane get away."

Endera laughed. "No. They infected her with a special poison I coated their teeth with. It will cause her unimaginable pain, and then she will die." She retracted her nail and gave Leo a shove. After that, they hiked in silence.

For the first time since they had arrived in Orkney, fear slithered into Leo's belly, chilling him, even though the baking sun made every step like walking in a furnace. Endera was unhinged and unpredictable. An Umatilla warrior did not let fear control him, but hiking up the steamy side of the volcano, Leo could sense his own doom with every fateful step.

Chapter Twenty-Nine

The cuff on Leo's arm glinted in the sun, the metal warm against his skin. Part of him wanted to rip it off and toss it into a deep crevasse, but that would be the coward's way out. And whatever he was, Leo was no coward. Still, it bothered him that Endera hadn't just taken it from him. Why not claim the prize for herself? Unless she needed him along for some reason. A bad one, he had no doubt. He worried about Jey, knowing in his heart that the boy's survival was as unlikely as his own.

Endera never spoke, never broke her stride, just moved silently and swiftly up the side of the volcano, dragging Leo along. Too soon, the looming opening of the Nifelheim yawned ahead. Leo followed Endera into the dark breach, bracing himself for what was coming. The witch snapped her fingers, and a torch sprang to life. Leo tugged the light from its mount and carried it high, casting a comforting glow on their path.

As they descended, Leo heard the rustling of wings. He cast a quick glance upward, knowing what he would find.

Shreeks.

Hundreds of the oversized bats hung upside down from the ceiling, their leathery wings folded back around their bodies. These were different than the shreeks they encountered flying through the woods. These pitiful creatures had once been human, according to Mavery, but the underworld matron, Sinmara, possessed the deed to their souls, trapping them in this place. Red eyes glowed down at Leo. He looked away, casting his gaze downward, but he could feel their stares.

They entered the main chamber where Sinmara held court. Leo saw her immediately, a bloated figure on a throne of onyx. The walls had been carved from the same black stone. A large pool of molten lava bubbled around her, sending up fumes of toxic gas. Columns of hardened lava rose up like fingers sticking out of the ground.

Sinmara was just as enormous as Leo remembered, with gray flabby skin that reminded him of a whale. The ugly grape-sized mole Mavery had torn off was back in place on her nose, pulsing with whatever slimy creature lived inside it. Oily hair was piled up on top of her head, giving it the shape of a beehive. On her lap, her pet, a black puma, purred as she rubbed its ears with her one good hand. A basket of snails, her favorite snack, rested on top of the puma, crawling with the slimy creatures. Her right arm ended in a withered stump, a lasting memory of their last visit when Rego had lopped it off.

"Endera Tarkana," she crowed, obviously delighted to see an old friend. But when she caught sight of Leo, her face flushed purple. "You!" she spit out. "How dare you return here?" A surge of lava sprayed out of the pool at her feet and came toward Leo.

He ducked, but Endera blocked it with a pass of her hand.

"Sinmara, enough. The boy is my guest."

Sinmara's bloated chest rose and fell as she gripped the side of her throne. "This boy made me lose my precious hand." She waved her stump at them. "Let's see how he likes having his limbs removed one by one."

Endera snapped her fingers at the underworld hag. "Ignore the boy, Sinmara. Focus. We have much to discuss and negotiate."

Sinmara continued to glare at Leo, but then a harsh laugh rippled through her ample chest. A smile lit up her face as she popped a snail into her mouth and crunched the hard shell. A spray of goo spattered Endera's bodice.

"Let me guess. You're here to bargain for your daughter. What was her name again? Pippin? Porter?"

"Perrin, you hideous wretch," Endera hissed, her face tightening into a grim mask of rage as she wiped away the gray goo.

"That's right, Perrin," Sinmara smirked. "There's a price to be paid to enter into my nest of souls."

"I have my own invite. I bring the Draupnir," Endera pronounced smugly.

There was a long moment of silence. Sinmara's mole pulsed wildly as she fought to keep her calm. "The Draupnir is guarded by a vicious beast—" Her eyes went to Leo and widened with sudden excitement as he turned his shoulder and showed her the golden cuff on his arm.

Lava rose in a dancing circle around him, lifted, it seemed, by the power of the cuff. As the heat rose, light reflected off the golden band.

Sinmara surged up, spilling the basket of snails and sending the puma flying. The creature yowled in protest and then stalked off. Sinmara was still bound by her thick chains, but she strained to the end of them.

"Ooh, isn't it a lovely thing?" Sinmara cooed. "I haven't seen it in centuries." She stretched her fat fingers out to him.

Endera slapped her hand away. "Hands off. I possess the cuff. That's all I need to enter the underworld."

Sinmara sniffed and returned to her throne, settling her girth onto the dais. The puma slunk back to climb onto her ample lap. "The black dwarfs crafted the cuff so Odin could go into the underworld and rescue his precious son Baldur and send him home," she sniped. "But not even Odin was immune to the rules. What goes in, comes out. Two of you go in, two of you go out."

Endera didn't look surprised. "I know," she said as calmly as if she was announcing the day's weather. "The boy will stay."

By the boy, she meant Leo. And by stay, she meant remain in the underworld. Which would pretty much mean Leo was dead.

The Sacrifice.

But not a willing one. He backed away from Endera the length of his chain. "I thought we had a deal. If I helped you, in exchange, when we got back to Skara Brae, you would take care of Catriona."

Endera gave a tiny shrug. "And I will. I didn't say you would be joining me."

At her words, Sinmara laughed, her throat jiggling with fat. "Then I will have my revenge," she gloated, stroking her puma with her good hand. The mole on her face had moved to her neck. It pulsated as she kept laughing.

"Sinmara, there's the matter of the door," Endera drawled.

The grotesque goddess wiped the tears from her eyes. "Of course. There are a few rules to go over. You can bring the child back as long as she's not too far gone. But first you have to find her."

"I'll find her," Endera said.

"Then proceed, the way is yours." She waved a hand carelessly. Behind Sinmara, a flaming hole appeared in the wall.

Endera walked toward the flames, dragging Leo along. He dug his feet in, but it was like trying to stop a freight train. All he got for his efforts were skinned knees and bruised shins from bouncing over the rough terrain. Endera relentlessly hauled him forward through the flaming entrance. His last hopes of escape died as the wall sealed shut behind them, trapping them inside.

Leo lay facedown on the cold, muddy floor, trying to slow his heart down. Was this it? Was his fate sealed like the solid wall that blocked his way out?

Jey's arrogant hawk-nosed face floated into his mind, bragging he was going to steal Keely away from him.

Jey would never give up like this. Jey would get to his feet and find a way out. Leo pushed himself up.

Endera ran her hand over the chain binding Leo, dissolving

it. No reason to tie him to her when there was no place to go. He rubbed his wrists. It had been hot in Sinmara's chambers, but in here it was cold and still, utterly silent.

"Move," Endera ordered, and she began striding away. Leo hesitated, turning his head in the other direction to see if there was an escape, but there was only darkness, and an eerie sense that eyes were watching him. He had no choice but to follow Endera.

Murky light made it possible to see their surroundings. The walls were made of a foul sludge that squirmed with subtle movements. Leo made out misshapen faces, mouths opened wide in agony as they passed. Grotesque hands covered in withered gray flesh reached out from the walls, grasping at Leo's arm.

Reaching for the cuff.

Whenever a hand would touch the golden band, a shock zinged to his heart, as if he had been stabbed with an icicle. Leo learned to pull away before they touched him. It was like they could sense the power of the Draupnir.

Leo focused on thinking of a way out of this mess, but so far his brain had come up with nothing useful. Every so often smaller dark tunnels led off to the side. Each time, Endera paused, considering, as if she were listening for something, and then she would continue on.

"She's not in there," she would announce. "Keep moving."

They continued on like this for an hour, stopping, listening, and searching. It was hard to breathe the musty moldering air. Escape seemed less and less likely the further they descended. After another slimy hand reached for him, Leo wearily asked, "If these creatures are dead, how is it they seem alive?"

Endera's words came slowly, as if she herself were feeling the effects of the underworld. "Death in our world . . . is a matter of stages. Creatures with powerful magic . . . they linger, clinging to this life as their magic drains away. Until the last drop is gone . . . they can be brought back." Her back straightened, and her pace picked up as if she realized what she had said. "Hurry up, we don't have a moment to waste."

Leo wanted to argue that he had no reason to hurry to his own death, but he couldn't stand the idea of being left alone in this earthen mausoleum, and so he followed her.

After an endless descent, they came around a bend into a large cavern. An enormous pool of water occupied the center bordered by a raised stone ledge. A triangle of crystals embedded in the ceiling glowed with a yellowish light.

"Here," Endera announced.

The water was cast in a yellowish glow. Under the surface, dark figures swam by, drifting in an eternal current. When the underground figures saw Leo and Endera, they wailed, silent mouths open. Leo stood transfixed, looking at the faces. They were begging to get out, pounding their hands against the invisible barrier as if it were a solid wall before being tugged away by the relentless current.

"How will you find her?" Leo asked.

"I have a piece of her I keep close. I am hoping it will help draw her to the surface." She lifted a heavy silver locket from around her neck that had been hidden by her dress. Opening it, she withdrew a tiny lock of hair and rubbed it between her fingers, dropping the fine strands on the water. She drew her hands in a circle over the surface.

Leo watched as a gray mist rose up, churning the water. Endera murmured strange words. Electricity crackled, making the hair on Leo's head stand up. Nothing happened. Endera stood poised. Minutes passed. He shifted on his feet, wondering what Endera would do if they didn't find Perrin. Would she lead him back to the surface? Or leave him here?

Then, like the strike of a rattlesnake, her hand went in and she grabbed one of the swimmers.

A dark wet head appeared above the water. Endera pulled, but the head didn't rise more than a few inches before sinking down again, as if being dragged back by a strong current. Here was his chance. Endera leaned precariously over the edge. One shove and she would be in the pool with the swirling dead. Leo raised his hand, taking a step forward, but Endera turned, her face a raw mask of pain. "Help me," she pleaded.

Leo teetered. Endera looked human, almost vulnerable. The object of her efforts, a dark-haired girl, screamed, her eyes wild and unfocused. This must be her daughter, Perrin.

Endera strained to pull the girl out, but she couldn't manage more than an inch or two before Perrin was tugged back down. Endera's shoulders hunched in defeat. "Please, I can't do it alone."

It was the last thing Leo wanted to do, but the girl looked so pitiful, he couldn't say no. Leo reached in and tugged on Perrin, getting one hand under her arm. He ignored the swarm of hands that grabbed at him, pulling him in.

Using his feet as leverage, he pulled upward until the girl's shoulders rose above the water. With one last tug, Perrin broke free, landing on the stone with a squelching burp.

The pale-skinned girl lay curled up on the ground, skin tinged blue. Her black garb clung to her. She was shivering and crying all at once. Endera covered Perrin with her cloak, and then the witch cradled the girl tightly in her arms.

"Mother, what are you doing here?" she said, dazedly looking around. "I was somewhere else. Where is this place?"

"Hush, Perrin. Everything's okay now." Endera's voice was husky with emotion.

But Perrin's eyes darkened. "No, it's not. Where are we? Mother, are we dead?"

"We are in the underworld," Endera said, tucking the girl's hair gently behind her ears. "But we are not dead."

"But I was dead," Perrin whispered.

Endera shook her head. "The Gungnir could not take your life. Not fully. You were not the intended target. So put it out of your mind. We leave now." She helped the girl upright. Perrin was shaky, but she kept her feet under her.

Leo looked back at the faces in the pool. They were enraged because one of their own had escaped. They pounded on the surface with angry fists. *What now?* he wondered. How were they going to get out of there, the three of them, when the cuff would only allow two?

Endera put her hand on Leo's shoulder.

"Thank you," she said softly. "Thank you for helping me get my daughter back."

It felt good. Saving the girl. Perrin must have been important for Odin to send Leo here. He had a moment's hope it was all going to work out. That being the Sacrifice didn't mean he had to endure a terrible fate. Maybe Endera had a scrap of humanity in her. A clever way to beat the rules that bound the cuff.

But he quickly found out that Endera was the same evil witch she had always been.

"Tragic, isn't it?" Endera said as they watched the faces plead for mercy.

Leo nodded.

"Pity you must join them."

The witch pushed Leo hard, sending him sprawling. His knees hit the edge of the pool. He flailed his arms, trying to stop his fall. With her other hand, she sent a blast of green fire at the Draupnir. The cuff glowed red hot, searing his skin before loosening its grip on Leo's bicep. She grabbed it with both hands, sliding it down his arm as Leo lost the battle for balance and fell forward into the pool.

Chapter Thirty

The Balfin ship was sleek and fast. In two days, Sam and his monstrous crew of Balfins had circled the seas around Garamond, but they weren't any closer to finding their destination: Odin's secret lair. Frustration made him want to tear a hole in the sky. They were wasting time. Every moment of delay was a moment Keely and the others were still in danger. Standing in the bow of the ship, Sam held the ancient navigation device up to the sun, cursing its lack of movement.

"Useless!" he said, throwing it against the gunwales. How had he made it work before? His mind was blank. Where was Mavery when he needed her?

The heavy armor he wore chafed at his joints. Catriona had outfitted him with the uniform of the Black Guard. Wearing the armor felt like its own betrayal. His heavy leather chest plate was adorned with silver fittings. The boots he wore were tall and well-made. Armguards laced around his forearms, embellished with sharp metal studs. Part of him wanted to rip it all off and toss it into the sea, but another part secretly enjoyed the power he wielded.

The brutish captain, steering steadily into the wind, grunted in surprise as the compass bounced off the wood and rolled back across the deck to stop at his boots.

"Give up?" he growled hopefully.

"No!" Sam shouted, seething with frustration that he, the most powerful he-witch alive, couldn't even break the small bronze-and-glass object. Furious, he snatched up the hateful thing and hurled it overboard as far as he could.

The compass swung in an arc, spinning wildly, and then boomeranged right back at him, bouncing onto the deck of the ship. Sam picked it up, looking hopefully over its weathered face. The needle lay motionless. Despair swamped him. Would he fail at finding Odin? Fail at saving his friends? Was all of this for nothing?

A sudden wind blew across the prow, sweeping across the sea and gathering a cloud of mist that hovered, green and opaque over the ship. Catriona's face appeared. "You waver," she screeched, her lips curled in contempt. "Use your magic. The dark magic I gifted you with. Break Odin's grip over the compass, or I will kill your friends myself!" The cloud burst into a spray of water that stung Sam's cheeks.

Sam straightened. He didn't want to tap into the magic Catriona had unlocked. It was too potent. Too addictive. It burned in his veins. He was afraid that if he let himself use it, he would enjoy it too much. He wouldn't be able to stop. *He would truly become Kalifus.*

He stared at the lifeless compass. He would have to risk it.

Holding the brass object up, he passed his hand over it, opening himself up to the new language that carried across the seas to his ear. Unfamiliar words that fueled him with a swell of power.

"Mordera saxus, mordera locus."

For several moments, the sea seemed to go quiet. The crew stopped their various duties, muttering nervously in their crude language. Suddenly, a blinding green flash of light enshrouded the compass, raising it off Sam's palm and turning it into a glowing orb. The Balfins watched in awe as the compass spun in a circle. The green glow intensified, and the compass spun faster.

Sam kept up the chant, repeating the four magical words like a litany, feeling a surge in power from within. Catriona's ritual had ignited the dark magic in him, and the stuff was potent. He could feel it changing him further, like a dial being ratcheted up three notches. The venom in him merged with the elemental magic that poured out into his chant, increasing its power.

The green energy extended from the compass to his hand and up his arm, through his armor, spreading into his chest. As the power surged through him, he shouted in exhilaration and threw the device into the air. At its peak, brilliant green light exploded in every direction like a fireworks display. The crew ducked as a shower of sparks fell on the deck. The compass landed with a thud, smoking and glowing.

Sam strode over and cautiously lifted it. The orb was surprisingly cool to the touch. Confidence surged in him as he studied it. The needle had finally changed direction. It now pointed at the symbol of an upside-down pitchfork, the symbol of Asgard.

"Captain!" Sam shouted with a grin, "We have our course."

The Balfins erupted in cheers, hooting and hollering in triumph. But within hours of their new heading, the seas grew heavy, slopping over the sides of the ship. As the wind howled, the crew dropped a sail to keep from turning over. Rain lashed the boat. It was as if Odin sensed he was coming and was driving him away.

Sam would not be deterred. Not by a little weather. While the crew huddled cowardly below, Sam stood in the bow, relishing the harsh ocean spray on his face. Time and again, Asgard changed locations, and each time, the compass vibrated in his hand and he shouted new directions to the captain.

The elements continued to worsen. Jagged lightning lit up the sky, striking within meters of the boat, lighting up the water. Once Sam thought he saw the shadowy outlines of an island, but then it vanished. They were getting closer, he told himself, clutching the compass tighter. His eyes never left the needle as he focused all his energy on hunting Odin down.

And then with a sudden shift, the seas calmed. The clouds parted, revealing a bright sun as if the storm had never been. Asgard rose from the sea, sparkling in the daylight. Sam recognized the outline of the island immediately. Checking to see his blade was in place on his hip, he climbed into a dinghy. As the crew rowed him to shore, nervous excitement bubbled in his veins.

He was back on Asgard. What would Odin do when Sam stood before him, armed with the ancient magic of his ancestors? Would he recognize the change in him? Sam was no longer that weak, scared little boy Odin had given his Fury to. He had tremendous power running through his veins. Odin would have to hear him out. He would make the god listen.

Sam jumped out in a foot of water before they had even beached the boat, and he stalked up the sand toward the dense fog bank, shouting at the captain to wait for him over his shoulder.

The captain's garbled voice stopped him at the edge of the jungle.

"How long?" he grunted.

Sam turned slowly. "Until I return," he said icily.

The captain looked uneasy, as if the place scared the pants off him. "And if . . . no return?"

There was no thought to his action. Power lurched in his veins. Sam strode the four steps to the boat, splashing angrily through the water to grab the captain by his ugly throat. "I. Will. Return. Do you hear me?" His voice spoke of the terrible things he would do to the captain if he did not obey. *Whose voice was that?* he wondered vaguely, as the captain nodded rapidly, his inhuman face suddenly frightened. *Mine or Kalifus's?*

Without another word, Sam left the crew and entered through the fog into Odin's realm.

He took in a deep breath and realized how much lighter he felt. The familiar jungle foliage tempted him to lower his guard with its lush plants, exploding with color. Purple flowers on stalks as tall as he. Orange and pink blossoms the size of basketballs. A songbird jumped on a low branch and sang a trilling melody, but Sam recognized its poisonous feathers. Last time it had embedded painful hooks in his skin. He sent a satisfying blast of witchfire at it, incinerating it on the spot.

He headed for the Yggdrasil tree. This time it was not hidden from him. Its bristling green branches towered from a distance. Jumping over logs and crossing streams, Sam kept at a relentless pace.

When he finally reached the base of the trunk, Sam came face-to-face with the giant snake that guarded the sacred tree. The reptile's fat coils wrapped several times around the trunk, yellow and red scales gleaming under the sun.

"You little thief," it hissed, raising its head to dart its tongue at the human who had stolen the Horn of Gjall. "You dare to return to this*sss* place?"

Sam had no time to argue with a snake, even if it was Odin's guardian. "I dare because I am a Son of Odin and I need to see him. Let me pass, or I'll show you a taste of my new power." He held out his hands, palms up, and two green flaming orbs appeared over them. "One for each eye."

The snake continued to glare at him, its tongue slithering in and out before it answered. "Odin *sss*said you would come. He awaits you."

Sam felt a stab of surprise. How did Odin know he was coming?

"Then get out of my way," he snapped, closing his palms. He stepped arrogantly up the snake's coils and lifted himself into the tree, climbing rapidly. Halfway up, sweating from the weight of his armor, Sam stopped to catch his breath. He caught sight of a pair of golden eyes glowing at him from a hollowed knothole in the tree. He leaned forward, searching the dark.

"Ratatosk?" he called, feeling a slice of fond memory. The squirrel had been a welcoming friend last time he had visited.

The golden eyes blinked at him, but there was no answer. Like the creature had somehow judged his character and found him wanting. Anger rippled through him.

Stupid squirrel.

Like Sam had ever had a choice since the day he had discovered his ordinary life back in Pilot Rock was one big fat lie. His destiny had been drawn out before he was born. Sam moved on, continuing his climb. The tree's leaves felt different this time—brittle, as if the branches were sickly.

Near the top, he could see the eagle sitting on the highest branch, sunning itself in the golden rays. He paused on the same branch he had stood on when Odin had given him his Fury. How long ago that seemed now.

"Odin," he called. "It's me, Sam Baron." He almost choked on his name. He repeated it again, to ensure Odin heard him. "Come on, Odin, Sam Baron. 'Member me? Robert Barconian's son? I really need to speak to you."

The eagle turned its gaze down at him for one long moment. Its topaz blue eyes blinked one time, and then the bird returned its attention to the sun.

Stunned at his dismissal, Sam shook the branch hard. "Odin, knock it off! Stop playing this stupid game. Did you really send Keely to the Vanir? You know she won't survive. And Leo, he's going to die in that underworld thanks to you."

Still, the god-bird acted as if Sam were invisible.

Sam climbed higher, determined to get Odin's attention. As he neared the top, he balanced carefully on a slender limb. "Look, just talk to me. Why would you put Howie in charge of Skara Brae? He can't even stand up for himself, let alone an entire city. The witches will destroy him. It's like you want my friends to fail."

The bird shook out its feathers but didn't transform back into the god Sam so desperately needed to talk to.

Infuriated, Sam stretched, reaching for the eagle's scaly legs. "You will talk to me!" he shouted. As his hands touched the pebbled skin, the branch gave way, snapping with a loud crack and sending him tumbling through the tree, bouncing from limb to limb.

Branches shattered as he landed on them, bruising his ribs, knocking the wind out of him. If not for his armor, he would have broken several bones. He hit the ground with a thud and went out like a light.

When he came to, Sam was engulfed by darkness. Groaning, he hauled his battered body upright. If Odin thought he was going to play his miserable mind games again, he was mistaken. "Odin!" he shouted as he stood up. "I demand to see you."

Silence. A fine tremor ran through Sam. He hated the darkness. He had spent enough of his life as a prisoner in Catriona's cell. Did Odin know that? Was he taking great satisfaction in using Sam's hatred of it now against him?

He drew his hands in a circle and cried out, "*Mordera luma*," calling a ball of light to his palm, illuminating his surroundings. He was in a cave. The ceiling had a familiar white lightning bolt etched into the rock. Sam remembered the rune stone the dwarf Rego had once given him.

Sigel, light of the sun.

Odin was taunting him. But Sam was determined not to be distracted. He threw his hands at the ceiling, wiping out the mark with a blast of energy, leaving a black smoke scar in its place.

Only one way led out of the chamber. A narrow opening that slanted downward. Sam strode toward it confidently. He picked his way over rocks, sliding down steep banks, descending farther and farther into this lightless hole Odin had cast him in. His armor was heavy, constricting his movements. He found himself cursing it time and again, even though it had surely saved him in his fall from the Yggdrasil tree.

He considered giving up, sitting down and waiting out Odin, but every second that ticked past was dangerous for his friends. After several long hours, he wondered if there was an escape. What if Odin knew why Sam had come and sent him here to wander in eternity? To die of madness? If that was the case, then why did he let Sam climb the tree just to be ignored by the eagle? No, Odin clearly had a plan.

He has plans within plans, Sam reasoned. *And he must know I'm here to demand answers.*

As he kept walking, drops of brackish water fell, hitting his head, rolling down his back. Each one felt like it was personally sent to annoy him. He grew angrier as the corridor got shorter, and dripping water continued unabated. Soon he was crouching down, his armor scraping the ceiling as he crawled on hands and knees to find an exit.

Frustration simmered in every fiber of his body. He would like nothing more than to blow the entire mountain of rock around him to pieces. What would it take to be released? What did Odin want from him before he would grant Sam an audience? He pushed on, more determined than ever to beat Odin at his game. As the tunnel narrowed to fit his body, his breathing grew labored, as if the oxygen was being squeezed out. The light that he carried dimmed, growing smaller until it extinguished with a gasp. Or maybe it was he who gasped at the impenetrable darkness.

The walls pressed in on every side. It was like being in the belly of Odin's snake, suffocating and narrow. Sam pulled himself forward, sliding along the cold slimy floor, gritting out each inch that he made until at last he came to solid wall. He scrabbled with his hands, searching for an exit.

The tunnel was a dead end.

He collapsed, resting his head on the unfeeling stone. Drip after drip hit his head, but he didn't care. This was it. He had failed in his mission. He was too tired to go back the way he had come. His breath came in gasps, sucking in the few molecules of oxygen left. Odin had sent him to his death. He could hear Catriona's drumming disappointment in him, her doubts in his powers clawing at his skin like sharpened nails, and he couldn't stand it. Raising his head, he put his hand before him, shouting out one last time, "*Mordera tentera.*"

A flash of purple-tinged witchfire stronger than he expected hit the stone wall, shattering it in a spray of gravel. Sam tumbled through an opening onto hard stone. Picking himself up, he dragged in a deep breath, grateful for the fresh supply of oxygen. Calling up his light, he held up his hand. The light cast long shadows.

The cavern looked strangely familiar. Looking up, Sam saw the scar in the ceiling where he had blasted the rune symbol countless hours ago. He howled in rage. He was back where he had started.

Sam was scraped, cut, and bruised, and he had gone nowhere. He wanted to pummel his head against the stone. He wanted to plunge that evil dagger in Odin's miserable heart and get it over with. Then he noticed something he had missed before: a glint from a black pool of water occupying one corner.

He knelt by the water, staring at the reflection. He half-hoped to see Vor's shining face appear, waiting to give him wisdom, but instead, a greenish glow swirled in the center, and then Catriona's withered face appeared.

She snarled at him, drawing one lip up over her teeth. "You waste time in this hole."

Sam gritted his jaw with disappointment, missing Vor. He kneeled down, gripping the sides of the pool. "I'm trapped here, I can't get out," he said.

Fire flashed in her eyes. "Odin plays tricks with your mind, Kalifus! I thought you were better than that."

"I am. I tried—" Dejection flooded him. He had walked hours and hours and gotten nowhere.

Catriona reached a hand through the water, bony fingers coming through the surface to grasp him by the nape. "Hear me, Kalifus. You have trapped yourself." Her cold rubbery skin felt real. "Use your dark magic. That is the key to unlocking your predicament. Wish yourself anywhere but here."

"I . . . it can't be that simple." He closed his eyes to stem the haze of rage that clouded his thinking. Clenching his fists, he dug his nails into his palms until they stung. "I wish I were on top of the Empire State Building," he shouted.

Chapter Thirty-One

Sam chose the most remote place he could imagine just to show Catriona this trick was useless. Opening his eyes, he gasped, his heart knocking against his ribs. He stood on the parapet of a building, a hundred stories above city streets. His arms pinwheeled as he tried to keep his balance, but too late. Sam plummeted.

This can't be real, he assured himself.

But the air rushed past him. The sounds of car horns and sirens and jackhammers assaulted his ears. Somehow, he was in New York City, and he had just fallen off the top of the Empire State Building.

As the sidewalk came rushing up to meet him, he shut his eyes and imagined that he was back in Pilot Rock atop the majestic red boulder. After a moment, when there was no impact with the ground, he opened his eyes. Amazingly, he found himself lying faceup on the famous rock, the sun warming his skin.

I can go anywhere, he realized.

Sam had no idea if this was the real Pilot Rock or just another mental projection, but that didn't stop a wave of longing from washing over him. What would it be like to be home? He stood and looked down at the city below.

He spotted the school, then the library where he had seen the Shun Kara wolves. And if he looked hard enough, he could even make out his house. His mom was probably there, sleeping away the day, getting ready for her night shift. Queasiness made him sway. He shouldn't be here.

This is not my home anymore. Sam belongs here, not Kalifus.

He was becoming Kalifus, he realized. With every use of his dark magic, Sam receded and Kalifus rose up inside him. He closed his eyes and imagined the Tarkana Hall where Catriona had given him his mission. But this time when he opened them, he was back in Asgard. He recognized the green field where he had once chased after his mother, before the Omera had snatched her away. The breeze blew across the flowers, bringing the scent of pollen. Had he wished to come here, or had Odin tricked him again? He couldn't be sure because suddenly, he wanted, needed to see his mother.

Sam listened hard. Maybe she was here. Maybe she had come back for him.

Foolish hope made his blood sing. Without thinking, he started running through the fields. "Mom, are you here?" He didn't care that the armor made him sweat and struggle. He found the willow tree where Abigail had once stood holding a purple insect. She had been here recently, he was sure of it. He could smell her perfume lingering.

Under the tree, a figure sat bent over a rock.

"Mom?" he called.

The figure turned. The wrinkled, gray face of Catriona peered at him, her green eyes glinting with pride. "I'm your mother now, boy," she cawed at him.

Sam jumped back, stumbling, dazed.

"Yes, Mother," he said, laboring to speak his mind. "I remember now." The words tasted like bitter paste, but he said them aloud, and the louder he spoke them, the more natural they felt to him. "I am Kalifus, your son."

"Who are you?" she repeated, circling him like a vulture.

"I am Kalifus," he affirmed, spinning to keep up with her, feeling dizzy.

"Whom do you serve?" she asked, poking at him with a sharp fingernail that sent a jolt to his toes.

"I serve you!" he shouted, feeling nauseous. He wanted to scream at her to stop, but he could not find the words.

"Why are you here?" she whispered.

That he remembered with ease. "I am here to kill Odin."

As he said the words, the world exploded around him in bright colors. The tree disappeared, and Catriona dissolved. In her place stood a giant beast. A bear, standing upright on two legs. It was cloaked in full armor, one eye patched, claws the size of daggers, and broad muscular shoulders. It growled a warning.

Sam backed away. He remembered a story Mavery had told of a giant bear on Asgard name Brunin. She had boasted it was two-stories tall and was Odin himself, but Keely had been uncertain. This bear stood just over seven feet. Could it be the same one?

The bear gave a mighty roar that fluttered the leaves in the tree.

"Odin? Is that you?" Sam stumbled over a rock but kept on his feet. He had been prepared to face Odin as an old man, not this giant mass of sinew and fur. The bear crouched low, as if it was about to pounce on him.

Besides the armor he wore, Sam had only a single weapon: the obsidian knife Catriona had claimed was cursed with dark magic. He drew it out, clutching it with a sweaty palm. It seemed pitifully small compared to this beast. Was this another of Odin's games?

"Tell me your name!" Sam shouted. When the creature roared again, he could make out one word:

"Brunin!"

Then it sprang at him, claws extended.

Sam defended himself, stabbing at it with his blade as he dropped back and rolled, but the bear was too quick for him, and he missed. It ripped his shoulder armor to bits as it passed over. Springing to his feet, Sam winced at the stinging scrape of its claws.

The pain shocked him. This was no game.

This was real.

Brunin roared again, shaking its shaggy head and leaping on Sam, pinning him back against a tree trunk with one massive paw. The claws pressed painfully into Sam's armor. Brunin roared in Sam's face, baring long canine fangs. Sam stared into the bear's fearsome eye, the one uncovered by the eye-patch, and recognition hit. The knife slipped from his hands, falling to the ground.

Odin and Brunin were one.

Before he could stop himself, he blurted out, "You let my father die."

The bear's single eye narrowed. Its heavy armor went up and down on its chest as it breathed heavily from exertion.

"You could have saved him, but you let him die," Sam said. Tears clogged his throat. "You could have given me the power, but you didn't care." He ripped the pouch that held Odin's ground-up stone from his neck and threw it on the ground at the bear's feet. "It's your fault he's dead! And now, you're sending my friends to their deaths. I hate you! Do you hear me? I hate you!"

Brunin's head hung for just a second, as if the weight of Sam's words were heavy. He released the boy, setting him on his feet. Then a dazzling golden glow formed around the bear and it shifted form, shrinking in size, losing fur and claws until a man appeared before Sam. He wore a crown of green leaves around his head and a white toga. His eyes were a blazing blue topaz.

"Hello, Sam."

At his words, Sam's anger evaporated and a weight lifted, like a fog clearing. Thoughts of Kalifus and Catriona and dark magic fled his mind.

"Odin!" Sam couldn't stop himself. He ran forward and threw his arms around the god, feeling sobs deep in his chest. "I'm sorry. I didn't mean it."

Odin's arms came around Sam, holding him upright. "No,

you are right," the god said wearily. "I could have saved him. But it was not meant to be."

He released Sam and beckoned him to sit down on the grass. Odin took a seat on a rock.

Sam stared up at the god. "What does that mean?"

"Some things are meant to happen as they do. I don't expect you to understand. But know that I am sorry."

Sam took in his words. "And Keely and the others?"

The god was silent, his eyes staring into the distance.

"Odin?"

The god turned his head toward Sam, his eyes suddenly cool. "You came here for a reason, Sam. You have set in motion a course of action which cannot be undone."

Dread gripped him. "What are you saying?"

"If you had stayed true to yourself, things would have been as they were, but instead you followed the witches' bidding." Odin's words were accusing, like Sam had somehow failed him.

"I did what I did so I could warn you," Sam said hotly.

"Perhaps." Odin rose. "But now the witches believe you are one of them. You did not withstand the test. You failed."

Sam scrambled up. "Failed? I did everything right! I refused to follow Catriona, no matter what trick she fed me into believing my friends were against me!"

"No!" The god bellowed so loudly the leaves on the tree overhead shook. "You surrendered to her the moment that witch showed you a future you didn't like. You let her in with your doubts. Even now, she worms her way into your heart." He snatched up the pouch Sam had thrown at his feet and opened it, pouring the grains of sand out onto the ground. "You destroyed your father's stone—his gift to you—all to prove you were a loyal subject."

"No," Sam swore, even as he weighed the truth of Odin's words. Catriona was like a sliver under his skin, throbbing painfully on the edge of his consciousness. "I did it to see you. To ask for your help."

"You came here to kill me. To destroy everything I have

built." Odin was relentless, probing Sam with his fierce gaze. "You are not a Son of Odin. You were never a Son of Odin. You have always been one of them, a witch. Born with a dark heart. Admit it, Sam, you like being Kalifus."

"No, I don't," he said, defending himself. But his head swam. *Was it true? Did he?* "I swear, I came here to warn you." This was not going the way he had expected at all.

Odin pointed at the ground to the weapon Sam had dropped. "Then why do you wield her enchanted blade when you know it was cursed by Rubicus before he died with an ancient magic that even I can't stop?"

Sam knelt down and picked up the dagger, hands shaking as he studied it as if it were for the first time. The symbols seemed alien to him now. "Because . . . she insisted . . . it was . . . to get her to believe me . . . that I was Kalifus," he whispered.

"Liar!" Odin roared, his eyes blazing blue fire. "You came here to destroy me." Odin began to glow with that golden aura as he transformed back into the bear. "But it is you who will be destroyed."

Sam backed away. "Odin, please, why are you doing this?"

Brunin roared at him. "Because you betrayed me!" He pawed the ground with one taloned paw, like a linebacker ready to tackle. Then Brunin charged, jaws open, letting out a terrifying roar as he leaped at Sam, teeth glistening. Their two bodies smashed into each other in the center of the grassy clearing, an explosion of fur, muscles, and brawn. Brunin wrapped both arms around Sam, his massive jaws inches from Sam's head. Sam blocked his descent with one armored forearm under the bear's chin, but he couldn't hold Brunin off for long. The knife was in his hand. All he had to do was thrust upward before the bear ripped his head off. But he tried one last time.

"Odin, please, don't make me do this."

But Odin was gone. The bear roared its rage and lowered its head to attack, and that's when Sam stopped fighting the darkness inside him.

Maybe Odin was right about him, and maybe he wasn't. But Sam wasn't going to go out without a fight.

He thrust upward with the blade Catriona had given him and plunged it into the heart of the beast. As the knife penetrated the bear's flesh, bright light exploded from the wound, blinding Sam as the life force drained out of the creature. With a wrenching groan, Brunin toppled on its side with a thump so loud the ground shook. A gust of cold wind blew across the clearing, and the world around Sam seemed to ripple.

Sam's chest heaved up and down with exertion. What had just happened? *You killed Brunin, idiot, that's what happened*, his mind graciously supplied. Not just Brunin. Odin himself. A bubble of hysterical laughter passed through his lips.

Blood streamed from Sam's wounds, his armor hung in tatters, but the pain was distant, as if it was happening to someone else. Spots danced behind his eyes as he rose to his knees.

What should he do? His head reeled with the impact of his actions. But some part of him surged up with a ferocious inner voice. *Catriona would want proof*, it whispered. Sam grasped the still-warm fur and used the cursed blade to saw off the bear's left ear, and he tucked it into his pocket.

Then, he fainted.

He awoke some time later in a pool of sticky blood. When he lifted his head, pain lanced where Brunin's claws had marked him. He spied the familiar pouch of his father's. His fingers crept toward it and clutched the soft leather. Sitting up, he slipped it back around his neck and searched for the slain bear. There was no sign of it anywhere. He reached into his pocket and felt the small scrap of Brunin's furred ear. So it was real.

He knew with certainty that he had killed Odin, because everything around him was changing. Leaves fell from the trees. Flowers wilted. Bushes withered. Not a single animal sound could be heard in the forest.

Asgard was dying.

The once-green grass beneath him became dry and brittle,

turning to dust under his feet. He clutched a fistful of it and watched it crumble between his fingers. The spark of life that had kept Asgard alive was out, thanks to him. He waited to see if he would feel something. Guilt. Remorse. But nothing came.

He staggered to his feet and started walking.

With every step, crushing loneliness settled over him like a dark cloud. His friends would never understand what he had done in their name. They would despise him. The only person who would accept him now was Catriona. She and the coven. That's where he belonged. To slither among the worst of the worst.

Sam was dead.

Kalifus lived.

Long live Kalifus, he joked with the lowest gallows humor he could muster.

In the distance, he spotted the mighty Yggdrasil tree, only it was no longer green and lush. Black rot climbed up the trunk, spreading like a fungus, consuming the tree. A giant branch broke off near the top, tumbling to the ground.

As he passed under the sacred tree, another branch fell, just missing his head. Out of nowhere, a tail came out, whipping itself around his feet and knocking him flat.

"What have you done?" Odin's guardian hissed, its yellow eyes penetrating as it raised its head to strike at him. "Where isss Odin?"

Kalifus scrambled back up. "He's dead. Odin's dead." Surprisingly, he could say it without emotion. Kalifus was much stronger than Sam.

The snake's eyes flared with surprise and fear. "It can't be," it hissed. "No mortal has that power."

"I am no ordinary mortal," Kalifus boasted. "I descended from Odin, and I share a bloodline with Rubicus."

"Traitor. He trusssted you." The snake lunged at him, but Kalifus dodged to the side, sending a blast of witchfire at an overhead branch and bringing it down on the snake.

He had no wish to harm the creature, so he began jogging

toward the shore, but the snake's tail whipped out and wrapped around his ankles, dropping him to the ground. Before Kalifus could fight it off, he was rolled inside the long coils. The snake squeezed harder, crushing Kalifus's damaged armor and choking the breath out of him.

"Let me go!" Kalifus demanded, pushing at the coils.

"Ssson of Odin, you will die," it hissed at him.

Kalifus couldn't get his hands to his knife. He tried to conjure up a spell, but he had nothing. It was infuriating. After everything he had been through, now it appeared this stupid snake was going to kill him. He could feel the rage building inside him. Sam would probably talk his way out of this, but Sam was gone. Kalifus closed his eyes and let the Deathstalker venom flow freely, mixing with his magic, turning his body into an inferno.

"*Mordera, erasmus!*" he called, easily tapping into the dark magic Catriona had shown him. When he opened his eyes, yellow fire blazed forth.

He directed a torrent of furious energy at the snake's gaping mouth. The snake let out a painful shriek, and the coils loosened long enough for Kalifus to escape. He staggered away, leaving the giant snake writhing on the ground.

Behind him, the giant tree shuddered and then, with a loud crack, the trunk split down the middle, dividing the tree and sending half of it falling straight for Kalifus. He broke into run, stretching his legs to leap over branches as the once-mighty tree came down around him.

By the time he emerged through the rim of fog, bruised and breathless, the island was crumbling apart behind him—literally breaking into pieces. The forest trees toppled over one after another. Chunks of the island broke off like pieces of an iceberg.

"Go, go, go!" he shouted to the mutated Balfins as he jumped into the awaiting boat. His crew rowed as fast as their bulky arms would carry them while all around the boat, Asgard was sinking, sending two-story waves at them. One crashed over their rowboat, sweeping a hulking ape-man overboard. His heavy armor swiftly carried him under the surface. Kalifus clung to the gunwales as the crew rowed harder until they bumped into the side of the Balfin ship. Strong arms reached down and pulled Kalifus onto the deck.

With a grunt of impatience, he shook off his rescuers and turned to watch the last shard of land collapse in on itself in a roar of rushing water and then disappear from sight. Kalifus closed his eyes, exhausted.

Odin was dead.

Asgard destroyed.

The captain thumped Kalifus victoriously on the back. But as he opened his eyes, watching the crew erupt into raucous shouts and jeers, a feeling of triumph settled in his stomach. He had been an outright fool to think he could ever turn back from the intoxicating power of using dark magic.

I killed a god.

He raised his fists with the crew and joined in on their celebration.

Chapter Thirty-Two

Catriona stood on the shore of the small cove in the early morning light. Her gray hair was tousled by the wind. Around her a black-clad row of witches lined the banks. A breeze blew over the ocean, bringing with it a gloominess, like the winds were keening their sorrow.

"Do you really think he did it?" Agathea snipped, pacing back and forth along the beach.

"We will see, won't we?" Catriona replied for the umpteenth time. A raven had brought word of the ship's imminent return and the destruction of Asgard, but she would believe it when it came from the boy's own lips. Even though she *felt* it, in every bone in her body. The shift in atmosphere. The departure of hope.

The end of tyranny.

"There, see? The ship comes," Lemeria said, clapping her hands. A ship entered the small cove bearing the black sails of the Balfins. It unfurled its sails and dropped anchor.

Of all the Tarkana witches, Catriona thought Lemeria showed the most promise, and the least amount of loyalty to Endera. She rewarded the young witch with a pat on the shoulder. "Yes, but is the boy on board?" She studied the ship with sharp eyes, searching for his slight form.

There, in the prow of the ship. The wind blew his hair back from his face. He wasn't skulking. He looked defiant. Proud.

He had done it. She was certain. The thrill of victory made her pulse race. Odin was dead, that insufferable god. And all that he had done to tamp down on the power of her kind had been erased. *I have avenged you, Father*, she thought to herself. Rubicus would be pleased.

Soon Skara Brae would fall when her army marched on its walls.

All of Orkney would crumble when it did.

And then Catriona would break the bonds of magic that separated Orkney from earth, allowing her rule to spread and grow with no bounds.

A rowboat was lowered and swiftly carried her prodigy to shore.

The witch boy splashed through the shallows to where she waited for him. She was excited as a schoolgirl.

"Kalifus, my son." She grasped his shoulder. "I heard the words the raven spoke, but I dared not believe it until I heard it from you. Is it true? Is Odin really dead?" She probed him with her magic, searching for deceit, for any trace of lies.

Kalifus fell to one knee, his arm across his chest. "I killed him myself," he said, laying the ragged ear of Brunin at her feet.

A wild cheer went up from the witches.

Catriona picked up the scrap of flesh, rubbing it against her cheek, smelling its rotted scent like it was the sweetest perfume. "How? How did you do it?" Her eyes glistened with a lust for blood. There was not a trace of deceit about him. Wickedness fairly oozed from his pores. Even his eyes were different. Yellow tinged the whites, a side effect of all that glorious Deathstalker venom inflaming the dark magic that ran through him. This powerful weapon truly belonged to her.

The witches gathered around him, crowding in to hear his tale. Kalifus glowed under their attention, relating in detail how he had destroyed their oldest adversary. He described the giant bear, how it had battled with him, and how he had defeated it with Catriona's enchanted dagger.

"This belongs to you," Kalifus said, pulling the blade out to return to her.

Catriona folded his hands around it. "No. It is a gift. Keep it. You have done well, my son. You will ride next to me in a place of honor as we take over this world."

The ensemble of witches let out a shriek of approval.

Kalifus smiled. "Yes, my queen," he said with a short bow.

The air burst with a loud crack and the smell of sulfur. Black smoke coiled around a woman, who tumbled to the ground. Her long black hair fanned out. Blood marked the white sand where she lay.

Catriona dropped to her side. "Ariane. What has happened to you?"

Ariane's face was gray and etched with pain. She was dying, the light in her eyes fading. "I have been searching far and wide for you. I've been . . . poisoned," she gasped out.

"Who did this to you?" Catriona cried, giving her a shake.

But Ariane shuddered in the grips of death, her eyes fluttering closed.

Catriona shrieked in her face. "Who did this?" Then, grasping the back of Ariane's head, she cast a spell, using her other hand to pull back, drawing the last gasp of air out of Ariane's chest.

"Ennnnderrrra . . ." Ariane breathed the name of the traitor and then went limp.

Catriona dropped her back onto the sand. The entire coven appeared shocked by the name Ariane had uttered.

Agathea spoke first. "I knew she was trouble," the witch hissed. "We should have taken care of her long ago."

Catriona ignored her. Rage blazed in her eyes. "Endera is no doubt going into the underworld after her daughter. If she survives the journey, we will deal with her. For now, our plan continues. Our army is ready."

She turned and marched to the top of a small rise. Kalifus

and the others followed. Below in a shallow valley, an army of transformed Balfins awaited. The ground was black with their movements as they swarmed and organized their ranks. Vena rode on the back of a large stallion, commanding them with a long silver whip she snapped over their heads, shouting orders at them and keeping them under her control. General Degroot seconded her orders, his silver helmet shining as he rode on his huge black horse among the rank and file.

"Aren't they marvelous?" Catriona crowed, clapping her hands in excitement.

Vena rode over to join them. At her side the Balfin general rode on a beastly horse with armor embedded in its flesh. Another of the monstrosities lifted her down from the saddle, setting her gently on the ground.

"General Degroot has trained his army well," Vena said. "And dear Sigmund led the way." She patted the hulking behemoth like he was a pet Rottweiler.

The General grunted loudly, slapping his arm to his chest, and bowed his head.

Vena laughed. "The Orkadians will fall like paper dolls."

"What of Paulina?" Catriona demanded.

"As you ordered, Paulina took a battalion to attack the Orkadian Guard on their mission to make peace with you. I assure you, there will be no survivors."

Catriona cackled in vicious glee. "Then tomorrow we march on Skara Bare," she shouted, raising her fist to the sky. Green lightning shot out of her fingers. The other witches joined in until the sky was ablaze with crackling electricity.

The Balfin creatures beat the ground with their lances and heavy boots, grunting and hooting in a glorious cacophony of noise.

Catriona grinned delightedly as Kalifus raised his fist with the rest of the witches and sent green fire into the sky to join with theirs.

Chapter Thirty-Three

Days of hard riding and limited stops had pushed Howie and Captain Teren's finest to the point of exhaustion. A pair of broken axles and several heavy rainstorms had delayed their travels to the seaport where Catriona was promised to be waiting to discuss a treaty. The High Council leader, Lord Drabic, stuck to his carriage, drinking ever-increasing amounts of the endless supply of wine he had brought. He was attended by his two servants and hardly stepped outside except to head straight for the tent they set up for him nightly, a silken pagoda that included a feather mattress and thick carpet for his tender toes. The rest of them made do with bedrolls around the campfire.

To Howie, it was an adventure of the highest sort. Here he was actually on a diplomatic mission to help end a war. No more working the Chuggies counter after school and having kids laugh at his dorky uniform. No more Ronnie Polk shoving grape-jelly sandwiches in his face. He was a Chosen One. He almost began to believe that Catriona was really going to be waiting for them at the other end, ready to sign a treaty. And then Howie's job as Protector would be a grand success without even breaking a sweat.

Scattered clouds threatened more rain in the coming days. On their left, thick forest encroached all the way up to the road. The sun had begun its descent when something in the air made Howie sniff. It was the faint smell of smoke. Like a bonfire. He had a sudden craving for s'mores.

Teren raised his hand and halted the caravan. Heppner pulled out a scope and searched the sky. "There." He handed the glass to Teren. "See that smoke?"

Howie craned his neck. A thin black trail wound up into the sky. The road ahead twisted and turned. It was impossible to see what was causing it.

"Wait here," Teren said to his other men. "Heppner and I will scout ahead."

Howie ignored the order and tagged along because he was Teren's squire, and he had a funny feeling running up his spine that made him want to stick close to their fearless leader. As they came around the bend, the horses reared up at the sight of a bonfire in the middle of the road. Someone had piled tree stumps and set fire to them, sending shooting flames crackling and popping as the dry timber was consumed.

They dismounted to study the raging fire.

"What in Odin's name?" Heppner said.

"It's a trap," Teren answered.

Howie felt the backs of his hairs stand up, as if unseen eyes were watching them from the woods.

The sound of hooves thundered toward them. Howie turned and saw Lord Drabic's carriage running wildly down the road. The coachmen were nowhere to be seen. The carriage headed straight for the fire.

Teren jumped into the middle of the road in the way of the stampeding horses, waving his arms and shouting at them to stop. They came to a shuddering halt, tossing their heads in terror. Teren threw open the carriage door. "Lord Drabic, are you okay?"

The portly Drabic tumbled out onto the ground. A large sword protruded from his back. His servants had vanished.

Before anyone could speak, galloping horses sounded again on the road. Teren and Heppner drew their swords. Howie just gaped as Teren's men appeared, riding fast and hard, looking like they were fleeing from a nightmare. Behind them was a terrifying sight. A horde on horseback followed them. They carried the black banner of the Balfin army. Only they weren't ordinary men. These were the monster men Beo had warned about.

They looked like sneevil-faced ape-men. Howie could make out misshapen faces and tusks that stuck out of their fat lips. Thick hair covered their heads and arms. Clawed talons that could rip flesh from bone gripped the reins of the beasts they rode. In their hands, they clutched double-headed axes and deadly maces. Their horses had been changed into something from a horror movie: beasts with breastplates and metal armor built into their hides. Alongside them, a herd of sneevils snarled and nipped at the horses' heels as they raced after them.

Howie struggled not to pee his pants.

"By the heavens, what is that?" Teren whispered.

"An abomination," Heppner said. "Coming our way."

"Off the road!" Teren shouted, snapping back to his senses. He gave Howie a shove toward the safety of the trees. The remaining men followed behind, abandoning their steeds and scrambling through the thickets as fast as they could. Arrows zipped through the air. Snarling sneevils chased alongside them. Howie looked in sheer terror as one of the men was brought down, then ripped to pieces by the beasts. This was nothing like a video game. This was real. Too real. He kept pumping his legs, trying to keep Teren in sight. They jumped over rocks and slid down banks. Ahead, a dark opening in a small knoll of boulders indicated a cave.

Shouting at the men to follow, Teren grabbed Howie by the collar and pushed him inside. The surviving men poured in, only a handful. Heppner stood at the entrance. Only four others had made it. Howie trembled with uncontrollable fear. Teren sent the men to search for another exit.

"I expected a trap, but not so soon, and not like this, with beasts I can't even describe," Teren said, pacing. "When Beo said monster men, I thought . . . I don't know what I thought, that the sailors had been bewitched."

"What were those things?" Heppner asked.

"Balfins, most likely, by their banner. The witches transformed them into something evil."

"They're coming," Heppner said from the entrance. He raised his crossbow and sighted out into the woods.

"Any other way out?" Teren asked, seeking guidance from the soldiers that returned from their search. They shook their heads.

Outside the mouth of the cave, the clearing was still. Teren joined Heppner and peered out. Howie peeked out from between them. A lone sneevil ran across the open ground. Teren drew a bead on it with his crossbow and released the bolt, striking it clean in the heart. It fell over, but then three more advanced. The ape-men filtered through the trees. Up close, they were even more frightening. Their shoulders bulged with muscles. They knocked down trees with a swing of a mace. Teren shot at one of the monster men, hitting it in the chest. It yanked the bolt out like it was a nuisance and kept coming.

Heppner let loose with his crossbow, sending an iron bolt straight into the head of one of the Balfin mutations. The creature fell down and was quickly run over by the sneevils.

"I've only got two shots left," Heppner said, "and there's a whole lot more than that out there."

Between them, they had a pitiful amount of arrows, and each man his sword.

The swarm of creatures climbed over rocks and moved carefully forward, avoiding the open. It was only a matter of moments before they sent the sneevils in and overcame Teren's sorry resistance.

Howie turned away, unable to watch. They were going to die. There was no last-minute save. They didn't have the manpower to fight this army. Tears burned his eyes as he thought of his parents. They didn't always do a great job showing him how much they loved him, but deep down, he knew that they cared. And they would never know what happened to him.

Teren turned to face Howie and the small band of men. "I don't know about you lads, but I'm not about to die in this hole. I say we go out there, and we give it our best. We take as many of them with us as we can and die in battle knowing that we gave our life in the discharge of our duty."

There were mutters of agreement. None wanted to die, no less in this dark hole.

Teren raised his sword, and they raised theirs with his. "To Orkney," he said, his voice thick with emotion.

They joined in, rattling their swords and shouting loud enough to shake the stone.

Howie started to draw the rusted sword that hung at his side, but Teren stayed his hand. "No, lad. You don't leave this cave. Hide until it's over. That's an order, squire," he added as Howie opened his mouth to argue.

As one, the soldiers emptied out and charged at the creatures, leaving Howie behind. He hovered in the entrance, wanting to follow but too scared to move. He grimaced as Teren swung his sword, taking off the head of the first ape-man. Another loped toward the captain, and he pivoted around, stabbing it in the chest. Two more came at him. Howie watched in awe as Teren relentlessly parried and thrusted, fighting his way forward.

On Teren's right, Heppner took out a pair before throwing his crossbow aside and running at them with his sword. Two of Teren's men went down. These ape-men had a vicious overpowering strength.

As another creature came at Teren, he ran it through with so much force his blade embedded deep in a tree. As Teren yanked on it, another of the creatures snarled and loped toward him. Teren was defenseless. Heppner was busy fighting off his own attackers.

Howie swallowed the lump in his throat. He thought about

Ronnie Polk and being pushed around and forgotten his whole life. Teren had trusted him, had given him a shot. Before he knew what he was doing, Howie charged out of the cave and ran toward Teren, screaming at the top of his lungs like a raving lunatic. Odin's second-hand sword clanked against his leg. Might as well give the old thing a workout before he was dead.

Howie gripped it, then started to pull it out. But a strange thing happened. As he withdrew it, gold sparks shot out in every direction. Blazing light flickered from a razor-edged blade. The plain hasp was now crusted with jewels. In a blink, it changed from a rusted heap to a glowing golden sword, whole and without decay or rust. It shone in the fading afternoon light.

A single act of bravery can turn rust to gold.

Fetch's annoying riddle made sense now. But Howie didn't have time to admire it. He kept running, holding the sword over his head, and made a beeline for the monster. The creature flinched at the golden rays shining from Howie's sword. Howie kept yelling, ready to take its head off, but just as he brought the sword down, a flash of blue light arrowed through the trees, incinerating the creature to trickling ash. Howie slashed air.

Staggering, he held up his hand to block the blinding light. What the heck had that been? The blue light moved off, flashing and sending screams into the air.

"Come on, lads, we have them!" Teren called, digging his sword out and rallying his men. He flashed a grin at Howie. "I thought I told you to stay in the cave."

"I was never good at taking orders," Howie said, grinning back.

As they pushed forward, Teren and Heppner took out two more of the apes. One dropped out of a tree, nearly squashing Heppner. Without hesitation, Howie ran it through with his golden sword, watching it grunt in surprise before toppling over. The redhead flashed him an appreciative grin.

Quickly, the forest emptied, leaving only grotesque bodies littering the ground. Blue fire continued to flash through the trees. Teren headed for the light with Howie and Heppner on his heels.

A woman stood in the clearing cloaked in black. Before her, a witch hung in the air. A flare of blue lightning held her there. The cloaked figure murmured words. The witch began to spin and whirl around, sending a strong wind. Then she exploded into a spray of green light. The remaining beastly creatures ran off, screeching into the night.

Teren held his sword, ready to slay this latest adversary. Howie did the same, clutching his awesome golden sword. Heppner stood at his other side.

"Nice sword," Heppner muttered.

Howie just grinned. Odin had climbed to a whole new level of awesomeness in Howie's mind.

"Show yourself," Teren ordered.

The woman turned, her face cloaked in darkness. "You would kill the one who just saved your life?"

Howie froze. He recognized that voice. Teren must have, too, because his face went white with shock. "My lady," he whispered. "Can it really be you?"

She threw back her hood, revealing herself. "Yes, Captain Teren, it really is."

Teren dropped to one knee. "My Lady Abigail. You have returned to Orkney."

Sam's mom smiled at Teren. "Oh, I'm back, all right. Now where is my son?"

Chapter Thirty-Four

Keely followed Rifkin because she had no choice. She wouldn't survive the glacial temperatures of Rakim on her own. How did the frost giants live here? They had to be like polar bears. Snow seemed to fall constantly, leaving her numb and chilled to the bone. Her cloak had a fur-trimmed hood, but it felt like the tip of her nose had frozen off. Her fingers were permanent chunks of ice. She stuffed them in her armpits to keep warm, praying she didn't get frostbite. Her once-new boots had split along the seams, letting snow in. And forget about her toes—she had lost feeling in them days ago.

Rifkin plowed through the snow just ahead of her.

"How much fa-fa-farther?" she asked through chattering teeth. She was plagued with worry about Mavery and Galatin, fearing for their safety and hoping they didn't think she had abandoned them.

"Not long now," he said.

Annoyance flashed through her. "You said that before. I'm hungry." She hadn't eaten a full meal in days; her pants hung off her hips. Hunting had been impossible with the loss of her bow.

He stopped abruptly and turned to grab her by the collar of her jacket. "You think you're the only one that's cold and hungry?" His eyes were bloodshot and sunken. His beard hung in frozen clumps around his jowls. "Even if we caught something, we couldn't cook it, or the smell of a fire would bring the Vanir on our heads. Or is that what you want? To be captured by them so you can join your friends in their prison awaiting a sentence of death?"

Keely wasn't afraid of Rifkin, but she didn't want to antagonize him. He was still her only hope. "No, I want you to take me to the Cave of Shadows."

"Then stop your bellyaching. We're wasting time."

"How do you even know where we're going? Every tree looks the same."

"Find the star, we'll find the Cave of Shadows."

Keely's pulse gave a leap. This was the secret Rifkin had been keeping about the location. "What star?"

"You'll see."

After that, Keely didn't complain and didn't ask how much longer. The trail broadened at the bottom of the valley, and walking became easier. Keely allowed herself a glimmer of hope that they might actually make it. So far they had managed to steer clear of any frost giants by staying off the main trails and sticking to the trees.

Keely followed in the steps Rifkin made in the snow and put all her energy into forcing herself to keep moving. She was dreaming about Chuggies and Howie's sizzling tower of fries when she ran into Rifkin's back. He had stopped in the middle of the trail.

"What's wrong?" she asked, grateful for the rest.

"Nothing's wrong. Everything's right as rain. There it is. See, I told you ol' Rifkin knew the way."

Keely followed his finger, and a gasp escaped her. Rifkin hadn't been lying. There was a star shining low in the sky. It twinkled like a living thing, visible even in the grayish light of day.

"Is that—"

But Rifkin cut her off. "Shh," he said, listening. Then abruptly he shoved her headfirst into a deep snow bank and dove behind the tree. Keely was buried under the snow when it happened. Hooves thundered down the trail. Something sharp clipped her on the side of her knee, and she cried out in pain.

A horse whinnied in surprise, and the hooves stopped their thundering. A deep voice rumbled, calling out. Keely's knee was bleeding where the edge of the hoof had connected with it. She could no more run away than she could make herself invisible.

A hand reached into the snow and grabbed her shirt, yanking her out. She came face-to-face with a frost giant.

He was as surprised to see her as she was to see him. He towered over her, standing well above seven feet tall. His shoulders were as broad as a barn. Shaggy hair was tied back with a leather band. A fur pelt was belted at his waist, leaving his arms bare. In his hands he clutched a deadly looking club.

They stared at each other for a moment, and then he let out a piercing whistle. It was answered from another clearing not far away.

The Vanir said something to her she couldn't understand. His words were harsh. He shook her and repeated the question. Then he lifted her like she was a ragdoll, hanging her several feet off the ground. A shadow moved behind him, and then his hand went slack. She slipped through his fingers, sprawling in the snow. Blood sprayed the white surface as the giant keeled over, Rifkin's knife sticking out of his back.

Rifkin held out his hand to Keely. She took it without a word.

She put her arm over his shoulder, and they limped over to the Vanir's horse. It was even bigger than a Clydesdale, with a bushy hair around its hooves and neck. It shied away from them, but Rifkin whistled softly, stroking it on the nose. It snorted but let Rifkin hold its mane. There was no saddle. Rifkin lifted Keely up and sat her on top.

He led the horse over to a rock and climbed up behind her, giving the animal a hard kick. It took off like a rocket, streaking down the trail. Keely grabbed the mane with two fists. Rifkin wrapped his arms around her and gripped the mane as well, tugging the horse to the right, away from the main trail.

They broke into a wide snowfield that fell away from the forest. Rifkin kicked the horse, urging it through the deep snow. They didn't have much time. Even now the sound of whoops in the forest alerted them that the Vanir were after them.

Ahead, the outline of a knoll came into view. Not a hill, but a rounded mound of snow. It was directly under the shining star, which was now much higher than it had appeared from a distance. Keely could just make out an opening of sorts down an incline.

Three arrows hit the snow in front of them. The Vanirian's horse snorted, rearing up. Keely couldn't hold on. She tumbled off, taking Rifkin with her into the field. Behind them came a short blast of a horn. They had been spotted.

Rifkin grabbed her, tossed her over his shoulder, and ran for the entrance.

He broke through snow with each step, but he grimly muscled his way on. Then he stumbled and fell, dropping her. She brushed the slush out of her eyes and let out a scream. Rifkin had an arrow sticking out of his back.

"Come on," he said, reaching around to yank the shaft out. "Keep moving." He struggled to his feet, swaying, then grabbed her arm in a viselike grip and dragged her forward.

There were a half dozen Vanir chasing them on horseback. They let loose more arrows. The shafts plonked into the snow. Keely let out a yelp as one grazed her.

Still, they limped on. They were so close. Below them, the opening was clearly visible now, a slash in the side of the mound at the bottom of this hill. It glowed faintly blue with a hint of the ice that lined the interior walls.

Another arrow whizzed by Keely's ear. Rifkin gave her a push, and she slid down the remaining slope, hitting the bottom of the hill just outside the opening. Rifkin came crashing down next to her, knocking her forward into the cave.

She passed through a film of icy mist. Keely could feel the difference in air pressure. It was quiet in here. The sounds of the Vanir pursuit were muffled and distant. She waited for Rifkin, but he didn't join her. Turning around, she saw him just outside the entrance. He was screaming at her. His face contorted in angry motions. He pounded against some invisible barrier with his fist.

Keely stepped forward, to see what was the matter. Before she could reach him, Rifkin twisted and turned, convulsing.

The Vanir had arrived at the top of the hill and filled him with arrows. He fell to his knees and then dropped forward facedown.

Keely reeled in horror, pedaling backward three steps. The Vanir streamed down the hill. They kicked Rifkin's body, rolling him over, then stared directly at her. Keely stood five feet away from them, but it was as if they couldn't see her. Some how she had broken through the veil that sealed the entrance. So Rifkin had been right. She was part Eifalian now, thanks to Mimir's tricks.

The men dragged Rifkin's body up the hill. Keely stared at the red stain in the snow and sank shakily to her knees. Even though Rifkin had been a traitor, in the end, he had protected her in his own way. First by telling Catriona she was dead, and second, getting her here safely. So what if it had been to line his pockets with treasure. In her gut she wanted to believe ol' Rifkin would never have actually harmed her.

The cave radiated a chill that pierced her skin. The walls were blue frost, glimmering with a faint reflection of light. Icicles hung down like warning spikes, threatening to impale her head. Jagged outcrops of rock encased in ice loomed in every direction.

She forced herself to stand and put one leg in front of the other, favoring her sore knee. A shadow appeared on the wall. Her shadow. She held up a hand and waved. The shadow waved back, as if it had a life separate from her.

Keely remembered: she was in the Cave of Shadows. It must have taken control of her own silhouette. She limped forward, and the shadow followed, matching her movements. The ground was hard and rocky. Ice covered most of it, making it treacherously slippery. She fell on her rump hard enough to knock her teeth back.

Keely gritted her jaw and stood up. She was getting angry now. This was too hard. For anyone. What was she fighting for? A magical realm she barely knew? She was tired, cold, hungry, aching, and she would have sold her soul to sit in a steaming bubble bath for two days straight.

"Enough!" she shouted. She let out a scream, sharing with the universe how frustrated and scared she was. It bounced back at her, echoing in the confines of the cavern. Her shadow covered its ears with its hands.

But her scream sounded puny next to the screeching roar that followed. The bellowing noise sent thundering shock waves through the tunnel, sending icicles crashing to the ground, splintering shards of ice everywhere.

Cold sweat trickled down her spine. Her shadow frantically pointed in the opposite direction, like it wanted to flee. She flashed on her vision of the eight-legged beast that guarded the place. Fleeing sounded pretty good. Run screaming from this cave and fling herself on the mercy of the frost giants.

Then she remembered: the Vanir had no mercy.

She sighed. *Enough pity-party*, she chided herself. She was here fighting not just for her friends, but also for what was right. Catriona was evil. She couldn't be allowed to win. Not as long as Keely still had life in her.

She looked around. There was nowhere to hide, and no one to call on for help. She would just have to face whatever happened and hope Odin had picked the right girl for the job.

Keely doggedly dragged herself forward, dreading what she would find. Her shadow was her only company, limping along beside her. She found it oddly comforting. The trail became steeper, and the icy blue walls pressed in closer. She tried to stay on her feet, but the ground was too slick. She ended up falling, rolling, and tumbling down a steep incline, bruising every inch of herself.

She stood shakily, hoping she hadn't broken anything. Her shadow looked woozy. With no wall to support it, it stretched out from her own feet across the floor, swaying side to side. She had rolled into a big blue cavern. In the center, a large spear of ice hung down from the rocky ceiling. It was a glittering icicle, reflecting the light of a million captured stars.

"Whoa," she said out loud. It was bright in here. Light shone on a smooth pond. Excitedly, she recognized it from her vision. The Moon Pearl had shimmered at the bottom of the clear water.

She didn't see the pearl, but she did see the moon. Or rather, its reflection. It shone brightly on the surface, as if Keely were out under a clear night sky instead of deep underground. She could pick out the detail of the craters and the shadows of the moon's face in the shimmering image.

Caught up in the beauty, Keely forgot about the horrible screech—until a large furry beast entered the cave from a round tunnel and shuffled toward her. It was the creature from her vision, a beast with eight legs. The legs on each side stepped in unison, moving the monster forward like a freight train. Its body was the size of a small house and was covered in thick white fur. Its head had a long snout that ended in a row of white teeth it bared at her. Strands of drool dripped from its jaw, as if it was dreaming about making her its next meal. Its ears were pricked up to a point, and its eyes were luminous and wide, staring at her with distrust.

Keely started to back away, but her feet wouldn't move. She looked down and saw that while she had been distracted, a solid rim of ice had formed around her boots. The ice swiftly climbed to her knees. It was rising higher with every second, inching its way up her body. At this rate, she was going to be encased in ice in moments. Her shadow tried to help, lifting from the ground to tug on her hand. There was pressure and coldness, but it couldn't budge Keely.

The beast drew close and gripped her shadow by the head with its teeth and tossed it high, flinging it into the water of the pond. It hit with a splash, black arms floundering, and then sank.

Chapter Thirty-Five

Keely's shoulders slumped. She had made it so far. Was this the end, then? Would Sam be lost to Catriona forever? Evil magic would erupt into her world, creating pandemonium. Everything she had seen in Mimir's vision would happen. All because she had failed.

"Why?" she cried as the beast inched closer to her. "Why are you doing this?"

It said nothing. Its eyes were golden with narrow black pupils. It didn't blink. It slowly ambled forward on its eight legs until it stopped a few feet away.

The ice had reached her waist now. "I know who you are," she said clearly, remembering the stories Rifkin had told her on the long frosty nights. "You're Audhumla."

Audhumla had been a giant cowlike creature that had nursed the creator, Ymir, with milk in the beginning of the world. The eight-legged beast lowered itself to the ground, its head level with Keely's. Keely looked from one golden eye to the other, trying to think of something that would matter. The ice reached her shoulders. In another minute, she wouldn't be able to speak or breathe.

"Listen to me. I am a Chosen One. I must see Ymir. Orkney is in danger."

The ice continued to climb higher. Audhumla appeared indifferent, waiting silent as a sphynx while Keely was slowly encased in an ice-coffin.

"Hey, I'm talking to you," she shouted. "The witches have taken my friend. Terrible things are going to happen if I don't stop them. Ymir can help us. Please, take me to him."

The creature let out a snort loud as a foghorn. Vapor steamed from its nostrils, sending a rolling gray mist across the chamber to the icy blue wall. Splotches of black ink pooled and took shadow forms and began acting out a scene. There were three young men in silhouette. They rose up with spears to attack a larger man with a crown on his head.

This was the day Ymir had been killed, Keely realized, remembering Rifkin's story. These were his sons rising up against him. Odin, Vili, and Vi, killing him with their long spears, then throwing his bones into this cavern, into a large pool. The shadow of an eight-legged beast wept next to the pool, crying huge fat tears into the pond.

"Bad things happened," Keely said. "Ymir was betrayed by his own sons. But you helped him create this world, Audhumla. You can't want to see it destroyed."

Treacherous ice reached her chin. It was getting hard to breathe. Cold filled her bones. Audhumla did nothing, just watched her with wary curiosity. There was nothing more Keely could say. The ice rose higher, sealing off her nostrils, covering her eyes, and encasing her completely.

There was no air. Ice pressed in on her. She couldn't even struggle. It was like being encased in cement, but she could still see Audhumla's golden eyes watching her. This was it. She was going to end up a Popsicle. And then her survival instincts kicked in. *Don't give up, Keely*, she told herself. *Fight it. You had enough magic to get in here. To start a fire. So use it.*

Mavery had said magic was needing something and believing it can happen. Right now, Keely needed a miracle. She concentrated on her fingers, remembering the sensation of starting the fire. A tiny tingle in the tips gave her hope. She concentrated harder, willing herself to heat up. Warm sparks shot through her bloodstream. The ice cracked, spreading tiny fissures like spider veins. She doubled her efforts, putting everything she had into it until the ice shattered into crystals. Keely staggered, dragging air into her lungs, feeling weak relief.

The beast blinked in surprise, then lumbered forward. Keely scrambled back, not ready for another attack, when its tongue lolled out and it lapped the girl, spreading thick saliva on her. The tongue was rough and prickly, but it made Keely warm up instantly.

The creature lapped Keely's face and her shoulder where she had been grazed with the arrow. A tingling feeling shot through Keely's body. The saliva smelled like dog breath, but it was healing her. Audhumla slurped at her knee, taking the swelling and the pain away with every lick.

Keely reached a tentative hand out to touch Audhumla's nose. "Hey."

Audhumla let out a blaring bleat in response, shaking the walls of the cave.

Keely flinched at the loudness, but then smiled. "You're not so scary once you stop freezing me to death. I think I'll call you Auddie." She looked around the cavern, searching for the source of the light, but it was as if the moon's reflection had been captured by the pond and held there forever. Auddie nudged Keely with its shaggy head toward the water.

She took a step forward. As she reached the edge, the water steamed and churned. Out of the center of the lake, a figure rose up. It was a man. A Vanir. He was as broad-shouldered as the ones Keely had seen. He wore a brown toga of soft leather. White hair grew to his shoulders. A crown of green leaves rimmed his head. He glided across the surface toward her.

"A visitor," he said with a touch of surprise, covering a slight yawn as though he had been awakened from a long nap. "I have not had one of those in eons."

"My name is Keely Hatch," she answered, hardly believing this was really Ymir. "I am from Midgard."

He studied her closely as he joined her on the shore. His eyes were a kaleidoscope of blue and green and gold. "An earth child who has Eifalian blood. How fascinating. What do you ask of the creator?"

"Orkney needs your help. My friend, Sam, has been taken by the witches. He's a powerful he-witch, the first in a long time. The witches are trying to turn him against Orkney. We can't let that happen."

"I fear you are too late." Ymir's face saddened as he waved a hand over the water. An image of Sam in black armor reflected on the surface. His face was angry and twisted as he thrust a knife into a giant bear's chest.

Keely gasped in horror. "No." She was speechless. Vor's words to Leo rang in her ears: *One of our own will be taken.*

What has Sam done? And then another thought punched her in the gut: *Is it too late to save him?*

For a moment, Keely felt all hope leave her. What was she supposed to do now? If Sam had really done this, then Catriona had already won. But something inside her refused to give up. She might be too late to stop them from turning Sam, but she could still prevent Catriona from getting everything she wanted. "Sam would never hurt Brunin. Not willingly. He's a true Son of Odin. But Catriona is going to use him to return her magic to earth so she can destroy everything Odin cares about, including mankind. I have to stop her. When I drank from Mimir's well, I saw a pearl shining in this pond."

Ymir's eyebrows shot up. "Ah, you seek the Moon Pearl." He studied the glowing image of the moon on the water. "You know, when I created this world, the sun got all the attention. Without it, humankind couldn't exist, but what of the moon? It serves no purpose but as a thing of beauty. You can look at it as long as you want." Ymir spoke wistfully, a small smile on his face.

Keely's mind was racing. "I thought it was the key to saving Sam, but maybe it's the key to stopping Catriona. Will you let me have it?" She waited, fingers crossed.

Ymir folded his arms. "The Moon Pearl contains the essence of my heart. I require something of equal value in return."

Keely's brain sputtered as she tried to think, but her possessions were meager as a beggar's. "I have nothing to give. I already cut my hair to gain wisdom."

Ymir's eyes probed her, glinting with sudden interest. "What I seek is not gold or silver, but far more precious. A secret chipped from the depths of your soul. What do you hide from the world? Only then can I judge your worthiness."

"I . . ." Keely tried and failed to speak. She wanted to deny she had a secret, but it sat there, lodged in her chest like a tumor. Ymir continued to look at her with those patient eyes of his, as if he already knew the truth, the same way King Einolach had looked at her. Maybe it was time.

Words tumbled out. "I tell everyone my mom died of a brain tumor, but it's a lie. It's my fault she's dead. She forgot to pick up my English project from the printer. I'd spent weeks on it, and it was due the next day." She saw herself yelling at her mom, who had one hand to her temple like she was in pain. "She had a headache. She got them a lot."

"Go on," Ymir said gently.

Keely shook her head, feeling the guilt sting every cell in her body. "She wanted to lie down and rest, but I threw a fit. No way Keely Hatch was going to get marked down a grade," she mocked as scalding tears rolled down her cheeks. "It was raining outside. Her car . . . it slid off the road into a ditch. She didn't survive."

"It seems an accident, was it not?"

Keely raised her eyes to Ymir. "Don't you get it? She wouldn't have even been out there if it weren't for me. She just wanted to rest, but no, I had to get my A. She was always forgetting things. It wasn't until after . . . that they discovered the tumor. They think it's the reason she lost control—but it's still my fault—"

Ymir interrupted with a gentle wave of his hand. "Death is inevitable. Have you considered she was spared the unnecessary pain of a long illness?"

Keely stared at him. The doctors had said almost the same thing, but Keely had never believed it.

Ymir put a hand on her shoulder. "You must learn to let go of the guilt or it will eat at your soul. Only then will you be worthy of the Moon Pearl."

Something in Keely's chest eased. Just saying the words out loud had suddenly made them less powerful, less painful.

"I swear I am ready. I can do this," she said with more confidence than she had ever felt before, but Ymir still appeared troubled.

"The Moon Pearl may help you with your friend, but surely you have bigger problems."

Keely frowned. "What do you mean?"

He sat down on a small rounded stone and motioned for her to sit across from him. "You have broken the treaty that kept peace between the Vanir and the Eifalians."

"But I haven't done anything."

"The treaty they signed was blood sacred. No Vanir has stepped south of the Skoll Mountains in ten centuries, and no Eifalian has traveled north. By coming here, you have violated that agreement."

Keely was getting tired of explaining she couldn't possibly be an Eifalian. "I told you, I'm from Midgard—"

He raised a finger at her. "Only the Eifalians have the magic to pierce the veil that seals my home. Audhumla was confused, sensing you were not as you appeared; it's why she acted to protect me. But you surprised her with your magic. Deny it all you wish, but you are their enemy."

Ymir waved his hand across the water, and a new vision began to play.

Men on horseback were mounting up and rallying with swords and deafening shouts. A battle raged, and the Eifalians died in droves as the Vanir ran them down with long spears. Then the vision shifted, and Keely saw the Vanir being killed by the Eifalian defenses. It was terrible. This was the start of the war she had seen in her vision at Mimir's well, but she now felt the horror of being the cause of it.

"I did this?" she whispered.

"It is one outcome. You have given both races an excuse to act on the hatred that has festered all these years."

"I can explain to them. They will have to listen. You can make them."

"That is not in my power. But . . . I have something that might help."

Ymir reached into his toga and withdrew a small flute carved out of several small bones lashed together. He ran his lips across the openings, and a beautiful sound filled the cave.

"Give this to the king who leads the Vanir. His name is Joran. Show no one else. Tell him, what is lost can be found. If he is the man I think he is, he will know what it means."

"And if he doesn't listen?"

Ymir put his hand to Keely's face and cupped her cheek. "Then your journey may end with your death."

She nodded as she stood, taking the flute and tucking it safely inside her shirt next to her heart. "What about the pearl?"

"You will find it where your guilt once was."

Keely reached into her chest pocket and felt a small bulge. Her fingers closed around the round, cool surface of the pearl nestled close to her heart.

"Thank you," she whispered, her eyes shining.

The eight-legged beast shuffled closer, waiting to take her back up to the surface.

She grabbed a fistful of Auddie's fur and then paused. Ymir stood by the pond. He looked wistful, as if he didn't want her to leave yet. "Can I ask another favor?" she asked.

"What is it?"

"If I don't make it back, can you let my dad know that it's okay? He shouldn't have to suffer anymore. He doesn't deserve that."

He thought about it a moment and then nodded. "I will see what I can do. Take care, young Keely."

As Ymir walked back across the water, he began to sink until the pond sealed up over him. The surface remained still and calm. The reflection of the moon was gone, Keely realized.

She took a deep breath.

Outside the cave, the Vanir would be waiting. It was time to rescue Mavery and Galatin and get back to saving Sam.

Auddie gave her a ride to the entrance of the cave. Keely slid off its back and rubbed its long snout. The creature nuzzled Keely, butting her with its furred head.

"I'll miss you too, Auddie." Keely planted a kiss between its eyes. On the icy wall, her shadow reappeared, waving goodbye. Keely waved back and then walked through the wall of mist that separated the cave from the outside world.

As soon as she stepped outside, Auddie disappeared. The entrance was dark and unreadable. Keely turned around and saw a ring of warriors waiting for her at the top, swords drawn. At her feet, she spied Rifkin's blade. It wasn't enough to stop the horde of frost giants that awaited, but she lifted it anyway. Then she took a deep breath, pasting on her best smile, and waved the sword.

"Hey there, I'm Keely."

They didn't smile back. Didn't move. Just watched as she hiked up the small hill to where they waited.

"I demand to see your leader, Joran, right now," she said, boldly holding the sword out in front of her.

They started laughing. Her feet went out from under her, and she found herself swept up behind a horse, tied over the end of it like a sack of potatoes. A bag was thrown over her head, blocking out the world.

At least they hadn't killed her on the spot.

Chapter Thirty-Six

Bouncing around on the back of the frost giant's horse, Keely had plenty of time to think about what awaited her once they arrived in Galas. Mavery and Galatin might not even be alive. Hope and despair seesawed her emotions as she waited in agony to see what her fate would be. Finally, there was a change in the sound the horses made, like they were clattering on stone. Chains clanked loudly, like something was being lowered, and then the hooves pounded on wood.

They must be entering the capital. Galas.

The horses finally came to a stop. Someone whipped Keely's hood off. She blinked in the sudden glare of sunlight. They were in a large open-air arena carved from blocks of warm sandstone. The stadium looked like it could hold a thousand people. The seats were filled with a sea of faces, mostly bearded and fierce as her captors. Snow crusted a muddy field. Keely's boots sank in, squelching with each step as she was frog-marched to a raised platform in the center. It was made of rough wooden planks. At the top, a man knelt, his hands tied behind him. His head hung down despondently.

Galatin.

Next to him was the tiny figure of Mavery. Even though Keely was thrilled to see them alive, she worried it wouldn't be for long. This looked an awful lot like a gallows. The giant standing with a large double-bladed axe in his meaty hands looked an awful lot like an executioner.

Keely's feet didn't want to move, but a frost giant dragged her up the stairs and threw her down next to Mavery. Guilt flooded her as Mimir's vision came back to haunt her, the one of Mavery's head on a chopping block. So far, she had failed miserably at stopping the terrible future she had witnessed.

Mavery's lips trembled as she stared at Keely, but she didn't speak. The girl seemed too terrified to open her mouth.

"Hey, it's okay. We're going to figure this out," Keely said, even though the sight of that axe made her knees turn to jelly.

At her voice, Galatin turned to look at her. His face was bruised and bloody. He looked defeated. As if all hope had been drained from him.

Drums sounded. Banging loudly like impending doom.

Across from the platform, a blood-red canopy covered a raised dais that gave a bird's-eye view of the arena. Two thrones that looked like they were carved from gold were positioned in the center. Behind them an array of padded chairs sat in a line. That must be the VIP section. A purple banner hung down with the symbol of a bear chasing the tail of another. A group of frost giants filed in, solemnly filling the row of seats. They wore fur-skin cloaks, but their chests were bare.

A brutish soldier stepped out onto the arena ground and blew on a large carved horn, blasting a long and low sound.

The crowd rose to their feet, growing silent as they waited.

A lone fly buzzed in Keely's ear. She focused on her surroundings, trying to think of a way out of this. Like Skara Brae, Galas was built into the side of a cliff above the ocean. Where Skara Brae was built of gray stone, the Vanir used a caramel-colored sandstone to construct their towering edifices. Their construction was square and massive like the people themselves. There was very little color besides the purple banners that rimmed the arena. Far below, the sea sent whitecaps crashing against the rocks. What she wouldn't give to be on a raft, sailing away.

The roaring of the crowd had her turning back. A giant of a man with a crown of leaves similar to Ymir's came out with a woman on his arm. He was even taller than the others, with an air of power about him.

He must be the one. Joran. The ruler of the Vanir.

Joran raised his hand, briefly acknowledging the cheering throng. The drums stopped, and the assembly of frost giants sat down. Joran appeared bored. Uninterested. He spoke to the woman next to him. Someone handed him a goblet. He drank it down in one gulp and handed it back to be refilled. The woman had long brown hair braided in a coil around her head. She was nearly as tall as he was, though lithe and clothed in a fine gown of shimmering yellow silk.

The black-hooded Vanir used his boot to thrust a heavy chopping block in front of Galatin. In his hands, he held a huge double-headed axe. He swung it once around his head, flexing his muscles.

"So I guess this is it," Galatin said, giving Keely a grim smile.

"We're not done yet," she said, desperately thinking of a way to save their lives.

"We're pretty done," he said as the Vanir shoved his head down on the block.

Keely looked over at Mavery. The witch-girl was frozen in a state of shock. She nudged her. "Hey, snap out of it. Help me create a distraction."

Mavery finally moved her lips. "Th-th-is—this is what you saw, isn't it?"

"It doesn't matter," Keely hissed, "because it's not going to happen. Use some of that witch magic of yours."

"I c-c-can't. I'm not that strong."

"Yes, you are. You're a great witch. Besides, I'm right here with you. We can do this together."

Across the muddy field, Joran laughed at something the

woman said. He drank from the goblet he held and picked at some grapes on a large platter a servant passed him. He paid no attention to the little drama being played out on the platform, where Galatin was about to lose his head, followed, Keely was sure, by her and then Mavery.

The executioner tested the axe against Galatin's neck. Weighing the distance.

"Now, Mavery," Keely said, scrambling to her feet.

Mavery stood up, shouting at Joran. "Hey, you big galoof!"

No one paid them any attention. The party went on. The head of the Vanir roared with laughter at something said to him.

That made Mavery angry. She stomped her foot and drew her hands over her head, throwing them forward. A clump of mud swept up from the floor of the arena and spattered across the front of Joran. The woman next to him shrieked as clumps of gooey, sticky earth clogged her hair.

The crowd gasped in horror.

Joran jumped to his feet and roared a command to the executioner. The giant raised the axe over Galatin's head, but Keely tackled his knees, knocking him off balance. He teetered, flailing his arms, then lost the battle for balance and fell flat on his back in the mud. Keely picked up the double-bladed weapon, struggling to hold it out in front of her as armed Vanir swarmed them. Mavery spat bursts of witchfire at them, but Keely put a hand on the witch, stopping her.

"Stop and hear me," Keely called out.

Joran held up his hand. "Wait," he said, standing from his seat.

"You speak English," she said, relieved. She turned to Mavery. "Help Galatin." The girl went to their comrade and untied his binds.

Joran wiped mud from his face with a cloth. "Of course I speak the language of our enemy."

"I am not your enemy."

"You are Eifalian."

"I am from earth, what you call Midgard."

"You lie." He turned. A servant passed him a familiar satchel. He dumped Keely's soul crystal and the phoralite into his large hands. "Are you saying these trinkets don't belong to you?"

Keely was exasperated. "Yes, they're mine, but—"

He cut in. "You were caught leaving the Cave of Shadows. Only those with Eifalian blood can enter. What more proof do I need?"

Keely gave up trying to convince him. "Look, we have bigger problems than some ancient treaty. The witches are trying to take over Orkney."

Joran dismissed her with a wave. "We have no quarrel with the witches."

"You will."

"We are far to the north."

"They will come for you. They won't stop until they control everything."

His face was like iron. "We will fight them."

"You will lose," Keely said.

"You speak treason!" he shouted. "For this alone, you shall die."

"I speak the truth!" she shouted back, finding her courage in her confidence that she was right. She dropped the axe, suddenly hating what it represented. Violence. War. "You will lose, because they will wait until you are done fighting the Eifalians. Then, when you are weakest, when you have lost so many, the witches will strike, and they will win."

He was silent a moment, swirling his drink. "What makes you so wise?"

"I drank from Mimir's well. I have seen the outcome. Unless I change things, that is how it will be. I spoke to Ymir," she added. "When I was in the Cave of Shadows. He had a message for you."

The Vanirian king's head rose sharply like a ferret who'd caught sight of a mouse. In an instant, he leapt over the side of the railing and strode across the arena. With a single bound, he was on the platform, standing next to Keely. She felt small next to him. She bit the inside of her cheek, refusing to show fear. He grabbed her arm, pulling her close.

Joran's eyes were a glacial blue, intently looking into hers, searching for deceit. "What did he say?"

"He said to tell you, what is lost can be found."

The king turned a deathly shade of gray. "You lie," he said hollowly, dropping her arm like it was a viper. "I should break your neck with my bare hands."

"He said to give you something." Keely reached in her shirt and pulled out the flute. She handed it to him. In his large hands it looked small and fragile. He could snap it in half with a twitch of his fingers, but Joran held it gently as if it were the most precious thing in the world.

He put his lips to it. He hesitated, closing his eyes. He drew in a shallow breath and then blew.

A few broken notes came out, and then he settled into a soft melody that drifted across the platform and up to the stadium. The audience fell silent. The woman he had been seated with rose to her feet, clutching at her bosom. Joran played the notes, lifting a song up that was haunting and sad. It made Keely's heart swell.

When he was done, he kissed the flute once and then turned to Keely.

"This belonged to my son. He wandered away one day and was lost in a storm. I have searched every end of Rakim for him. To bury him and find peace. You have given me a great gift. How can I repay you?"

"Don't go to war," she pleaded.

He hesitated. She was winning, she was sure of it. Joran was going to listen.

But then a horn blast came from the harbor below. A whistling sound followed. Keely ducked as a dozen flaming arrows fired over their heads to embed in the wooden gallows.

All eyes turned to see the source. Where the sea had been

wind-whipped and empty, it now held a dozen ships, all carrying the green Eifalian banner. A row of archers lined each deck, bows nocked with arrows.

"You might not be Eifalian, but they are," Joran said fiercely. He waved his hand at his men, ordering them to gather their weapons. Buckets of water were thrown on the flames, dousing them quickly.

Keely grabbed his arm. "Wait. Let me speak to them."

He pierced her with his gaze. "I cannot show weakness to my men. They would turn on me like a pack of wild sneevils."

"For your son," she implored. "Let no one else lose someone they love."

His nostrils flared with impatience, but he steadied himself. "I will give you one hour, till the sun sets, to convince them to surrender. But your friends stay here."

"Okay. One hour." Keely backed away, looking at Galatin and Mavery, for support.

Galatin winked at her, his arm around Mavery. "Go on, then. You know what to do."

Chapter Thirty-Seven

Keely jumped buoyantly off the platform and followed after the pair of escorts Joran sent with her. She had to trot to keep up with their long legs as they marched quickly down the rutted trail that led to the docks.

She could do this. The Eifalians would listen. They were a peaceful people.

Frost giants lined the rails of every ship, staring down at her silently as she walked down the long dock. One of the escorts beckoned her to get into a small rowboat. She jumped in and sat down as they quickly rowed toward the closest Eifalian warship.

The waves tossed the boat around, but the frost giants cut through the water with hardly a grunt. Anxiousness made her nauseous. There wasn't much time. If she didn't make something happen fast, Joran would attack, and once the war began, it would never end until both sides had been depleted. There would be no winners. Ymir had made that clear.

They bumped into the side of the Eifalian ship. Ropes dangled down to secure their dinghy, and arms reached out, pulling her up onto the deck. The Vanirians refused to get on their enemy's boat, waiting alongside. Keely's legs felt like rubber. The Eifalian High Council representative, Gael, walked toward her in his flowing green robes. Next to him trailed a small white-headed boy.

"Theo," she cried, running and giving him a hug. "I was so worried about you."

He was awkward at first, holding her off. Then he relented and let her embrace him. "Someone had to come save you again," he boasted. "I told you going north would cause trouble."

"Yes, you did, and I probably should have listened. But I had to get the Moon Pearl."

"And did you?" Gael asked.

She nodded, patting her pocket. She was afraid to touch it out of fear of using up its magic. "It's here. But I broke the treaty. They think I'm Eifalian."

"Theo told us about the troll hags. They would have reported an Eifalian girl to the Vanir. We guessed that whether or not you made it to the Cave of Shadows, the Vanir would attack us. They have been waiting for centuries for an excuse to strike at us."

"So you struck first," she said.

He nodded.

"But you can't go to war. You must come speak to Joran. He will listen."

"She is right," came a voice. Gael's father, King Einolach, emerged from the ship's cabin. "I, too, have read the auras. You are not the only one who can see things, child." His long hair blew in the wind. He held his mother-of-pearl staff. It glowed blue and pink in the fading sunlight of the day. "We don't have much time," he finished.

"Then we should go," Keely said.

"Father," Gael said, "you are not leaving the ship."

The king's eyes narrowed slightly. "You are not king yet, Gael. I know what I am doing."

Gael put a hand on the king's arm. "But you can't." Silent words passed between them that Keely couldn't grasp.

When King Einolach spoke, his voice was heavy. "There are

things a king must do, and this is one of them. You will understand one day when you are king."

Einolach was going to face the Vanir alone. Even Theo guessed it.

"No, Grandfather, please, don't go." The boy hugged him tightly around the waist.

King Einolach held Theo a moment and then knelt down. "You must be brave, Theo. There is much to be done. This girl needs our help. I want you to stay strong. Be mindful of your lessons. Don't let bitterness into your heart, or it will root there."

Theo nodded. "Yes, Grandfather."

The king stood and faced Keely. "Shall we?"

"Father, I'm coming with you," Gael said.

But Einolach shook his head. "I forbid it. Only the girl and I return—as it must be."

Gael took his father's hand and pressed a kiss to his ring.

"Do not strike first," the king said. "If they attack, you must defend. But only defend. No offensive."

"I will do as you ask," Gael said.

Einolach clasped his shoulders. "I am proud to have you as my son, Gael."

"Thank you, Father."

They touched their foreheads together. A gleaming aura circled their heads tinged orange by the setting sun.

Time was running out.

"We have to go," Keely said.

King Einolach let himself be lowered into the boat. Keely joined him. The Vanirian escorts rowed them swiftly back to shore. Keely was nervous, but hopeful Joran would be reasonable.

Less than an hour had passed, but when they entered the arena, everything was different. The Vanir had emptied the stadium and now stood in orderly lines, fully armored, ready to do battle, shields out. At the sight of the Eifalian king, the air grew silent. A pin drop could have been heard. Keely escorted the king through the mud, holding his arm and helping him up to the platform in the center. Joran awaited them, standing patiently, as if he hadn't moved since Keely had left an hour ago.

Joran sized up the much older king and then nodded ever so slightly.

King Einolach did the same, keeping his shoulders high as his chin ducked.

Joran spoke first. "The Eifalians have broken the blood treaty."

King Einolach agreed. "We have. Although the reasons were good, the fault is ours."

"What reasons are these?" Joran said.

"The child saw a vision of a future, one where Vanir and Eifalians are no more."

Thunder crossed Joran's brow. "This is not possible. The Vanir have been here since the beginning of time. Ymir himself was a frost giant."

King Einolach nodded patiently. "And the Eifalians have also existed since the dawn of time, even before we were brought to the Ninth Realm to preserve our magic. It is unfortunate that it brought our people into conflict."

"Rakim is our land. You invaded it."

"I cannot disagree, but we had no place else to go. We needed a wintry home, and this place suited us."

Joran looked surprised. "So you don't deny it."

"I cannot deny the truth of my ancestors' decisions any more than I can deny what the child has seen, for I have seen it myself."

Joran's brow darkened again. "What does this mean?"

"There is much danger ahead. I sense a new evil coming, something that none of us will be able to stop unless we work together."

Keely flashed on those malicious eyes she had seen in Leo's quest. With her new instincts, she knew this was the evil the king referred to.

"You have no proof of this," Joran scoffed.

"None. But heed my words, Joran. War is coming, but not with the Eifalians."

"So you will pay the price to keep the peace?"

King Einolach hesitated, and then he nodded.

Joran's jaw worked as he took it in. "Then it shall be so." He clapped his hands twice sharply, gathering the attention of the assembled crowd.

"The king of the Eifalians has offered himself as a sacrifice to restore the blood treaty between our people."

A wave of horror washed over Keely. Her mouth fell open. She should protest, cry out, but the power of speech had deserted her.

The bloodthirsty ranks of Vanirian soldiers grumbled.

Joran held up his hands. "I cannot break the laws of the treaty that binds us. If he offers himself, the treaty is restored."

Mavery buried her face in Keely's waist.

"What's he saying?" she wailed. "I don't understand. I thought you were going to fix it."

Galatin lifted the girl up, prying her hands gently off Keely, and carried her off the platform.

King Einolach turned to Keely. He pulled the giant opal ring off his finger and pressed it into her hand. "Give this to Gael. Tell him to go home."

She started to protest, her brain trying and failing to come up with another answer. "But you can't—"

"I must," he said quietly, putting his hand on her shoulder. "You saw as clearly as I what the war would do. Would you rather all those innocent lives were lost?"

She shook her head. Tears ran down her cheeks. "But you're innocent. This is my fault. I shouldn't have asked you to come."

"No. There is no fault. It just is. Go on, now. You must get that Moon Pearl back to Skara Brae."

Galatin waited for her at the bottom of the stairs, holding Mavery in his arms. The girl was sobbing into his shoulder. Galatin put one arm around Keely and escorted her away from the arena. She craned her neck around and watched as King

Einolach folded his robes neatly and knelt down, laying his head on the chopping block.

Keely turned away. She couldn't watch. She buried her head into Galatin's side, wrapping her arms around his waist and letting him lead her down the hill toward the ships.

As the sun sank below the horizon, Keely tried to remember everything good in her life: the smell of her father's cologne, the crisp feel of a new book, Sam laughing at something she said. But eventually, the sobs took over, and all she could do was shake.

She had come here to help Orkney, and instead, she had nearly started a war and caused the death of a king.

Chapter Thirty-Eight

Leo floated.

He tried to remember where he was, how he had gotten into this strange pool, but he was too tired. He wasn't troubled, though. The water was neither hot nor cold. Figures brushed up against him, bumping him as they swam past. His arms were curiously weak, as if he had no control over them. He could stay here forever, in this nothingness. The only sound he heard was a peculiar thump, like the slow beat of a drum. Leo had played the drums in the tribal ceremonies back home. His father had taught him.

Thump, thump. Thump, thump.

His mind drifted back until he was there, alongside the Blue River, standing in the cool shade of the tall sugar pines, waiting for the celebration to begin. The annual salmon ceremony welcoming the great fish back from their journey south.

Thump, thump.

He saw himself beating the drum, as his father and the other members of the tribe performed the ancient ritual honoring the food that would feed their tribe another year.

The drumbeat was getting slower, and his father and the others turned to frown at Leo.

Thump . . . thump.

Leo tried to lift his arms, but they were limp, boneless. It was like time had slowed down to a near stop.

Thump . . .

Leo opened his eyes. There were no drums. The sound was his heartbeat. And it was fading. A spurt of adrenaline shot through him. He swam, pulling with his arms, moving past other figures that pulled at him. He brushed them off, kicking hard. He had no idea of a destination; he just had to move.

He caught a glimmer of light ahead, a change in the water color. Leo headed for it, straining upward, and then broke through the surface, flinging his wet hair out of his face. He was in another chamber. Leo paddled to the side and pulled himself up over the ledge, then looked back into the water.

Leo's heart sank. It was like peering through a looking glass. He could see the first chamber where Endera had shoved him in. Only now he was on the other side. A figure jostled Leo, and he looked around, suddenly realizing he wasn't alone. Around him, the newly demised moved closer, reaching for him. They were in various stages of decay, gray skin slowly melting away. Leo took a step back. Was he one of them now? Dead?

Fear made his heart kick in his chest, and with that reminder, hope returned.

I'm alive.

Leo backed away, searching for an exit. The room was circular, with tunnels leading in every direction. He chose one at random and ran.

The dead chased after him. He brushed off their grasping hands, striking at them when they got too close. They fell easily but got back up, continuing their pursuit as if he had something they wanted.

His legs tired, and his muscles burned, but he managed to keep ahead of his followers. Finally, when the sounds of pursuit had faded, he paused to rest. He put his hand on the wall to catch his breath, only to feel a hairy scalp under his palm.

He reared back, seeing a gray decaying face under a mat

of stringy hair. The flesh was rotting away, but there was still a semblance of a nose and high cheeks. The lower lip and chin were gone, revealing jawbone. The eyes flew open, a brilliant green that reminded him of that witch Ariane's.

"Where is my body?" the head screeched, eyes flickering left and right.

Realizing the thing had no limbs to attack him with, Leo stepped closer. "Who are you?"

"I am Nestra, one of the great Volgrim witches!" Her eyes bored into him, commanding him with the same arrogance he had seen in Ariane and Catriona. "Save me, boy, and I will grant your every desire." A worm crawled out of one nostril and made its way up her rotting cheek.

Leo backed away as four more worms burst out of the mud and began their trek across her face. More worms emerged from her matted hair, wriggling into her ears. Revolted, Leo fled as she screeched after him in fury. He kept running until her screeches faded away. He came to a fork and chose the right tunnel.

And ran smack into a half dozen of the living corpses. They spied him and began shuffling toward him, making excited moans. Leo spun and retreated back to the fork and headed down the other tunnel. It was steeper than the others. There was less and less light with every step, and the air felt even more cold and empty. The sound of his heartbeat, the one constant that told him he was alive, grew fainter. It grew harder to breathe in the thin air.

After traveling only a dozen yards, Leo's lungs burned, and he had no choice. He had to stop. As he dragged deadened air into his failing lungs, a whisper drifted to his ears, like a ghost was calling him.

"Psst, you there. If you want to live, come inside."

Leo turned his head to find the source.

There. A dim hole in the wall. An opening, down low. He staggered to it and crouched, peering inside. It was a cavern with light. Maybe air.

"Come closer. Don't be shy," came the voice. "No one will bother you in here."

The sound of shuffling footsteps came down the tunnel. The army of dead were on his trail. Leo made his decision. He crawled through the hole into the cavern.

Leo stood up, straining to see in the faint light. In the center, a man stood chained to a large rock. He was shirtless, wearing only a rough pair of ragged pants that went to his thick calves. His hair was bushy and long. Glittering eyes sparked with curiosity, searching Leo up and down like the boy was an apparition. Heavy chains wrapped around his ankles, around his wrists, around his waist, even around his neck. All strung through bolts sunk into the stone walls.

Thankfully, the air felt lighter in here. Leo could actually breathe. He began to feel strength flow back into him. He was safe. For now.

The man flashed a mischievous grin at Leo. "I must say, it's been an eon since I saw something so precious as another living creature." His eyes had a glint to them as if he found being locked up down here entertaining. He wasn't very tall, but he had wiry biceps that flexed as he pulled on his chains.

"Why are you chained here?" Leo asked, stepping back when the man swung his arms close.

"Don't be afraid. It's not like I can break free." He rattled his chains loud enough to wake the dead. "Believe me, if I could, I would have broken out of here ten centuries ago."

Leo sat down, crossing his legs, and closed his eyes. He needed to meditate. To think about what to do. How was he going to escape this underworld prison?

"You got anything that can break these?" the man asked hopefully, pulling on his chains.

"No," Leo answered, keeping his eyes closed.

"What did you do to end up here?"

Leo concentrated on feeling his heartbeat. It grew steadier as he centered his energy. He needed to find a path that led upward. Maybe this odd person could help him. He would play along. He opened his eyes to study the man. "I trusted a witch," he answered.

The man laughed harshly. "A very bad idea."

"What did you say your name was?"

"Let me free, and I'll tell you." The voice was coaxing, but underneath, it was hard, cold. Evil.

Warning tremors ran up Leo's spine. The man was dangerous. A predator. It felt like he was locked in the same cage as a lion. One that hadn't been fed. "Tell me who you are, or I'll walk out of here," he said firmly.

The man's bushy eyebrows rose in a plea. "Don't rush off. My manners are just rusty. Can't blame a fellow; it has been centuries since I entertained. Name's Loki. My dear friend Odin banished me here a long time ago. Then I think he forgot about me." The man picked at his nails while he said it, like it was no big deal.

A chill ran through Leo. "You're Loki? *The* Loki?"

"In the flesh." His grin just grew wider. "So you've heard of me."

Now Leo knew why Keely had warned him so strongly about what he was up against. He might not have read as many mythology books as Keely, but every kid in the world had heard of Loki, God of Mischief, enemy of good. "Why did Odin put you here?"

"Oh, I'm sure I deserved it." Loki laughed, winking at Leo. "I might have killed Odin's son Baldur by accident. His Almighty was not pleased. Baldur was always his favorite."

Leo struggled to his feet. He was better off taking his chances with the dead than staying in the same place as this prince of evil. "I have to go," he said, stepping backward toward the entrance.

Loki's eyes narrowed into mean slits as he read Leo's intent. "If you walk out of this room, the dead will overwhelm you in minutes and drain every precious ounce of life out of you. There will be nothing left of you but a lost soul. Is that what you want?"

Leo hesitated. "No. But I can't stay here."

"I can help you escape. Break these chains." He rattled them at Leo.

"No." Leo's decision was firm. Releasing Loki was a bad idea.

"Find a rock and smash them. The links have rusted. Do it," Loki urged.

Leo stepped back further. "My father says, you shouldn't make a bad thing worse."

Loki dropped his chin to his chest as if he were disappointed in Leo. "Fine, you're right. We should both just give up. As a matter of fact, I'll call the army of the dead for you." He began to yodel loudly.

"Stop it!" Leo turned to listen at the door for the sound of the dead returning. In that moment, he hated himself. He didn't want to die. He would do anything to keep hope alive, even if it meant helping Loki escape. "How do I know I can trust you?"

Loki shrugged. "You can't be sure, but I give you my word. You cut me loose, and I'll show you the way home."

Leo hesitated. Loki would probably leave him behind the first chance he got, but Leo couldn't think of any other options.

"And you're sure that you know the way out."

The man tapped his head. "Got it right here, chief."

Leo shook his head, thinking this was a very bad idea, but he began to search for a bludgeoning rock. He found one about the size of a football. He checked the links in Loki's chain. The God of Mischief was right. The chain was heavily rusted in parts. Leo bashed on the chain with the rock. The clang didn't seem to draw any attention. Loki had been rattling his chains for years. He bashed them again and again until, with a spray of sparks, one of the links finally broke. The chains fell away in a pool of steel. Loki stepped forward, looking shocked at his freedom. Then he grinned an evil grin.

"There's something I should tell you," he said, flexing his arms.

"What's that?" Leo rested his hands on his thighs, out of breath.

"You were right. It was a very bad idea to trust me," Loki drawled, grinning from ear to ear.

Dread bloomed like the sour taste of bile. Leo dropped into a fighting stance, but Loki acted first, punching Leo once in the stomach. It felt like the kick of a mule. Leo dropped to his knees, fighting to breathe. "Stop," he gasped. "Take me with you, or I'll die here."

Loki chuckled. "I'm the God of Mischief, not good deeds." Then he lifted the rock Leo had used to free him and let it drop on Leo's head.

The impact knocked Leo facedown. Dazed and stunned, he managed to roll onto his back. He was dizzy, seeing double. His head throbbed, but his body felt numb. He couldn't move his limbs. All he could do was stare up at the ceiling. It extended much higher than he had realized. A narrow shaft went up hundreds of feet. He squinted, trying to focus. Was that a blue circle?

For one crazy moment, Leo thought he saw a raven. Or was it two of them? They flew up the shaft, spiraling higher and higher until they disappeared into the blue circle.

His eyelids drooped as the dizziness grew. Leo fought to stay awake. He wanted to sleep, but if he did, he knew he would never wake up. Not this time. The blue circle fascinated him. What was it? He raised a hand, wishing he could touch it. As he did, a white butterfly landed on the tip of his finger. It fluttered its wings at him, delicately balanced.

Get up.

The voice clanged like a fire bell in his head.

Get up. Climb.

And then the butterfly fluttered off, heading upward for that blue circle.

Leo forced a smile. He wasn't going to die here. Not today, anyway.

Chapter Thirty-Nine

Howie held clumsily onto the reins, holding on for dear life as Teren drove them like a madman back to Skara Brae. Their surviving group was pitifully small. Besides Teren and Heppner, there were two badly shaken Orkadian soldiers and Sam's mom. Lady Abigail, as she was called. She was a lot different than the mom who used to burn their grilled cheese sandwiches. This Abigail rode like she was born on a horse, a taut and steely look to her face as she repeatedly questioned Teren about the events of the past few months and the fate of her son.

Howie told her he hadn't seen his bud since returning. Abigail asked him questions about his arrival in Orkney, raising her eyebrows at how Odin had flushed them back, and she didn't laugh a bit when he told her about his Chosen role.

When the gray walls of the medieval fortress came into view, Howie nearly wept with relief, not just because it meant he had survived his first real test as Protector, but also because if he didn't get off the back of a horse, his butt was going to break in half. A slender dark-haired figure jumped up and down in the ramparts, waving a white handkerchief excitedly at him.

Abigail rode up next to him. "It seems you have a fan," she said warmly.

"Yeah, me and Selina, we're tight." Howie glanced over at Sam's mom. Now that he knew she was a witch, he wondered why he had never noticed before. Her eyes sparkled with a fiery green that was definitely witch. And her hair was as raven black as every other witch he had met. There was a power about her that was obvious when you just looked. "Hey, Mrs. Baron, I mean, Lady Abigail—"

She cut him off. "Abigail is fine, Howie. We don't stand on ceremony here in Orkney."

"Fine, Abigail, ma'am, I've been meaning to ask, it's just . . . what took you so long to come back? I mean, Sam's been here a while. He could've used your help." Howie couldn't hide the accusation in his words.

Abigail shook her head sadly. "You think I didn't try? I spent every day conjuring up ways back here, but nothing worked. When Chief Pate wa destroyed the stonefire, he cut off our only known portal. If I had known Chuggies had a magic drain, I would have eaten there every day," she teased.

Howie frowned. "So how did you do it?"

"I rebuilt the stonefire." Her voice was proud.

"Say what?" Howie pulled up his horse to gawk at her.

"It was Chief Pate-wa's idea. I used every ounce of magic I had to piece it back together."

"So we can go home when this is over!" Howie was jubilant, but Abigail dashed his hopes.

"No. Unfortunately I could only hold it together for the one trip. But don't worry, Howie. We'll find a way to send you home."

Before Howie could tell her how awesome that sounded, a bird dive-bombed out of the sky and nearly took his head off. Lingas flapped around his face, trying to smother him with affection or claw his eyeball out, Howie wasn't sure which.

"Calm down, I missed you too, bird face," he said, as the iolar settled on his shoulder, nipping at his ear over and over again as if she just couldn't help herself.

They entered through the tall gates into the main plaza that fronted the Great Hall. The windows and doors had been boarded up in anticipation of the coming skirmish, not that a few boards would stop the destruction that loomed. Selina flew down the steps from the ramparts, practically knocking Howie over as he dismounted from his horse.

"Oh, Howie, you're alive. I didn't think—I mean, I knew you could do it, but I—oh, I'm just glad you're back."

Howie blushed to the roots of his hair as she showered kisses on his cheeks.

But not everyone was happy to see them safely returned.

The weasel of a High Regent, Lord Orrin, came stomping across the square, his long red robe flapping behind him. He was followed closely by the dour-faced Emenor. Both men looked fit to be tied.

"What's happening? Where is Lord Drabic?" Orrin demanded.

Teren's voice was neutral as he stroked the muzzle of his horse. "As I predicted, it was a trap. The witches ambushed us on the road. Drabic was killed."

Orrin ignored the accusation in Teren's words and pointed at Abigail. "And who is this?" he demanded.

"Lord Orrin, meet Lady Abigail Barconian," Teren said with more than a hint of smugness.

Orrin's eyes bulged as he took in the words. "Barconian? But that's . . . she's . . . she's a witch? How do we know she can be trusted?"

"Because I say so," Teren answered with steel in his voice.

Orrin's face flushed red with outrage at the Captain's insolence. "Need I remind you, Captain, that with Drabic gone, I am in charge of this city?"

Before Teren could point out all the reasons Orrin was unfit to watch over a pack of hyenas, Emenor pushed past and grabbed Teren by the arm. "Are the rumors true? That there are monstrous men out there?"

Teren nodded, his face haunted. "Aye. The witches have turned your kind into something . . . unspeakable."

Emenor blinked several times, as if he couldn't quite grasp what Teren was saying.

Speria appeared over the top of the rampart.

"Captain Teren. Hate to break up a reunion, but you're gonna want to see this."

The group quickly joined Speria. A walkway ten feet wide ran along the length of the wall that protected Skara Brae from intruders. Howie squinted at where Speria was pointing. Something moved on the edge of the horizon like an undulating wave of black ants.

Howie cupped his hand over his eyes to block the glare. Whatever it was, it was moving this way. Fast.

"What's happening?" Orrin demanded.

Speria handed Teren a spyglass. The official studied the oncoming horde then slowly lowered the scope, his face gray as putty.

"Look for yourself." Teren handed Orrin the spyglass.

Orrin held it up to his eye, put it down, then looked again. A single muscle ticked in his cheek. He passed the scope silently to Emenor.

The Balfin gasped as he stared through the glass, putting a hand to his throat. "By the gods, what have they done?"

Howie snatched the scope from him and twisted it until it came into focus. There were hordes of the Neanderthals they had met in the woods. So many they couldn't be counted. Then he saw something even worse than his worst nightmare.

His buddy Sam. Out in front. Leading them. Dressed head to toe in black armor, his dark hair falling over his forehead. He looked grim as death. It felt like a blow to Howie's stomach. He passed the scope to Abigail, who visibly paled at the sight of her son.

"Your orders, sir?" Teren said archly to Orrin.

Orrin kept staring at the approaching storm. Then, without a word, he turned and walked away, disappearing down the steps.

Emenor trembled. "They've transformed my brothers into monsters. We are all going to die." His voice bubbled with hysteria. His eyes darted wildly from Teren to Speria. "We're doomed!"

Teren popped the babbling Balfin in the chin with his fist, a stiff uppercut that dropped Emenor like a stone.

"Take him to the armory and shackle him," he ordered Heppner. "He'll just get in the way." Heppner dragged the unconscious man away.

A rattle below drew their attention. Howie leaned over the rampart and watched as the heavy iron gates rolled up. A lone horseman bolted out of the gate before it was hastily lowered again.

Orrin.

He whipped his horse hard, turning left—away from the fight.

Teren just grunted. "So I guess that settles who's in charge."

Abigail stood staring at the oncoming horde. Her hands were white-knuckled as she gripped the balustrade. "Sam is out there. We can't attack them."

Teren addressed her, his voice gentle. "My lady, if he is with them, he is not Sam. Not anymore."

She shook her head emphatically. "No. My son is not lost to us. I refuse to believe that. Let me go down and face him. I can bring him back."

Teren shook his head. "Look at that line of witches. The moment Catriona sees you, she will try to destroy you. You are powerful, but alone against Catriona and her horde, it is too dangerous. And it will put Sam's life at risk if he tries to help you."

She stared at her distant son, then sagged in defeat. "I will stay back. For now." She turned to Howie. "Tell me again what Keely is doing."

"Keely went to get some Moon Pearl from Ymir. It's supposed to help us bring Sam back."

"Okay, so we just have to hold out until she gets here."

Teren's voice was despondent. "Abigail, we have no idea where Keely is. Or if she even lives. We don't have the manpower to fight that army. At the first attack, we will be overrun."

Abigail's chin was firm, her gaze steady as she met Teren's. "You have me. I may be rusty, but I still have a trick or two up my sleeve. And the Falcory will come, as will the Eifalians. We are not alone in this, Teren. Our friends will not desert us in our time of need. We just need to buy some time. Howie, Odin chose you as Protector. We could really use one of your clever schemes."

Howie's mouth opened and closed. Everyone was waiting for him to say something. "Well, I'm not sure . . ."

Sam's mom gripped his arm. "Think, Howie. Odin must have believed you were special to have chosen you."

Howie's brain hummed like a high-tension wire. He tried to think of all the things he knew about battle. Heck, he had played umpteen hours battling imaginary creatures in video games. To win, he usually upgraded his weapons cache and out-battled his opponents. His hand went to his waist. Odin had already given him the ultimate upgrade . . .

"Well, I could go out there with my sword."

"That rusted thing?" Speria said, scowling with doubt.

Howie grinned at Teren, who nodded his permission. As he gripped the handle and pulled it out, gold sparks shot in the air. Blazing light flickered from its razor-edge blade. Once again, it had changed from the rusty old heap Fetch had given him into a glowing golden sword, shining in the fading afternoon light.

Speria's eyes grew as big as silver dollars. "By Odin's blood," he breathed, awestruck.

Even Selina looked impressed. "Now that's a fine blade." She reached out a finger to trace the edge.

"That's Tyrfing," Howie said proudly. "Did I mention it was made by a pair of black dwarves and had an evil curse on it?"

Abigail nodded encouragingly at him. "Okay, Howie, the sword will help, but it won't stop an army. We need something to slow them down. Any other ideas?"

Howie scratched his head, coming up blank. And then a light went off. "Hold on. Just hold on a minute. Nobody move."

He left them staring at him strangely as he raced down the steps across the square into the Great Hall, heading for the residence quarters. He pounded down corridors until he skidded to a stop at Teren's door. He threw it open and raced to his bed, throwing back the covers. He lifted the pillow.

There it was.

The Horn of Gjall.

He lifted it, kissing it once, and then scurried back to the impatient group on the rampart.

"Got it, oh yeah, say, 'Howie, you're the man!'" he shouted as he gasped for breath.

"What in Odin's name?" Teren's voice was awestruck. "It can't be." He reached his fingers out to touch the horn.

"That's the Horn of Gjall," Abigail said with a fierce mixture of hope and awe. "Howie, where did you say you got these gifts from Odin?"

Howie shrugged. "Long story. A little green guy named Fetch gave me the sword. The horn's from Mimir. He and I were joking about calling up an army of the dead. I guess that old dude doesn't kid around. Look, I think I'm supposed to blow on it." He put it up to his lips, but Teren stayed his hand.

"Do you know what the horn does, lad? When you blow on it?"

Howie nodded. "It calls up some kind of undead zombie soldiers."

Teren's hand was like an iron manacle on his wrist. "And you're sure this isn't some plan of the witches'?"

Howie studied the old thing. Mimir had given it to him, so he figured it was part of Odin's master plan.

"Well, I guess we'll find out." He licked his lips once and then took a deep breath. He held up his sword for courage as he blew a long blast. At the sound of the first note, the sword began to send out golden sparks. As everyone looked on in awe, Howie blew the horn again. A golden beam of light shot out from the sword, stabbing at the ground below just outside the walls of Skara Brae. Howie stopped, and they all waited, holding their breaths. A large crack in the earth appeared, zigzagging in a line. Then the earth split apart, opening a chasm. A skeletal head appeared, looking around, and then pulled itself out of the earth. It was followed by an unending line of skeletal men, trailing swords and wearing tattered uniforms over their bony remains.

They filed out in procession, dragging their jerky frames into formation.

"By the heavens, I have never seen such a sight," Teren exclaimed. "Those are Huns. You can tell by their armor." Ragged fur trimmed their pointed helmets, and long beards drooped down from the sides of their skeletal jaws.

What had Fetch said? That some king named Agantyr had destroyed an entire army of Huns with the Sword of Tyrfing on its last evil quest? Howie's respect for Odin's gift rose to new levels because he had no doubt the sword had helped conjure up this batch.

Selina clapped her hands. "Amazing," she murmured. "Way to go, Protector."

Heppner slapped Howie on the back.

Speria looked dour as ever. "Don't celebrate till we know whose side they're on," he grumbled.

Howie's initial excitement turned to mounting unease as reality set in. *I've just called up an army of dead Huns I have no idea how to control, so I can go after my best friend and his witch buddies,* he thought to himself. *Why couldn't I have been picked as the Sacrifice?*

The assembled squad of skeletons looked up and rattled their swords at Howie. They seemed to be waiting for him to come down.

He straightened his shoulders, holding the golden sword with a sweaty hand. "So I guess I'll just go down and introduce myself before my best friend gets here and tries to destroy us."

"I'll go with you," Selina offered.

"No way," Howie said. "You stay with Teren and help." He looked at Teren as he pointed at Selina. "She's a better swordsman than any one of your recruits."

"The fight's going to be over before it's begun." Teren spoke with little enthusiasm. "My men are scattered around Garamond fighting battles. We've only a handful of recruits on hand. That and a legion of dried-up bones aren't going to win this battle."

"Don't be so sure." Selina nodded over his shoulder. Behind them, a group of men had assembled along the narrow rampart. Howie recognized Milligan, the weathered farmer who had given them a ride to Skara Brae.

"We reckon we're in this, we might as well fight," Milligan said. Behind him stood bakers still in their flour-covered aprons, the blacksmith with grease up to his elbows, more stable boys, even the old apothecary—all nodding firmly in agreement. "So we'll fight if you'll have us." He gripped a pitchfork.

Teren grinned. "It would be my honor to stand with you. But first, I have an important honor to bestow."

The captain shrugged out of his armored chain mail and red Orkadian vest and slipped them over Howie's head. The chain mail went to Howie's knees. Teren drew his sword and tapped Howie on both shoulders. "I hereby induct you into the Orkadian Guard."

Howie felt a grin split his face from ear to ear. The feeling was better than anything he had ever experienced. Better than winning science fair sixth-grade year. Better than the kiss he had gotten at science camp. Better than anything he could ever imagine feeling.

Teren's eyes gleamed with hope. "I think I have an idea how we can use Howie's army and give those witches a fight they won't soon forget." Teren explained his plan. Once they had agreement, it was time for Howie to head out.

"Don't be afraid, Howie," Abigail said, putting her arm around his shoulder. "I'll be watching over you. Just promise me you won't take Sam's head off with that sword."

Howie clutched the powerful weapon in his hand, swallowed back his fear, and made his way down the steps, marching past a sea of frightened faces until he reached the front gate. With every step he felt as if he were striding closer to his death.

He hesitated in the archway of the gate as it rattled up. The moldering band of skeletons grunted with shouts of huzzah when he appeared, eyeing his sword like it was a beacon from the heavens.

One of the skeletal figures strode forward to meet him as he crossed the bridge. A thick Fu Manchu mustache marked its skeletal jaws. A rotted velveteen robe trimmed with dark fur was flung over its bony shoulders.

"*Ta nar khen yum?*" it barked at Howie.

"Yo, skeleton-face. How's it hanging?"

The zombie leader looked at the other men, then thrust his sword in Howie's face.

"*Ta nar khen yum?*" it shouted, breathing clouds of dust in Howie's eyes.

Howie coughed at the centuries of bad breath. "I get it. I'm as confused as you. Here's the thing. Odin made me Protector, and I could use some help."

At Odin's name, the leader quieted down.

"Odin?" it muttered.

"Yes, you know Odin?" Howie asked.

The skeleton shouted nonsense, and then the entire crowd of skeletons moved in around Howie like an angry mob.

"Okay, bad idea, no Odin. Back off." He wielded the sword, swinging it awkwardly over his head, and they stepped back, clearly afraid of the golden blade.

"Does anyone here speaka the English?" Howie asked.

A skeleton thrust its way through the crowd.

"I speak your language," it muttered between clenched jaws. Its teeth were rotted along bare jawbone. Armor hung in tatters over a bony chest. A broken clavicle bore the round mark of a spear. "I am Blad."

"Great," Howie said. "Can you translate what the boss man here is saying?"

The lead skeleton began shouting. "*Ild bidend khorigdlyg ezemshdeg. Ild temtsekh, bid gargasan bolno!*"

Blad nodded and turned to Howie. "General Octar says that cursed sword led to our death. Why would we fight for you?"

"Uhm . . ." Howie had no idea. "Well . . ."

The Huns pressed in closer. Bony fingers went to their dirt-crusted swords. Howie began to sweat. "Tell Octar-man, you tell him . . ."

Howie began to cluck like a chicken. "What's the matter, Octar-man, you afraid of a few witches?" Howie continued to squawk, flapping his arms and dancing in a circle. The Huns drew back, looking at each other like he was crazy. "I thought you were Huns," he taunted. "I thought you were the baddest army on the face of the earth, but I guess you're just a bunch of sissy pants."

Blad translated Howie's words. Octar shouted in Howie's face. Dirt flew from his dried-up lips. Whatever he was saying, the Hun-master was not happy.

Howie stopped his dance. "What did he say?"

Blad put a bony hand on Howie's shoulder. "He said you are crazy. But he will fight."

Howie gaped. "He will?"

In reply, General Octar shouted, "*Kherev tiim bol. Temstel!*"

Howie didn't need a translator to know *temstel* meant *fight*.

"*Temstel*," he answered, waving the sword over his head.

"*Temstel!*" the group shouted, joining their swords with his.

At that moment, Howie would have given his life for a cell-phone camera and enough Wi-Fi to post this picture of him commanding an army of Hun skeletons all over the Internet.

"Bring it in, my Hun buddies. It's time to make a plan."

Chapter Forty

A rush of excitement filled Kalifus as the red flags of Skara Brae came into view. It had been an age since he had been to this city that was his second home. A wave of nostalgia rolled over him as he remembered Teren and his other Orkadian friends and the good times they had shared. Those days were gone forever now. Kalifus squashed the sappy feelings and gripped the reins tighter. By end of day, Skara Brae would be in shambles, and Kalifus would be celebrating its destruction.

He rode by Catriona's side. Her back was ramrod straight, eyes facing forward. The Balfin army marched behind. Such ugly hairy brutes with twisted faces and ropy, muscled bodies. Vena had made them nearly invincible. The once-harmless Balfin puppets had become snarling monsters that knocked down trees with mere swings of their meaty paws.

The day was bright and sunny, the air crisp with the light winter chill. Weather in Skara Brae was mild, even in the middle of winter. By nightfall, smoke would be rising from the turrets of Orkney's last stronghold. With Teren out of the city and probably dead by now, there would be no one left to lead the defense.

Catriona raised her hand to stop the horde. Before them, less than two football fields away, the walls of Skara Brae shimmered. The flags snapped sharply, like rifle shots in the afternoon breeze. The ramparts appeared empty. Where were the sentinels? The manned towers? Had they given up already? A slow smile crossed Kalifus's face. This was going to be a blowout.

The Balfins spread out, loping across the fields in waves, halting a safe distance from the walls. Catriona rode through the center, heading straight for the wooden gate of the main entrance to the city. Kalifus accompanied her along with Agathea and Beatrixe. Vena stayed back with her creations, cracking her whip over their heads as she marshaled them into position.

They had no siege weapons. They didn't need them. Their sheer numbers and potent magic would provide all the offense they needed.

Kalifus squinted as a tiny figure came into view. It couldn't be. Standing outside the gates of Skara Brae. All alone.

Howie.

He should be holed up in an underground bunker, quaking with fear. Not brazenly loitering outside the gates of the city. A murmur of unease made Kalifus wary. Howie could be bait. His eyes scanned the area, searching for any sign of a trap.

They rode up to where his old friend stood, gangly arms hanging awkwardly at his side. Howie had walked a stone's throw from the castle and was completely unprotected. He had an old rusted scabbard looped through his belt. It was so long it dragged in the dirt, leaving a trail of dust. The armor he wore was two sizes too big. The red Orkadian vest hung to his knees. Chain mail sagged off his shoulders. He looked like a scrawny kid standing up to an army that would as soon tear him to shreds.

Laughter rippled through Catriona as she halted her horse. "Is this the boy?" she asked Kalifus. "The one Odin named Protector?"

"That's me," Howie answered before Kalifus could speak. A stupid grin was plastered to his face. "I'm the Great Protector." He turned toward Kalifus, waggling his fingers in a salute. "Heya, Sam, how's it hangin'?"

"My name is Kalifus," he snapped back, dismounting from his horse to eyeball his old friend, walking in a half circle around him. "Is this some kind of joke? You couldn't defend a flea from a dog's scratching."

The rest of the coven chuckled.

Howie joined in the laughter. "Yeah, you're probably right, Sam, I mean, Mr. Kalifus, sir. But I'm not worried about a dog. Just the yellow-bellied coward standing in front of me."

Kalifus's rage flashed into a boil. Did Howie not understand what he had done for him? For all of them? He threw out his hand and lifted Howie as if he weighed nothing. He twisted his fingers so the boy felt his choking power.

"You dare insult me?"

"Yeah, I dare." Howie grabbed at Kalifus's hands, prying at them. "I dare, because I'm your best friend."

"I despise you," Kalifus swore, staring into Howie's glasses. Kalifus's own red-rimmed eyes stared back in the reflection.

"Enough," Catriona said, sounding bored. "Kill him."

Obediently, Kalifus threw Howie back so forcefully that the boy tumbled head over heels in the dirt. Gathering his energy, Kalifus sent a blast of witchfire to annihilate him, but Howie rolled away faster than Kalifus expected, and his blast struck dirt. Howie looked up at him with hurt in his eyes.

"Why are you doing this, Sam?"

Blood pounded in Kalifus's ears. Next time he wouldn't miss. "The Orkadians are too weak to rule this land. Power belongs in the hands of those willing to seize it."

Howie got to his feet, brushing off the dust. "Yeah, well, the Sam I knew stood up for the underdog."

Kalifus stalked forward and shoved him. "Sam is dead! I killed him, the same way I killed Odin. And now, I'm going to kill you." Kalifus enjoyed the shattered look of pain on his friend's face. The hapless boy looked like he was about to burst into tears. Twin balls of witchfire appeared over Kalifus's hands. This time, he wouldn't miss. He drew his arms back.

Howie shrugged scrawny shoulders, his chin sagging in defeat. "Then I guess there's only one thing left to say."

Kalifus paused. "What's that?"

"Your buddy Fetch says hello." Howie's chin came up, and his eyes sparkled with a fierceness that was out of place for Kalifus's meek and mild friend.

Confusion raced through Kalifus as he remembered Odin's little green-furred helper. "Fetch?"

Howie drew his sword from the rusted scabbard at his side. Only the blade wasn't actually rusted. As he pulled it out, the sword transformed, glinting in the sunlight and nearly blinding Kalifus with its brilliance.

Catriona let out a strangled shriek of pain and rage.

"Behold the Sword of Tyrfing," Howie shouted. "I command my awesome army of Huns to attack."

Behind Howie, bony apparitions in tattered uniforms clambered to their feet, skeletal men that took form in the light of day. They had been hidden in shallow earth under piles of brush. From the rampart walls, a row of men popped up armed with bows. Immediately, arrows flew over their heads, aimed at the witches' army. Catapults filled with flaming tar pitch were launched, rocking the ground with the force of their impact.

It was a trap.

Howie had tricked them. Veins pulsing with outrage, Kalifus spun, intending to erase the scrawny boy, but he was gone.

"Howie! Get back here!" Kalifus shouted, but the little coward had scampered off back to the safety of the castle. Kalifus sent blasts of witchfire after Howie's back, but they fell short.

The Balfin baboons were running every which way in a panic. Billowing smoke rolled over the fields. A flaming ball of pitch landed in the dirt next to Catriona, sending her flying backward as she was sprayed with burning tar. Kalifus was there to lift her to her feet. The Balfins engaged the army of dead Huns with swords and double-headed axes. The Huns crumbled under the mutant Balfins' superior strength, but their numbers seemed endless. For every ten knocked down, twenty more Huns appeared. Vena used her whip to stop the Balfins from fleeing the battlefield, urging them to keep fighting.

"Steady," Catriona called out, grasping her hands into clenched fists. Agathea took a stance to her left. Kalifus joined her at her other side. Next to him, Beatrixe and then Hestera, Lemeria, and the other Tarkana witches lined up.

"On my order, we combine our magic to erase these despicable creatures from the face of the earth," Catriona bellowed. "Are you ready?"

"Ready," Agathea said.

Beatrixe grunted in her mute speech.

"I'm ready," Kalifus said, folding his hands to gather his magic.

"Ready," Hestera said, cracking her old neck as she took a stance.

And so it went down the line.

The witches stood shoulder to shoulder and blazed the army of the dead with a steady hail of green witchfire.

The Huns kept up the attack, fighting through the Balfin lines to get to the witches. Catriona and her closest allies released a hail of unstoppable magic that wiped out every bloodthirsty Hun skeleton that approached them. Kalifus was enjoying this. Power engulfed his veins as he unleashed with every cylinder he had. It was a rush like nothing else. With this new magic of his, he could take down an entire row of skeletons with just a pass of his hand. But after several long minutes, even Kalifus tired. His arms felt weak, his knees shaking so bad they could barely hold him up.

Next to him, he could see Beatrixe struggling. The mute witch had resorted to spraying the swarming bones with the acid that spouted from her fingertips. Several Huns broke through the Balfin line and swarmed over her. She disintegrated two of them, but one managed to run her through with a sword. Kalifus blasted it away, but another came. Before he could obliterate them, Beatrixe had five swords in her. She went down screeching in wordless agony under their attack.

"Don't falter!" Catriona screamed. "Destroy them all." Catriona appeared tireless, blazing a steady trail that wiped out every skeleton in her path.

The line of witches kept blasting, but one by one they tired, dropping their hands in exhaustion. Lemeria was taken down next, her simpering giggle stopped mid-syllable when a tottering skeleton ran his sword through her throat. Catriona blasted him to bits, too late to save her favorite Tarkana witch.

The skeletons dwindled in numbers, but a fresh batch broke out of the earth, staggering toward them. It was down to Kalifus and Catriona.

They took out the first row, but the next wave was on them so quickly. Hestera cowered behind Kalifus, but he had nothing left to fight with. Even Catriona seemed to have run dry. Her green witchfire sputtered and went out. A Hun charged her, broad sword held high over its head. It was shrieking at her with its dried-up tongue poking out, shouting, *"Temstel!"*

The Hun swung the blade around to bring it down on Catriona. Like a match to dry grass, Kalifus erupted into fury. No way some ancient pile of bones was going to take out his queen. His exhaustion faded away, replaced by a high-octane venom-laced fuel that raced through his veins. Just as he had done back on Asgard, his eyes shot flames out like laser beams that destroyed the skeleton mid-swing. He turned his attention to the oncoming horde and blasted every last Hun zombie that remained.

Kalifus was left shaking and gasping for air as the Balfins grunted and kicked at the skeleton remains on the ground.

"You have proven yourself, Kalifus," Catriona crowed with pride. "Truly you are my son."

Kalifus glowed, but he said nothing, tipping his head in acknowledgment.

"We rest for now," Catriona called to her remaining coven. "We lost dear Beatrixe and Lemeria. Tomorrow, we will take our revenge."

Vena rode up on her horse. "We cannot withstand another battle like that," she said, whipping her hair out of her face.

"Too right," Catriona agreed. "And it's too risky to just conjure ourselves inside. They could have an even nastier trap waiting." She turned to Kalifus. "Do you have another way in?"

An idea sprang into his mind. Without a word, he strode away from the walls toward the distant trees. Catriona followed. He whistled sharply three times as they approached the woods.

"What are you doing?" she asked.

"Getting us a ride," he said. They waited under the trees for long minutes until a shadow passed overhead. An Omera settled down in the clearing with a thump. Its black wings arched high before settling down at its side. It bared its fangs at Catriona, but Kalifus ignored the danger and strode over and rubbed his old friend's nose. "Bring the others," he whispered. "Bring them all."

Without a sound, the Omera took flight, winging through the trees.

Chapter Forty-One

The Eifalian armada was a dozen ships strong. Each ship held a hundred skilled archers. The sleek crafts cut through the water cleanly and swiftly. Time was running short. If they didn't reach Skara Brae before the witches took over, Keely's journey would have been for nothing. The king's sacrifice, in vain. The wind was icy as it whipped across the front of the boat. Keely showed her face to the elements. The biting cold kept her from choking with fear over what was to come.

Galatin joined her at the railing. "I never properly thanked you," he said stiffly, looking out over the water.

"For what?"

"For saving my life. First with the troll hags and then with the Vanir."

She shrugged. "You would have done the same."

"All the same, I underestimated you. I thought I would be the one taking care of you."

"You never did finish what you were going to tell me. Why we left Torf-Einnar in such a rush."

He laughed ruefully. "I was going to warn you that Rifkin was a traitor. I overheard him having a conversation with a pair of ravens. Didn't take a genius to figure he was working for the witches. If the king read our auras again, he would have known my suspicions, and we would have never left Ter Glen. Rifkin was the only one who knew the way to the Cave of Shadows. I figured I'd let him lead us to it, and then I would deal with him. I didn't count on getting beaten by a troll hag and being trussed up by the Vanir."

Mavery joined them, snuggling up under Keely's arm. "Are we there yet?"

"We're passing Pantros," Keely answered, slipping her arm around the thin shoulders of the witch-girl. Theo took a silent stance next to Mavery, his slender fingers gripping the rail.

They looked out over the water. The moon shone down, reflecting off the sea like a white carpet. In the distance, the dark volcano on Pantros loomed ominously.

"What's that?" Mavery asked, pointing.

In the light of the moon, a thin trail of smoke rose up from the shoreline. The smoke was odd, billowing and then stopping, then starting again.

"It looks like someone is signaling," Galatin said.

"Who would be signaling from that dark place?" Theo asked.

Dark place. Keely's pulse jumped. "Stop the ship!" she cried, running back to the helm where Gael stood overseeing their course. "We have to go to Pantros."

Gael looked up from his navigation charts. "Why in Odin's name would we go there?"

She grinned. "Because Leo's signaling us."

Dawn crept over the horizon with slivers of tangerine and gray, lighting the dark-amber sky and rousing Howie from his slumber. He rubbed the sleep from his eyes. He was still up in the ramparts. The cold stone bit into his hips as he threw back the light blanket that covered him. Teren and Abigail were looking out over the massing Balfins, as they had been doing all night.

Howie had stayed with them, until he had fallen asleep on his feet and Sam's mom had pushed him into the corner and ordered him to get some rest. Lingas cawed at him from her cage, protesting her confinement. Howie tossed her a piece of jerky and then joined Teren at the wall.

Overnight, the Balfins had fashioned rough catapults out of trees. They were dragging them into position. There were also several long logs with small boulders lashed to the ends. They looked like they would make excellent battering rams. Skara Brae was like a medieval Fort Knox. The walls were more than four feet thick. But the gate was made of iron-reinforced wood. Scant protection against Sam, aka crazy-Kalifus, and his army of ape-men.

"Any sign of our backup team?" Howie asked.

The veteran soldier shook his head. "Something's not right," he muttered.

"I agree," Abigail said, her eyes searching the throngs for her son.

"They're getting ready. Rouse the men," Teren ordered, laying out his supply of iron bolts for his crossbow.

Howie put his fingers between his lips and let out a low trill. An answering call sounded down the ramparts, and another farther on. The men were awake and ready.

As the sun crept above the horizon and formed a round orange ball in the sky, the Balfins launched their first missile. It was a boulder the size of a washing machine. It smashed into the corner tower and sent men pinwheeling through the air, splintering the wood.

Abigail created a blue sphere of energy she launched back, disintegrating the first catapult. Howie ran along the ramparts, handing out arrows, refilling crossbows, and shouting words of encouragement. Milligan made a fine lieutenant, marshalling the other farmers to help man the catapults. The walls held as the replacement soldiers did their part to hold the line. One of their own catapults was destroyed by a lucky shot before Abigail blasted the Balfins' machine to bits. A wave of ape-men braved the arrows and swarmed the wall, carrying a rudimentary ladder. The mutant Balfins began to climb.

"Selina, help me with this," Howie called, throwing the girl a thick glove and putting one on himself. They each took one handle of a large pot and carefully carried it to the ledge. Hoisting it up, they tipped it over, dropping boiling tar into the face of the first snarling Balfin. He fell back, screaming, taking out a line of Balfins below him. Abigail used her magic to disintegrate the ladder to ashes.

The fight went on for what seemed like an eternity, but it was probably less than an hour before it all went wrong.

The Balfins increased their onslaught of boulders flung at the castle. They mostly crashed harmlessly against the solid wall, but some got through and caused minor damage. Howie was pulling a dazed farmer out from under a fallen beam when it hit him.

Where was Sam?

The witches weren't down on the battlefield. He dropped the farmer, ignoring his yelp, and turned to warn Teren, but he was too late.

Shadows blanketed the sun. The sound of beating wings filled the air. And then from over the trees of the forest, two dozen Omeras appeared, long forked tails streaming behind them. Their black bodies alone were a fearsome sight, but each Omera carried a trio of witches, all spraying the ground with their nasty green witchfire. They were winging straight for the walls of the Skara Brae stronghold. The Omeras were fast, easily dodging the few arrows that were launched. The witches leaned over the side, sending Teren's men diving for cover as they blanketed them with witchfire.

They landed in the center of the town square, at the steps of the Great Hall.

Howie peered over the rampart, feeling gutted as he watched Sam jump down from an Omera.

Teren came to kneel by his side. "Stay down," he whispered, motioning his men to stay out of sight.

The other witches descended from their Omeras and took up position around the square. The Omeras took off, circling overhead.

Catriona strode to the middle of the square. "We have won," she shouted, spinning in a circle. "Surrender before the clock strikes noon, and we will spare the lives of your citizens. Attack us, and I will burn this city to the ground."

Howie looked at the clock tower on the Great Hall. They only had a few minutes.

A girl emerged from the armory and ran at Sam, bearing a sword like she wanted to take his head off.

Selina.

Howie lurched up to warn her, but Sam had already seen her. With a wave of his hand, he sent her flying away from him; she crashed into a pile of barrels and lay motionless. Teren yanked Howie back down.

Sam stood by Catriona, searching the deserted ramparts as he shouted for Howie. "Great Protector, get down here before I blast this girl to ashes!" He held a ball of his nasty witch magic over his hand.

"Tick, tock," Catriona said. "Listen," she put a hand to her ear. A loud banging noise echoed in the square. "Soon your gate will be in pieces, and then even I won't be able to stop those brutes from destroying everyone in this city."

Teren turned to Howie. "Howie, can you go down there and distract Sam? We must defend the gates."

Howie blinked at him. *Distract the psycho witch who was my best friend?* "Sure, Teren. I can do that."

Teren nodded, gripping his shoulder before shouting at the men, "To the gate, lads," Heppner and Speria led a group of men along the rampart toward the battering noises.

Abigail turned to head down the stairs to where Sam waited, but Teren grabbed her arm. "My lady, we need you at the gate. We'll never hold off that horrid army without magic."

Her eyes were hollow. "Not this time, Teren. I will speak with my son."

Teren pleaded. "Abigail, I beg you. None of us will survive the horde out there if they breach our walls. The people of Skara Brae need you more than Sam. There is still a chance that our allies will arrive in time, but it won't matter if we're all dead."

The banging on the gates intensified, shaking the ground under their feet. Teren's men continued to fire on the ape-men who approached the wall.

"It's okay, Mrs. Abigail," Howie said, gripping his golden sword, "I got this. I'm not afraid of Sam."

Abigail cast one last lingering glance at her son's figure below, then reluctantly let Teren drag her away. "Buy me some time to seal the gate," she called over her shoulder. "I can get through to him."

Howie waited until they were gone, and then he stood at the railing that faced the square. Lingas squawked forlornly at him from her cage. He rubbed her head with his knuckles. The way he figured it, Keely should have been here by now if she was coming. The only thing standing between Skara Brae and total destruction was Howie. His hand went to the Sword of Tyrfing at his side. If it came to it, he would do what had to be done.

Howie forced his trademark grin. "Chillax, Sam, I'm right here." He slowly climbed down the steps.

Chapter Forty-Two

As Howie ambled across the open square, Kalifus sent a blast of blazing fire at the boy's feet, making Howie stumble and fall back on his rear. "You traitorous worm, you think you're so clever. Who's going to save you now, Howie? Where's your zombie army now?"

Undeterred, Howie pushed himself up to face his friend, clenching his fists. "Doesn't matter, dork-face, because you're the one who needs saving."

Kalifus snorted. "From who?"

"Me." Howie's face tightened, and his hand went to his sword, clearly intending to run his old friend through with it, but when he reached for his hilt, it was empty.

"Looking for this?" Catriona held the Sword of Tyrfing. It glinted in her hands. She ran one finger along the blade. "This blade took the life of my father. It is only fitting that you, Kalifus, should use it to take the head of Odin's chosen hero."

Kalifus took the sword, holding it out before him. It was a thing of beauty. The hasp was encrusted with rubies and emeralds. The blade itself was long and unscratched, glinting with a sharpness that left no doubt it could cleave a man's head.

Agathea swooped in, chucking her fingers under Howie's chin. "Cut him in pieces and we can feed him to my sneevils," she cooed. "They hunger outside the walls."

Kalifus nodded, ignoring the pleading look in Howie's eyes. He gripped the sword in both hands, raising it over his head.

"Don't do it, Sam," Howie begged, trying to step backward, but a wall of witches moved in behind him, blocking his way. "I'm still your best friend."

"Best friend? You were going to kill me!" Kalifus blasted back. His arms trembled with rage. His friend didn't look brave anymore, just scared, and terribly hurt, like a light had gone out in his eyes. A ripple of doubt made him pause. He shook his head to rid himself of it, then doubled his grip on the sword. He could do this. It would be his final test to himself, to prove who he really was. He shut his eyes, to block out Howie's face. Then, taking a deep breath, he raised the sword high, prepared to swing the blade with all his might.

Before he could twitch a muscle, a blast of witchfire burned his hands, sending the sword flying from his grip. His eyes flew open. The sword clanged across the paving stones to land at the feet of a lanky young witch.

He gaped in surprise.

Perrin Tarkana.

Kalifus growled in disbelief. It couldn't be. She was dead. He had killed her. So why did it make him strangely happy to see her?

Because a sister witch was restored, he told himself. He had a right to be pleased. More green lightning flashed across the open space. Catriona squealed in outrage as she was zapped on the rear end.

Behind Perrin, a smirking Endera stepped from the shadows of the blacksmith shop into the square.

Forgetting Howie, Kalifus crossed to Catriona's side, taking a protective stance. Agathea crouched on the other. The remaining witches fanned out, forming a wide circle. They ogled the group in the center eagerly like they were about to witness a playground fight.

Catriona's eyes glittered with malice as she stared down her opponent. "You dare show your face after killing Ariane?"

Endera sent another blast of fire at Catriona's feet, making her step sideways. "That hag deserved it," she said, sauntering forward slowly.

Catriona's eyes turned red at the arrogance in Endera's voice. "She deserved your allegiance," she hissed, but then she vanished. She reappeared in a cloud of gray smoke behind the upstart, sending fingers of glowing fire at Endera.

Endera disappeared before it struck, reappearing on the other side of the square. "She was weak. Like you. Not fit to lead this coven."

Kalifus made a movement toward her, but Catriona held up her hand, staying him.

"And you think you are fit? The coven follows me." She looked around the tight circle of witches. Their faces gave away nothing. Unease made Kalifus shift on his feet. He couldn't tell if they were on her side or not. Hestera's face was like pudding, her lips pursed in a straight line.

Catriona changed tactics, flinging her arms wide. "Let us not fight on this glorious day. Let us celebrate our victory."

"Our victory came with a price," Endera challenged. "You promised me Agathea's life."

Agathea's chin dropped as she hissed at Catriona. "How dare you!"

Catriona waved her off. "It meant nothing. Endera doesn't have the power to take your life." She turned to Endera. "Agathea has the blood of Rubicus. We are sisters in every sense. She's not as weak as cousin Ariane."

"Watch me." Endera snapped her fingers, disappearing in a black cloud of smoke.

In an instant, she appeared at Kalifus's side, slipping the enchanted obsidian blade from his belt. Before he could react, she pivoted and thrust it upward into Agathea's chest. The witch screamed, her body arching. Catriona released a bolt of green lightning at Endera, but the deed was done. Agathea's lifeless body crumpled to the ground, the blade embedded deep in her chest.

Catriona screamed loudly in rage and anguish, sending a giant wall of fire at Endera. She rolled nimbly to the side so only the edges of her skirt caught fire.

"Mother!" Perrin stepped into the circle, sending a blast of witchfire at Catriona, but the girl's magic was weak. Catriona batted it away and released a rolling ball of green fire at the young witch.

Kalifus stepped in to deflect it. "No. She is a witch, one of us."

Endera laughed behind his back, patting down the flames. "What's the matter, sister? Your pet not behaving? Tsk, tsk, I'd say you're losing your touch. Too bad he wasn't so protective of his warrior friend. I had to leave him behind with Sinmara."

Kalifus felt like he had been punched in the gut. Leo left in the underworld? Across the square, he locked eyes with Howie. His old friend shook his head, like it was all Kalifus's fault. Guilt made him uncomfortable and angry. If they had just stayed back in Pilot Rock, none of this would have happened. He seethed at the unfairness of it, his skin prickling with anger. He stepped forward to battle at Catriona's side, but she held him back with one hand.

"No, Kalifus, this is between me and Endera. So this is what it's come to, Endera," Catriona said haughtily. "A battle for the right to lead. Very well. You shall have your fight." The clock began to strike the hour. "Before the clock is done chiming, you will be finished, and my army will be inside the gates. I hear their battering ram now."

Kalifus had almost forgotten the battle raging outside. The relentless banging had grown louder, the shouts of the Balfins raised in ever-increasing volume. He frowned. How was Captain Teren holding the gates? Those Balfin apes should have knocked it to pieces by now and joined them in the square. He was tempted to go check, but he didn't dare leave Catriona in case Endera's cronies got it in their mind to back her.

The clock gonged again. Ten more to go. Catriona pointed one gnarled finger at Endera. "Let everyone in Skara Brae watch me destroy you once and for all," she called. "And when I am finished, my hold over this coven, and this world, will be absolute."

"Mother, be careful," Perrin warned, but Endera raised her hand to silence the girl.

"No. She is right. It is time we put this to an end. Catriona has tainted this world long enough."

Two more gongs echoed.

"Watch carefully. You don't want to miss this." Catriona was cocky, arrogant.

Endera held two glowing spheres over her hand. They sparked and crackled with energy. "Oh, I won't miss." She drew back and flung the fireballs at Catriona. Catriona never moved, never flinched. The balls were aimed straight for her head. At the last second, she lifted her palm and caught them, extinguishing them with a flick of her wrist.

"Is that all you've got?" She covered a yawn with one hand.

Endera's face turned red. "No, you old crone, I've got more. A lot more." She swung her hands in a circle, creating a vortex of witchfire like Kalifus had never seen. It was a cyclone, swirling and blowing, growing larger and larger until it towered three stories over them. It swept forward, consuming Catriona inside it. Kalifus stood by, horrified and helpless. Endera glowed triumphant, and then the cyclone went out with a sputtering gasp, and Catriona stood there, unharmed. Kalifus relaxed, grinning.

Catriona brushed her hands down the front of her dress. "I am immune to your pathetic little spells, Endera. Have you not yet grasped the power of my dark magic?"

"How could you . . . that's impossible." Endera's face was shocked.

"Nothing is impossible for me, dear." Catriona flung her arms wide and cried out, *"Mordera, cirrus exodi!"*

Kalifus watched in awe as the skies grew dark and a curtain of gray clouds moved in. A sharp wind blew across the square. Inside the clouds, a swirling bolt of energy formed.

Endera backed away. "Stop. Enough."

Catriona's eyes were wild with vengeance. "Not until you've taken your medicine, Endera."

As the last gong rang out, Catriona raised one fist and then threw it forward. From the turbulent center of the cloud, a jagged bolt of lightning cut through the air, headed straight for Endera.

Endera threw her arms up in defense, but the lighting pinned her in place, illuminating her with white fire. Her body jolted and spasmed, her back arching sharply as thousands of volts of electricity slammed into her. Her hair stood up wildly as the current ran through her. Her mouth was wide open in a silent scream. Endera's body began to smoke. Her clothes burst into flame. Catriona clapped her hands twice, and Endera simply exploded into a cloud of ash.

"That's for Ariane and Agathea," Catriona spat.

Immediately, the dark clouds parted overhead, dissipating into nothing.

"Mother!" Perrin ran forward, but there was nothing left but a pile of ashes.

Kalifus would have cheered, but he was struck silent by Perrin's obvious grief. The girl dropped to her knees, wrapping her arms around her stomach.

Catriona threw her head back, laughing loudly. She raised her fists in the air, whirling to face the coven. "Bow to me and call me your queen, or face the same fate."

Hestera was the first to acquiesce, dipping her chin to her chest. She was followed down the line by every single Tarkana witch, save for Perrin, who continued to kneel in shock.

Catriona gloated. "Is there any who challenges my right to lead? Anyone?"

Silence. Not a sound escaped the coven.

Catriona began to smile in triumph when a splash of sticky mud sprayed her face.

She blinked as gooey sludge dripped from her hair.

There was a giggle from behind an oak barrel. Kalifus could think of only one person who would dare throw mud at Catriona.

Mavery.

He turned and searched for the little imp. There, by the black-smith's shop. He blasted the barrel, exposing her hiding spot.

"You missed, troutface," Mavery said, giggling behind her hand and not looking in the least bit frightened.

"What are you doing here?" Kalifus asked. Before he could recover his wits, an arrow landed in the dirt at his feet.

"Hey, lunkhead, miss me?"

That voice. Kalifus recognized it. He turned slowly.

A girl stood at the top of the steps to the Great Hall. She was dressed in a green velvet cape over fur-trimmed boots. Another arrow was nocked in her bow, a full quiver slung over her shoulder. Her white hair stood up in tufts. She looked tired, but a fire burned in her eyes.

He found he was gawking. Keely had transformed into a completely different person. Not just her appearance. She had a fierceness about her, but at the same time, an aura of grief hung over her, as if she had paid a high price to be where she was. A splinter of pain pierced his heart. He had missed her, he realized.

"Impudent wretch!" Catriona was fuming as she wiped mud from her face. "Kill that witchling," she barked at Kalifus, but Kalifus was frozen in place, his gaze locked on Keely.

Catriona snapped her fingers at a coil of rope. The rope whipped up and danced around Mavery like a whirling tornado. Before the girl could move, she was wrapped like a mummy all the way up to her neck. Rope stretched across her mouth, gagging her screams. Catriona flung her wrist, and the rope dragged Mavery along the ground and then whipped up and looped around a beam in the blacksmith shop. She hung upside down, swinging by her ankles as if she were in a cocoon.

Kalifus felt another splinter pierce his shell. He should help Mavery. But he couldn't bring himself to move. His eyes were glued on Keely.

Catriona planted her hands on her hips to study the earth girl. "My, my, how Odin's Chosen Ones have failed. The warrior boy is lost in the underworld. The other had his pathetic army defeated. And the one you tried so hard to save," she patted Kalifus on the shoulder, "is loyal to me now."

"Sam will never be loyal to you," Keely said. "He's one of us. And Leo's right here."

From the shadows of the Great Hall, a pale figure stepped forward. Leo had a bruise on his temple, and his eyes were sunken, but he was alive. Kalifus felt an impulse to run to him, but Howie was there, slapping Leo on the back, nearly knocking the boy over as they celebrated. Jealousy ran through Kalifus. He had once been part of their tight little band.

Keely marched down the steps, shadowed by Leo and Howie. They made a solid line facing off against Catriona and Kalifus.

"I don't believe you," Keely said. "Sam would never hurt me, would you, Sam?"

"My name is Kalifus," he said, but it was an effort. Seeing Keely had unsettled him, made him uncertain. More splinters dug into his gut. He felt like he was bleeding internally.

"Who's Kalifus?" Leo asked.

"I am Kalifus." He rapped his fist to his chest for emphasis, or maybe to remind himself. "How did you get into the city?"

"We came in the back door," Keely said. "You know, scaled the cliffs, risked life and limb. All to get to you."

"Join us," Leo said. "We're on your side."

His side? Kalifus almost laughed aloud. If Leo only knew what he had done, who he really was. *A murderer*. He might think twice about trying to save such a lost cause.

"I'm willing to give you a second chance," Howie said. "Even though you did try to kill me," he added dryly. "Just step over here away from that ugly witch and join us." He held the Sword of Tyrfing pointed squarely at Catriona.

A tiny sliver of hope no bigger than a single atom flickered to life in Kalifus. Maybe it wasn't too late for him after all. But the next instant, the crushing weight of his guilt extinguished the light. He dug his fingernails into the skin of his palms, needing the stinging pain to add weight to his words. "I don't need your help or your pity. This is who I am. You're all just too dumb to see it."

Keely had been optimistic that once Sam saw her, he would miraculously bounce back to his normal self, but it seemed there was still a lot of work to do. He looked hollow, his skin pale, his eyes yellowed with whatever toxin was inside him. She tried humor, forcing a chuckle out. "Got it all under control, do you, Sam? Catriona is about to take over Skara Brae, and when she's finished, she's going to use you to help her return Orkney and all its magic to earth. You know what that means? She's a psychopath, Sam. Our entire world will be in danger. You have to stop this." Keely's hand went into her pocket and clasped the Moon Pearl. It felt cool and smooth under her fingers. Somehow she had to get it to Sam.

Before he could answer, Catriona pushed him aside.

"We've wasted enough time for one day." Catriona raised her hand, and three single bolts of green lightning shot out, wrapping around the throats of Keely, Howie, and Leo. The bolts lifted them off the ground so that their feet dangled. Catriona called over her shoulder. "Hestera, make yourself useful and take the coven to dispense of the Orkadians holding the gate. The time for mercy has ended. I want our sister Vena to see this victory."

Hestera grumbled, then motioned to the loitering coven. They hurried across the square toward the sound of the banging—all but Perrin, who remained in a daze on her knees.

The lightning sizzled and crackled around Keely's neck but didn't burn. Instead it tightened, slowly squeezing off her windpipe. Howie was kicking and choking next to her. Leo alone was calm.

"Don't struggle," he urged. "Conserve your strength."

Catriona raised her other hand and drew her finger in a circle. A ring of fire sprang up around them, orange flames leaping tall. She splayed her fingers out and then slowly drew them into a fist. The circle grew smaller and smaller until the three heroes writhed and twisted in the flames that threatened to ignite their clothing.

"Join me, Kalifus," Catriona shouted, her eyes glittering with triumph.

Keely's eyes reached out to Sam, urging him to look at her. If he joined Catriona, her heart would break. He began to raise his hand.

"Don't, Sam!" she cried. But Sam wasn't Sam anymore, she realized with a sinking heart. Fire burned from his palm, cutting a traitorous trail across the cobblestones until it joined with Catriona's stream. Keely's pain intensified until her whole body felt like it was being stabbed with tiny knives.

"Why shouldn't I?" Kalifus shouted. His yellowed eyes reflected the poison that raged inside him. "This is who I am. Who I have always been. A Son of Rubicus."

Keely fought with every last ounce of strength she had. "No. You're Sam. The guy who copies off my Algebra notes and stands up to bullies. You can't give up on yourself, Sam."

But her friend's expression didn't change. "Sam is dead. Kalifus has risen to take his place," he said.

The words sounded like nails on a chalkboard to Keely's ears. Catriona cackled with victorious glee as her and Kalifus's combined forces intensified until the pain was unbearable.

As Keely's strength faded, her hand opened up, and the Moon Pearl slipped out. It fell to the ground and rolled through the flames straight for Sam. Hope skyrocketed in her as he knelt to retrieve it, but before he could touch it, a sharp pointy boot came down on it, grinding it underfoot.

Keely's last shred of hope was crushed under Catriona's heel.

But then a strange white vapor swirled around Catriona's feet. Ice sprang up, climbing up her boot and pinning her in place.

Anticipation made Keely grin. She knew what was about to happen. The Moon Pearl was encasing Catriona in ice, the same way Audhumla had done to her back in the Cave of Shadows.

The witch magic choking them was cut off as Catriona struggled to free herself. "What is this magic?" She zapped her feet, but the electrical bolts ricocheted off the ice. She turned to her protégé. "Help me, Kalifus! Stop this magic."

Kalifus-Sam had to release Keely and the others to add his powers to hers. Grateful to catch her breath, Keely waited to see what would happen. The ice rose quickly, passing Catriona's knees to reach her waist. The two witches tried futilely to blast it away, but it simply raced faster until it reached Catriona's neck. She managed to screech out her rage before the ice swallowed her up, silencing her.

"What have you done?" Kalifus-Sam roared, advancing on Keely.

"I'm trying to save your butt," she shouted back. "So why don't you stop acting like a jerk."

Catriona's eyes glowed under the ice. Water ran in rivulets down the sides. The Sam imposter returned to her side, trying to blast his way in.

Keely stepped closer. "We don't have much time. Catriona will be free in minutes." The ice was melting fast. Cracks formed and spread in the surface. Keely put a hand on Kalifus-Sam's arm, feeling the scorching heat of his anger. "Fight the darkness inside you, Sam. I know you can beat it."

"You don't understand." He dropped his palms, putting out

the witchfire, and reeled away from her. "You don't know what I've done." His voice was etched in pain.

"You killed Brunin," Keely said calmly.

Kalifus-Sam turned red-rimmed eyes to her. "You know?"

"Ymir showed me," she said. "I'm sorry that you had to do that. You must have had a good reason. The Sam I know would never hurt someone he cared about like that."

"I went there to kill him!" he shouted. "Odin is dead. Asgard is gone, destroyed. By me!"

"Catriona poisoned your mind. She's to blame— "

Catriona's ice block splintered with a loud crack, and panic rose up in Keely. The witch would be free any second, and she still hadn't changed Sam's heart.

She grabbed Sam by his chest plate, dragging him close, braving an up-close look at those yellowed eyes. "Look, you, I faced troll-hags and frost giants to bring back the Moon Pearl, but I realize now, it won't save you. That's not what this was about. Odin could have gotten the Moon Pearl anytime he wanted, but he sent me because somehow he knew, I needed to face my past. And when I did, I was finally free. That's what this is about, Sam. You have to face the past and deal with it."

"Yeah, bro," Howie chirped up. "I've been scared of my shadow my whole life. I thought it was a joke when Odin chose me as Protector, but look at me now." He flexed newly formed muscles. "I've taken down Balfin ape-men."

Then it was Leo's turn. His chocolate brown eyes were warm as he looked at his friend. "I thought I had no honor because I wanted to run away from my tribe, but I was willing to sacrifice everything to save this realm. That's all the honor I need."

Kalifus-Sam only looked angrier, his cheeks flushing scarlet. "Great! You all did smashing! But Odin told me I failed his test. Get it?" he shouted. "I. Failed."

"No." Keely shook her head. "No way. Odin didn't do all this so you would fail. Come on, Sam, use your brain. He would have never let you get close to him unless it was the outcome he wanted."

"So what," he sneered, "he just let me stick a blade in his heart?"

Keely threw her hands up, exasperated. "Who knows? What do you have to face in your past? Did you ever forgive yourself for what the red sun did? Or for not saving your father? Maybe Odin wanted you to learn how to forgive yourself, so he gave you the ultimate test."

Perrin pushed Keely aside. The lanky witch thrust a finger in Sam's chest. "Look, if I can forgive you for putting a spear through my chest, I think you can lighten up a bit. I wish I had friends like this."

Kalifus-Sam remained silent, but his eyes flickered left to right, as if he were processing their words. Before Keely could plead her case more, Catriona's ice exploded into a burst of stinging ice shards.

"Wretched child, there will be no mercy for you!" Catriona was livid. Ice dripped from her hair. Her chest heaved up and down. A fireball instantly appeared over her hand. "You dare test me with Odin's magic? You will burst into flames and burn for eternity." She drew her arm back and launched her projectile at Keely.

Keely braced herself for the impact when a funny thing happened. A dome of energy sprung up around them. Catriona's witchfire bounced off the defensive shell back at her, zinging her and making her shriek in pain.

Keely's eyes flew to Sam's, and he winked at her. Joy shot through her.

Sam was back.

Chapter Forty-Three

Sam cracked his neck. "I have been wanting to do this for weeks." He clapped his hands sharply and then threw them out, sending Catriona flying backward, tumbling head over heels. Keely's words had finally sunk in. And not a second too soon. There was so much truth in them, he didn't know where to begin.

Catriona was on her feet in an instant. "Traitor!" she screeched. The old witch flung her arms out and clapped her hands together, sending another bolt of lightning out of the sky straight down at him.

Sam pushed the sizzling burst away, turning it back at Catriona. The impact sent her rolling across the paving stones, leaving her crumpled and broken, stringy gray hair strewn across her face. He waited for her to get up, but for the moment, she lay motionless.

He dropped the energy bubble that encased his friends. Keely rushed forward, throwing her arms around him. "Sam!" she shouted.

"Hey, Keely, took you long enough to get here."

"Is it really you?" Her eyes searched his face.

He smiled wryly. "I thought Sam was gone forever. But what you said, it finally made sense. Not that I don't think you make an awesome Protector, Howie, but we both know he should have chosen Leo."

Leo just grinned. Howie tried to look offended, but then he high-fived Sam. "Dude, you are so back. I love it!"

"Did you really call me a dork-face?" Sam said, fake punching Howie in the stomach.

Howie batted his hand away. "Did you really call me a traitorous worm?"

Sam reached out to clasp his shoulder when a bundle of skirts hit Howie and knocked him aside.

"Howie, you all right?"

Sam watched as the girl he had threatened earlier took Howie in her arms and hugged him. But Howie didn't seem to mind. Not at all.

"Hey, Selina. It's cool. My man here, Sam, is back among the living. Everything's going to be okay now."

"Really? Because he looked like he wanted to kill you," she said with disdain as she looked at Sam.

Sam laughed. "Trust me, the longer you know Howie, the more you want to kill him."

The two friends grinned at each other.

"We still have to deal with Hestera and the other witches," Sam said.

"Uh, I think we have that covered," Keely answered.

Sam's eyebrows went up. "Do tell."

She looked proud as she saucily announced, "Well, while Leo and I were keeping you busy, Gael led his Eifalian troops to help man the ramparts. Look."

Sam followed her gaze. At the top of the ramparts, Gael stood gazing down at them. Galatin stood at his side. Over their heads, black-winged Omeras took flight with witches clinging to their backs. Hestera had led the coven in full retreat.

"Well done, Keely!" Sam said.

The sound of Mavery's muffled squeaks and shouts sent them running to the blacksmith's. Sam blasted the rope to shreds, and the cocoon dropped to the ground. Arms flailed as Mavery wriggled out of her coils. She immediately began to pound Sam on the legs. He deflected her blows as he knelt down in front of her. "I take it you're mad at me?"

Tears streaked her muddy face. "You nearly blasted me to pieces."

"But I didn't. Hey, I told you a million times, I can't figure this witch stuff out without your help."

Her lips quivered as she tried to stay mad, and then she relented and threw her arms around his neck. "I'm glad you're back."

"Me, too."

A blast of witchfire spat into the ground next to them. Sam sighed. Without even turning, he knew Catriona had recovered.

"Guys, this is my fight. Leo, Howie, go see what Gael and Teren need. Keely, you keep Mavery out of trouble."

"Let me at her," Mavery argued, wriggling to get free, but Keely dragged her to the shelter of the blacksmith shop.

Sam turned. The gray-haired witch stood waiting, hands planted on her hips. A streak of mud creased her cheek, and her hair was askew. But a raging fury made her bristle with energy. "We are not finished, Kalifus. You think you can just walk away from me? You are mine. My son. My creation."

"My name is Sam. And I am most definitely not your son," Sam said, taking a stance to face her. "I just forgot who I was for a while. But I had good reason. I thought it would save my friends, but turns out, they didn't need saving at all." Her toxic magic burned like acid in his veins. He would do anything to rid himself of it.

She stalked forward, pointing an accusing finger. "You killed Odin. You did that for me!" She thrust her hands out, blasting him with a violent tirade of witchfire, rolling him over and over across the paving stones.

When she stopped, his whole body was numb. Getting zapped was like sticking a finger in a light socket. He was really tired of Catriona calling all the shots. He pushed himself up to a sitting position. "I killed Odin because I had to choose between him or me," he said. "And I chose me. But enough of this child's play." He climbed to his feet. "I command you to end this."

"Command me?" Her face was a mask of contempt. "Foolish boy. Who's going to stop me? I made you. I can destroy you."

Sam focused on calling on his Volgrim magic, trusting he could control it. He sent three balls of witchfire at Catriona in rapid succession. They were different than the others, their fiery green edges tinged with a malevolent shade of bruised violet that hinted at the deeper power he now carried. The first two missed, but the third one hit her on the shoulder, sending her reeling backward. "You can't beat me," he boasted, moving closer. He drew two more balls of the powerful new witchfire he possessed and launched them. "Remember? You gifted me with your putrid Volgrim magic. Like it or not, my powers are as strong as yours. So go ahead and try, but I will beat you."

He chanted in that strange language Catriona had given him. The language of her dark magic. He drew his hands around him, planting his feet firmly. "*Mordera, mordera senvindium fray.*" He repeated the phrase, his voice rising to the last word, then raised his leading leg and stomped down hard, thrusting forward at the same time with his palms. The ground cracked beneath his feet, zigzagging straight for Catriona. A sound like a thunderclap split the air.

Catriona was thrown off her feet. Rocks tumbled from the wall. The queen of evil looked shaken, but a crafty light came into her eyes as she sprang back up. "So arrogant. We'll see how you feel when I strip my beautiful magic away." She flung her bony fingers forward and proceeded to barbecue Sam, searing him with matching sizzling grape-colored fire shooting from her fingertips. Sam screamed in agony as smoke rose from his limbs. He dropped to the ground, rolling from side to side to escape her retribution.

"*Mordera exodiam,*" she chanted.

Smoke the color of rotted jookberries began to filter out of

Sam's nose. He gritted his teeth against the pain, willing himself not to fight back. The smoke pooled in a cloud over his head, draining the poisonous magic from him. Catriona inhaled deeply, drawing the cloud toward her and sucking it into her greedy lungs until every last drop of the tainted smoke was completely gone. She lowered her hands and sighed contentedly, as if she had just eaten a fine meal. "Now, you are nothing."

Sam lay on his back, still and motionless. He blinked, looking up at the sky. The sun was yellow, the blue sky cloudless. His head felt clear for the first time in weeks. He wanted to shout with joy. He sat up. "Phew, that's better." He pushed himself to his feet, swaying slightly. "Now that I have your nasty, disgusting, revolting magic out, I can get back to being me."

"You tricked me," she said, gasping in disbelief. "You wanted me to leech it from your system."

He grinned at her, shrugging impishly. "I have all the magic I need from my mother and father. So let's do this." Instinctively, he reached for his leather pouch, the one that held the ground-up dust of Odin's Stone. He opened it, about to pour the last grains of sand into his hand, but instead the original shard rolled out. He stared at it in shock, and then a grin crossed his face.

Leave it to Odin to surprise him once again.

He put the shard back in the pouch, sealed it, and swung it around his head. He closed his eyes and called on his deepest light magic. Wind whirled around him. "*Fein kinter, testera, testera, Catriona, venimus. Dispera, dispera, mora nae mora,*" he shouted.

Catriona held her arms up to block the wind, holding her position. Using her magic, she picked up a pitchfork from a hay wagon, sending it straight for Sam's heart. Sam raised his hand and stopped it, sending it into a wooden post with a loud thunk. The old witch sent a pair of oaken barrels next. He couldn't move fast enough and they knocked him off his feet, bruising his ribs. He rolled to avoid another blast and sent a bolt of green fire at her head. She dodged it easily and flung him backward with a flick of her wrist, sending him crashing into the wall. Sam saw stars, and his left shoulder sent out shooting pains. She sent the pouch flying from his hands to skid across the paving stones.

Catriona looked bored. "You are nothing but a weak and pathetic boy. You have all the power of a toddler."

Sam forced himself back on his feet, ignoring his aching ribs and throbbing shoulder. He saw a short double-headed axe embedded in a post. He called it to his hand, gripping it tightly, then heaved it at Catriona. It spun across the open space, spinning head over tail. A foot away, she clapped her hands, turning it into a cloud of dust.

Catriona stalked closer like he was prey. "You should have never given up your dark magic." She thrust her palms out and trapped him in a blaze of emerald and amethyst witchfire. Shooting pangs of agony made him arch and writhe.

Sam fought to push back her magic with his own, but his arms were starting to shake. She was right. Without the aid of Catriona's dark powers, he was quickly running out of gas.

Mavery ran out of the blacksmith shop and sent a blast at Catriona. The hag was forced to turn her attention from Sam to send the little witch flying head over heels across the square until she tumbled in a heap in front of a spice shop. Keely emerged, running to help Mavery to her feet. They took cover behind some casks in front of the shop.

Sam gasped for air, grateful for the reprieve. But a loud rattling came from the armory. The door flew open. Metal objects began to hurl through the air. A sledgehammer flew out and came straight at his head. Sam ducked, but he couldn't avoid the pair of flying shears that cut across his thigh, splitting open his skin. Pain fogged his head. He felt warm blood run down his leg.

Catriona conjured more objects, sending a spinning helmet that struck his temple, making him see double. A stack of metal shields came at him like flying saucers. He flung his arms up, and they banged and bruised his forearms. And then the swords came at him. One after another, as if she were emptying the armory.

Sam blasted the first two away. The third he leapt over. The fourth he couldn't avoid. It embedded in his thigh, bringing him down to the ground. He yanked it out, his whole body in agony. His father's pouch lay on the ground a few feet away. He tried to drag himself forward, to use the precious magic in it to help him. His fingers closed around it, but before he could swing it, Catriona ground his wrist into the ground with her pointed boot.

Her face was gloating, eyes shining with victory as she stood over him. "Now I will do what I should have done that first day. Erase every trace of your existence!"

Sam braced himself for the burst of witchfire that would turn him to ash, but before Catriona could raise her hands, a puff of smoke exploded in the square. A woman appeared in a heavy cloak, sending crackling blue fire at Catriona. "Get away from my son," the woman commanded.

Through the haze of pain, Sam's heart leaped into his throat as he recognized her voice.

"Mom!"

It was his mother. Here in Orkney. How was that possible?

Catriona turned her fire from him toward the newcomer. "How dare you attack me!"

"I'm his mother," Abigail said calmly, releasing a torrent of blue fire at the old witch. "His real mother. So get away from him before I send you back to the dark hole you emerged from."

"He is mine!" Catriona screeched, blocking Abigail's attack with her own.

Their magic met in the middle, sending a wall of flames shooting up fifty feet high. The blue and purple magic intertwined. Abigail was strong. But even Sam could see her arms were trembling. He struggled to get to his feet, but his leg wouldn't hold him. Then Keely was at his side, running a pink crystal over his wound.

"What are you doing?" he asked.

But she ignored him. She probed with her fingers. He felt a tingle, and then the crystal glowed a faint pink. His eyes bugged out. *Did Keely just use magic?* But the wound, while still painful, was better. She tied his leg off with a strip of fabric and lifted him to his feet.

"She needs you," Keely said. She helped him limp over to Abigail's side. His right leg throbbed, but it was bearable. Sam raised his hand, joining his witchfire with hers. At his side, Mavery took a stand. The girl had a scrape on her cheek, but her chin was determined. Her magic was small, but every little bit helped.

They were holding their own, but Catriona seemed to be getting stronger, while they were using up all their strength. The smell of crackling electricity and sulfuric heat filled the air. And then Catriona unleashed another wave of magic. Did the witch have an unlimited reserve? They were losing, slowly being driven back. They needed more magic. They needed another witch on their side.

"Need some help?"

The voice came from Perrin. Revenge fired her eyes as she joined them. She tilted her head and rubbed her hands together and then flung them outward. Instantly their tongues of witchfire strengthened as she joined them. Perrin was powerful, Sam realized, especially when she was angry.

They were gaining on Catriona, driving her backward.

Sensing she was losing, Catriona suddenly directed all her power skyward.

"I call on the father of witches, Rubicus. Send down your guardian Safyre Omera to defend me," Catriona shrieked.

A blast of crimson lightning split the sky. A distant figure unfurled from a curl of black smoke that streaked across the horizon. They heard the beating of wings as the creature descended over the ramparts. It was an Omera, a giant one, ancient-looking, with battle scars crisscrossing its chest. Its eyes glowed ruby red as it blasted the way in front with fire, searing everything in its path.

"What is that?" Keely asked.

"That looks like a fire-breathing Omera," Sam supplied. "We should run."

"No," Keely said calmly. "No running."

She scrabbled in the dirt, getting down on her hands and knees as she searched.

"What are you doing?" Sam eyed the approaching monster. Had Keely lost it?

"There!" Shouting with triumph, she opened her hand. She held a large white pearl. It was muddied, and cracked, but it still held an opaque glow.

Keely held it up in her fist. "I call on Ymir, ancient guardian of this land, to defend us." It took a moment. Then a streak of ice blazed across the sky and hit the ground at their feet, sending dirt and mud spraying. A furred white beast as large as a school bus shook itself free of the clinging mud.

"Holy cow!" Sam said in awe.

"It's Auddie!" Keely cried, grabbing Sam's arm and jumping up and down with excitement. "She's Ymir's guardian."

The beast stalked forward on a crazy set of eight legs, long sabretooths drawn as she faced Catriona. Sam was beginning to like the odds.

As the Safyre Omera passed overhead, ready to incinerate them, Auddie belched, sending a blast of frozen snow across the arena. The ice cloud put out the Safyre's blaze, leaving only a black spit of smoke.

Catriona shrieked in frustration and launched herself into a thin red streak, zinging up to the ancient Omera. She appeared on its back and urged it forward for another pass.

Auddie buried her head as she pawed the dirt.

"Uh, Keely, is she going to do anything?" Sam asked.

"I hope so."

They waited as Catriona bore down on them. Everything burned in the Safyre's path, until Catriona was nearly on them.

The white creature didn't move. They were going to be incinerated.

"Run!" Sam shouted.

"No, wait." Keely ran and leaped on Auddie's back.

"Oh, great!" Sam muttered. Since when had Keely turned into such a fearless warrior? He followed her, leaping on behind her. "I hope you know what you're doing!" He grabbed a fistful of fur as she urged the beast on.

"Come on, Auddie. You can do this."

Auddie bleated and shuffled forward on her eight legs, moving like a freight train, heading straight for the oncoming creature.

As the fire was about to hit Auddie and cremate them all, Auddie let out a mighty burp. A frigid cloud billowed out of her mouth, enveloping the blazing fire. Catriona was forced to leap from the back of the giant Omera, which was unable to stop before it entered the icy cloud. The creature instantly turned gray, dropping from the sky like a rock to crash into the ground, shattering into pieces. Catriona rolled across the muddied paving stones, screaming in outrage at the destruction of her fire-breathing pet.

Sam leaped off Auddie's back, looking up at Keely. "Wait here. This is my fight." He caught sight of his mother across the square. She nodded at him, giving him the encouragement he needed to face his biggest enemy. "We are finished," he said to Catriona.

The witch swayed a bit, but she was still powerful. She used both hands to unleash her destructive magic at him. "No," she cried, "you need me."

Sam was done doubting himself. He held up his hand and simply stopped her, pushing her magic back at her so that she sniveled in pain.

"I made you who you are," Catriona wailed.

He pushed harder, sending a blast wave at her that knocked her off her feet and into the dirt.

"No. My parents did that. I am Sam Baron. Son of Robert and Abigail Barconian." Sam's mother came over to his side, standing shoulder to shoulder with him. He turned and smiled at her. She handed him his father's pouch, and he almost laughed aloud with joy as he gripped it.

Catriona crawled forward, pointing a finger at him. "But you share the blood of Rubicus. You are one of us."

"I will never be like you," he said, letting the last trace of his rage wash away like the tide receding from the shore. "You put me in a prison. And now I intend to return the favor."

Sam closed his eyes and thought of the black hole he had been locked in. He swung the pouch holding Odin's Stone over his head. He thought of the darkness as he muttered the words that flowed through him. His mother's hand rested on his shoulder, giving him courage. He created a vortex that spiraled and spun behind Catriona, slowly drawing her backward. She clawed at the earth, trying to stop herself from being sucked into it.

Sam pushed harder. He saw the stone walls of his prison. The dark airless atmosphere. The dripping water. He imagined his poisonous companions waiting for her. He imagined it all as he pushed her through and then let go, collapsing with exhaustion as the black void spun and whistled and then disappeared with a snap.

When it did, Catriona was gone.

Chapter Forty-Four

Sam gasped and nearly collapsed. If it hadn't been for his mother's arms squeezing him tight, he probably would have fainted right there.

"Mom!" He wrapped his arms around her. "Are you really here?"

"I'm really here, Sam." She held him away from her. "Look at you. I swear you've grown two sizes."

He grinned. "I've missed you, too."

"I told you I would find a way to you." She swept him in close, pressing him tight to her chest.

They stood there like that for a long moment, but there was no time for a reunion.

Leo whistled from the ramparts. "We've still got a problem up here."

Keely and Mavery joined as they climbed the stairs. Sam's body was aching and bruised, but Keely had somehow managed to heal his leg enough so he could limp along. Leo and Howie stood next to Sam's buddies, Speria, Heppner, and Galatin. The men each greeted him with a hearty slap on the back, jolting his bruised ribs, before returning to stare glumly out over the black sea of Balfins that spread out below them. The monstrous army

chanted and stomped the ground as they prepared a new battering ram for the front gate.

The war was not over yet.

The last Volgrim witch, Vena, rode tall among them, cracking her whip over their backs as she urged them on. One of her
generals, a Balfin with a tall silver helmet, rode at her side, bellowing at his fellow ape-men.

Twelve hundred Eifalian archers lined the walls, firing tire-
lessly at the horde below, keeping them back from the barrier.
But there were only so many arrows, and there were too many
of the ape-men to count.

Gael stood by a young Eifalian boy, his hand on the boy's
shoulder. Gael's aquamarine eyes looked Sam over closely, and
then, for once, they warmed. He nodded at Sam. "It is good to
see you are back, Samuel Barconian. My nephew, Theo."

Sam stuck his hand out in a greeting. "Hey."

Theo's eyes glowered at him. His uncle squeezed his shoulder, and the boy begrudgingly shook his hand.

Captain Teren arrived out of breath. "Glad to see you came to
your senses," he said to Sam. "The gate still holds, thanks to Lady
Abigail's enchantments, but I don't know for how long it will last."

"What's the plan?" Sam said, rubbing his hands together. "I
say we go out there and take the fight to them."

"We don't have enough swords to fight that lot," Speria
said dourly.

"Yeah, what we need is a miracle," Heppner said.

"I could blow the Horn of Gjall. It worked last time," Howie
said eagerly.

Teren nodded his approval. But when Howie put the horn
to his lips, no sound came out. He tried again, blowing so hard
his face turned red, but not a sound escaped. "I guess it's broken," he said disappointedly. The horn vibrated in his hands like
a jumping bean, and then a pair of bronze wings sprouted on
either side of the horn. The wings began to flutter, and the horn
rose in the air, hovering a moment before flying off into the sky.

They watched it go as if it carried their last hope with it.

"Look, what's that out there?" Leo pointed.

A ball of dust rolled through the center of the black army. A tight pack of horses led by a redheaded dwarf.

Rego. And a small band of Falcory.

"Give them cover fire," Gael ordered. "Drive those beasts back." The archers began firing furiously on the massed group of Balfins pounding on the gates. They dropped their battering ram and scrambled for shelter.

Abigail and Sam did their best to spray witchfire at the Balfins chasing the band. One of the ape-men pulled a Falcory from his horse, but the rest continued on.

Teren called down to his men. "Open the gates on my command."

Abigail quickly removed her enchantment, a blue glow that surrounded the gate. At the last second, Teren called out, and the gate opened just wide enough for the small band to roll through; then it slammed shut again, and the gate began to glow blue. A pair of Balfins managed to break through, but they were quickly dispatched by what looked to Sam like a crowd of angry farmers.

Sam raced down to the square. He spied Beo slipping off his horse, favoring one leg. Next to him, a younger version of Beo had his arm in a sling.

But Sam only had eyes for his stalwart friend. "Rego, you're alive!" Sam grasped him in a bear hug.

"No good way to kill a dwarf," Rego muttered. "But they tried. Tiber and I were sucked into a cloud and thrown clear across the desert. A witch named Ariane tied us up and was about to turn us into stew when Beo's son Jey came charging into the camp waving his javelin around."

"Where is Tiber?" Sam asked, searching the few riders for a familiar face.

Before Rego could answer, they were attacked by a crazy bird. It was a baby iolar no bigger than a rooster. Rego started laughing. "Lingas. There you are, you pretty girl." The bird settled on Rego's arm and rubbed her head on his chest, cackling with what sounded like delight. Then Rego's face grew grim. "Tiber didn't make it. He died saving my life from a ball of witchfire that would have turned me into a pile of ash."

Sam's heart fell. Tiber had been a good friend. A stalwart soldier. Loyal to Orkney with every cell in his body. For a moment, Sam wished he could have prolonged Catriona's suffering a bit longer before banishing her.

The dwarf looked around the nearly destroyed square. "Seems like you made quite a mess here."

"Nothing I couldn't handle," Sam said, winking at Keely as she joined them.

She snorted. "No. He just about killed us all. But what else is new?"

"Dwarfmaster, you're back!" Howie high-fived Rego. "I see Lingas is . . . uhm . . . happy to see you. That's cool." Howie shoved his hands in his pockets, looking like he had lost a friend, but he brightened when the bird hopped across and landed on his shoulder, fondly pecking at his ear.

Rego laughed. "I'd say she's found herself a new owner."

Teren marched up, a hopeful look in his eye. "What about the Falcory tribes?" Only four warriors accompanied Beo.

"We have three hundred warriors riding hard. Still a day away," Beo said.

"In a day's time, we'll all be dead," Teren said grimly.

"Where's Leo?" Jey asked, his sharp eyes searching the crowd.

"I'm here."

Jey turned at Leo's voice, and the Falcory boy's face lit up. They slapped each other so hard on the back, Sam was surprised they didn't break any ribs. They broke into chatter about how they had both survived their ordeals, which seemed to involve a giant beast shaped like an iguanadillo and equal amounts of evil witches out to kill them.

Renewed pounding on the front gate brought them all back to the present. The Balfins were back to relentlessly ramming it.

Abigail wrung her hands. "My magic won't hold against that much longer."

Howie raised his hand. "I've got an idea. It might sound crazy, but I think we should open the gates."

Everyone looked at him.

"I . . ." he flushed beet red. "You know, so they can run into our trap. Then, *pow*," he punched one fist into his other palm, "we take them out. Meanwhile, we send out a hit squad and surprise attack from the side." Lingas let out an approving squawk from his shoulder.

A sharp look of appreciation came into Teren's eyes. "The boy has a sound idea. But how will we sneak out of the city? The walls are too thick."

Mavery tugged on Sam. "You can do it, Sam. With your magic. Remember?"

The witchling was right. Sam had once opened a hole in the wall for them to escape the city.

Teren quickly organized them into squads. Half would stay inside the walls and battle the Balfin mutants who came in, and the other half would go out onto the battlefield and take them on.

There was no dissent. Their ragtag band gathered in the square, checking armor, fidgeting. Sam shed the armament of the Black Guard and put on his red Orkadian uniform. It felt oddly comforting to have his outside appearance match the inside.

Keely rubbed the snout of that strange creature, Auddie. "This is no fight for you, girl." She sent her home with a kiss on the nose. Auddie flew up into the air in a white streak, disappearing from sight.

As Sam strapped on his armor, his mom appeared at his side. "I'm not letting you out there with those monsters," she said fiercely.

Sam couldn't remember the last time he had had someone to worry about him. He kissed her on the cheek, acting braver than he felt. "You know I have to go. For this to work, you're needed here helping Gael. Trust me. I've got this."

She hesitated and then cupped his face with her hand. "You're just like your father. Don't you dare do anything stupid. Stay with Rego."

Perrin stood to one side, wringing her hands as if she wasn't sure where she fit in.

Sam led his mom to her. "Mom, meet Perrin. She's an amazing witch. She can help you."

He beckoned Mavery over. "You, too, kiddo, they'll need your magic." Mavery's eyes lit up with pride.

Abigail linked arms with the girls and led them away.

Sam joined Teren as he stood before the men. Teren raised his sword over his head. "For Tiber, and all whom we have lost in this war!" he shouted.

Sam raised his sword. Keely held up an Eifalian bow. It was tall as she was and strung tight. A quiver of arrows hung over her shoulder. He hadn't quite gotten used to her silver white hair, but he liked this fiercer side of her. The girl who had once kept her nose in a book was long gone. And then it was time to go.

"Be safe," he said.

She smiled. "Ditto." She threw her arms around his neck, hugging him tightly. "I believe in you," she whispered, then stepped back.

Leo hugged Sam tight, then took Keely by the elbow and led her away. Leo's eyes were haunted, like he had seen unspeakable things. Sam wished there was time to talk things over.

"Come on, compadres," Howie said, clasping the golden sword. "We've got some ape-men to put down." Howie had locked his sidekick iolar in her cage to keep her safe.

Selina flung her arms around Howie, kissing him soundly on the cheek. "Watch your back, Howie. I wish I could go with you, but these farmers can't hold a sword on their own."

Howie turned beet red. Sam rolled his eyes, yanking Howie

out of his daze to hurry after Rego and Captain Teren. There were two dozen soldiers with them, including Heppner and Speria. That, and Howie's golden sword. It wasn't much, but it would have to do.

They moved quickly down the deserted streets. Not even a stray dog loitered in the alleys. Every shop window was boarded up. Captain Teren had ordered those unable to fight to take refuge in the Great Hall, sending them down into the underground caverns that ran beneath it. They moved into the lower part of town where the air was danker and the smell of sewage filled the air. Sam turned down a familiar alley that dead-ended at the exterior wall.

"This the place?" Rego asked, looking skeptically at the stone wall.

Sam ran his hands over it, feeling the rough stone. It felt pretty solid. How had he done it last time? He grasped his father's pouch, searching for confidence. He swung the pouch over his head and called, "*Fein kinter, terminus.*"

There was a swirl of wind. Sam swung harder, holding one hand up and pushing, feeling the magical force leave his body and travel through space to the wall. He imagined the stones rearranging themselves, imagined them disappearing. The stone began to blur, like someone had smeared the surface. It was working. He pushed harder, and a gaping black hole opened up.

Howie high-fived him. "Dude, that is so righteous!" He dove through the hole headfirst.

The rest of the men climbed through, gathering close against the outside wall. The Balfins were preoccupied with the gate. Keely had a spyglass on them from the rampart. When Sam gave the signal, Galatin would open the gate, letting half the Balfin army inside the city. The ragtag army of farmers were hunkered around the square, with Leo, Jey, and the Falcory in position above with Gael's archers. Once they closed the gate, Sam's squad would attack their flanks.

They didn't stand much chance of winning, but they were planning to do a lot of damage before the war was over.

Even though Keely was used to magic by now, she was still amazed by the black hole that appeared in the wall. She waited for Sam's signal, crouched down next to Leo. On her other side, Jey kneeled so close she could feel his breath on her neck. The Falcory seemed determined to get her attention, helping her up the steps and offering to shield her if any arrows came. If things weren't so serious, she would find his attentiveness amusing. Especially because it got a rise out of Leo.

Picking Leo up off of Pantros had been the high point of this whole experience. The joy of seeing him standing on the shore, waving his arms as they rowed toward him.

Keely had clasped him in her arms, but something had been missing. A part of him lost. She didn't know what it was, but he wasn't quite himself. Not yet.

She tensed. There. Sam had waved a red handkerchief. Keely gave a thumbs-up to Sam's mom, who waited by the gate. Abigail made a cutting motion with her hands, removing the blue aura that protected the barrier. Galatin threw the lever on the pulley that held the gate closed. The chains shot sparks as it rose up with a crash, and a teeming mass of Balfins charged in.

The ape-men poured into the center of the square, looking around in confusion as they found it empty. Once the square filled, Galatin gave a sharp whistle, and the gate came crashing back down, sealing the rest of the Balfins out.

On cue, the Eifalian archers popped up under Gael's command and began firing on the armored beast-men. Keely and Leo joined in, firing furiously. Even Theo had a bow, firing arrows by his uncle's side. Jey's injured shoulder made him unable to hold a weapon, but he fed them an endless supply of arrows. Keely's arm ached as she nocked arrow after arrow, steadily drawing a bead on the mass of creatures below. She couldn't think of them as people, only monsters that wanted to kill them.

The Balfins began to panic as the arrows found their targets and dozens fell to the ground. The rest tried to flee, but the farmer squad, led by Milligan and Selina, had erected barricades at every exit. They began pelting the Balfins with rocks, jabbing at them with pitchforks if they came too close. Galatin lent his sword to the fight, making sure none of the apish creatures breached the barriers.

Abigail and Perrin added fierce witchfire, blanketing the intruders with blasts that sent them spinning through the air. Even Mavery helped with tiny bursts.

Keely's heart swelled with hope. Things were going well. There was an aura of defeat in the Balfin rank as more and more of them fell to the ground. And then one of the Balfin apes boasting a tall silver helmet grunted loudly in a guttural language, brandishing his sword. He had an air of authority about him. On his command, Balfins began scaling the inner walls to get to the archers. Abigail and Perrin knocked them down with witchfire, but they kept coming. Helmet-head led a pack of soldiers for the stairs that led to the ramparts. One by one his consorts fell, but he urged more of them on. Gael's men were too busy fighting the ones breaching the walls to deal with this new attack.

Keely braced herself, with Leo and Jey on either side, as the silver-helmeted leader burst onto the rampart. Lingas squawked ferociously in her cage, batting her wings at the door to get out. Ape-man's face was drawn into a snarl. Tusks jutted up from his lower jaw as he screamed gibberish at them, spraying them with spittle. His eyes were red under heavy lids. Sparse hair covered his face and his head.

Before Keely could release an arrow, Jey shouted, foolishly running headlong at the helmeted Balfin with only a hunting knife in his hand. The Balfin threw the boy into the rampart wall with one swing of his meaty paw like Jey was made of paper. The boy crumpled to the ground.

Helmet-head roared, throwing his head back with triumph, and then swung a mace in a circle, aiming straight for Leo and Keely.

While Balfins poured through the open gate, Captain Teren ordered his group to move in closer, crawling on their bellies. Sam and Howie were sandwiched between Rego and Teren.

Teren turned to them, speaking in a whisper. "Howie, with me, I'll need that sword to watch my back. Rego, you keep an eye on Sam. Be ready on my command."

When the gate slammed shut, they leaped up in a single line and charged forward.

"This one's for Tiber!" Teren shouted, cleaving the first Balfin with his sword.

They had the benefit of surprise and managed to break through the ranks. Sam fought alongside Rego, admiring how the dwarf made mincemeat of the Balfins he faced. His arm never seemed to tire. Howie was like a wild man, swinging that powerful golden sword of his like he had been practicing his whole life, mowing down every ape-man that got close. Heppner and Speria fought side by side, bantering and bragging to each other over who was the better swordsman. Sam added his witchfire to the attack, pleased at how long he was able to sustain his magic.

A pair of apes came at Rego from behind. Sam blasted the first one, sending it spinning. The other one carried an axe it swung at Rego's head. Sam tried to send another blast, but he tripped over a sneevil that tried to gore his leg. He turned his witchfire on the beast and then looked up, sure Rego was going to be skewered, but the dwarf had impaled the beast by thrusting his sword behind him without even looking. He winked at Sam and lifted him to his feet.

"Got to have eyes in the back of your head. Keep your wits about you."

Sam grinned. This was working. The Balfins were getting nervous as Teren's line of Orkadian soldiers mowed through the ranks. For a moment, it seemed as if they had a chance, but a fresh wave of Balfins swarmed over them, separating their line. Sam lost sight of Rego. He saw two Orkadian soldiers go down, unable to help them in time. He was all alone, surrounded by sneering mutated Balfins. He swung his rock and pushed them away with magic, blasting them when they got close, but more kept coming.

Vena was doing this. He had to get to her. Stop her.

He fought his way across the battlefield, searching for her tall figure.

The crack of the whip and smell of sulfur led him to her.

"Vena, Catriona is gone. Stop this!" Sam shouted.

Venomous rage made Vena's face purple. "Then I will finish this in her name."

She snapped her whip over his head, lashing at him. Sam ducked and rolled, coming face-to-face with a sneevil. He quickly rolled again and came up behind Vena. Only Vena had moved. When he reached for her, he found only air. Confused, he turned and saw her standing behind him, a devilish smile on her face. In her hand, she held one of the Balfin's curved blades.

"And now, witch-boy, the last hope of Orkney will fall under my blade." She lunged forward, aiming the tip of the blade for Sam's gut.

As the barbed end of the mace came swinging toward her head, Keely arched back, touching one hand to the ground. Leo spun on his heels, ducking out of the way. When Keely rose, she had an arrow nocked in her bow, same as Leo. In tandem, they fired, burying a twin set of arrows in helmet-head's chest. He reeled backward, eyes wide with shock, flailing his arms. He knocked over the cage that held Lingas and then crashed to the stone.

Lingas broke free, arrowing for the sky.

The Balfin apes behind helmet-head stopped in their tracks, staring at their leader in confusion. Leo and Keely used the moment to run at them, shaking their bows in their faces. The Balfins turned and ran, scrambling down the steps and making a run for the gate.

Galatin reeled up the gate as a stream of Balfins fled the square and ran for their lives. The farmers broke from their hiding positions behind the barriers and began chasing them. Gael's archers continued to fire at them as they fled.

Leo hurried to Jey's crumpled form, but Keely cast a worried glance over the battlefield. Where were Sam and Howie?

Sam's life flashed before his eyes. He saw the glint of the tip about to enter his guts when someone tackled him and knocked him to the side.

Howie lay on top of him, eyes shining behind his glasses. "I got this, bro."

Before Sam could argue, Howie was up, pointing his golden sword at Vena. "Looks like it's you and me, witchy-poo."

Vena grinned at Howie, an evil look in her eyes. She thrust forward with the blade. Sam could hardly believe his eyes as Howie neatly parried and pivoted around her like a gymnast. He blocked her thrust and then brought his sword up and into her belly before she knew what was happening. Her eyes widened with shock. The curved blade slipped out of her hand. Then she fell backward onto the battlefield with Howie's sword embedded in her. The golden sword shot out beams of light in every direction before disappearing in a blinding shower of golden sparks. Howie stood over her, eyes fierce as he locked gazes with Sam. "Friends stand together," he said, "to the end."

Out of nowhere, a Balfin ogre charged Howie, taking him down like a linebacker. The ape-man was familiar. Sam recognized Sigmund, the one that always stayed by Vena's side. Sigmund howled with grief. He wrapped meaty fists around Howie's throat, trying to choke the life out of him. Before Sam could blast him off Howie, a bird dropped like a rock from the sky and attacked Sigmund, biting and clawing at the ape-man's head. He swatted it, knocking the bird to the ground, and went back to choking Howie.

An arrow zinged over Sam's shoulder and pierced the hulking Sigmund through the heart. The Balfin toppled off Howie with a resounding thud.

Sam turned to find Keely standing fifty feet away, coolly nocking another arrow.

A horn sounded, piercing the air with a long low blast. Every Balfin ape paused, turning to see what the noise was. Along the edge of the forest, a great army appeared. Half-naked men on horseback. Correction: huge half-naked men on really big horses. They blew their horn again and then stampeded across the valley. Sam didn't know if they were good guys or bad guys, but as they ran down the Balfins, it became clear they were fighting for Orkney.

"What did I miss?" Howie said woozily as Sam helped him to his feet. Lingas squawked a greeting, flying up to nestle on his shoulder.

Keely ran up, pointing excitedly with her bow. "Look, the Vanir. They came."

With reinforcements at hand, Teren rallied his remaining men. The captain was a mess, a gash running across his cheek and one arm hanging limp, but that didn't stop him swinging his sword with his one good hand.

The Vanir were an even match for the brute strength of the Balfin apes. But the frost giants had better weapons and were clearly more skilled in battle. They were led by a giant man with a golden crown, who roared out orders to his men. The battle boiled over into a swarm of clashing swords that glinted in the afternoon light. The air was filled with clanging metal crunching against bone followed by yowls of pain.

And then it was over. The few remaining survivors disappeared into the woods, pursued by the ruthless Vanir. As the dust settled, the large frost giant wearing a golden crown rode over on his horse. He jumped down and stood over them.

"Thank you, Joran," Keely said, flinging her arms around his waist.

He patted her gently. "You were right, young one. This world is our world. It must be protected."

"We will need your help again," she said, pulling back to stand by her friends.

"The Vanir will be there," Joran promised, bowing his head before he leaped on the back of his horse. He blew once on a large curved horn, sending a deep booming call to his men. In moments, the valley had cleared of the giant men.

Rego and Teren hurried up as Joran rode off. Both men had shocked looks on their faces.

"Were those . . ." The normally unflappable Rego was speechless.

"They're huge," Teren added, eyes agog. "And their horses . . . did you see?"

"Yup," Keely said. "Those were the Vanir."

"You're on a first-name basis with a bunch of frost giants?" Sam said, elbowing her. "And you can shoot an arrow better than I can. Any other surprises?"

"Did I mention I'm part Eifalian now and I have magic?"

They laughed as they walked back to the gates. Selina found Howie the moment he entered the city, practically squeezing him to death. Abigail beamed down at Sam from the ramparts. He gave a short wave before he was tackled by a tiny mud-caked figure.

"We did it, Sam." Mavery's small face was streaked with dirt, but her grin was the same. Perrin trailed behind her.

Sam ruffled Mavery's hair. "Yeah, we did. Thanks to you."

Perrin punched Sam on the arm. "Good job, brother."

He winced, rubbing his arm. "Did you just give me a compliment?"

She grinned. The smile transformed her face. "Maybe."

"Things are looking up," Sam said. "The witches are defeated."

"You're a witch," Howie reminded him.

"Correction: The bad witches are defeated, and things can go back to normal."

"Not normal," Keely said slowly. "We're still stuck here in Orkney. And you killed Odin," she said gently, "or did you forget?"

The group of friends waited for his answer.

Sam grimaced. "No, but I can't change that. You were right, what you said to me about facing the past. Vor warned me that I had to surrender to the darkness to win. I didn't understand what she meant, but ever since I came into my magic, I've been afraid of what I would become. That if I let my guard down for a second, the darkness would swallow me up. Well, now I know what the worst of me looks like, and you know what? I'm not afraid anymore."

Leo came down from the ramparts, one arm under a woozy-looking Jey. "We have a bigger problem than getting home," he announced. "When I was in the underworld, I met someone. I can't remember his name. I think he hit me in the head with a rock." He scowled, rubbing his temple. "All I know is, I messed up big time, but I don't know how."

They looked at each other grimly.

Sam spoke first. "Look. We'll deal with it as it comes. But I promise you, we'll figure out a way to get you home. Now, unless I'm mistaken, it's time for the kitchens to reopen. A feast is in order to celebrate our victory!"

"I could eat an entire cow," Leo said, rubbing his stomach.

"I could eat an entire herd of cows," Jey boasted, grinning as Leo wrestled him to the ground. Howie and Sam piled on. Mavery laughed herself silly.

Keely and Perrin exchanged looks. "Boys," Keely said, hooking arms with the girl.

Chapter Forty-Five

Catriona opened her eyes and shrieked. She recognized the underground stone walls. She had kept Kalifus here for weeks. Defiance rose in her like the temperature on a summer's day. This stone prison wouldn't hold her.

"Let me out," she screeched. "I am Catriona, the greatest of witches."

She rattled the door, but no one came.

"I demand that you release me," she screamed again, spittle spraying from her lips as she threw her bony frame against the door. Nothing. She collapsed against it. Would she spend eternity here alone? What of her plans to rule Orkney? To rule the world of men? She could not be defeated like this. She would not be.

A rathos emerged from the shadows, an old one by the looks of its silvered back. It squeaked pathetically at her, running to her feet and winding itself around them. She kicked it hard, flinging it against the stone wall. It hit with a thunk and fell to the ground, then transformed into the familiar hunched figure of her cousin Bronte. Horrified by her carelessness, Catriona rushed to her side, but the old witch disintegrated into a cloud of ancient dust.

Catriona rocked on her knees, heartbroken and alone.

And then like manna from heaven, a sliver of light marked the floor as a slot opened in the door. A wild-looking eye pressed up to it.

"Hello, pretty," a voice called.

"Who's that?" Catriona rushed the door, peeking through the small slot.

"A friend in need. And you seem in need of a friend."

Catriona turned on her charm. "I can be a very powerful friend. Get me out of here, and you will be rewarded."

The eye blinked. "Perhaps we could make a trade."

Excitement made Catriona scratch at the door. "Yes, anything."

"I will provide you with an escape in exchange for that talisman of Odin you carry in your pocket," the mysterious voice said.

Catriona backed away, clutching the tattered scrap of fur she kept hidden in the folds of her skirt. "No. You can't have it."

"Then we are at odds."

The slot closed with a snap.

Catriona flung herself at the door, pressing her face against it. "No, come back. Please, we can negotiate, surely."

The slot slowly reopened. "You have one thing only I desire. Pass it through, and I will give you salvation."

"You will let me out of here?"

"The means to leave this cell," the voice said cryptically.

Catriona rubbed the ear and then decided it was a useless piece of sentiment. She shoved it through the opening. Fingers twitched as it grabbed it from hers.

She pressed her hands against the door, waiting. "There. Now, give me my release."

A familiar object appeared in the slot. "Here, my pretty, enjoy."

The black obsidian blade of Rubicus clattered to the ground. Catriona stepped back, away from it.

"What is this?"

The voice chuckled with mirth. "Why, it's your escape."

Outraged by this deceit, she sputtered, "How . . . how can I escape with this?"

"That's for you to decide." The slot snapped closed.

Catriona sent a blast of witchfire at the door, but nothing came out of her fingertips. She shook out her hands and tried again. Then she howled with rage. How dare they strip her magic! Her most precious gift shriveled to nothing.

The whisper of sound behind her froze her in her tracks. "Who's there?" she called.

She turned her head at the skitter of tiny feet on the rock. It couldn't be. They wouldn't dare challenge her.

The first sting made her flinch. The second, and she let out a shriek. Then the scorpions covered her body, and she went down in a teeming mass of stinging carapaces.

Epilogue

The towering silver acanthia tree sat high on a hill over-looking Skara Brae and the distant ocean. The wiry figure of a man sat on the limb, swinging his legs, whistling to himself. In his hand, he clutched a precious scrap of fur he had acquired in trade. Below him, his empire spread out like a ripe plum ready to be plucked from the unsuspecting. He felt so free. No one criticizing him. Telling him he was wrong. Telling him he was to blame.

His years of imprisonment were over. Odin was dead, killed by someone he trusted. He clenched the scrap of fur tighter.

Revenge really was the sweetest of nectars.

"The king is dead," he said, cackling to himself. "Long live the king."

Loki, God of Mischief, threw his head back and began to laugh.

Chaos had returned to Orkney.

From the Author

$\mathcal{D}$ear Reader:

I hope you enjoyed *Kalifus Rising*! It has been an incredible journey creating the Legends Orkney™ series. Sam took quite a dark turn in this story, but in the end, I loved how he was able to come out of it intact. My favorite character arc in this story has to be Keely's. She really gets a chance to be a strong female character. Howie and Leo make a pretty good showing as well!

As an author, I love to get feedback from my fans letting me know what you liked about the book, what you loved about the book, and even what you didn't like. You can write me at PO Box 1475, Orange, CA 92856, or e-mail me at author@alaneadams.com. Visit me on the web at www.alaneadams.com and learn about the interactive digital game app you can download on your smartphone.

I want to thank my son Alex for inspiring me to write these stories, and his faith in me that I would see them through. A big thanks to my team at SparkPress for their unfailing marketing support. Go Sparkies!

The adventures of Sam and his friends are not over. Look for the third book in the series to come out in 2017!

To Orkney! Long may her legends grow!

—Alane Adams

About the Author

Alane Adams is an author, professor, and literacy advocate. She is the author of the Legends of Orkncy fantasy mythology series for tweens and *The Coal Thief, The Egg Thief,* and the forthcoming *The Santa Thief,* all inspirational picture books for early-grade readers. She lives in Southern California.

SELECTED TITLES FROM SPARKPRESS

SparkPress is an independent boutique publisher delivering high-quality, entertaining, and engaging content that enhances readers' lives, with a special focus on female-driven work. Visit us at www.gosparkpress.com

The Red Sun, by Alane Adams. $17, 978-1-940716-24-4. Drawing on Norse mythology, *The Red Sun* follows a boy's journey to uncover the truth about his past in a magical realm called Orkney—a journey during which he has to overcome the simmering anger inside of him, learn to channel his growing magical powers, and find a way to forgive the father who left him behind.

Wendy Darling, by Colleen Oakes. $17, 978-1-94071-6-96-4. From the cobblestone streets of London to the fantastical world of Neverland, readers will love watching Wendy's journey as she grows from a girl into a woman, struggling with her love for two men, and realizes that Neverland, like her heart, is a wild place, teaming with dark secrets and dangerous obsessions.

Wendy Darling: Seas, by Colleen Oakes, $16.95, 978-1940716886. Wendy and Michael are aboard the dreaded Sudden Night, a dangerous behemoth sailed by the infamous Captain Hook. In this exotic world of mermaids, spies and pirate-feuds, Wendy finds herself struggling to keep her family above the waves. Will Wendy find shelter with Peter's greatest enemy, or is she a pawn in a much darker game, one that could forever alter not only her family's future, but also the soul of Neverland itself?

Runaway Daughter, $15, 978-0-9893159-9-9. Kamada lives in a world of magic, gremlins, fairies, an talking objects that shield her from a society where men act like they own the women walking down the street. She knows she does not belong, and to escape, Kammy wants to leave India to go study in America.

The Revealed, by Jessica Hickam. $15, 978-1-94071-600-8. Lily Atwood lives in what used to be Washington, D.C. Her father is one of the most powerful men in the world, having been a vital part of rebuilding and reuniting humanity after the war that killed over five billion people. Now he's running to be one of its leaders.

Within Reach, by Jessica Stevens. $17, 978-1-940716-69-5. Seventeen-year-old Xander Hemlock has found himself trapped in a realm of darkness with thirty days to convince his soul mate, Lila, he's not actually dead. With her anorexic tendencies stronger than ever, Lila must decide which is the lesser of two evils: letting go, or holding on to the unreasonable, yet overpowering, feeling that Xan is trying to tell her something.

About SparkPress

SparkPress is an independent, hybrid imprint focused on merging the best of the traditional publishing model with new and innovative strategies. We deliver high-quality, entertaining, and engaging content that enhances readers' lives. We are proud to bring to market a list of *New York Times* best-selling, award-winning, and debut authors who represent a wide array of genres, as well as our established, industry-wide reputation for creative, results-driven success in working with authors. SparkPress, a BookSparks imprint, is a division of SparkPoint Studio LLC.

Learn more at GoSparkPress.com